Lizzie

After the War

Nancy B. Brewer (signature)

Nancy B. Brewer

Lizzie

After the War

Nancy B. Brewer

Cover Design by Sean Snakenberg, Brentwood
Cover Photography by Vernon A. Brewer, Jr.

PUBLISHED BY
BRENTWOOD PUBLISHERS GROUP
COLUMBUS, GEORGIA 31904

Books by this author
Published by Brentwood

Carolina Rain
978-1-59581-573-6

Beyond Sandy Ridge
978-1-59581-641-2

Letters from Lizzie
978-1-59581-714-3

A Doll Named Fannie
978-1-59581-569-9

Quotes and Poems in Black and White
978-1-59581-663-4

Garnet
978-1-59581-696-2

The House with the Red Light
978-1-59581-680-1

The Two Faces of Nina Grey
978-1-59581-750-6

Lizzie After the War was published by arrangement with Nancy B. Brewer, Inc. Except for review, no part of this book may be reproduced, scanned, distributed in any printed, or electronic or audio form without permission from the author.

To order additional copies of this book or other books by author:
www.nancybbrewer.com

Retail orders: msnancybnc@aol.com

I Have Seen Miracles!

Lizzie After the War *is a work of historical fiction. It is the author's desire to give you a true sense of time. Therefore, names of real people and places have been added. However, the storyline is imaginary. Any resemblance to any persons living or dead is purely coincidental.*

Dedication

I hold the hand of a strong, but gentle man.
A man who is never too proud to step forward,
and brave enough to sometimes walk behind.

I dedicate this book with respect and devotion
to my husband,
Vernon.

Chapter 1

Happy Birthday

I awake this morning to the dull ache in my back, which has grown as familiar to me as an old friend. I used to tease and say to my husband Joel, "My body is like a small train wreck, but as long as it keeps going down the track, it is a good day." He would laugh, but the compassion in his eyes was always my best medicine.

"Rebel Number Four" is waiting patiently by the door. I named him "Rebel Number Four," for he is the fourth of his kind I have given the name "Rebel." To many he may be just a hound dog, but to me he is a champion and a friend to the end.

The house is damp and cold. I stumble to the bedroom window and part the lace curtains. It is raining again. We have been without sunshine six days in a row; perhaps the sun will never shine again.

Joel's robe is hanging on a hook on the bedroom door. Slowly I lift it to my nose and stroke the fabric. His scent is still there, woven among the threads.

The aroma of freshly brewed coffee is calling me to the kitchen and I make my way down the hall. Joel's robe is too big for me, which causes me to nearly trip over Rebel prancing in front of me. I stop to brace myself against the walls, which are painted with the fingerprints of family.

It is not easy to master a smile, but I give it my best try and sit down at the table. Dovie looks up at me and starts to speak, but when she sees me in Joel's robe, she shakes her head. I know she would like to scold me, but for the moment she holds her tongue and pours my coffee.

Dovie should know by now that I don't care for conversation in the mornings and especially not now. But she is just like her mother, who never took subtle hints. When I see her pull up a chair next to me, I know her lips will start flapping. *"Miss Lizzie, we gots some fresh eggs and I's made up some sweet rolls. After yous has your breakfast, whys don'ts we ride over and see Ma? She's a been askin' bouts you."*

"It's raining," I reply.

"Well, da carriage has a good-enough cover," she encourages.

"I'll have one egg and half of a roll," I answer sharply, hoping to shut her up. She sits on for a moment until I turn my head and stare out the window.

"Yous ain't gonna melt," she says, going about her work. Soon she starts to hum, as she always does when she is annoyed.

My mind starts to drift to thoughts of Dovie's mother, Cindy Lou. She was the only slave that came to North Carolina with me from Charleston. We lived through the war years and suffered the gains and pains side by side. Toward the end of the war, I gave her to the employment of Dr. and Mrs. Cotton. It was there she met her husband, Homer. Mrs. Cotton was an artist. She often stated that Cindy Lou could be a fine artist too, if she had the training. When Mrs. Cotton died, she left provisions in her will for Cindy Lou. In addition, she made arrangements for Cindy Lou to be enrolled in Barber Scotia College for Negro women here in Concord.

The years following the war were changing times. I was pleased for Cindy Lou, but at that time her financial profile far exceeded mine. *One should never underestimate the power of fate.*

I hear a clang in the kitchen and turn slightly to watch Dovie cooking. Yes, she is a better-looking version of her mother. She favors her Aunt Violet more with soft saddle-colored skin and delicate proportions. Even as a young girl, her mother possessed an awkward combination of features and poor carriage. I am not sure if it is age or education that did the grooming, but her mother is a most presentable Negro woman these days.

Dovie is the oldest of six children. Three years ago when Dovie's father died, she came to live with us as our housekeeper. She is almost 20 years of age now. I suppose she will be staying here, unless she can make better use of herself.

I return to my coffee and notice a fly has settled on the edge of the table. Quickly I swat it with the newspaper. Dovie stops, views my action, but turns back to her cooking.

Her father was a clever craftsman and cabinetmaker. He had been a long-time employee of a wealthy enterprising Negro man by the name of Mr. Warren C. Coleman. Homer helped build over 100 small rental houses on the outskirts of town, down by the depot. The area is commonly referred to as Coleman Village, where most of the colored population resides. Most of the houses are minimal and little more than shacks. Yet Homer's position and Cindy Lou's money afforded them to build the "big house," as their home is referred to by the other Negroes.

Unfortunately, Cindy Lou's money is long gone and she is without Homer's salary to support the five children remaining at home. She works full time at the college, takes in laundry and stays up half the night washing and ironing.

I find myself staring down at the dead fly lying on the floor. I wonder if Dovie detests flies as much as I do, since it was the supposed work of a fly that brought about the peculiar death of her father.

Before Homer died, he was helping Mr. Coleman build a cotton mill, which was to be fully operated by Negroes. Apparently his saw slipped, resulting in a cut to his upper leg. It was an ordinary wound, so I was told, not too deep or threatening.

Under normal circumstances, Cindy Lou, having worked as a nurse's assistant during the war, was capable of taking care of such a wound. Cindy Lou thought it would be best to allow the wound to dry out and heal. So for several days before she left to go to work, she bedded Homer out on the porch, leaving the wound uncovered. She did not take into consideration it was the better part of July, right in the middle of the dog days of summer. When she came home on the third day, Homer was burning up with fever and she sent for the doctor. His examination revealed that while Homer lay sleeping, flies had infested the wound, laid eggs and infected Homer's body with the screwworm. By the next morning, Homer was dead.

I am still staring at the floor when Dovie shoves the plate of hot food in front of me. "Here you go, Miss Lizzie!"

It smells inviting, but the fly has robbed me of my appetite. I manage the roll. After a few bites of the egg, it begins to lay heavy on my stomach and I empty the balance of my plate into Rebel's bowl. Again, Dovie shakes her head.

"Go on to see your mother, Dovie," I say, picking up my cup of coffee. "You may take the carriage. I will be fine until you get back." I leave her standing in the kitchen with her hands on her hips. The door slams behind me.

I wander into the keeping room and flop down in the faded velvet chair next to the fireplace. On the table beside me is a stack of unopened sympathy cards and letters, all addressed to me, Theodosia Elizabeth Simpson. A few of them are perfumed in fancy sleeves. Mother used to say, "One should never perfume or squander money on fancy papers. Sensible persons will ridicule you; and besides, it is a waste of good perfume."

What can even the kindness of words do for me now? After six week of suffering in the hospital in Asheville, Joel is dead, and most of me died with him. I lay down the unopened letters and assume my daily position of staring at the ceiling.

Dovie calls out as she leaves, but I do not answer. Rebel jumps up in my lap and my eyes settle on the painting over the mantel. For an unknown time I sit with my eyes fixed on the young woman in the portrait. I study the lines of her face, her hollow cheeks, sparkling eyes and radiant hair. There she hangs with the kiss of youth on her lips. It is as if she never existed at all. That girl has vanished and left me in her place.

I rise from my chair and approach my former painted self. On closer look, I note the soft sensual smile painted on my face and my hands politely folded. I reach up and place my hand over the hand in the portrait. The contrast fills me with rage. Without thought, I pick up the candlestick. I have intent to throw it through the canvas, but a force stops my hand in midair. I turn quickly, but I am alone. As if by magic or supernatural occurrence, my mind suddenly recalls the birthday poem Joel last wrote for me:

Shall I whisper in your ear,
or shout it loud and clear?
There is no need to fear my dear,
for your beauty grows with each and every year.

A smile comes to my lips followed by a tear dripping down my cheek. I suddenly find myself laughing as I speak directly to the painting. "You are safe today, my dear. I will leave you to haunt these halls, but maybe tomorrow you will not be as lucky." Then with the arrogant posture of a once Charleston Belle, I make my exit.

I now find myself standing in the front hall facing the "room." The French doors are closed and the glass is in need of cleaning, but I can clearly see inside. There is his chair, his pipe and his "Field and Stream" magazine lying on the table. It has been three weeks since I returned from Asheville and I have not braved through those doors.

Something inside of me forces my trembling hand onto the doorknob. I quickly pull open the door. The sunlight streaming in from the large oval window temporarily blinds me. To my amazement, it has suddenly stopped raining. When my eyes adjust, I can see tiny particles of dust dancing across the room.

Next to the window are my desk and the old typewriter. My family spent many hours in this room. Joel would play games with the children while I worked on composing letters and poems. When I had nothing in my head to write, Joel would read to us from his Sherlock Holmes books.

For a brief moment I smile thinking of those happy days. That was then, but today this room holds nothing for me any longer, nor do I have anything left to write. Even if I did, who would care or even turn the pages?

Angered by my loneliness and driven by self-pity, I am compelled to leave the room. As I make my exit, for some odd reason a book falls off the shelf directly in my path. I bend down with intention of placing the escaped book back on the shelf. Once the book is in my hand, I discover it is a book of poetry by Ella Wheeler Wilcox. The book was my gift to Joel last Christmas. It is inscribed on the front leaf: *With all my love to my own dear husband, Joel. Yours forever, Lizzie.*

The price of this book was dear, but it was many times repaid. It became Joel's favorite and he could quote almost every line. Joel's bookmark is still in place and I flip open the book to see these words underlined:

I will not doubt, though all my ships at sea come drifting home with broken mast and sails; I shall believe the hand which never fails.

"Thank you," I whisper, but I am not sure if I am speaking to God or Joel. I think it is both.

Looking back over the room it suddenly offers me a new comfort. I walk over, take my old seat at my desk and dust off the keys of the typewriter. It has been too long; surely the keys are stuck with age.

A rush of excitement fills my being as I slip a fresh piece of paper over the roller. Yes, I have a story just waiting for me to write! As to who will read it, it matters not. The story will be patiently waiting until the day it presents itself to the eyes of its beholder.

I place my hands on the keys and that old familiar sound of the keys clicking is like music to my ears. I begin:

October 6, 1892
Today is my birthday and I am now a half-century old.

Chapter 2

All in God's Perfect Timing

My first day's attempt at writing my journal consists mostly of putting paper in the typewriter and pulling it out. I suppose once it is finished it will be regarded by most as little more than a novella. But to me it will be so much more. For what it is worth, in black and white, on bounded pages, it will contain the story of my life.

When Dovie returns from her mother's, she finds me in the front room with a pile of crumpled-up papers on the floor next to me.

"Yous alrights in there Miss Lizzie?" she asks. The sun had just slipped behind the trees and evening cast its dark, smoky shadow. Without asking, Dovie walks over and turns on the lamp. I can feel her looking over my shoulder, attempting to read what I have written.

I turn my head and look directly at her. The light is like mirrors flickering in her dark, misty eyes. "Yes, Dovie, I am alright. If you don't stop fretting over me, I am going to have you committed to the mental hospital in Morganton." It is my first attempt at a joke since Joel's death. Dovie was not sure whether to laugh or cry.

"I hears you," she says, bending over and collecting the wads of paper around me.

"Leave it be," I said, fanning my hand at her to go on. "I have set my mind to writing a book. I expect this is how this room is going to look until it is done. Now you run on and fix us some supper. I am famished."

October 7, 1892

The next morning Dovie finds me in the kitchen preparing my own breakfast. I am groomed and dressed appropriately for an outside excursion. She looks me over, but says nothing. She is surprised by my cheerful tone when I speak. "Come on in Dovie. Sit yourself down. I have made plenty enough for both of us."

"Is you alright, Miss Lizzie?" she asks, fearing I may have finally lost my mind.

"My, my, Miss Dovie, will you please just stop asking me that!" I say, and plop her plate down in front of her.

She eats in silence, glancing up at me every now and then as if she expects me to do something crazy at any moment. As soon as I finish my breakfast, I jump up from the table and make the announcement. "I will be going out for the morning."

"Is you alrigh...," Dovie breaks in, before she catches herself. *"Dos you want me to come along?"*

"No, that will not be necessary. Expect me back early afternoon," I call out, leaving her sitting alone in the kitchen.

It felt good to be out of the house. Fall has always been my favorite season. I readied my buggy and was heading down the main road before eight. It has always been my belief that crisp fresh air is the healthiest for humans and animals alike.

Today the sky is as blue as the sapphire earrings Mother gave me on my 18th birthday. They belonged to my grandmother. How Mother made her decision which daughter to give them to will always be a mystery. I suspect it was not much of a contest. Back then Mother had plenty to share. The war cost all of us many things, but those precious earrings survived. We all thought Papa was being overly cautious the day he buried our valuables in a little metal box under the rose bushes. We were wrong. In my case, they are the only jewels I own. Someday soon, I will have to decide who will receive them, Victoria or Tessie.

I sat back in my seat and let my mind drift back to the years following the end of the war. For two long years Joel struggled to recover from its devastating effects. Finally in 1867, Joel, like many men, sold farm and home to settle in Concord.

In those days you could throw a stone from one end of this little courthouse village to the other. When Joel said we were leaving Stanly County to move to the city, I was hoping to find a bit of Charleston. I did not expect just a couple of clapboard buildings, dark muddy streets and only a few hundred residents. It was foolish of me to think otherwise. Nothing will ever be as grand as Charleston before the war.

What Concord did have to offer was the cotton mill and that meant jobs. Working in a cotton mill was not Joel's dream, but we were grateful for the food it put on our table. Those of us that depend on the cotton mill for our livelihood have become a close-knit community.

Today I am headed for the new mercantile to purchase paper and ink for my typewriter. I take in the fresh air and ride along striving to bring my mind to a state of tranquility.

As I approach town, I admire the newly constructed homes on the main road and my mood begins to change. Old images of our plantation begin to flash through my mind. Few people here know Papa was once one of the richest men in Charleston. Joel and I seldom spoke of my privileged years. I have no regrets spending the last 25 years as the wife of a good, honest man who earned his living over a cotton loom.

My attention is quickly brought back to the present when my horse rears up in protest to the approaching steam trolley. Concord Railway Company built the track right through town to haul people to the depot. It is referred to as the "dummy line." I can see why. The "dummy line" is out of commission half the time and I can walk to the depot faster than it can carry me.

Poor Bella will never get used to them. The old girl is up in age and she is entitled to retire to a nice pasture somewhere, but I am not ready to give her up. My husband Joel was a fine horseman. It almost seems like blasphemy to turn to this modern transportation.

My eyes begin to tear thinking of the old days. On a beautiful day like this, Joel and I would ride across the meadow to our secret spot down by the creek. We always went on pretense of hosting a picnic or taking a swim, but we both knew it would end with fulfilling the passions of our young love.

"Stop it!" I say aloud to myself. I know I must gain control of my rambling mind. When I pull up in front of the store, I pull out a little flask in my purse and take a sip. Papa always said a little bit of brandy was good for almost everyone.

I adjust my hat, tie off my horse and walk to the front door. I nod at the two old gentlemen playing checkers on the porch and step back to marvel at the new screen door. "Keeps the flies out," one of the men calls out to me.

"If there is one thing I hate, it is a fly in my house," I say, thinking of Cindy Lou's husband.

17

The other man looks up at his friend. "Flies trouble us not by their strength but by their multitudes." He pauses and then ends with "Just like Yankees." They both laugh, even though it may not have been intended as a joke.

I see Mrs. Waddell sitting behind the counter nervously looking over a stack of papers. When I open the door, she looks up over the top of her glasses and raises her brows. "Lizzie! What a surprised to see you out and about so soon."

"Nice to see you too, Edna," I answer sweetly, even though she is looking at me disapprovingly. I quickly dart down the first aisle, hoping to escape one of her prying conversations. But, as soon as I hear scuffling footsteps closing in on me, I know I will not be that lucky. Then a high-pitched voice calls out, "Can I help you dear?"

I inform her I have just come out briefly to pick up a bundle of paper and an ink ribbon for my typewriter. She stares at me for a moment and says, "This way."

Up and down the aisles I follow her, trying to divert my eyes away from her large derriere bouncing up and down like a ball. At last, she ends the search and leaves me waiting while she goes to get Oliver. I would rather not deal with the husband, but it appears it will be unavoidable.

I am not to wait long before I see the husband coming up the aisle unrolling his sleeves. He pauses briefly, unties his apron, tosses it back to Edna and runs his hand through his greasy hair. "Good Morning Mrs. Simpson. How may I be of service to you?" he asks, extending the same greasy hand to me. "You know our motto, if Waddell's does not have it, nobody does," he says smiling, exposing his gold tooth.

"For sure," I reply. I avoid the handshake by digging in my purse to present to him the typewriter ribbon for his examination.

He looks displeased. "My dear lady, these old ribbons are hard to find. Surely you are not still using an antique typewriter like this."

"Do you have the ribbon?" I ask firmly.

"Waddell's is not in the habit of carrying old-fashioned merchandise," he says bluntly.

I thank him for his time and turn for the door. Mr. Waddell chases after me. He winds up tripping over his wife and skating into a display of Pears' soap. I glance back just as the advertisement sign tumbles to the floor. "Wait," he calls out. "Mrs. Simpson, I feel I would be doing you a great disservice to let your delicate little finger tips continue to receive such abuse. Come let me show you what modern technology has to offer."

I pause and cut my eyes his way. He seizes this as an opportunity to take hold of my arm and direct me across the store. "Might I say, Mrs. Simpson, you have not aged a day since I first saw you. Why, if I could bottle your secret, I would be a wealthy man." He then looks over his shoulder to gauge his distance from Edna. "Any word of advice for my wife?" he whispers.

Before I can comment on how distasteful I find his little joke, I see Edna making a jealous approach. She is all aware of his flirtatious nature. Oliver quickly lets go of my arm and stands proudly in front of a brand new roll-top desk. With an arrogant little nod, he sits down and opens the desk, exposing a modern typewriter unlike any I have ever seen.

He sees he has my attention and lifts his hands high in the air as if he is a pianist preparing for a concert. Slowly he lowers his fingertips onto the keys and in just seconds a line of crisp clear words appear on the paper. He presses one key and the carriage returns. Quickly he jerks the paper out. "See," he says. "Simple as A, B, C!"

"So quiet," I say in awe. "Where is the foot pedal?

"My dearest, there are no foot pedals like the old models. You have just witnessed the technology of the modern Remington typewriter. Would you like to give it a try?"

It is difficult for me to hide my smile at his offer, but I shake my head no. "Mr. Waddell, I am sure without even asking I cannot afford such a machine. I would only be wasting your time. If you do not have the ink ribbon I need, I must be on my way."

"Now Mrs. Simpson, you owe it to yourself to give it a little try. It won't cost you a penny. And besides, I would like your opinion of its performance. "

He pulls the chair out and I walk over slowly and sit down. "So many keys," I say, feeling a bit overwhelmed.

He reaches over me and presses a single key marked "shift." "See this one. It makes capital letters." Then he inserts a fresh piece of paper welcoming me to begin typing. I am much impressed with the ease of the keys. With little effort the machine is clicking along at amazing speed.

When I look up, I realize I have been so engrossed with the device that I did not notice that Mr. William Lee has joined Mr. and Mrs. Waddell. I am embarrassed to see I now have an audience of three. To add to the awkwardness of the moment, Mr. Waddell attempts to introduce Mr. Lee, who interrupts with "We've met."

Surely he should know that a gentleman never makes such a statement. It could only lead to gossip and Edna Waddell thrives on gossip. She is delighted with the possibility of a newsworthy story, which is obvious by her giggling and wayward glances.

I suppose for all intent purposes, Mr. Lee and I could be a likely match. He is of handsome stock, a middle-aged widower and a successful attorney. A match if I was interested, but I am not. I have barely put my late husband in the ground. The last thing I want is gossip or romance. Yet, I wonder what could have possibly planted such a thought in my head. His smile makes me uneasy and I shift in my seat. "Oh yes, Mr. Lee helped facilitate my late husband's will."

"The pleasure was all mine," he says, turning and smiling at Mr. Waddell.

Why did he have to say that? Mrs. Waddell will have a story going all over town before sunset.

Mr. Waddell clears his throat. "Mr. Lee is interested in purchasing the Remington typewriter for his office."

"Well I was not actually," Lee declares. "But I figured the only way I was going to shut you up was to come take a look at it. I will admit, now that I have seen it in action, I am indeed interested. The only trouble being, I would have to employ the skills of a fine operator like Mrs. Simpson. With big old hands like mine, I am not too fitting for that kind of work."

He holds up his hands in the air and I take notice. Mr. Lee is a big man. His physique is more suited for a lumberjack or farmer than an attorney. He begins to laugh and I realize I am eyeing him and I quickly turn my head.

Mr. Waddell is itching to close the sale and applies a bit of pressure. "Mr. Lee, I only have one typewriter. In all fairness I must give Mrs. Simpson first option."

I quickly respond. "Like I said, Mr. Waddell, I certainly cannot entertain the idea of purchasing such a machine. If you have a buyer in Mr. Lee, by all means feel free to secure the sale." With that said, I attempt to squeeze out of the chair between the two men.

"Hold on there, Mrs. Simpson," Mr. Lee says, placing one of his large hands on my shoulder. "You have a need for this machine and so do I. You can operate it, but I cannot.

What do you say if I buy the machine and have it delivered to your house this afternoon?"

"Why ever would you do such a thing?" I ask, hearing my voice tightening up.

"It will be a business deal. You'll prepare my legal documents and in turn you can make use of the machine whenever you wish."

"Mr. Lee, I hardly think I am qualified for such important work."

"You pass the test by me," he says, giving me a little wink. Without looking at me again, he tells Mr. Waddell to deliver the typewriter to my house. There are no formal goodbyes and he turns to leave, picking up his pace as he nears the door.

It is my intention to put a stop to this nonsense. I start to follow him, but Mrs. Waddell takes hold of my arm. "Now Lizzie, those that are in the state of widowhood must resist the temptations of their youth," she whispers to me as if I am a foolish schoolgirl chasing after a beau.

I cannot hide my disgust at her remark. "Mrs. Waddell, if I need your advice I will ask for it." I do not wait for her response and quickly make stride to catch up with Mr. Lee.

When I run out of the store, the screen door slams behind me and wakes up the two old men on the porch. Mr. Lee has already mounted his horse, so I must raise my voice. "Mr. Lee, may I speak with you before you leave?"

"Sorry Mrs. Simpson, I am in a bit of a hurry. I am late for my next appointment." Mr. Lee pulls back on the reigns. "I'll be by your place this evening to discuss your salary and drop off your first assignment. Oh, I can stay for dinner, but don't worry about fixing up something fancy." He tips his hat and calls out to his horse, "Walk."

I am left standing on the porch to watch the backside of him bouncing in his saddle as he rides away. The old men settle back down in their rockers and I look back at the store. Edna was watching, but when she sees me turn, she slips behind the curtain. I straighten up my waistcoat and make my way to my carriage. There is nothing left to do or say. It seems I have been shanghaied into being Mr. Lee's secretary.

Once on the road again, I begin to run the events back over in my mind. If I understood correctly, Mr. Lee is not only going to allow me to make use of the typewriter, but he is also going to offer me a salary for the work I will be doing.

I could certainly use a little extra money. My finances are manageable on what Joel had saved, but there is little leeway for extras or unexpected burdens. I ponder over the strange events and come to the conclusion it is all divine providence. It is all in God's perfect timing. I shall accept it with a cheerful heart.

I am eager to make quick my return home and call out to Bella to pick up her speed. In record time I arrive home. Once I walk through the front door, my excitement fades. It is hard to break old patterns. Before I can gather my senses, I think to myself, *"I must tell Joel my news."*

Once opening this door was a promise of happiness. Now my surroundings seem to have appointed me the keeper of sadness. For over 25 years these walls housed a family. Now the children have all left home, Joel is dead and I am alone.

I drop my purse on the hall table, hang up my hat and call out "Dovie!" With my shoulders stooped, I walk across the hall to the keeping room. There hanging over the mantle is my painting. She is always overseeing, like a ghost from the past. I want her life again, my children to be young and most of all, my husband back from the grave. Within moments, Dovie appears at the door. I ask her to bring me some boxes.

"Yes Ma'am, I's be rights backs just as soon as I's turn offs da beans."

"Is there anything other than beans for supper?"

"No Ma'am," she replies, looking puzzled.

"Well, see if you can bake some cornbread. I think there is a jar of apples in the cupboard. Please make a pie. We are having a guest for dinner."

"Yes'um," she mutters and disappears out the door.

The sadness returns and I begin to feel my energy leaking out with my tears. "Daylight is burning!" I say aloud, trying to shake off the mood. I have too much work to do today to indulge in mourning. The old typewriter will have to go to the attic and the front room is covered with months of dust and scattered papers.

Today my housecleaning is a journey pondering over the past. I spend the entire afternoon in my old housedress with my hair tied up in a handkerchief. Bit by bit I sort through the pieces of my life.

The doorbell rings just as I am sealing the last box, which contains all of Joel's pipes. The deliverymen have arrived. I let Dovie go to the door and quickly pull the handkerchief off my head and untie my apron.

For a split second more I look over the room again. I will have them place the desk by the window, so I can watch the sunset on the days I work.

Dovie shows the men in. I begin to give them instructions, but the front door being propped open serves as an open invitation for Mrs. Davis and her daughter Lilly. They stop in the middle of the hall blocking the way of the men coming up the steps. "Do not tell us you are moving away, Lizzie," Mrs. Davis begins to pry.

"No, No," I assure her and take hold of her arm to pull her out of the way. I am frantically trying to answer all the questions coming at me at one time. "Yes, over there sir, by the west window. It is only a delivery Mrs. Davis. Yes Lilly, it is a new typewriter."

In all the commotion, Rebel races down the hall barking. In seconds, he manages to intertwine himself under the men's legs. We all hold our breath as the men struggle to keep from dropping the desk.

"Down Rebel!" I scream and reach out to grab his collar. He leaps forward and I land on my knees with my hair flopping down in my face. Just when I think things could not be more out-of-hand, I look up and see Mr. Lee standing at the door. I ask myself, is this all in God's perfect timing?

When I close the door behind Mr. Lee, it is after 8 o'clock. I am grateful to finally be alone. I take a deep breath and go to the kitchen to pour myself a glass of brandy. I sit down in my chair, close my eyes and reflect back on the events of the evening.

I knew that once Mrs. Davis and Lilly laid their eyes on Mr. Lee, they would overstay their welcome. Dovie had to reheat the beans so many times that they were mush and the cornbread was dry. The apple pie was unaffected and hopefully it was Mr. Lee's last memory of the meal.

Today Dovie restrained herself from asking a single question about the typewriter or Mr. Lee, but that will only last until morning. I will also be willing to bet that Mrs. Davis will be over bright and early with her share of questions too. She never misses a single opportunity to prospect a potential husband for her daughter.

Poor Lilly has a sad story. At age 14 she married a young man by the name of Virgil White. Shortly after they were married, he enlisted in the Mexican War and was later killed.

Mrs. Davis is convinced that Lilly will receive a handsome widow's pension someday. According to Mrs. Davis, unless Lilly is to marry a wealthy man, it is not worth risking the supposed pension. Therefore, for the last 40 years Lilly has remained Lilly White, the widow of Virgil White. Lilly works in the mill and the mother takes in sewing and tends to children.

Sadly, it is not just Lilly her mother's good intentions have affected. There is Henry Hickey. Henry has been the doting suitor of Lilly for the past 25 years. Henry is a sawed-off little man, but what he lacks in stature he makes up in character. He is not a wealthy man by any means, but he holds a steady job with the railroad. If Lilly's mother had not meddled, Lilly would have married Henry years ago. Maybe today they would have a family of their own.

Although Mrs. Davis does not find Henry a suitable husband for Lilly, she has no trouble finding him a suitable handyman. Henry takes on her assignments cheerfully, hoping that someday she will change her mind.

Lilly may have been a beauty once, but age and hard work are beginning to take their toll. Lately I have noticed Mrs. Davis seems to be particularly nervous about Lilly's appearance. Perhaps she is nervous the pension is never coming. She is insisting on dolling Lilly up in youthful fashions. Recently she has even resorted to such theatricals as false hair and rouge. It is not becoming and only results in making poor Lilly look silly and a source of gossip.

Just last week at church I overheard some of the women whispering as Lilly walked by. "Hold on to your husbands, ladies. No telling what a woman like that will do."

"Someone should ask her to leave. It just ain't decent for a woman her age prancing around like that," another lady spoke out.

I interrupted with "Is this not the Lord's house ladies? My Bible says the Lord welcomes everyone to his home."

I find myself laughing aloud as I recall the looks on their faces when I walked down the aisle and took a seat next to Lilly. Who would dare say another word? Yes, everything is in God's perfect timing. I take the last sip of my brandy and head down the hall for bed.

Chapter 3

A Day's Work

It is 5 o'clock in the morning and my eyes fly open, the same as they have for the past 25 five years. Although I could easily sleep as late as I please, old habits are hard to break. I lie in bed listening to the rain on the roof, seemingly to peck out a lonely tune. *"No breakfast for hungry children need be prepared. No lunch for a working husband need be packed. No, No, Theodosia, you are all alone, and alone you will always be."*

I wander into the kitchen where I have coffee and the last of the apple pie for breakfast. One good thing about my present state and age, the old rules do not apply. I can eat and drink as much as I like. I don't have to dress until noon or not at all if I please. I can stay up all night or go to bed before dark. Who is to know or who is to care. There is only Dovie here now and if a better offer comes along, she will be gone too.

I have three children. Victoria, who will soon be a woman of 30, is as independent as any man. Then there is Robert, age 26, who is the image of his father. Just like his father, he tries to take on the whole world. Lastly, there is Tessie, who for the whole of her 24 years has been a little worrier.

My children's stories are their own now. They must write their own futures. I can only write about their past, which I will do.

I pick up my coffee cup and head to the front room to start my new job. I am wearing Joel's robe again and my hair is uncombed, hanging down around my shoulders. Just as I cross the hall, I run into Dovie. *"Mornin' Misses Lizzie,"* she says, backing up to eye me over. *"Folks might be stoppin' in todays. Don'ts you wants to fix up a bit?"*

I look across the hall at the painting of myself hanging over the mantle. "I suppose," I mutter under my breath, turning back toward the bedroom.

Something told me she might be right. I fully expect to see Mrs. Davis and Lilly today and I do not care how they see me. However, professionally speaking, it would be distasteful should Mr. Lee stop in and see me in disarray.

Last night he provided me with a drop box for my porch. He will stop by every afternoon to pick up and drop off my next day's assignment. At the end of the week he will place a check in the box for the work I have completed. It was Mr. Lee's idea and it seems like a workable plan. Even though I consider him likable, he is a bold individual. I am not sure he will be so respectful of my privacy.

Just before 6 o'clock, I open the doors to the front room, which I am now calling my office. As soon as I sit down at the desk I feel a sudden chill. Is the room too cold or is it a ghostly haunt that sends a shiver down my spine? Either way, I am in need of comfort and I light a fire.

As I am waiting for the room to warm up, I pull back the curtains and stand by the window. It is not yet fully daylight, but the streets are busy with people hurrying along. Most are heading for the cotton mill to make their 12-hour shift. It always saddens my heart to see the number of children among them. It is the way of things here and the poor have little choice. I will always believe that children are designed for green meadows and play, not for factories and cotton dust.

So brief does the rose of childhood bloom,
Yet, with tender hands and love a mother gladly tends.

Oh well, I suppose every day above ground should be considered a blessing.

The instruction manual is lying next to the new Remington typewriter. I pick it up, thumb through the pages and think of Joel. If he were here, he would insist that I read every word before I press the first key.

I can almost hear Joel's voice cautioning me as I lay the manual down and proceed to feed the first piece of paper in the machine. The paper does not feed in as I expected. Then again, what does work exactly as you think? An hour later, I have the paper inserted correctly and it is all for the good.

"There," I say aloud. "Just like Mr. Waddell said, simple as A-B-C. Reading the manual would just have been a waste of time. I am confident that I will have Mr. Lee's reports typed by noon and have the rest of the afternoon to begin writing my own book.

The sun is now streaming through the window and the room is nice and warm. Dovie comes in, refreshes my coffee and then quietly closes the door behind her. It is time to open Mr. Lee's envelope of work. There is a handwritten letter enclosed:

Dear Mrs. Simpson,

I am most happy to have you as my secretary. I had interviewed several other ladies for the position, but found not one suitable candidate. As you will see this position requires a sensible individual who is not prone to gossip or idle talk. Mrs. Simpson, I consider myself a good judge of character. In you, I see such qualities, which is evidence of a fine and proper upbringing. I hope this position will serve you well. As you know, I lost my wife six years ago and I was thankful to have my work to divert my thoughts. I have often said some folks work to live, while others live to work. I look forward to working with you. Do not hesitate to contact me should you have any questions or concerns.

Sincerely,
Mr. William T. Lee

There appears to be two reports which are held together with straight pins. In addition, there is an unopened package of waxed carbon paper. Although I had seen this duplication paper, there has never been an opportunity for me to use it. I open the package and read the card inside:

Rogers and Rogers Company Inc.-Makers of the finest quality inks, carbon papers and typewriter ribbons. We are the modern way to do business. Rogers' duplication carbonated sheets are available in both blue and black ink. Type it once and make up to three copies. Instructions: Applying enough pressure is essential in order to produce a good quality copy. Since typewriters and operator's techniques vary, we suggest using a practice sheet first, before using your finest paper.

I had not budgeted a practice time in my day, but it might be wise. I remove the clean sheet of paper and insert a used sheet with the carbon paper behind. Three hours later, I have discovered the paper has a tendency to slip, tear or otherwise malfunction. Making corrections is not an easy task either. You must carefully lift the layers, apply correction ink, and allow it to dry completely before continuing. With this lesson learned, it is nearly noon and I break for lunch. By 1 o'clock, I return to my desk, feeling refreshed and ready to tackle the reports.

Report number one: My instructions are to make six copies of a Mr. Charles Caldwell's handwritten will: one for the file, one for the wife and one for each of the four children. Even with the carbon paper I can only produce three copies at a time. Therefore, it is necessary to type the entire will twice. After three start-overs and numerous minor mishaps, the clock strikes 4 o'clock as I am completing the first report.

Sitting so long has left me feeling stiff as a board. I stand up to stretch, pick up the second report and walk over by the window. I discover it is lengthier than the first, but thankful only three copies are required. With respect for the time, I return quickly to the typewriter.

I begin typing: I, Mr. William T. Lee, attorney at Law, have been retained by Mrs. Daisy Jones Wilson. The plaintiff is suing her estranged husband, Mr. Pleasant Otis Wilson, for divorce. The grounds for said divorce are as follows: adultery, mental and physical abuse and fraud against her good name.

I quickly find myself engrossed in the report. I now understood Mr. Lee's concern why his secretary of choice could not be of the nature to gossip.

It appears that Mr. Pleasant Otis Wilson was partaking in an ongoing affair with an unnamed woman. Mrs. Wilson claimed that the alleged rendezvous took place after the woman, a nearby neighbor, turned her horses loose. The wild horses served as a signal between the two offenders. Mr. Wilson played the good neighbor, corralled the horses and returned them to his waiting mistress. Mrs. Wilson later stated that her husband would be gone for hours and sometimes even overnight. Her depression over the ordeal nearly drove her out of her mind. Neighbors said she hardly knew if it were day or night. When she became bedridden, it provided the perfect opportunity for Mr. Wilson to have her committed into an asylum. Poor Daisy may have spent the rest of her life there, if she had not convinced one of the nurses to send a letter to her son in Boston. The son came home and discovered the other woman living in the household with his father. He pieced together the facts and is now assisting his mother in the case against his father.

The room is dim when I finish the report. I am alarmed to find it is nearly 6 o'clock. I had been so immersed in the story that I lost track of the time. What if Mr. Lee has already come by and found the box empty? Jumping up from my seat, I quickly prepare the envelope and head for the drop box.

Just as I open the door, I see Mr. Lee stepping up on the porch. "Good evening Mrs. Simpson," he calls out, in a carefree sort of tone.

"Oh, a good evening to you too. Here are your reports, sir," I say proudly.

Before he reaches for them, he stops and looks at me inquisitively. "My goodness dear lady, you have put in quite a day's work."

Suddenly becoming aware of my appearance, I push my hair out of my eyes and smooth my skirt. "Not so very much, but it did take some time to learn the machine."

"Indeed," he says smiling. He thanks me and turns to leave. "Oh, I almost forgot to give you tomorrow's assignment." He reaches in his coat pocket for the envelope. "I am afraid I must offer my apologies, but these will be dull in comparison to the ones you prepared today."

I knew exactly what he meant and we shared a laugh. Our eyes met for a brief moment and I felt like I was sharing a secret with an old friend. The moment is short lived. He announces that he must be going and to expect him around the same time tomorrow. For some reason I feel almost duped as he hurries off to his carriage.

There is a little click and the streetlights come on. I can now clearly see there is a woman waiting in the carriage. I hear her laugh as he jumps in next to her. The scene catches me by surprise. I pause and watch them ride off down the street.

Just as I turn to go inside, I see a dark couple walking arm and arm toward the house. In the dim light, I cannot identify the figures. I pull my shawl up around my shoulders and walk cautiously to the front gate. At closer look, I realize it is Dovie and some unknown young man. I quickly turn to go inside. I was hoping she had not seen me, but I hear hurried footsteps coming up from behind. I know she thinks I will be angry, but I am not.

"Misses Lizzie," she breathlessly calls out, rushing in the door behind me. *"I's was just..."*

I stop her in the middle of her sentence and pat her on the shoulder. "You don't owe me an explanation, sweetheart."

She smiles at me for a moment and then gives me a big hug. *"I's saved you supper."*

I follow her into the kitchen and she dishes out a bowl of stew for me. When I sit down to eat, she says goodnight and goes to her room. I eat slowly pondering over the day. Things had not gone like I planned. I had hoped to start on my book today, but my eyes are way too tired for that now. Oh well, tomorrow is another day. I call for Rebel and he comes running. "Hey boy, let's call it a night."

Chapter 4

My Story Begins

Four weeks have passed since the typewriter arrived. I admit I struggled the first week. I ruined paper, ink ribbons and nearly pulled out my hair. The second week I opened up the manual and studied it like the Bible.

I decided if this was going to be a real job, then I needed to set up a regular work schedule. I allowed time for lunch, a walk in the afternoon and scheduled breaks to prevent fatigue. Lastly, to reduce the stress I put aside my idea of writing my own book until I had mastered the job at hand.

Mr. Lee was right; this work is healing. It has given me a sense of purpose and a reason to get up each day. I still miss Joel terribly, but the work fills up some of the lonely holes. The worst part of my day is going to bed alone and waking up in the morning to an empty bed. They say time is the only thing that will heal a broken heart. In my case, I think the best I can hope for is that time will seal the cracks.

By noon, Mr. Lee's work is typed and ready to deposit in the drop box. When I step out on the porch, I spy the newspaper on the walkway and venture out to collect it. It is then I see Mrs. Davis standing in her front yard. Today is testimony to her recent frail and unkempt appearance. Her clothes are wrinkled, her stockings sagging and her gray hair is flapping in the wind. She has attracted my curiosity as to what she is looking at on the roof. Then I hear her shout out, "Henry! Did you find the leak?"

"Not yet, Mrs. Davis, not yet!" Henry calls back.

Mrs. Davis sees me and waves. I smile and do the same. Fall is in the air and it makes me think of the holidays. This will be my first Thanksgiving without Joel. I could impose myself on a nearby family. My sister Sallie would welcome me at her table, but she has a small herd of her own to feed.

Robert and Tess have their own children and in-laws to host celebrations. They would gladly include me, but the merriment might be more than I could appreciate at this time. Then there is my oldest, Victoria, who is living in Charleston. She has chosen not to marry and at her age it is doubtful she will. She appears to be happy; therefore, I have resolved to be happy with her choice. *I am reminded that the children we birth do not belong to us. They belong to God. We are simply the vessels through which they arrive on this earth. We are appointed to care for and guide them; however, we must recognize when the time comes for them to govern their own lives.*

By the time I am back in the house, I am lost in thought. I walk across the hall, sit down at my desk and carefully analyze the situation. I wish the holidays would come and go without notice, but that is not likely to happen. There will be decorations and wreaths on doors and neighbors hosting parties and socials.

There is time to plan a trip to Charleston, but I would need to write to Victoria right away. With the money I have earned the train ticket should be affordable, but there is still more to ponder. My mind is racing and I think of the money I am earning again. Another check will be dropped off today. If I shop wisely, I could have all of them here for Thanksgiving and Christmas dinner. Joel loved big family gatherings and I could host it in his memory. If he is looking down from heaven, he will be most pleased.

About an hour later, I attach Rebel to his leash and open the front door. It is a satisfying feeling to be armed with my newly written invitations to each of my children and my sister Sallie's family. The rusty hinge on the gate is stuck again, which causes me to scuff my knuckles. I quickly forget about my minor injuries as Rebel pulls me down the street. He knows the way to the post office.

For the first time in many weeks, a happiness comes over me like a veil of peace falling gently around my shoulders. Walking along I am smiling and planning the events in my head. I will ask Cindy Lou and Violet to come help with the cooking. Even though Victoria is busy with her work, surely she will consent to come and stay at least until the New Year. I must not think of what has ended, but of new beginnings and new traditions.

When I return home, I settle down at my desk and put a fresh sheet of paper into the typewriter. Writing my book has been on my mind for weeks. It is not without thought that I begin. I have arranged all my scrapbooks and diaries in chronological order on the shelves next to me. They will serve as my outline and assist me in recalling detail and forgotten memories.

It is my plan to begin in 1867 when Joel and I first moved to Concord. I will end in the present. I type the header in bold capital letters.

CHAPTER ONE

My hands freeze on the keys as I recall my days at the Miss Talvande's Academy in Charleston. I can almost hear Miss Valdo's voice. "Now ladies, let it not go without note, the most important words of your composition are contained in the very first paragraph. If they are not well thought out to lead to intrigue, then your readers will be apt to consider the entire manuscript nothing but rubbish."

Funny how things from the past seem to be buried in your mind. The only reading audience I expect to secure at this point is my children. Therefore, my job will be to engage them. What could intrigue them more than buried pieces of the past?

I suppose they should know the truth. What if they discover these things on their own, long after I am dead? It is best if it comes from me. If I am to be convicted, at least I can offer up my own defense.

Knowing now that I must begin the book with a prologue, I insert a clean sheet and type a new heading:

My Life Before You

Dedicated to my children: Victoria, Robert and Tessie

My darling ones, before beginning this book I am faced with the task of revealing some pieces of the past. I beg each of you to employ understanding. Victoria, I am afraid this will apply especially to you.

When the war first began, we thought it would be short lived. The thought of the young men marching off to protect our cause inspired excitement and romance. My sister Sallie became a war bride and my baby sister, Annabelle, announced that she, too, was in love. She begged Papa to allow her to marry Thomas. Papa gave his consent with the stipulation that she wait until her 18th birthday.

If only Papa could have predicted the future, perhaps Annabelle would be alive today. The young lovers' passion soon resulted in Annabelle being with child. In Papa's anger, he packed her up and delivered her to Thomas in North Carolina. Right before the baby was due, she contracted typhoid. She died delivering the baby.

That was a lonely time. I lost one sister to marriage and the other to death. I was sure I would never marry. The man I loved was married to a woman who had been an invalid of the mind for many years. Most men would have felt it honest to divorce such a wife and marry another. I respected him more that he did not.

There were a few suitors—an attorney who I ousted after his character turned sour. The second was a doctor.

We were not much more than friends when he was killed in the war. Unbeknownst to me he had drawn up a will leaving all his earthy belongings to me, including his home in downtown Charleston.

The next two years were like a hurricane that never ended. When Papa left for a war mission, I moved into the doctor's house and mother went to North Carolina to stay with my sister Sallie.

Papa's mission failed and he was captured. I was left alone and defenseless, making me the perfect target for the handsome Edmond Cook. I thought he loved me and I agreed to marry him. When I discovered the truth about him I was already carrying his child.

A year of tragedy and marital abuse ended with a great climax. It was near the end of my pregnancy and I was restricted to bed rest. However, when I heard screaming I carefully made my way downstairs. To my horror, I saw my drunken husband in the process of accosting poor Cindy Lou. I reached for the fire poker and struck him on the head, rendering him unconscious.

I pulled Cindy Lou to her feet and we fled to my house in town. The excitement of the event brought on my labor. That evening, November 1, 1863, I gave birth to a baby girl, who I named Victoria Frances.

Victoria, as this story unfolds you will understand why I chose to protect you from this information. It was not until I had recovered from the delivery I learned that Edmond was dead. My only intention was to protect Cindy Lou, not take Edmond's life.

I, being the widow and the mother of a newborn baby, was never questioned. It was a terrible sin for me to carry and it has taken many years for me to accept God's grace of forgiveness.

By the time Papa was released from the Yankee prison our plantation was in ruins. With the threat of Sherman's Army approaching, we left Charleston to come to North Carolina.

After moving to North Carolina, I discovered the wife of the man I first loved had died. In letters, we planned to marry when the "Great Rebellion" ended. I think the happiest day of my life was the day I became Mrs. Joel Simpson. This is the man all of you knew as Papa.

The pages that follow will be our journey of the life we built together here in Concord, North Carolina. These pages will reveal fragments from the past and events that occurred along the way. Some happened during your tender years that you could not comprehend.

My children, I am proud that you have grown to be honest and stately into adulthood. I pray my words fall upon your ears as gentle as the sweet Carolina Rain.

With all my love and respect, your own true mother.

Theodosia E. Simpson

1867

It was a heavy decision for Joel to sell all that belonged to him and his father and move to Concord. For weeks after moving, he labored if he had made the right decision to raise our children, Victoria and Robert, in the city. I labored with him in spirit, but on November 19, I was also laboring with the delivery of our third child.

We were as settled as we could be in a new home and community. Joel had made his inquiries as to the best doctor in town before he moved our family. After meeting Dr. Baker and learning he served in the Confederate army, Joel secured his services.

The city doctor's delivery fee was $2.50. Joel began making payments of 25 cents a week. He hoped to have the entire bill paid before the baby was due.

However, Robert and Victoria came down with a mild case of whooping cough. This resulted in draining the entire balance at Dr. Baker's office and leaving us in arrears.

There was no more money for doctor fees. So I suggested that we consider the Indian woman from Stanly County that delivered Sallie's children. She never asked for money and was happy to accept food and clothing in exchange for her services.

Although Joel and I had confidence in her gentle skills, it would mean she would have to agree to come to Concord and stay in our home until the baby was born. It would not be an easy task to convince her to leave the seclusion of her little home on the banks of Rocky River.

A week before the baby was due, Joel finished his shift in the mill and rode out for Stanly County. He arranged for Lilly to come and stay with me while he was away. He promised he would only be gone the extent of two nights. If he could not find her or convince her in that length of time, he would sell his horse and hire the city doctor.

The first night Lilly came to spend the night was like a little party. Lilly invited Henry over for the evening and Mrs. Davis brought in supper. Henry played his guitar and after the children went to bed we all played a card game.

I went to bed too after Mrs. Davis left and Henry and Lilly enjoyed the rare opportunity to be alone.

I fell asleep quickly, but I kept waking up with reoccurring dreams. One, I recall clearly seeing myself standing on top of a tall mountain and then suddenly I began to fall. I woke up in a cold sweat and for the balance of the night, I tossed and turned with pain in my back.

I was exhausted when morning came and appreciative that Lilly had already attended to the children. Breakfast was on the table and waiting for me when I walked in the kitchen.

"Sleep well?" she asked.

"Yes," I lied.

She looked at me with her head held sideways. By the looks of me, she knew that was not the truth. The breakfast started down satisfyingly, but after a few bites, it seemed to disagree. Feeling afraid I would become sick, I left the table.

Victoria took little notice of my sudden departure, but Robert began to scream. "Mommy, Mommy!"

By the time I reached the hall, the entire contents of my stomach were now on the floor.

Lilly helped me into bed, cleaned up the mess and tried to appease the children. I dozed off after that, but I awoke with sudden pains in my stomach. I looked at the clock and it was after one.

I got to my feet and went to the kitchen. I was praying it was only hunger pains and not the onset of labor.

Lilly and Mrs. Davis were in the kitchen drinking coffee and the children were taking a nap. After a bowl of soup and several cups of coffee, my strength was restored. I dismissed the earlier episode to something I had eaten.

By the time I bathed and dressed, I felt better than I had in several weeks. I convinced Lilly of the same and she went home to help her mother with the laundry.

Thinking it may be our last warm day of the season, I dressed the children to go outside to play.

For an hour or two Robert and Victoria entertained themselves toddling around on the front lawn pretending to be looking for gold nuggets.

I was immensely enjoying the sunshine from the front porch swing. I looked up from my knitting occasionally to make sure my two little angels were not in harm's way.

Victoria discovered a ball, which had rolled under the porch and crawled in after it. The bouncing ball gained the attention of "Rebel Number two" who was lying at my feet. Before I could grab hold of him, Rebel had knocked Robert off his feet and ran off with the ball. Robert was only two years old. His feelings were easily hurt as well as his behind.

I jumped to my feet, but I stumbled and lost my footing on the front steps. It was only a minor fall, but the sight of seeing their mommy spread out on the ground caused both children to scream.

Henry was next door painting Mrs. Davis' porch and came to my rescue. Once on my feet I realized my water had broken. I am not sure which was worse, my embarrassment or the fear I would be in labor soon.

Henry sent Victoria for Lilly and helped me inside. The balance of the afternoon I spent in bed, sipping hot tea and praying that the labor would hold off until Joel returned. The intermittent sharp stabbing pains told me it was not likely.

Shortly after 4 o'clock, the pain in my back was constant and I was certain I was in labor. Joel was still not home. Although Mrs. Davis felt she could deliver a baby, she was uneasy with the responsibility.

Unbeknownst to me, Henry had left to go for the doctor. By the time Dr. Baker arrived, I was well into active labor and happy to see him. In fact, at that point I would have been willing to offer him anything we owned to deliver the baby.

Several hours of intense labor passed and the baby had not come. I could hear him talking over me and Mrs. Davis was crying. I was so weak I was afraid I was dying.

Sometime after that, he raised my head up so he could be sure I could see him. He explained to me the baby was turned in a position that would not allow it to be born. He was going to have to take the baby by Caesarean birth. Since Joel was not here, he would have to have my permission to perform the procedure.

I asked him if he had performed the procedure before. He answered "Yes." However, when I asked if the mother and child survived, his reply was, "If we do not take this chance, Mrs. Simpson, you and the baby may die."

I had little choice. I agreed, but I insisted on seeing my children before he administrated the chloroform.

It was daylight when I awoke. I was grateful to be alive, but troubled not knowing the outcome of my baby. I tried to rise and found to my surprise the Indian woman was seated next to me. She cautioned me not to get out of the bed. Then she immediately left the room. Seconds later Joel entered with our baby in his arms.

I was to learn that Joel arrived with the Indian woman moments before the doctor was to begin the surgery. She insisted on evaluating the situation and the doctor reluctantly agreed. Later he was quoted to say he had witnessed a miracle performed by the hands of this woman. Until then, he would have never thought it possible under such circumstances a baby could be delivered naturally.

The doctor never charged us a penny for that day. Our new baby girl, Tessie May, was not only a gift to us, but also to the many lives saved by the lesson learned by the good doctor.

I only bother to tell the events of that day to show how blessed we were. A mother quickly forgets all her suffering once she has babe in arms.

I was a little slow in recovering, but by Thanksgiving I was able to prepare the holiday meal.

It was unusually cold for November that year of '67 and the ground was covered with a light snow. Joel had already put in a full day's work hauling in wood for the fireplace and stove. Every time the door opened the wind whipped in, nearly cutting us to the bone.

We had invited Lilly, Henry and Mrs. Davis for dinner. When they came in, they mentioned a boy tracking across the back yards.

"A young boy?" Joel asked, thinking of the cold.

"Yes," Mrs. Davis replied. "I'd say about 10 or so. He was poorly wrapped and carrying a wee little dog under his arm."

"His folks may have sent him on an errand," I said, going to the window to take a look.

"Well, maybe so," barked Mrs. Davis. "But somebody should have bundled him up better. This is pneumonia weather."

45

I gazed across the yards. I saw a few tracks leading around to the barn, but there was not a soul in sight. After a few minutes, a crying baby and a hungry family to feed, I forgot about the boy.

It was not until Joel went out for more wood that we were reminded. He said he saw a boy down by the barn. He called out to him, but the boy took off like a rabbit.

"He might not be alone, Joel," Henry cautioned. "I've seen a mess of freeloaders lately. The other day down at the railroad, I counted 15 fellows jumping out of an empty boxcar."

"I expect they are coming here to work in the Brumley Gold Mines," Joel replied.

"I reckon so, Joel, but folks with no homes are the desperate sort. They could be up to no good, stealing chickens or who knows what. Get your rifle and let's take a look around."

"Nothing to worry about," Joel said, smiling as he shut the door behind him.

Lilly was terribly nervous over the ordeal, but I was not. I assured her Joel was capable of taking care of himself and little Henry too for that matter.

She laughed, but her hands were shaking, causing her to drop a cup. When it hit the floor, the handle broke off. Instantly, her eyes filled with tears.

"Not to worry darling," I told her. "It is only an old cup and besides, I am sure Joel can glue it."

She handed me the cup and the broken handle. On the bottom, it was marked Havilland & Co. Limoges France.

I smiled, but it was I who could have cried. The china had belonged to my mother. Even after all our trials, not a single piece had been broken until now.

My mood was quickly restored when I turned around to see my two children sitting at the table and baby Tessie in her cradle by the fireplace. Even if the cup was pure gold, it could not compare to the beauty of their little faces.

"They're coming!" shouted Mrs. Davis. "And they got the boy with them."

In walked Joel, Henry and one frozen little boy with a very wet and smelly dog under his arm. I am not sure who was shaking the most, the dog or the boy.

Joel told the boy to have a seat by the fireplace and he would see if he could find some dry clothing for him. The boy obeyed, but never looked up once at the rest of us in the room.

Henry walked across the floor and in a low voice said, "Looks like the boy has been abandoned." The boy heard him and he began to weep.

Mrs. Davis was a kind woman, but the tone of her voice is always domineering. "Boy," she said, towering over him. "What is your name?"

The boy looked up at her. He was a handsome child, with clear blue eyes and fair hair. His lips were so badly chapped from the cold he could barely speak. "Les Lester."

"Lester who? Boy, what is your full name?" she asked firmly.

"Les Lester," he said clearly.

"Les Lester, is that all of the name you have?"

"Yes Ma'am, as far back as I can remember."

Before she could ask any more questions, Joel was back. "Come on son, lets see if we can suit you up," he said quietly.

The boy stood up to follow Joel and put the dog on the floor. The dog began shaking and splattering dirty water on the walls. The dog, now warm and smelling food, was running all over the room. The children thought it was great fun, but I did not. I now had a broken cup and muddy walls to clean.

Not knowing what to do next, we took our seats at the table. In a few minutes, Joel returned with the boy. The boy was wearing much-too-large pants and shirt and smiling like a mule eating saw briars.

"I would like to introduce our special guest for dinner, Mr. Les Lester," Joel said, as he pulled back his own chair for the boy to have a seat.

As soon as the boy sat down the dog jumped in his lap and extended his nose over the table. Again, the children found it far more entertaining than the rest of us.

"I bet your little dog is hungry," Joel said. "Let's get a bowl for him, too."

"Rooster will sure be beholding to you sir. Me and him ain't had nothing to eat in a couple of days."

"Rooster?" Henry asked the boy.

"Yep, I named him that, cause his hair sticks straight up on top just like a rooster."

Joel put some scraps of meat in a bowl and handed it to the boy for the dog. The boy shoved a handful of the niblets into his own mouth and then set the bowl down for the dog.

The boy ate like a starving soldier. When he was finally full, he and the dog lay down in front of the fireplace and went to sleep.

All the while I took note of Henry and Lilly looking over him. Lilly covered him with a blanket and Henry said, "How could anyone run off and leave a fine little boy like this."

"They should be hung; it is a downright crime," Lilly replied, wiping the tears from her eyes.

By the end of the evening, Henry took ownership of the boy. The father never came back for him. Henry, with Lilly's help, raised him. I will always believe they thought of him as the child they never had together.

Chapter 5

The Trouble With Hats and Handkerchiefs

Monday, November 23, 1892

It is too early for the stores to be open, but I am perched on the sofa and ready to leave once the clock strikes 8 a.m.

The house is still and there is not a sign of life in the kitchen. Dovie is not one to sleep in, but my guess is she is counting on the fact I usually do.

I have my suspicions that lately she is spending some of her nights out. Seconds later the door slowly opens and I see her sneaking in the front door carrying her shoes. It is confirmation of my theory.

"Good morning," I call out to her. She nearly jumps out of her skin. If it were possible, she would have turned white as a ghost. I can hardly contain my laughter. "Mind telling me where you have been?" I ask, in a make-believe stern voice.

"I's-I's been-been out for a walk. You knows a body can'ts gets enough fresh air," she answers nervously.

"I see," I say, looking her directly in the eye. "Seems mighty cold to be walking around barefoot."

"I's don'ts mind it," she replies. Before I can say more, she slips out the door promising breakfast will be ready shortly.

I let her go about her business, but I intend to address this later. She is 20 years old. I am not her mother, but I do feel responsible for her. I do not intend to preach, but like the old saying goes, if you can get the milk for free, ain't no use to buy the cow.

In a few minutes, I hear the pots and pans rattling. I was not hungry, but now with the sweet smell of bacon coming from the kitchen, I am starving. She is likely to outdo herself in an effort to distract my questions. Good for me, I think smiling. I hope she makes hot cakes, too.

While I am waiting for Dovie to call me for breakfast, I think of my plans for shopping that day. Robert and Tessie have accepted my invitation for Thanksgiving dinner. They have declined my offer for Christmas, saying they have promised that pleasure to the in-laws. It is disheartening to think I will not see the grandchildren for Christmas, but I will not think of it for now. I am happy knowing Victoria is due to arrive tomorrow. Her letter is in my pocket and I take it out again to read.

The Charleston Female Seminary

151 Wentworth Street
Charleston, South Carolina
Mens sana in corpore sano
"A sound mind in a sound body."

November 17, 1892

Dear Mother,
When I received your letter, I planned to go at once to Miss Kelly and request for time off to come to North Carolina. I felt it likely she would grant my

request. Over the past ten years, I have asked for few favors. In addition, most of the girls would be going home for the holidays.

However, that same day I learned that Beatrice Kohn had been relieved of her position and Miss Kelly had hired a northern girl to replace her. I must admit that halted my intentions. Most southern girls prefer marriage to the teaching profession, but there seems to be a trend for the reverse for northern girls.

As you know, I am an activist for the equality of women. I support the right for women to vote, hold office and above all have access to higher education. I think the time has come that man can no longer think of women as property, or just something pretty to look at. We must be allowed to seek our own destinies and receive equal pay for a day's work.

You and I may not always see eye to eye, but I know if you were in my shoes, you would ask the same question. Just what does a Yankee girl know about teaching young ladies to be Southern Belles?

With the fear I could be so easily replaced, I felt it not wise to ask for a temporary furlough. I stuck your letter in my pocket and forwent confronting Miss Kelly. The next morning Miss Kelly sent word she wished to speak to me. I left my class fearing the worst. I keep telling myself that Miss Kelly was a fine Christian woman and surely she would not dismiss me without reason.

Much to my surprise she has summoned me to award me. She remarked on my fine performance and dedication. She said I was overdue a recess and granted me time off until the first of January with pay!

After I regained myself and started for the door, she called me back. "Victoria, you must have dropped this letter in the hall." I realized she must have taken the liberty to read your letter, but with the outcome, how could I be angry? So darling Mother, expect me to arrive in Concord Tuesday, November 23.

Arrivederci until then!
Victoria

I fold up the letter and visualize my oldest daughter in my mind. She is taller and fairer than myself. Still, no one can deny she is my daughter. Victoria was a serious child. "Just because" was never good enough for her. She had to know why. Joel always said she was one pigheaded little girl. Even so, she has finished up to be a respectable young woman. I suppose with such an independent nature, she may be wise not to marry.

There is a gentle tap on the door and Dovie tells me breakfast is ready. I lay the letter down and follow her into the kitchen. I am right. She has outdone herself, hot cakes and all. Most mornings she pulls her chair up to the table and talks my ear off, but today she eats standing up by the stove. I finish my meal in silence and pretend not to notice. When I am finished, I fill Rebel's bowl with the scraps and turn to leave. I stop for a moment and give thought to what I should say. "Dovie, do you know about the birds and the bees?" I ask.

She looks up at me puzzled, *"Yes'um."*

"Perhaps I should ask that in a different way: "Dovie, do you know how babies are made?"

"I's knows dats too. It tells it in da Bible. An angel came unto Mary and told her she was gonna have a baby."

"Do you think that is how all babies are made?" I asked, fearing it might be true.

"I reckon so," she answers.

"Good Lord!" I shouted, and stomped out the door.

"Yes he is!" she calls back to me.

I knew that tonight I would have to break the news to Dovie that is not how babies are created these days. Why Cindy Lou has not explained this to her is beyond me. Then the thought crosses my mind; maybe she does not know either.

My plans were to do my shopping and be back before noon, but now I am running late. I will be hard pressed to get Mr. Lee's reports typed in time for his pickup.

I am alone and the chore of hooking my horse and carriage up is my own. It is a cold damp day and not the best for climbing in and out of a carriage. Riding down the road the cold ache in my back returns. I seldom think of the day I walked in on a thieving scalawag some 25 years ago, but today I am reminded of the bullet lodged in my back.

With several new stores in town, I had hoped to do some comparison shopping. Now I have lost the interest. I will do my shopping at Patterson's on Main Street and then cut across to the meat market to buy a turkey for my family and one for Cindy Lou's.

By the time I turn onto Union Street, it is raining. The streets are bare except for a few Negroes carrying wood and supplies into the fine new houses. My mind drifts back to holidays on the plantation. How my life has changed. When Joel was living I never missed the old days, but lately I have begun to miss it all. I have dreams of Mammy. Her hands are always working—making bread, sewing or combing my hair.

Last night I dreamed Papa and Mother were alive and well. I cannot understand why suddenly my past is haunting me.

I am almost to town when I see a carriage pull up in front of the mayor's house. W. G. Means and his wife, Corallie, step out. Mr. Means is wearing an impressive overcoat and top hat, and across Corallie's shoulders is a lovely wool cape with a fur piece.

Mrs. Means was instrumental in founding the Episcopal Church and Mr. Means is an attorney. They have four or five children, but the only one I know by name is Gaston or "Bud" as he is called. He has a reputation as being abnormally smart, but a rather peculiar lad with big ideas. I wonder what will become of that boy.

After leaving the meat market, I start out for the post office. It is doubtful I will have mail, but it will be nice to see Miss Mary Dusenberry, the postmistress. I am barely on the road when my stomach begins to growl. I try to ignore the empty feeling in my stomach, because lately I have put on a few pounds. Since Joel died, eating has almost become a hobby to me rather than a necessity.

However, as I pass by the hotel I smell the aroma of fresh baked bread. I decide I will not deny myself a small bowl of soup and at least one of Mrs. Brown's yeast rolls. After all, at 50 years old, who do I have to impress.

I pull up front of the hotel and a Negro boy runs out to take charge of my carriage. Mrs. Brown greets me at the door and seats me at a small table by the window. The hotel is actually the Browns' home and they also own the livery stables around back.

I order a cup of coffee while I am waiting for the soup and entertain myself by looking out the window. Across the road is a row of professional offices. Mr. Lee's office is the one next to the end.

My thoughts drift to the day Joel and I came to see him, just before we left to go to Asheville for his treatment. Joel joked and claimed he had been meaning to draw up a will for years. But his constant coughing was a reminder of the seriousness of the event. I honestly believe Joel had already given up hope. Yet for my sake, he would not admit it. Maybe if I had God's eyes and could have known the outcome, I would have never insisted he go to Asheville.

Not now, I think to myself. Tears are not for public display. I reach in my purse for my handkerchief and blot my eyes. I take a sip of coffee and open the newspaper lying on the table. I have just begun to scan over the headlines when I hear someone call out my name. "Lizzie, is that you?"

I lift up my eyes and standing over me is Miss Kelly. She was my children's teacher. Our pleasant conversation is quickly interrupted once Mrs. Harris walks up and taps Miss Kelly on the shoulder. She turns smiling, but her smile quickly fades when seeing the angry look on Mrs. Harris's face.

"Miss Kelly," she begins. "My grandson just informed me that you are instructing the children to recite a Pledge of Allegiance to the union flag. Is this true?"

"Yes, Mrs. Harris, that would be correct," Miss Kelly responds, and takes hold of the table bracing herself for an attack.

Mrs. Harris's face is beet red when she points an imposing finger in Miss Kelly's face. "My dear teacher, do I need to remind you how many men died fighting for the Confederacy and those that were not killed swore their allegiance at Appomattox? So I hardly think our children should have to do it again!"

"Mrs. Harris, do I need to remind you that the year is 1892?"

"Well, do I need to remind you, Miss Kelly, that James P. Cook, the superintendent of the schools, is a close and dear friend of mine? I wonder what he will think of this?"

"Well, I suggest you find out for yourself in today's paper!" Miss Kelly says, reaching over me and collecting the newspaper lying on the table next to me."

Mrs. Harris refuses the paper and storms out of the dining room. Miss Kelly winks at me and politely excuses herself, promising to stop by and see Victoria while she is in town.

I glance around the room and I am thankful the guests seated nearby seemed to be engrossed in their own conversations.

My soup arrives along with two hot yeast rolls dripping with butter. Again I pick up the paper and begin to read. I see at once why Miss Kelly suggested that Mrs. Harris read the paper. According to an article on the second page, Francis Bellamy has written this Pledge of Allegiance. It was published in the September 8, 1892, issue of *The Youth's Companion*, to serve as a celebration of the 400th anniversary of Christopher Columbus's arrival in America. Thus in October of this year, it was approved to be recited in the public schools. It does seem odd that the parents were not consulted on this matter first.

I see out of the corner of my eye that Mrs. Brown is escorting a couple to a table. I am more concerned with finishing the last bite of my second yeast roll to look up, until I hear a familiar voice. "Yes, I'll have coffee and the lady will have tea."

It is Mr. Lee. His back is to me, but I can see the woman clearly. She is pretty enough and fashionably dressed, but her large hat is out of proportion for her petite frame. Looking at her's makes me think of the little box hat on my head. She is most likely thinking mine is too small for my frame. I now wish I had not eaten that second roll.

I cannot just sit here all day, but I am embarrassed for Mr. Lee to see me. I scan over the dining room paths. I have no choice but to walk right past them wearing my too-little hat.

I quietly open up my purse and leave the money for my tab on the table. Then with as little action as possible and in a discreet manner, I begin my exit. I pass the table and it looks like I will have a successful escape, until I hear "Mrs. Simpson!" I turn quickly as if I am caught by surprise.

Mr. Lee excuses himself from the table and rushes up to greet me. He is smiling like a politician. You know the kind of smile that is not directed at one person, but is meant to be broadcast to anyone who is watching. "Miss Simpson, may I speak with you for a moment?" he asks, taking hold of my arm and directing me toward the door.

I fear he wants to express his concerns that while I am out lunching, his reports are waiting. I am preparing my speech as we walk. I will assure him if the reports are not completed by this afternoon, I will hand deliver them to him first thing in the morning.

Once we are outside and he could talk freely, he still speaks in a whisper. "Mrs. Simpson, I stopped by your home early today to tell you since it was a holiday not to bother with the reports until Monday. I also wanted to drop off one of my mother's pumpkin pies.

I started to say thank you, but I could see he had more to say. "Your colored girl told me you were out for the morning and then she fell at my feet weeping!"

"Weeping?" I ask in complete shock.

"Yes! It took me a minute to find out what was wrong. Apparently a beau of her's was arrested by a group of men and thrown in jail last night."

"Did she say what for?" I ask, forgetting myself and taking hold of Mr. Lee's hand.

Mr. Lee pats my hand. "You best sit down while I tell you the rest of the story." We walk over and sit down on the wicker settee. Although it is cold outside, suddenly I am excessively warm.

"Well," he begins. "It involves Darlene Candleberry. She claims earlier on that same afternoon she was on her way to see her sister when the colored boy approached her and made an attempt to assault her virtue."

"Do you think it is true?" I ask.

"Well, your Miss Dovie certainly does not think so. I have to admit she offered up a convincing argument on his behalf. She claims he is a good Christian boy and is studying to become a preacher down at the African Methodist Episcopal Church. I hope you do not mind, but I took the liberty to pay the boy a visit in jail."

"I am sorry if you have been misled, Mr. Lee. Dovie does not have a nickel to her name and certainly cannot pay for legal services. If you will send me the bill, I will reimburse you for your time."

"No, no, Mrs. Simpson. I am not asking for payment from you or the girl. I was strictly acting as a Good Samaritan. After talking to the boy, I think he is indeed innocent. He said he was on his way to church and just happened to be behind Miss Candleberry when she dropped a fancy blue handkerchief. He picked it up and tapped her on the shoulder to offer its return. The girl flew into hysterics and took off running down the street. That night when he was having his evening meal, the men knocked his door down, handcuffed him and took him to jail. It was not until the next morning he discovered why he was arrested."

"What makes you so sure he is telling the truth, Mr. Lee?" I ask.

Mr. Lee smiles, reaches into his pocket and produces a fancy blue handkerchief with the initials D.C. "The boy still had the handkerchief in his pocket. As soon as I finish my meal, I will go over to the girl's home and see if I can clear up this matter. With any luck I will have the boy out of jail by this afternoon."

"I am most grateful to you for your time and I know Dovie will be too. I am sure she will be happy to come and do some domestics for you in exchange for your kindness."

"Speaking of time," Mr. Lee laughs, "I must get back to my lunch."

"Yes, you must not make your lady friend dine alone. She is likely to be angry already." With that statement, I jump up to leave.

"She does not mind, as long as I am paying," he says boldly. To his comment, I must have looked stunned. "But then, what is a big brother for?" he says, and winks at me.

"Oh, I see," I laugh nervously.

"The stable boy had watched me come out and has my carriage waiting. I climb in and take a big breath. "So, Mr. Lee has a little sister," I whisper to myself as I take hold of the reigns.

I call for Dovie as soon as I open the door, but she does not answer. I step in the kitchen and on the table sits the pumpkin pie, but no sign of Dovie. Thinking she may be in her room, I walk upstairs. She is not in her room. A fear comes over me. What if she has done something desperate? Maybe she has run away or God forbid something worse? I open her wardrobe. I am somewhat relieved to see her clothes and belongings are still there.

With no help, it is up to me to bring in the groceries, put up the carriage and attend to the horse. I had arranged for Cindy Lou and Dovie to be here to help with the preparation for the meal tomorrow. Oh well, I suppose the only person in this life you can really count on is yourself.

I spend the rest of the afternoon slicing, dicing, mixing and preparing a meal for nine adults and five children. I am not sorrowful of the work and it helps to keep my mind occupied. One thing for sure, I am most grateful Mr. Lee has forgiven me of my clerical duties until Monday.

After I have done all I can do in the kitchen, I am left with the task of polishing up the house for guests. However, Dovie being a steady and excellent housekeeper, there is little to do. A little past five my work is done and I fix myself a bite to eat. The clock strikes seven and still no word from Dovie. I go to my office and attempt to start on the reports, but I am too worried to organize my thinking. Eight o'clock, I try reading. By nine, I decide that it is time to go to bed.

I have just put on my nightclothes and I am brushing out my hair when I hear a knock at the door. I am alarmed. If it were Dovie, she would have used her key. It is way too late for a sensible guest. Something must be wrong. I tuck my pistol in the pocket of my robe and go to the door.

"Who is it?" I say, before unlocking the door.

"It's me, Mr. Lee," comes the reply.

I am stunned why he would be calling this time of night. I fear it is bad news about Dovie and unlatch the door.

I am fully expecting to see Mr. Lee step in, but instead a young Negro man comes through the door. I am just before screaming until Mr. Lee steps in behind him and closes the door. "Can we talk?" he asks.

Sometime in my life, I must have been in a more awkward situation. Nevertheless, tonight, standing here in my nightclothes with Mr. Lee and an unknown Negro man, has to be at the top of my list.

Even so, I nod and motion for them to have a seat in the front room. "May I get you something: water, coffee or perhaps a brandy?" I ask.

"Yes, I think for me a bit of brandy would be in order. How about you Jasper?" The young man does not respond and remains staring at the floor. "Bring him a cup of water," Mr. Lee says, as if he is speaking for a child.

I return with the drinks, feeling sure I have put two and two together. The young man must be Dovie's beau.

Mr. Lee lifts the brandy to his lips and drinks it in only two gulps. "Another?" I ask, reaching for the glass.

"No, no, I am good," he says, and clears his throat. "Mrs. Simpson, this is Jasper, the young man that I spoke to you about. It took some doings to get him out of jail. When I first arrived at the Candleberry's home, I spoke only to Mrs. Candleberry and Miss Darlene. I was certain Miss Darlene realized she had overreacted to the situation. However, she was too embarrassed to give up her story in front of her mother. As an attorney I am used to this type of circumstance, so I continued to interrogate the witness for over an hour. She held fast to her account, until her father came home and saw through the story too. He insisted she confess to the truth. Afterwards, Mr. Candleberry went with me to the sheriff's office to drop the charges. At that point, there was no reason for the sheriff to hold Jasper. I was hoping to leave Jasper here with you and the girl."

"Why on earth here?" I ask, wondering why I am to be involved in this.

"The sheriff suggested that he lay low until this thing blows over. Once people find out what happened, everything will be alright. But since this is a holiday, the newspaper will not be out until Monday. If the Klan is on to this, the first place they will go looking for Jasper is down in Coleman town. He would not be safe at my house either, since my name has been linked to this case."

"I see, but I have not seen Dovie since I left the house this morning," I sadly admit, biting back the tears.

Mr. Lee turns to Jasper and starts hammering him with questions. "Do you have any idea where this girl could be? When was the last time you saw her?"

Jasper hangs his head down and puts his hands over his ears to close out Mr. Lee's words. Mr. Lee then gets down on his knees so that he can look Jasper directly in the face. "You don't want anything to happen to the girl, do you?"

Jasper is frightened and it appears his eyes will soon pop out of his head. *"Nos, Nos I sho don'ts!"* he shouts out.

"Then just where the hell is she?" Mr. Lee shouts back, causing Jasper to retreat to his stumped-over position.

I can clearly see Mr. Lee is tired and has lost patience with him and I take over. "Jasper, Dovie is like a daughter to me. If you know where she is, please tell me."

Jasper looks up at me with tears streaming down his face. *"Just after dark, Dovie comes to the Jailhouse window. She says dat she done and rounded up a whole bunch of colored folks. Soon they'd be a comin to bust me outs of the jail. She says they will have a fast horse and she and me will run away and never come back. I's told her not to start up no trouble on my account. But she runs off and I ain't seen her since."*

"Fools. The sheriff will have them all arrested!" Mr. Lee says and stomps his foot.

"Somebody is a likely to get kilt!" Jasper cries out.

"Jasper, do you know where they were to meet up?" I ask.

"Down at the African Church is my guess," he responds.

"I'll have to go down there and see if I can stop this," Mr. Lee declares, and reaches for his hat. Jasper gets up to go with him. Mr. Lee shakes his head. "Jasper, you stay here. You are the last person that needs to be down there in this mess."

"Then I'll go with you," I say firmly.

"A woman! I will not hear of it!"

"Mr. Lee, you may be a smart man, but you are a fool if you think they are going to listen to a white man they don't even know. Dovie and the others trust me and they will listen to me!"

"I don't like it, I don't like it at all," he says, and starts pacing the floor.

"Well, the way I see it Mr. Lee, you have little choice. Wait here while I go change my clothes."

Before we leave the house, Mr. Lee cautions Jasper not to open the door to anyone until we return. I feel some uneasiness leaving Jasper alone in my home, but some situations call for blind trust.

On the way across town, Mr. Lee mentions what a cold night it has turned out to be. Other than that one remark, he says nothing until we see a row of lanterns bobbing up and down on the road in front of us. "That must be them."

"Block the road and let me out," I tell him. In the dark, I cannot see his face, but I know he is looking at me. "It will be alright," I assure him, even though I was not so certain.

He hesitates for a moment and then turns the carriage sideways, creating a roadblock. I jump out and stand where they can see me. "Dovie!" I shout out. "It is me, Lizzie." The lanterns come to a halt and I see a row of dark faces looking back at me.

"Dovie!" I shout again. "Jasper is free, everything is alright!" There is a sudden hum of low voices. A few minutes later, a lantern starts toward me. I am hoping to see Dovie, but instead I see a stranger, a large Negro man.

Mr. Lee becomes anxious and jumps out of the carriage to stand next to me. When the man is at arms reach he calls out, "I am the Minister Jones of the African Church. I wish to hear what you have to say."

As Mr. Lee and he begin to speak, I see Dovie standing in the crowd. I leave my position, walk over and put my arm around her. "Let's go home dear; it has been a long day."

Chapter 6

The White House Cook Book

8 a.m. Monday, January 2, 1893

Today I will be taking Victoria to the train station to return to Charleston. This will be the first occasion I have had to wear the new hat she gave me for Christmas. I laugh as I place the hat on my head. I step back from the mirror to take a look. It is a handsome hat, adorned with a gorgeous array of feathers and bows, but it is large.

When I first took it out of the box, my face must have dropped. Victoria took one look at me and knew exactly what I was thinking. We may differ in opinion on various subjects, but there are times we can read each other's minds. "Mother," she said. "Large hats are all the style in Charleston. The old rule that just large ladies should wear large hats no longer applies."

We have had a brilliant visit. With all the festivities, the holiday passed by so quickly. It all has ended with an unexpected finale, the wedding of Dovie and Jasper.

Two days ago, I overheard Dovie and Victoria talking about marriage. Dovie said she told Jasper to find someone else to marry. It just would not be right for her to leave Miss Lizzie all by herself. Who am I, the keeper of lonely souls?

I certainly did not want someone else to be unhappy at my expense.

The next day when Jasper came to see Dovie, I met him in the hall. "Jasper, these walls sure need painting. There is a hole in the ceiling and the roof is leaking. There is way too much to do around here for just Dovie and me. Lately I have been thinking if Dovie could find herself a handy husband, my worries would be over. You do not know anyone, do you?

Jasper took the bait. Reverend Jones at the African Church married them the next day after the Sunday service. It was a warm and natural feeling to be there with Cindy Lou's family. We were not black or white people. We were just people bound together by love and understanding. As I walked out of that church, I felt like I had rediscovered my inner peace. The church I go to puts too much emphasis on silly things, like the color of choir robes or who plays the piano. I may just forsake my old church and join these people in their house of the Lord.

That night before I fell asleep I laughed, thinking about what Cindy Lou said as she placed a white lace handkerchief on Dovie's head to walk down the aisle. *"All girls look innocent in a white veil."*

On Christmas day, we were surprised with a visit from Mr. Lee and his mother. I found her to be an interesting conversationalist, but not nearly as much as Victoria found Mr. Lee. Politics, to be exact, was their common interest. They debated the rights of Negroes and women, labor laws, the pros and cons of the government taking control of the railroads, telegraphs and telephones and even the temperance movement. Ironically, this discussion was all over a bottle of sherry.

They discussed the radical Republicans' tactic of "'waving the bloody shirt" to gain votes and lastly the re-election of Grover Cleveland. This reminded Mr. Lee of the reason for his visit. He leaped from the settee and within seconds he returned with a present for me, beautifully wrapped in gold gilt paper.

I was a little reluctant to accept it, until he assured me it was only a small token of his gratitude for the work I had performed. I opened the package and discovered an edition of the "White House Cookbook" published and dedicated to the White House bride, Frances Folsom Cleveland. The mention of her name ignited a whole new topic of conversation in which his mother was well versed.

According to her, President Cleveland was 27 years old and a friend of the family when his future bride, Frances, was born. Twenty-one years later, on June 2, 1886, at the White House, President Grover Cleveland, age 49, married Frances Folsom.

I admit I am enjoying talking to Mrs. Lee about the White House socials and teas. However, Mr. Lee soon grew fidgety and said it was time for them to leave.

Thinking back to that afternoon, I realize he now addresses me as "Lizzie" and no longer "Mrs. Simpson." I presume there is no need for formalities with business associates. Even so, I think I will not address him as "William."

When I hear a knock at the door, my daydreaming ends and I return to the present.

"Mother, are you ready? Jasper has the carriage waiting."

I dread opening the door, knowing this will be the end of the holiday. Victoria will climb on the train and I will make my lonely journey home. I step back one more time and look in the mirror. Yes, a hat like this frames the face nicely, but now I need a stylish new wardrobe.

Just as we open the front door, there stands Lilly preparing to knock. "Oh, hello Lizzie," she says, giving Victoria and I a broad smile. I notice she is carrying a small suitcase. "I was hoping to visit with you and Victoria before you left for the train station. I have some marvelous products to show you."

"What sort of products?" Victoria asks.

"The finest cosmetics and creams in the world. I have something for all your beauty needs: pancake makeup, perfumes, rouge, skin-lightening creams, even hair remover, should you need it," she says, and begins to open the case.

"Lilly," I say, taking hold of her hand to stop her. "I see you did not put much stock in my advice. I hardly see how you can support yourself going door to door selling beauty products. Please tell me you have not quit your job."

"Oh Lizzie, it is a woman's world these days. Isn't that right Miss Victoria? When you see what I have to offer, you will want to purchase the full line of products. I might go as far as to say you will want to become a beauty consultant for Madame Phoebe Products as well," she boasts. Then she leans back with her hands on her broadhips exposing her flat chest.

"Lilly, Lilly, Lilly," I scold. "I bet it cost you a month's worth of paychecks to buy that kit. When I return I will take a look at your products, but I assure you I am not signing up to be a sales representative."

The promise of later seems to satisfy Lilly and she picks up her little suitcase. "I'm off to visit Mrs. Harris; she is one that can really use some beauty products!"

Victoria and I are laughing as we climb in the carriage. "No truer words have ever been spoken," I joke, and take hold of the reigns.

Four o'clock, I return home and my sunshine is gone in more ways than one. It is raining again. On the lighter side, the rain will most likely discourage Lilly from visiting.

I see the fire has burned down in the front room. The house is cold and damp. There is only the faint odor of the breakfast remains coming from the kitchen. My first thought is to call out for Dovie. I reconsider. They are new-lyweds and eventually they will tire of "the experience," as my sister Sallie calls it.

I pause in the front room, take my hat off and walk up to the mantel. "Hello Lizzie," I say to the painting of myself. "Do you remember those honeymoon days?"

For a moment I could have sworn she winked at me. I walk out of the room shaking my head; must have been a twinkle of light flickering in from the window.

My stomach calls me in the kitchen, but I am sorry to find all that is left of yesterday's chicken is a greasy pot soaking in a pan of water. My search for the leftover pota-toes and peas quickly leads to more empty dishes. At that point, I consider myself lucky to find one slice of bread, some blackberry jelly and an apple.

Providing a roof over Jasper's head is one thing, but at this rate, he will eat me out of house and home. I did not take that into consideration. Now it must be addressed promptly. Jasper works for Mr. Roberts at Brentwood Press. He can certainly contribute something toward the grocery bills.

Fear crosses my mind regarding the honeymooners. Lord forbid I am stuck with a house full of colored children to feed and clothe too. "One day at a time Lizzie," I pray.

There was only a single report to type last week and nothing was dropped off this week. Mr. Lee informed me his workload slows down this time of year. He laughed when he told me his theory. "When it is so blame cold out-side, people are less likely to go out looking for trouble. But by spring, the natives will be stirring."

Once I finish the small feast, I start down the hall with plans to work on my book. I am disappointed to find there is no fire in my office or wood in the box. This forces me to wrap up, go out in the rain and fetch a load of wood. I am miserably cold when I return to start up the fire.

The little chair by the hearth holds me prisoner until the room is warm enough for me to move about. I have just settled down and put my first sheet of paper in the machine when I hear Dovie coming down the stairs.

"Miss Lizzie, is yous home?" she calls out. I do not answer, but wait for her to find me on her own. She goes in the kitchen and soon I hear the sound of pots and pans banging together. What she has found to cook is beyond me, but in a few minutes I smell something sweet.

Dovie is as fat as a match. You might think she would be light on her feet, but she is a heavy walker. I hear the dishes rattling in the cupboards as she stomps down the hall. She walks into the front room, stops and touches my hat. She calls out again, *"Miss Lizzie."* Again, I do not answer. From my chair, I see her pull back the door and peek behind. Did she really think I would be hiding behind the door?

Thinking I will make amusement, I slowly rise from my chair and conceal myself behind the curtains. I hear her enter the room. She looks at the fireplace, sees the newly collected wood, but no Lizzie. "Lordy, Lordy," she mumbles.

Just as she turns to leave, I start to moan softly. She whips around, sees no one and lets out a scream. I am beside myself laughing when I step out from behind the curtain. *"Yous ain'ts funny, Miss Lizzie. I's for sho thoughts it was da ghost da chillin' say da seen."* Even though she has tears

70

in her eyes, she bites her lips to keep from smiling.

They say there is a fine line between laughing and crying. Perhaps this is a release of all my trapped emotions, but I cannot control my laughter. I am even unable to show remorse when Jasper comes running down the stairs.

I did not mention my unsatisfying supper to Dovie. I sit down at the table and enjoy a plate of her apples fried in bacon drippings and a hot biscuit. When Jasper has eaten his fill, he slips back upstairs. As soon as Dovie finishes her duties, she joins him.

Rebel follows me into the bedroom and waits patiently for me to change into my nightclothes. I gather up a blanket and pillow and Rebel is on my heels. I open the front door to allow him to make one last passage across the yard. He is back in short order and the two of us withdraw to the office.

I throw a few logs on the fire and spread the blanket out on the sofa. This room is my friend and will be my place to work, sleep and think. From now until spring, I will submerge myself in the completion of my book. It will be my mission.

Here I can hibernate from the world, taking only breaks to eat, drink and sleep when necessary. Perhaps I will spare myself the agony of unnecessary grooming. When I have finished the book, I will order myself some new clothes and emerge like a butterfly out of a cocoon.

Until I am finished, I will avoid visitors like the plague. Dovie can turn them away and Jasper can take care of all my errands. With that thought, I sit down at the desk and begin to exercise my mind. Rebel stretches out in front of the fire and I say to him, "This is going to work out just fine."

Just as I begin to type, I hear a thumping noise overhead. I have only to reason quickly and I know the cause.

Dovie's bedroom is directly overhead. Rebel raises his head and begins to growl. "Settle down boy, I am afraid we will have to get used to this."

Once I resume typing, it drowns out the noise and he lowers his head and returns to his sleep.

1868

In my last chapter, I spoke of how we came to Concord and of the joyous birth of Tessie. I also told you about the boy, Les Lester. Lilly and Henry took joint ownership of the boy, but three nights a week I schooled him, teaching him to read and write.

The boy lived with Henry in a little house down by the depot. It was not a desirable neighborhood, consisting of poor white and colored families.

Henry worked for the railroad. Until the day he retired, he left every morning before dawn to walk up the railroad track 12 miles and back. If he had to replace many spikes, it was sometimes midnight before he got home. Then he would do it all over again the next morning. No matter what the weather, Henry was dependable. He said his job was the most important job on the railroad. Just one loose rail and a train could go off the track.

Poor little Les was only 10 years old when we found him, but he went to work right away in the mill. He would dress himself, walk to Lilly's house for breakfast and then they would go to work together.

I will always question why Lilly allowed her mother to manipulate her over the supposed widow's pension she would someday receive. If Henry and

Lilly had married, they could have made life much easier on Les. Lilly and her mother are like family to me, but I consider both of them somewhat foolish and selfish.

Those early years after the war, Concord was occupied by Federal troops. We went about our business as normal as possible. Just as it is with all people, there are good and bad. There were Yankees here who were just doing their job. Others felt it was their right to cause conflict with the citizens.

Joel said that a government that had to be held together by the bayonet was not much of a government. His belief was the less animosity we offered, the sooner the Yankees would be gone.

Unless you have lived through those dark days, it is hard to explain the force of unbalanced power that governed the Southern people.

The Yankee government placed Negroes in positions of power. Many could not even read and write. Some used the power to better themselves; others used it as a weapon, while others were little more than pawns of the Union.

We were flooded with carpetbaggers and scalawags looking to make their fortune from others' misfortunes. Henry Hickey was one of the victims. Joel would have been a victim too, if Henry had convinced him to invest in railroad stock that turned out to be a hoax.

If a town has a railroad, the population will grow. There were desirables coming to town to work in the mills. But there were whiskey drinkers, gamblers and gold miners too. Joel felt it was not safe for a woman to go out alone and he always carried his pistol.

Around the same time North Carolina was readmitted into the Union in 1868, the federal military presence began to dwindle. However, I can recall seeing troops passing through even as late as 1877.

Those early years of reconstruction were hard years. Never let anyone tell you that you cannot survive on love, for that was just what we did.

After Joel and I married, I did not follow politics very closely. I could not cast a vote and I was busy raising three children. I suppose I felt Joel kept up with things enough for both of us. So, forgive me if I do not tell you all.

Shortly after we came to Concord, Joel joined the Masons. It is a secret society. Contrary to some peoples' beliefs, it is not part of, or involved in, the Ku Klux Klan. I never saw Joel leave the house in a white robe and conical hat. To the best of my knowledge, he was never involved in any of the Klan's activities.

I will speak very little of the Klan, for very little is what I know. I heard the arguments for and against the Klan. Some people believed it was a necessary evil to gain control over a corrupt government. During reconstruction, Southerners felt the federal government all too often turned a blind eye to crimes committed by Negroes, Yankees and white scalawags. Others strongly protested the Klan, claiming it was solely operated by white supremacy Democrats and was nothing more than a terrorist organization.

In defense of all that happened following the years after the war, we were a nation of wounded people. The scars were fresh. Even now in 1893, they have only begun to heal. Sometimes I wonder if they ever will.

Even before most of the southern states were restored to the Union, Congress passed complicated amendments to the Constitution.

Since Lincoln's 1863 Emancipation Proclamation only mentioned slavery in the southern states that were in rebellion, slavery was still legal in other states.

Lincoln feared the presence of slavery could hinder his re-election. He insisted that passage of the 13th amendment to abolish slavery in all states be added to his platform for the upcoming election.

Lincoln was re-elected, but on April 15, he died from an assassin's bullet. The 13th amendment was not passed until December 6, 1865.

After Lincoln's death, Andrew Johnson stepped up as President. Some of the South felt that he offered a ray of hope, but there was much friction in Washington. In 1867, there was an attempt to impeach President Andrew Johnson.

In 1868 the 14th amendment was passed, granting equal rights and citizenship to all persons born in the United States, including freedmen and former slaves.

Confederate President Jefferson Davis was at last released from prison and Ulysses S. Grant was elected as the 18th President of the United States.

....

I pull the last page out of the typewriter. I can no longer scold my eyes to stay open. It is 3 o'clock in the morning. I feel satisfied with tonight's work and curl up on the sofa with Rebel. In the morning, I will begin with the year 1869.

Chapter 7

A Cold Winter Day

In a few short hours, daylight peeks in through the curtains. I attempt to stretch my legs, but Rebel is curled up in the bend of my knees. When I give him a nudge, he growls at me. The room is cold and smells like a burned-out fire.

I shiver as I cross over to the fireplace and manage, in the dim light, to stub a frozen toe. When I cry out, Rebel jumps up and begins prancing around the room. We both need to attend to our morning rituals. With the quilt wrapped around my shoulders, I struggle out in the hall. The hanging edge of the quilt becomes a tail for Rebel to tug me to the front door.

When I open the front door, Rebel runs out barking at the mules pulling Captain Odell's wagon past the house. As if I need a reminder of how cold it is, I am forced to step out on the porch to call him. A few of the bundled-up passengers wave. They are on their way to work in the mill.

Captain Odell's "scooter" is able to make it up and down the hills in the snow. He picks up his workers and delivers them home after their shift. The mill might have gone under had Captain Odell not bought it in 1877. Since then he has added three more mills, with over 20,000 spindles and 800 or more looms.

After the scooter passes, I tiptoe to the edge of the porch for the newspaper that is partially covered in snow. When I step back inside, Dovie is standing in the hall with her hands on her hips. *"You's going to come down with da death rattle,"* she warns.

Before I can answer, Rebel, who is now as frisky as he is wet, runs between her legs and into the kitchen. *"Miss Lizzie, puts some shoes on dem feets!"* she says, and goes back to her cooking.

She is right. I read in the newspaper just last week about three people who died of pneumonia and there is an outbreak of scarlet fever in Salisbury. I slip on a pair of cashmere socks and my boots and head to the bathroom on the back porch. We have had indoor plumbing since 1889. It is a luxury, but today the pipes will be frozen.

I enter the kitchen and spread out my newspaper on the table. When I hear a cup of coffee set down next to me, I expect to see Dovie standing there as always. I am surprised to see Jasper. He goes over to the stove and takes over the cooking. He is expecting me to question him. *"Dovie took sick; she bes back down in a bit,"* he says.

"Would you like for me to check on her?" I ask.

"Nos, she says it be something she ate," he answers, stirring eggs into the iron skillet.

"Jasper, would you please return the lamp oil we bought last week to Craven's and ask for a new jug? The lamps are so dim; the oil must be poor quality."

I look up and Dovie walks in slowly and sits down at the table beside me.

"Are you feverish?" I ask.

"Nos, I's all rights now," she replies.

"Dovie, do we need anything from the grocery?"

"Flour," she says, jumping up quickly and running back up the stairs.

I look at Jasper and he shakes his head. He sets a plate of eggs down at the table for me. Then he prepares a second plate to take upstairs. "Jasper, stop by the post office. On your way to town let Mrs. Davis know you will pick up their mail too. I'll leave $2.75 on the table for the flour." He nods and disappears up the stairs. I am happy to return to reading my paper and sipping my coffee.

On the front page, it says January 1893 is one of the coldest winters on record for Concord. It is bad news for the poor and the elderly. The churches are asking for donations of wood, food and clothing. They advise saving old newspapers to line the inside of coats and pad mattresses. On the lighter side of things, the ice farmers will have a large crop this year.

I scan over the front-page headlines:

Hoop Skirts of 35 years ago are back in style.

TC McBryde is a horse dealer, not a tax collector.

Railroads delayed 6 hours today.

Forest Hill colored barber, known as Pethal, is missing.

Mary Anna Custis Lee, daughter of General Lee, sets sail for Cairo, Egypt.

Mt. Amoena Female Seminary came near to burning down. Defective fireplace, with rats found to be the trouble.

I turned the page and began reading about a scam. *Mrs. Blackwelder of 56 Spring Street said an unidentified man sold her a cord of wood. That evening, just after dark, the man returned and stole the wood he had delivered earlier. She reported this to Sheriff Morrison who says there have been some similar incidents reported lately. According to Mrs. Blackwelder, the man accused was tall, thin and balding. She said she thinks the man was a Yankee because he was smoking rolled cigarettes.*

Dovie comes back in the room shyly and sits down at the table again.

"What's da paper says today?" she asks. Although she is capable, she does not often read.

"Oh, this and that," I reply. "Hey, listen to this! Mrs. Yates gives birth to her 24th child."

"Hows can da be, one woman have that many chillins?" Dovie asks, as her eyes widen.

"The paper says she was married at age 14, she had five sets of twins and the oldest is 27," I explain, and turn the page.

Dovie jumps up as if she has a bee in her bonnet. She stands there in deep thought for a moment before she speaks. *"Da poor woman should have jumped in a hole and hid from da man of hers."*

I laugh at her joke, but she is serious. She begins clearing the table as if she is angry. I now know that Dovie understands how babies are made. This seems like a perfect opportunity to share with her a married woman's secret.

After several minutes, I am finally able to explain to her the function of the rubber sheath. She seems a little put off by the idea, but laughs when I tell her in the old days we made them out of animal intestines.

After our little chat, she turns to go back upstairs. I have my suspicions it is with intentions to share this information with Jasper. "Dovie," I call out. "Tell Jasper to ask for 'Rubber Goods for Gents' at the drug store or the cigar store."

She hears me snickering. But with a little luck, I have just controlled the size of my household. That is, if Dovie's upset stomach does not prove to be morning sickness.

The kitchen door is jammed again and I have to give it a heavy push. When I barge through, I see the front door is open and Dovie is running down the stairs. She darts out the door, letting me know she is going into town with Jasper. Don't forget Mrs. Davis' mail," I remind her and proceed toward my office. Once she is gone, I call out across the hall to myself in the painting from 28 years past. "Good morning pretty, just look what a sight you have become." From her perch above the mantle, she stares at me blankly as if she is mocking me. Pulling my robe together, I cross the hall scolding Rebel for nipping at my bootlaces.

Once the door is closed to my office, I feel like Rebel and I are the last beings on earth. Dovie has left a pitcher of water and cookies on the table and to Jasper's credit, the wood box is full.

I scan over my old scrapbooks on the shelves and select the one marked 1869-1870.

On the first page were two newspaper clippings:
March 4, 1869. President elect General Ulysses Grant breaks tradition. He has refused to ride to the Capitol in the carriage with outgoing President Andrew Johnson. Conflict is evident and Johnson does not attend the inauguration.

Grant fears the carpetbaggers will rob the White House before he can take possession. The carpetbaggers he refers to are his own greedy politicians full of plots and schemes to deplete the treasury.

Lying loose in the scrapbook is a letter from dear Dr. Francis Holloway. I open it to read:

The Revolution.

"The true republic—men, their rights and nothing more; women, their rights and nothing less."

March 26, 1869

Dear Lizzie,

It seems like a hundred years since that day in New York I accepted your offer to come to Charleston, South Carolina. I was confident in my skills as a doctor, but accepting such a challenge as a Negro woman was a leap of faith.

I have to admit, the story of how you suddenly became the heiress of a home and a medical clinic was astonishing. However, perhaps more intriguing was your determination to keep your friend's clinic running in spite of his death. Somehow, your story had my destiny written all over it.

Those war years were certainly not without trial and tribulations. I must say, my time with you will always be the golden years of my life. You were wise to deed the house and clinic to me when you left for North Carolina. The Union would have surely seized the house otherwise. You are always welcome here and when my time on earth is over, it will return to you or yours.

Enough of the past, I am writing to you about the present and the future. Not just our future, but also the future of all women. In January at the National Women's Rights Convention, I met a group of strong-minded and intelligent women. I have since allied myself with "The National American Woman Suffrage Association," headed by Susan B. Anthony. It is exciting working with women of such morals and zeal for the justice of not only women, but for the equal rights of all people.

If the 15th amendment is ratified and the Negro man is given the right to vote, women should have the same rights.

I have leased a one-room apartment here in New York where I will be staying for the next several months. The space is tight, but it is outfitted nicely, thanks to the cabinet bed. It folds out at night for sleeping and then converts into a desk for the daytime. The bed was designed by Sarah S. Goode, who to my knowledge is the first Negro woman to receive a patent on an invention.

I have much work to do here. I am helping with the rallies and writing articles for a women's rights newspaper, called the "Revolution." We are the voice of the modern woman.

Lizzie, I believe in our lifetime we shall see that women will no longer walk a step behind men, but by their side. You may have heard of a woman by the name of Victoria Claflin Woodhull. She is making great strides for the sisterhood of women. Mrs. Woodhull and her sister own a respectable brokerage firm here in New York City, which proves the capabilities of our kind. Say you did not hear it from me, but there is talk that she might be the first woman candidate for the United States presidency.

When I leave here in early spring, I will be going to Washington for a women's convention. I will write again soon.

Pray for my health and safety, as I will yours.
Dr. Frances Holloway

I carefully fold the letter and place it back in the scrapbook. Perhaps I will never read it again, but all of Dr. Fannie's letters are precious to me. Although I was not to see my friend Fannie for many years, her letters are part of my story. Here in Concord, I often felt like I was cut off from the rest of the world. Fannie's letters were my living eyewitness account of history as it unfolded.

In reverence to the moment, I pause and say a prayer. *Dear Lord, you alone know our past and our future. The events of our lives are written in your book. We must accept that all unfolds in your time, not ours. Please help me to be grateful for your many blessings and accept the things that I cannot understand. Amen*

I pull the curtains back so that I can look out over the newly fallen snow and place a sheet in the typewriter to begin my work.

1869-1870

I will begin this chapter telling about a man that some called a devil and others celebrated, Jesse James.

My husband Joel read every article he could find on the escapades of Jesse James and his brother Frank James. For many of the former Confederate soldiers, Jesse James was a modern-day Robin Hood. He was a rebel proclaiming revenge on the federal government for their sins against the South.

During the war, Frank James rode with Quantrill's Raiders and Jesse was tagged with a group of bush-whackers led by Bloody Bill Anderson.

After the war, Jesse and Frank began their career robbing federal stagecoaches and banks. In Missouri, on December 7, 1869, they robbed the Daviess County Savings Association. Jesse suppos-edly shot and killed the cashier. Jessie was then officially labeled an "outlaw" with a reward on his head. The James brothers joined up with Cole Younger and became known as the James-Younger Gang.

There were many reasons people found the activities of the James-Younger Gang so fascinating. For Joel, I think it offered some excitement from his everyday life.

No one in his or her right mind would ever want to relive the war years. However, for men like Joel, working in the mill, day in and day out, was a battle itself. The shifts were long, the pay low and there was little chance for advancement.

A country defeated by war is a depressed country. North Carolina lost more men in the war than any other state. There were sweethearts forever lost in mourning, wives without husbands and children without fathers.

Many of the men carried the physical scars of missing arms and legs. Others suffered in private, hearing their own voices cry out in the middle of the night. For those that had a wife and family to offset the agony, it was easier.

Even after the government pardoned all participants in the late rebellion, many of the men could not bear the enemy inside. No one will ever know the tortuous battle in Walter Howard's mind the morning he left to go hunting. He was found dead two days later, killed by a self-inflicted gunshot wound.

The economy was poor in Concord. Joel sometimes would voice regrets for selling his land and moving here. He would say that at least if we had stayed in Stanly County, we could have lived off the land. We would be free of the Yankee soldiers watching over us day and night.

I think what he worried most about was the children's safety and mine while he was working.

December of 1869, he sold one of his horses. My Christmas gift that year was a bird's head grip, Smith & Wesson 7-shot revolver. It proved to be a good investment and I still carry it today.

When Joel mourned to be back on the farm, I had only to remind him of the hardships that Sallie and her husband Ransom were facing. Ransom could not afford to hire farmhands. By his own two hands alone, he had to feed his family. In addition to food, he must raise enough cash crops to pay his taxes.

With the deflated price of cotton after the war, farmers were forced to supplement their income with new crops such as soybeans, peanuts and tobacco.

Jobs were hard to find, especially with 35,000 freed slaves who were homeless and looking for jobs too. Many of the slaves would have been happy to stay on the plantations or farms and work for their keep, but with the new laws, it was complicated. With all the new government regulations on sharecropping or hiring Negroes, many of the farmers were afraid to take the risk.

Speaking of taxes, in April of 1869 a new educational tax revenue act was passed. All males of sound mind and body between the ages of 21-50 were required to pay a tax of a dollar and 5 cents just for living. New taxes were placed on real and personal property, even stocks and bonds.

In addition, we were now required to give the government 2 1/2 percent of our annual net income. Joel said if the government could determine every time a man made love to his wife, they would tax him on that too.

Times were changing and with change comes uncertainty. Men were bitter and afraid of losing control over their own lives and their women. Even though the war was over, the war between the sexes had just begun.

When the 15th amendment was at last ratified on February 3, 1870, giving Negro men the right to vote, women now were demanding their rights as well.

Being a happily married woman, I was never party to women's suffrage issues. Still, Dr. Fannie's letters and views were of keen interest to me. I will say now that I secretly felt she was well justified in some of her thinking. Occasionally I would share Dr. Fannie's letters and my own opinions with Joel.

I will never forget the fury of emotions sparked by the minister's service on the evils of unsexing women. He preached that giving women the ballot would be like casting a lamb into the den of lions. It was God's plan for women to be the guardian angels of the home and family, not of public affairs. He warned this imbalance of nature would be the end of domestic peace. Joel was a good man and husband, but I could clearly see he followed the same belief. My better judgment sealed my lips on such subjects.

In March of 1870, I received this letter from my sister Sallie in Stanly County.

Dear Lizzie,

I should have written you sooner, but it has been such a state of affairs. I will begin first with the bad news. We buried Ransom's father four weeks ago. As you know, his health has long been deteriorating. Although Mrs. Huneycutt is well, she is not able to do much because of her bad hip. For several months, they had housed a man and woman in exchange for maintaining the farm and helping with the household.

Ransom had hoped they would stay to take care of his mother as well. However, when Ransom was called, you will not believe what he saw. The plow was left out in the rain rusting, fences bro-

ken down and livestock walking freely over the lot. The house was upset and the woman was taking a nap. Lastly, he found the man was intoxicated.

Needless to say, he threw them out and we have sold the farm. Mrs. Huneycutt has now taken up permanent quarters at our house. It is all for the better and she is helpful with the children.

Ransom's brother does not know of his father's passing. Several months ago, Thomas and his wife went to the church to hear a young man speak who was recruiting couples to go to Brazil. According to the man, the Brazilian government had pledged to provide transportation, money, food and supplies to aid Confederates in settling in their country. Thomas and Betty Jo bought into the idea and they left over six weeks ago. We have not heard a word from them. I don't suppose Betty Jo has written you?

Well, one reason I am writing you, dear sister, is to invite you and the children to summer with us here in Stanly County. I must admit I have an alternative motive as well. With the sale of the family farm, Ransom's mother has encouraged Ransom to reopen the dry good store! There will be much work to do, stocking the shelves and setting up displays. You are so talented at arranging things; please say you will come help. Mrs. Huneycutt can watch the children and we can have our days free. Joel can bring you and come back on the weekends to visit. It will be like old times, horseback riding and going to the mill for picnics.

Please let me know as soon as possible. Ransom will be going to Charleston and then off to New York to stock up on the latest merchandise.

With my greatest hope of spending a special
summer with you, I will close for now.

Love, Sallie

Joel was gracious. We both agreed that a summer in the country would do all of us good. Even though he missed us during the week, the weekends more than made up for the loss.

So, the first of May, we packed up the children and went to Sallie's. Even before Ransom returned from his buying trip, the packages began to arrive. There was something for everyone. Joel was pleased with the blue denim waist overalls, made by the Levi Strauss Company.

When the store was stocked, we had a grand opening party. For the first time, the people of Stanly County were introduced to the hot dog, deliciously stuffed in a bun and topped with sauerkraut.

One of the weekends that summer, Joel took me to Rocky River Springs Resort for an overnight stay. We never had a honeymoon and with three children later, it was well overdue. To this day, it escapes me how he afforded such a luxury. It was an elegant hotel and we enjoyed soaking in the mineral springs. As an added treat, Ransom gave us a bottle of Pemberton's French Wine Coca.

I must say I enjoyed the wine immensely. It's rich taste was almost sinful. Later when I discovered the ingredients to be a blend of alcohol and cocaine, I understood. In view of what my mother went through with her addiction to Laudanum, I never touched it again.

That summer Ransom received a letter from Thomas and I received one from Betty Jo. Thomas sent an angry response after he learned that the family farm had been sold and his mother invested the money in the dry goods store. For many years I assumed, since this was Betty Jo's only letter to me, she was angry too.

July 30, 1870

To my dear friend Lizzie,
*   As you most likely know, I am writing you from the other side of the world. Thomas is happy here in Brazil, but I am homesick in the worst of ways.*
*   I did not come to see you before I left on purpose. I feared you would talk me out of going. If I had refused to go with Thomas, then we would still be where we belonged. Now it is doubtful we will ever step foot in Stanly County or see you again on this side of heaven.*
*   The trip here was hell and I mean hell. Most of what the Brazilian government has promised has turned out to be false. We knew we were in for trouble as soon as we boarded the ship.*
*   The voyage was 20 days and nights in the open air with little shelter. Of the 150 passengers on board, most of them were Negros, Indians and half-breeds. Among the whites were six Confederate men and myself and one other woman. The rest were criminals hoping to escape justice. The boat was filthy and they fed us out of large bowls, forcing us to take handfuls of the slop in our hands like animals.*
*   Several of the passengers died on the boat. Once we finally arrived in Brazil we were provided only half of the supplies we were promised. Then we learned the American Colony was still a distance away. I am not a weak woman, but the insects and heat were nearly unbearable for me.*
*   After three days of hard travel, we arrived at the American Colony. The natives here are helpful and*

the countryside is beautiful. Thomas is still con-
vinced this is the land of milk and honey. I can only
say in view of what we have all suffered, we deserve
paradise. Well, I close now with hopes of happiness
for you and your family.

Your true friend,
Betty Jo

Lastly, I will close this chapter on a solemn note:
Joel named our son after the great General Robert
Edward Lee. Sadly, General Lee departed this earth
on October 12, 1870.

....

By the time I have finished typing, my neck is stiff and
my stomach is growling. I fear I have become glued to the
chair, but I am able to stand. When I open the door into the
hall the house is quiet, but I am pleased to see Dovie has left
my supper in the oven.

After Rebel and I have taken care of our needs, we curl
up on the sofa in the office for sleep. I turn off the light and
close my eyes.

Dear Lord, so many souls have walked upon this dusty
old earth. Sometimes it seems as if we are all just gliding
through life only to find the grave our end. Save me from the
sin of despair. Open my eyes to see clearly the path you
have laid before me and joyfully I will follow. Amen

Chapter 8

Saved by the Skin of Her Teeth

January 28, 1893

Rebel woke me early the next morning barking and bouncing against the office door. Assuming he is under distress to go out, I jump to my feet, grab my robe and open the front door. He runs out to the edge of the lot and barks at Mrs. Davis' house.

The houses here on Peachtree Street are close together. So when something is out of the ordinary it is pretty easy to determine. There is a horse tied in front of Mrs. Davis' house and a carriage I do not recognize. It is 7 a.m. and Lilly should have left for work. Mrs. Davis would not entertain guests at this hour.

I fear that something is wrong and run inside to dress. I am pinning up my hair as I step out of the bedroom. Dovie is standing by the window looking out. "Do you know what is going on over there?" I ask.

"No, but Jasper says da black carriage been over dar since early dis morning."

I grab my coat and start across the yard. The remnants of the old snow have left patches of muddy ice on the ground. Just as I start to step up on Mrs. Davis' porch, I slip and fall. I am not injured, but when I walk across the porch, my wet skirt leaves a trail of frozen grass behind me.

I ring the doorbell and Henry Hickey opens the door. "Please come in Lizzie," he says softly. Now I am certain something is wrong. As long as I have known him, only once have I known him to miss a day of work.

Mrs. Davis' house is always dark and gloomy. It typically smells of fried food and dusty old things. But today I detect a different smell. I know the smell; it is smell of an undertaker. Someone is dead.

"Mrs. Davis?" I ask.

"Yes," he says, looking me directly in the eye.

"Henry, what in the world happened?"

"Your man brought the mail by yesterday afternoon and there was a letter for Lilly from the government. Mrs. Davis was afraid to open it and worked herself into a frenzy by the time Lilly got home from work."

"Was it Lilly's widow's pension?" I ask.

"Yes. I reckon the excitement was too much for the old gal. When I stopped by on my way home from work, she was mostly dead then. I went for the doctor and he said she had suffered a stroke. She never gained consciousness and the doctor declared her dead this morning."

"Where is Lilly now?" I ask.

"She is upstairs lying down. The doctor gave her something for her nerves. She would probably like to see you, if you are up to it."

"Of course," I said. Henry guided me down the hall. Movement caught my eye in the parlor as we passed by. I wish I could have stopped my eyes from looking into the room. The undertaker and the doctor were wrapping up Mrs. Davis' body to take her away.

The scene makes me feel faint. As I follow Henry up the narrow stairwell, I must hold to the railing. Henry knocks on Lilly's door. "Lilly, Miss Lizzie is here to see you."

In seconds a weak voice calls back, "Send her in."

Henry opens the door, allows me to enter and closes it behind me. Lilly is sprawled out on the bed, her hair twisted in a knot on top of her head and her clothes wrinkled. "Lilly, I am so sorry," I say, sitting down on the edge of the bed and taking her hand. She looks up at me and I recognize the narcotic glaze in her eyes.

Lilly reaches under her pillow and hands me a letter. "Read it," she says.

My eyes scan over the words until they settle on the sentence reading: *To Lilly Davis White, the widow of Private Virgil White, a military monthly pension of 4 dollars and 5 cents is hereby granted.*

"Lizzie, I killed her! All the same as if I would have taken up a gun and shot her," Lilly blurted out and then fell into my arms weeping.

I gently push her back, so I can look her in the eyes. "Lilly, the doctor said she had a stroke."

"No! There is more. When I opened that letter, I flew into such a rage as I have never before," Lilly cried.

"Well indeed, I can see why; it must have been a shock," I say, trying to calm her.

"Lizzie, mother and I quarreled. I said awful things and accused her of ruining my life for less than the price of a sack of flour and a pound of bacon. She grabbed her chest and fell to the floor right in front of me, never to speak a word again."

"It was not you dear," I say, and gather her up in my arms like a child. "She was 86 years old and nature recalls its own. You know that darling."

"You think so?" she asks, looking at me, as if I know the plans of God.

"It was just her time and nothing more. She loved you and

she would not want you blaming yourself." I take my handkerchief out of my pocket and wipe her eyes. "Why don't you lay back and try to get some rest," I say, and smile. She obeys and I spread a blanket over her and turn off the light.

Just before I leave, she whispers, "Lizzie, say nothing of what I told you to Henry."

"I will not," I assure her.

When I go back downstairs, the doctor, the undertaker and the body are gone. I am relieved, although the smell is still lingering in the air. I look around for Henry, but I do not see him. To go roaming over the house would be distasteful, so I resolve to leave without notice.

I have just opened the front door when I feel an icy hand on my shoulder. I jump back and start to scream, but I see it is Henry. "Lizzie, can you stay for awhile? I would like to ask you some questions."

"Have you had breakfast?" he asks. "I can offer you some sweet bread and coffee. I will not keep you long."

I can see he looks desperate and I follow him into the kitchen. He sets the plate of sweet bread on the table and pours me a cup of coffee. I accept the coffee, but politely refuse the bread. I have not an appetite for it, knowing Mrs. Davis must have made it yesterday.

"Lizzie," he begins. "As you may well guess, Lilly is not business savvy. Her mother took care of all the finances. Do you think it would be out of line for me to step up and take care of the funeral arrangements?"

"No Henry, I do not," I reply. I take a deep breath, relieved that the purpose of his conversation is not to query me on what Lilly said upstairs.

"Then there is the matter of the will, settling the estate and so on. I suppose I should handle all that too." Henry closes his eyes and rests his head in his hands.

"Does Lilly not have a brother?" I recall.

"Yes. This morning Lilly told me where to find her mother's will. It was then that we discovered the brother was left out of the will and everything is to go to Lilly."

Henry reaches in his vest pocket and hands me a hand-written will, dated and signed by Mrs. Davis two years ago.

"Henry, this could be trouble. I suggest you say nothing about this to anyone before you speak to an attorney. Take everything over to Mr. William Lee's office. He will advise you wisely."

"Thank you Lizzie. Can you sit with Lilly this afternoon while I take care of things?"

"Yes, just let me know when." I end the conversation and set my coffee cup on the counter.

When I return home, I break the news to Dovie and Jasper. Dovie is not one to take bad news well. I instruct Dovie to prepare food and for Jasper to go inform the neighbors of Mrs. Davis' passing.

I return to my office and with the best of my ability, I try to apply myself to my writing. I take out a stack of clean paper and sort over my notes and scrapbooks before I begin.

1871-1872

It appears to me that man must always have war. When one great rebellion ends, another will begin. Do they fight for a great cause or is it egos that must be conquered?

Following The War Between the States, the popularity of homesteading in the West was growing. The railroad industry was booming and the limitations of travel were decreasing.

Whites, Negroes and immigrants were heading west in pursuit of gold and cheap, fertile land. One of the problems the settlers faced was the Plains Indians.

In the 1870's the newspapers were scattered with reports of outlaws, political upsets and the continuation of the Indian Wars. There were stories of Jesse and Frank James and names like Geronimo, Crazy Horse and Sitting Bull.

Joel questioned why they called the Indians "savages" and not our government. Where in the Bible does it say there is glory for any soldier, black or white, in destroying another man's way of life?

Like most southerners, Joel believed the Homestead movement was all a government ploy to drive the non-tax-paying Indians off their land and replace them with tax-paying citizens.

During Grant's administration, the North's economy was growing by leaps and bounds, while most of the South was still starving. Mark Twain said it was the beginning of America's Gilded Age. It was confirmed by the emerging of the super rich, the Vanderbilts and Rockefellers.

Joel remembered General Grant and his compassion for General Lee at the surrender at Appomattox. He did not think he was the driving force of Washington. It was the greedy politicians that had their hands in everyone's pocket.

It was doubtful that even Washington could keep up with all the new tax laws and acts passed. One thing for sure, it appeared whatever the government did, it was for their advantage only.

Anything and anyone was subject to be taxed, even peddlers, gypsies and fortunetellers. There were fees for getting married and fees for dying.

Even though the federal government was raking in money, the 18th president of the United States was not without his share of hardships and scandals.

The effects of the French Civil War of 1870 were felt all over Europe. However, when Europe ceased minting silver coins and replaced them with the gold mark, the silver market crashed in America. This, combined with the reduction of money supply, high interest rates, heavy debts and expansion of the railroad, created the panic of 1873.

It is not my intention to write a history book or bore you with the retelling of such national happenings. Yet, in brief, I must, for our daily lives were so affected by those formative years following the war. The simple fact the southern people survived is proof of our strength and a promise for our future.

....

It is 3 o'clock in the afternoon when I pull the last page out of the typewriter. I am satisfied with a good day's work, but a little worried. Henry should have come for me hours ago. I hope Lilly has not spent the morning alone while Henry was out making the funeral arrangements.

It is always hard to know what to do in these circumstances. Part of me says respect their privacy and wait for Henry to come for me. Yet I am afraid they need me.

After a quick bite of food, I wrap up and go over to visit. When Henry answers the door, I find Lilly sitting nicely on the sofa. She looks worn, but calm. My assumption is her stability is due to the medication the doctor has given her.

"Please come in and have some tea," she says smiling. I slowly walk in and sit down. She pours me a cup of tea and offers me a piece of the sweet bread. For the second time that day, I politely refuse.

Henry has an odd expression on his face when he joins

us. I look back and forth at the two of them. I feel it is up to me to break the ice. "Well Henry, have you made arrangements?"

"Nope," he says and starts to smile.

"Tomorrow will not prove too late. Things like this are hard," I say, tapping Lilly gently on the knee.

Then I hear a voice rattling down the stairs. "Lilly, bring me my snuff!" The familiar tone of the voice causes me to lose my breath and I fall back against the sofa. Henry runs over and sets me up again. Lilly jumps up and runs upstairs.

"Henry, I must be ill. Please help me across the yard. I need to go home," I say, trying to regain my stance.

"No, no, you are fine. Please let me explain," he says, holding me down so I cannot get up. "This has turned out to be the most extraordinary day of my life. After you left my intentions were to allow Lilly to sleep awhile before I awoke her. I was just before waking her when I heard the doorbell ring. It was the doctor. He asked about Lilly and was relieved to hear she was sleeping. He then told me to hold the door ajar and ran back to his carriage. Seconds later, I see him and the undertaker bringing back Mrs. Davis' body. I am stunned, but upon their request, I allow them to carry her back to the bedroom. I am fearful that my delay has caused them reason to doubt the financial arrangements. Even though I had given my consent for the undertaker to sell her teeth to the dentist, perhaps the teeth were rotten. Shortly I am to learn that an unspeakable thing nearly occurred. The undertaker reported that since we had not made all the final arrangements, he commenced to remove the teeth first. To his surprise, the body was unusually warm for a six-hour corpse. After holding a mirror to Mrs. Davis' mouth, he discovered it was fogged with the breath of life! He sent for the doctor and with some care, he was able to resuscitate her. It appears she did not have a stroke, but was in severe shock, which rendered her comatose. The doctor says she will recover."

"That is extraordinary!" I find myself shouting.

"Yes, it is. I suppose if her teeth were not to be sold, he would have gone straight ahead with the embalming."

Lilly returns smiling and I say my goodbyes and promise to check on them in the morning. As I make my way across the yard, I run my tongue over my teeth. I am thankful for my own teeth. If mine all fall out, I will eat soup.

Chapter 9

A Wake or Wedding

January 28, 1893

Seconds after I awake, I am in a panic. My bare feet hit the cold floor and I run through the hall calling, "Jasper! Jasper!"

Fearing I am responsible for a disaster, I look out the window. A fresh new trickling of snow is falling, but I do not see a soul on the street. It is early and perhaps there is still time.

"Dovie! Jasper!" I call out as I am running to the bedroom to get dressed. There is no answer. I can only assume they have gone to visit Dovie's family, as they do every Saturday. It will be dark before they are home. I must handle this on my own.

I dress quickly, throw on the same dress from the day before, wash the sleep out of my eyes and make no attempt to pin up my hair. In a few minutes, I am out on the street, knocking on the doors of all the neighbors. Not a single door is answered.

My final destination is Mrs. Davis' house. Mrs. Eudy, from two doors down, opens the door to me. When I step inside, I see a large table set out in the hall covered with an assortment of food. The parlor is filled with neighbors and friends standing around and chatting. I am too late, the wake has begun.

Mrs. Eudy extends her hand, encouraging me to join the

others. For a second I wonder if they know, but then I see Mrs. Davis. She is dressed in her robe and seated comfortably by the fire. I hear a roar of laughter when she announces, "I am glad to be alive and witness this nice turnout for my wake."

Her son Lawrence is standing next to her. He is a baby-fat man with frail hands and a soft airy voice. Joel would say a man like Lawrence has a "streak of lavender." His expression was not intended as a compliment.

I mingle my way through the crowd to speak to Mrs. Davis. When she sees me, she reaches for me. "Lizzie, don't look at me like you have seen a ghost. Come here and give me a kiss darling," she jokes.

The houseful of neatly attired people reminds me that I am hardly dressed for a party. I slip around the outside of the crowd with plans to go home and return more suitably dressed.

As soon as I have freed myself to the hall, I hear, "Psst, Lizzie, come upstairs with me." I look up and see Lilly midways on the stairs. She is wearing a light-colored summer frock, no shoes and her hair is hot ironed into ringlets. She does not wait for my response and runs up the stairs giggling.

I have no choice but to follow. Her bedroom door is open, but as soon as I enter, she closes it quickly behind me. "Lizzie, have you heard the news? Mother has given her consent for Henry and I to be married."

"Congratulations! When will the wedding be?" I ask.

"Did you not hear Henry's announcement? Since everyone is here, we are having the wedding ceremony this very day. Henry will be back with the minister any moment!"

"Lilly, are you sure? A wedding under these circumstances hardly seems proper."

"Lizzie, everyone seems most agreeable with the idea, even Mother. Once the new wears off of her born-again triumph, she may change her mind."

I laugh, "You may be right, Lilly. Henry has waited a long time."

Lilly looks at me for a moment and then sits down on the bed. "Speaking of waiting," she begins, "I have something to confess. I was only 14 when I married Virgil White. When he left to go to war, he left me just as he found me and I have been that way since. Lizzie, do you know what I mean?"

"Lilly, let me get this right. Are you telling me you are over 50 years old and still a virgin?"

To my question Lilly drops her head and answers, "For the most part, yes."

She sees that I am somewhat shocked and her eyes start to tear up.

"Well, either way it is a personal choice, Lilly," I say, and walk across the room to look at myself in the mirror. I take up her hair brush and begin pinning up my hair.

"What do you mean a personal choice?" she says, jumping off the bed to stand before me.

"I just assumed that you and Henry...well, you know." I try to explain. It is clear by Lilly's expression she is contemplating a series of questions in her mind. I feel myself freezing up, waiting for her to start querying me about marital activities. I am much relieved when Henry calls through the door. He has returned with the minister.

"Lizzie, please say you will stand up for me," she begs. I smooth over my dress and she assures me I look fine. In view of the unorthodox state of things, I shake my head to agree.

The ceremony takes place in the parlor in front of the fireplace. By this time, the whole house is packed with friends and family. They all came out on this wintry day with intent to attend the somber event of Mrs. Davis' wake. As fate would have it, they are now witnessing a wedding. I would not tell Lilly this for the world, but it is doubtful her wedding would have drawn such a crowd.

With the knot tied at last, people are laughing and celebrating. In the midst of all this, I see Mr. Lee has just arrived. He is standing around looking bewildered. When he spots me, he makes his way through the crowd toward me. "Lizzie, Henry Hickey left a note for me. Something about a will; it looks like there is some misunderstanding."

The look on his face makes me laugh. "Mr. Lee, it is a long story and one better told over a glass of brandy. Would you care to join me next door and I will explain."

As we are leaving, we are stopped in the hall by Lilly, who is holding a tray in her hand. "Sweet bread?" she asks.

"No thank you. I never eat sweet bread." I lie, but it may be the truth after today.

Mr. Lee appears to immensely enjoy my sharing of the events that have occurred since yesterday morning. Sitting there with him and enjoying a glass of brandy is a pleasure all its own.

Before he leaves, he apologizes for the lack of work and offers me a salary advancement. I assure him it is not necessary and that the break has given me time to work on my book.

When I walk him to the door, a sort of uneasiness develops between us. We fumble for words as if both of us have lost our social graces for proper goodbyes. In the awkward space of no words, I reach out for the door knob and open the door for him. Very gently he touches my shoulder. "I hope to see you again soon, Lizzie."

I watch as he crosses the road to his carriage. I feel my face flush and suddenly I am too warm. I close the door and loosen my collar; it must be the midterm of life mother described. In view of the morning's excitement, I determine a nap is well deserved.

I do not think for the time I rested that I actually went to sleep. I slipped into the place somewhere in between, hearing noises next door and my heart racing in my chest. After an hour or so, I rose and looked out the window. The snow has stopped and the last of the guests next door are leaving.

Looking over the house, save Rebel and myself, there is no one here. Still I have the oddest feeling someone is watching me. I have that feeling often. which inspires the next chapter for my book.

1873-1874

Christmas of 1873 was the same as all Christmases have been since the beginning of the war. There were no elaborate decorations or grand social events. By this time most of the memories of those things only existed in my dreams of Charleston.

Please do not take me wrong. I am not bitter for myself. I had my taste of it all, but sometimes I was remorseful for my children. I did not dwell on what we did not have, but what we had. Our children were happy, surrounded by love and the security of a father's undying affection. But love and affection alone will not put food on the table.

The efforts the North had made to rebuild the South were put on hold when the silver crash hit. As a result of the frail economy, the mills in Concord had gone on short time. People were in a panic. Some of the men took railroad jobs and families moved away.

The only reason I think we managed to pull through that winter was Joel's hunting skills. From October through November he spent almost every weekend in the country with Ransom, trapping and hunting. By Christmas they had made a fair amount of money selling the hides and furs.

In spite of the depression, Santa Claus came through for the children that year, bringing each of the girls a doll and Robert a box of celluloid toy Indians and soldiers.

Until Miss Kelly opened her school, I taught the children at home. In the winter their studies occupied a good part of their days. When the weather was mild they could play outside. But North Carolina is known for its damp, rainy winters.

A little boy trapped in a house with two sisters was testy. In an effort to amuse them, I suggested we explore the contents of the attic. I had only been up there myself a few times and I was interested to see what was stored under those dusty rafters.

When Joel bought this house, it had been empty since before the war. In 1867, when we decided to move to Concord, Joel was able to buy the house, along with most of the furnishings, at the auction.

We knew little about the widow that lived in the house before us. According to Mrs. Davis, the woman had no children, but on occasion a niece would visit her. When she died, no one knew how to contact the niece. After a couple of years, the county took over the house. I suppose that is why most of her things remained with the house.

The attic trunks were filled with old clothes, hats and linens. They held the girls' curiosity for only a day or two. Robert, on the other hand, found the attic to be a whole new world. I am not sure if it was such a great adventure or a haven away from his sisters.

I could hear him talking to an imaginary friend. At first I saw no harm in it. Then he started slipping part of his supper upstairs for his friend. I disapproved of that activity on two accounts: it was a waste of food and it would encourage rats.

Robert told us elaborate tales about his friend he named Moses McGraw. According to Robert, his friend Moses was a soldier in the first war, as he described it. He fought Indians and soldiers in red coats.

I began to get concerned when Robert wanted to spend all his time in the attic. He talked foolishly about Indians killing people and scalping the hair right off their heads.

Joel laughed, but he agreed to talk to him. The talk did not go well. Joel insisted that Robert admit Moses McGraw was only make-believe. After two hours, Robert still held on to his story. His friend was real. Joel lost his patience, sent Robert to his room crying and locked the attic door.

I recall the incident well. I was angry at Joel for losing his temper and he slept on the sofa that night. The next day, Joel and I put it behind us, but not Robert.

For the next three days he moped around aimlessly. He did not want to play outside or with his toy soldiers. The depression even spread to the girls. I tried to break his somber mood by reading to him and baking him a special little cake, but nothing I did seemed to make a difference.

On the fourth day I could bear it no longer. After Joel went to work, I searched all over the house for the attic key. After an hour of searching, I decided that Joel must be keeping the key in his pocket. Joel knew I was weak when it came to Robert and I would likely give in.

That same night the children went to bed as normal. Joel turned in early. I stayed up a couple of hours longer reading the book Mrs. Davis had loaned me, "Little Women" by Louisa May Alcott. When sleep became unavoidable, I blew out the light and started down the hall. For some strange reason as I passed by the attic door I saw it was standing open. My first thought was the wind had blown the door open, but then I saw the key in the lock.

Intrigued, I then assumed Joel had gotten up in the middle of the night to go to the attic. When I started up the stairs I could see the faint glow of a lamp burning. After a couple more steps, I heard Robert's voice.

I had all intentions to tan Robert's little hide. I was sure he had found the key and snuck up in the middle of the night, until I heard a faint hum that sounded like a man's voice. Now I was frightened.

I stopped for a moment thinking I should go for Joel. Yet, for some reason I felt an urgency to continue up the stairs. To this day, I will never be able to explain what I saw when I got to the top of the stairs.

In the middle of the floor was a small table with two chairs. In one chair sat Robert and all around the other chair was a glow of soft light.

I must have stood there behind the rafters for four or five minutes. During that time, I witnessed the glow changing shapes several different times and I could have sworn I saw the faint image of a man's face.

When I tried to lean forward for a better look, I stumbled and Robert looked up and saw me and called out, "Momma." At that very moment the glow disappeared.

It was as if some spell had been broken. I walked over to him and thought carefully before I spoke.

"Darling, it is too cold up here for you. Your father would not approve of you burning a light; that is how fires get started."

"Yes Ma'am," he replied, and reached out and took my hand.

We walked down the stairs without saying a word. When I got to the bottom of the steps I took the key out of the door. "Now, tell me where you got the key so I can put it back before your father misses it."

"Oh, I did not take the key Momma. Moses McManus woke me up and said he had unlocked the door."

I hardly knew what to say. I tucked Robert back in bed and kissed him good night.

When I turned to leave Robert whispered, "Momma, I won't be going to the attic anymore. Mr. McManus said it was time for him to go be with his wife. He told me to tell you not to worry about things when Daddy was away. He'd be looking out for us."

A chill ran down my spine, not because I was afraid, but because I believed.

I laid the key on the kitchen table. I tossed and turned that night debating how I would explain to Joel what had happened. He would never believe this story and Robert was sure to be punished for taking the key.

As always I was the first up the next morning. I was dreading seeing the key lying on the table, but to my surprise it was not there.

Joel liked to sleep late. I never had to wake him. The smell of bacon frying was his alarm clock. Shortly I looked over and he was sitting at the table reading the newspaper. After breakfast, he got up to leave for work. He turned to me, "Lizzie, I think Robert has been punished long enough. Tell him it is alright by me if he wants to play in the attic today. The key is over the door frame in the hall."

"You are a good daddy," I said, as he leaned over and kissed me on the cheek.

As soon as the door closes, I go at once to check the door frame. I cannot reach the top of the frame and I am forced to climb up on a chair. I run my hand over the dusty ledge. The key is there.

I unlock the door slowly and start up the steps. My knees are trembling in anticipation of what I might find. In my timing, the sun is just rising and highlighting the contents of the room.

The room is quiet and nothing appears out of the ordinary. I walk slowly over to the table and stroke the chair where I had witnessed the vision the night before.

I opened up a few of the trunks and rummaged through them briefly. I started to laugh and I took a deep breath. I felt relieved. I came to the only reasonable conclusion. I must have been half-dazed by the hours of reading.

My theory was quickly tested when I spied a letter lying on the floor right at the top of the stairs. I was certain it was not there before.

My logical mind tried to reason that I must have jarred the letter loose from the rafters, bumping around through the trunks.

I reached down, picked it up and walked over to the window to read it. The writing on the envelop was faded. I strained my eyes to read the name on the cover and opened the letter.

12 October 1780

Dear Mrs. McGraw,

I regret to inform you that your kind and noble husband Moses McGraw has been killed. Your husband fought bravely against the Tories. In September his company commanded by Major John Phifer left on expedition to the Blue Ridge Mountains.

Unfortunately, while crossing the French Broad
River, the men were ambushed by the Cherokee. It
was there that your husband met his end. Moses
McGraw will be remembered by all his fellow soldiers
as a trustworthy and faithful friend.

> *God be with you,*
> *Your obedient servant,*
> *Captain John Barringer*

Until now, I have never shared what happened
that night with anyone. Robert's supposedly imaginary friend, Moses McGraw, became a family joke and
a scapegoat for unexplainable happenings around the
house. With time, Robert forgot about that night, but I
never have. I sometimes wonder if Moses is still here
watching over me now.

....

I remove the last page. I stand up and stretch while
debating if I should begin another chapter tonight. Several
hours ago I heard Dovie and Jasper return home, but they
did not disturb me.

The house is quiet. I open the front door for Rebel and
head for the kitchen. I heat up a pot of coffee and some
leftovers. I sit down with my plate and plan to read over
the paper and take care of my own necessities.

When I hear Rebel at the door, I walk outside for a
moment and look across the yards. All is quiet at Mrs.
Davis' house. Just hours ago Lilly and Henry were married. Tonight they will spend the bridal night under Mrs.
Davis' roof. It would not be to my liking, but nowadays
people do what they have to do.

I am feeling refreshed and return to the typewriter. I
have just begun to collect my thoughts when I hear the

noises from above. Dovie and Jasper again. God in heaven, does no one use a bed for sleeping anymore.

I turn off the light, close off the office and go back to my own bed to sleep.

Chapter 10

Bloody Cotton

Wednesday, February 1, 1893

Early yesterday morning I decided to walk to the cemetery. It was a sunny morning and I spent it strolling over the gardens. When my legs gave out, I found rest on the bench on the hilltop. I remained there for the balance of the morning. My lonely eyes looked over the graves. I wept. It was Joel's birthday.

On my way home, the sky began to gray. The evening became just another monotonous rainy day. In spite of my somber mood, I had planned to work on my book. These were the only words I had to share on January 31, 1893.

My days are filled with emptiness,
Of loneliness and memories,
And sometimes I must slip away.

I wander to the garden,
Where I sit upon the hill,
And dream of yesterdays and you.

Yesterday, my words flowed free,
Yesterday, the rose was a blooming,
But today the petals wash away,
Lost in the Carolina Rain.

Today, with hope and prayers to ward off the devil's evil gloom, I commence my day. My mother used to preach the importance of appearances. With that in mind, I dress in one of my nicer housedresses and arrange my hair as if I am expecting visitors.

After breakfast, I go straight to my office and take out my scrapbooks of 1875-1876. As I flip through the pages, once again a ghost from the past whispers. A letter from Dr. Fannie falls in my lap. I read over the letter once and then determine it is a good opening for the next chapter of my book. I open the curtain to let in the light and sit down at my desk and slip a clean sheet in the typewriter.

1875-1876

Dear Lizzie,

If there is a newspaper there in your little town of Concord, I hope you are following our progress.

Lizzie, I have always considered you a progressive thinker. I have a feeling, if it were not for that husband of yours, you would join us. Promise me this, that you will not hinder your girls from taking their rightful place in the world. They are the bud of promise for this corrupt world.

I am no longer working at the Revolution Newspaper. It has been sold. The two most crippling factors of its demise were the economical depression and the lack of support from the Republican Party.

In my previous letters I may have spoken favorably of a woman by the name of Victoria Woodhull. Now I know different. In brief, she is of low-breed, uneducated and her fame may have been excelled by

her bedroom skills. Her views on free love and specu-
lations of her own external marital affairs have left a
sour taste in the mouths of those who previously sup-
ported her.

Even with all the setbacks we have endured, I
have not abandoned my work for Women's Suffrage.
Several months ago, you may have read about Susan
B. Anthony and five other women who were arrested
for attempting to vote. Yours truly was one of the
five. We had hoped to gain national awareness with a
public trial, instead of just a slap on the wrist and a
hundred dollar fine. Well I will close now, leaving you
to return to your life of domestic bliss. Beware! One of
these days, I will surely show up on your doorsteps!

I forever pray for your health and happiness.

Your friend,
Fannie Holloway

Often I would receive two letters a week from Dr.
Frances Holloway. Sometimes mid-1875, her letters
were replaced by the new post cards. I was the closest
thing Fannie had to family. No matter how great your
accomplishments, they are small unless you have
someone to share them with. I was honored to share
Fannie's accomplishments and now I will share them
with you.

Anyone who picked up a paper knew about
Victoria Woodhull. In fact, she received more cover-
age than Lincoln's assassination. She had outsmarted
the system.

Since women were not allowed to vote, no one
dreamed that a woman would run for president.
Therefore it was not illegal. She may have been regarded
as a saint for her policies on an eight-hour workday and
equal pay for women, but her personal life flared tem-
pers and earned her the name of Mrs. Satan.

The arena for talking politics was the churchyard. Joel listened, but said little. He said it was a waste of a man's time talking about things he could not do a thing about.

President Grant was unable to turn the country around his first term. What makes him think he can do it in a second term? It is hard to fight a war when your soldiers are crooks and thieves. A wise man knows when it is time to give up and go home.

I wish I had a penny for every time Joel ended the churchyard conversations by saying, "Best not worry about your neighbors. Make sure your own fences are high enough to keep your horses in and low enough to keep your hogs from digging out."

Only I knew how troubled Joel was about the things he had no control over. In a working man's logical mind, he could not comprehend the concept of free trade. It was just bad business importing foreign cotton, while local farmers' cotton lay rotting in the fields.

Joel worked in the cotton mill and part time at the sawmill. When that was not enough, he helped Ransom on the farm. I worried about him. He had become serious and weary. I suggested that I go to work in the mill too, but he would not hear of it.

Finally, he did agree to allow me to take students in for piano classes. I made some inquiries concerning the going rates for piano lessons. The piano tuition per 12-week semester at the girl's academy was $12 and at Miss Kelly's $9. Based on that I felt I could make a fair go of it offering my lessons at 35 cents each, or $4.20 a semester.

I ran a small ad in the paper and the next week I had two eager students, which doubled to four the following week. Word spread and in no time, I was teaching two or three students a day.

The piano business was a blessing and my children soon became immune to the unmusical sounds they were subjected to several days a week.

Every lesson I taught on that old piano I thought of Mother. Countless were the hours she spent sitting on the bench next to my sisters and me. She encouraged every note with the patience of Job. She said it was important for a young woman to strive to become an accomplished pianist, as well as develop a pleasant singing voice. The gentlemen would enjoy it and others would admire us. Sallie proved to be gifted. I was learned, but poor Annabelle was tone deaf and had the voice of a screech owl.

It was from the piano students that the children gained interest in the graded school. Fall of 1876, they were enrolled. Victoria was 12, Robert 10 and Tessie 8.

The children adjusted well to the public school, except for Tessie. She said she could not bear for the teacher to call on her to read. Luckily, the teacher discovered that she could not see the chart. A trip to Dr. Morris' office was confirmation and Tessie came home with her first pair of spectacles.

With my income, things were a little easier. I was relieved when Joel gave up the job at the sawmill. He was a good craftsman, but the war had claimed two fingers on his left hand. Working around saws required a steady hand and I worried that his grip would slip.

Speaking of accidents, the cotton mill had its share too. Hands and fingers were lost, caught up in the machinery. If the possibility of entanglement was not enough, the noise and the flying fragments of yarn were also a threat to one's health.

The loosely written laws on child labor were rarely enforced. In North Carolina, it was supposedly illegal to work children under the age of 13 or work any child more than 66 hours a week.

However, for orphans like Les Lester, there were no age limits or restrictions. When the inspector showed up, under-age children were hidden or simply brushed off as visitors or helpers; therefore, not accountable as real workers.

Les started off as Lilly's helper. He was above average in wit and was soon given his own job as a sweeper, then promoted to a scavenger. Scavengers had to be small enough to crawl under the running machines and clean up under the whirling motion of the wheels.

Les never complained about his lot in life, nor did his work hinder his studies. When I started teaching piano, I could only school him once a week. I was amazed at his progress. He said he practiced his multiplications lying there flat on his back, listening to the hum of the machines.

By the time Les was 15 he was working alongside the men. He was an uncommonly handsome boy, which had not gone unnoticed by the young girls. It was nearly impossible for me to keep up with him in lesson plans. I was afraid he would surpass me. I secretly sent out a few inquiries to the local academies on his behalf. If they were offering any scholarships, surely this young man was deserving.

For most of April 1876 Les had been working overtime and missed his weekly lessons. He sent word with Joel to assure me he was following up with his studies at night.

On April 25, two days before his 16th birthday, Les began his new job as supervisor of his department. It being a coveted position and a considerable pay raise, there were a number of men in line for the job. Nevertheless, with Les's experience and work ethics he was selected as the best candidate.

Men like Joel, who had been in the war, understood that sometimes the best soldiers were mere boys. Lilly and Henry were proud of Les, but I personally hoped that the new position did not lock him into a career working in the mill.

That morning, I walked to the edge of the porch with Joel as he left for work. I watched him pick up his step to catch up with Lilly and Les. For some odd reason, Les turned around and blew me a kiss. I responded with the same.

I got the children off to school, set about my household chores and had just walked out to the garden when I saw Joel coming down the street. It was only 11:00 and too early for lunch. When Joel saw me he threw up his hand, but he turned down Mrs. Davis' walk. Something was wrong. I untied my apron, threw it across the front porch railing and ran across the yard.

When I stepped up on the porch, the front door was wide open and I walked in. I saw Joel and Mrs. Davis in the hallway. I could see the look on Mrs. Davis's face, but Joel was turned. I demanded to know what happened.

Joel turned around and I saw his shirt was covered with blood. I recall my knees going weak and I collapsed to the floor when Joel told me Les had been hurt.

He sat down on the floor beside me and put his arm around me. He said he had seen the whole thing. First, he heard a child screaming. When he looked up, there was a crowd gathering around one of the machines. A little girl's pigtail had gotten caught in the machine. Everyone watched in horror as her little head banged up and down between the machine and the floor.

The next thing he knew Les broke through the crowd. He slid under the machine and cut off the little girl's hair, releasing her just in time to save her life. The crowd was cheering as the little girl climbed out. In the excitement, Les must have forgotten his size and reared up too high. The machine came down and mangled his shoulder.

Joel said when they hauled Les off to Dr. Baker's, he was conscious. It was hard to tell how badly he was injured because of all the matted cotton and blood. Lilly sent Joel to let us know what happened and to go find Henry.

Mrs. Davis came over and spent the afternoon with me and together we waited for the news. The children were already in bed when we heard a carriage pull up. Joel and Henry were following behind on horseback. Mrs. Davis sat down and began to weep, saying repeatedly, "They are bringing poor Les's body home."

I saw I was not going to gain control over her, so I ran out across the yard by myself. Joel waved and I saw Lilly getting out of the carriage. As I approached, Joel gave me his halfway smile. Joel and I had been through so much together and I knew that smile. It was good news.

The doctor said he was a strong and healthy boy, but it would take sometime for him to recover. He had lost a lot of blood, but if infection did not set in the wounds, he would heal.

Lilly and I took turns sitting by Les's bedside day and night. On the second day, he would take water and by the third, he was taking broth. Once word got out what had happened, there was a steady flow of people coming in to hold his hand and pray for their young friend. The whole town regarded him as a hero. They brought food and dropped money in a jar to pay for his medical bills.

Each time the doctor came to visit, Les would ask when he would be able to go back to work. The doctor would just say, "We'll talk about it when you are stronger."

None of us had the heart to tell him the doctor said he was not certain if and when that would occur. There was muscle and tendon damage to consider.

Being the kind boy he was, he worried more about others than himself. I was there the day the mill manager came to see him. Les was delighted when he learned that Joel would be paid for the workday he missed and Lilly would receive her salary while she was out taking care of him.

The manager asked Lilly to step out in the hall with him. When Les drifted back off to sleep, I slipped out to go home. Lilly called me in to ask my advice. It appeared that the manager was there to offer a settlement for the boy's disabilities.

In front of the man, I cautioned her not to sign anything in haste. Even though $100 was a lot of money, it would hardly replace the use of the boy's arm. It was not my place to say more and I left the two of them alone. Lilly could not withstand the man's pressuring and the papers were signed before Henry came home.

Joel and I were heartbroken for Les. A month passed and his left arm was still too weak to lift a cup to his mouth. I tried to keep Les's spirits up, by taking him lesson plans. When I returned he had not even looked over them. Now, Lilly regretted even more that she had signed the papers.

It was the 2nd day of July and the children and I were sitting on the front porch. A fancy buggy stopped right in front of the house and a well-dressed man stepped out. He inquired if I was Mrs. Simpson. I replied that I was, but I feared he might be a tax collector.

I was greatly relieved when the man identified himself as Mr. Henry Thomas Jefferson Ludwig, head professor of North Carolina College in Mt. Pleasant.

He informed me he had come to speak to me about Les Lester.

Since Les's accident, I had completely forgotten about the school inquiries I had made on his behalf.

The man told me he found my letter of interest, but with limited funds for scholarships he had filed it away. However, Les Lester's name came up again when a well-known gentleman, who preferred to remain anonymous, came to visit the school. The gentleman said he was prepared to pay for the boy's tuition and board for as long as his grades were reflective of hard work. Under those same conditions, if Les was of the mind to seek higher education he would also stand good for that as well.

I was so overjoyed that I jumped up and hugged the poor little man, nearly knocking him off his feet. I quickly explained the accident and together we went next door and shared the news with a very happy young man.

I have my suspicions, but we never found out who the man was that paid for Les's education.

I have spent many words in this chapter telling you about what happened to Les. However, I should not close without telling you that General Custer was killed June 25, 1876, along with every man in his company in the Indian battle of Little Bighorn.

....

With one quick stroke, I pull the page out of the typewriter. Enough for today, I think to myself. I stand up, arch my back, then lean forward and dangle my fingers to the floor. I read it was good for fatigue. Rebel jumps down off the sofa and begins to bark at the queerness of my actions.

I look at the clock. Lilly and Henry will be here shortly to pick me up for the town meeting. When I open the office door, I am hoping to smell supper cooking. If it is ready, I can swallow a few bites before I leave.

I find the kitchen is cold. I call for Dovie, but before I can start up the stairs Henry knocks on the door. I purposely did not want to see anyone yesterday, but for over a week she had hardly hit a lick in the kitchen. I run my hand over the dusty bureau in the hall. I fear she has gotten lazy since she has married.

Henry knocks again and I grab my cape and open the door. When I step up in the carriage, Lilly turns around and waves. For the first few minutes, we ride along in silence. I am in deep thought about Dovie and Jasper. Do they think my house is a hotel? I have never felt like this before about Dovie. It has always been fair exchange, her room and board for housekeeping and domestics. I thought Jasper would be a good addition, but perhaps I am wrong. Joel would not be pleased, knowing I was allowing them to use me. I must attend to this matter as soon as possible.

Henry interrupts my thoughts with an abrupt sentence, "Oh the perils of modern life!"

"What are you talking about?" Lilly asked.

"Henry slowed down the horses and glared over at her. "We lived through the war, but this damn so-called 'progress' is going to be the doom of society. Electrical wires, machinery, natural gas explosions and not to mention all the railroad accidents. Why, if a man makes it to be an old man these days, he has done something."

Lilly nudged Henry on the shoulder and tried to laugh. She pulled her cape up over her shoulders and leaned back to speak to me directly. "Lizzie, I hear tell that Miss T. M. Dunn is offering china painting classes. I will sign up if you will go with me."

Before I can answer, Henry shouts out, "Rolled cigarettes! I tell you, people better take heed to what they are submitting themselves to." As soon as he stops the carriage, he points to a man standing out front of the town hall smoking.

"Henry, you have been awfully nervous lately," Lilly says, and pats him gently on the knee.

He helps us out of the carriage and makes a beeline for the door. Lilly takes hold of my hand and urges me to lag back. "I am not sure if marriage is agreeing with Henry."

"Maybe he is suffering from gas. Do you think it is your cooking?" I tease, and we walk in the building trying to stifle our laughter.

The room is crowded and we are unable to find three seats together. I am forced to take a seat in the row behind Lilly and Henry. I can see Lilly's shoulders shaking and I know she is still giggling. Henry looks over his shoulder at me, suspecting I am at fault. I wave at him and grin. He turns around quickly. Lilly's head bobs up and down as he leans over to speak to her.

When the meeting is called to order, I turn my head slightly to acknowledge the man sitting next to me. "Were you saving this seat for anyone?" I asked.

He smiles and raises his eyebrows, "Yes," he says bluntly.

I feel the heat come to my face and I start to get up. He reaches over and touches my arm. "I was saving this seat for the prettiest lady in the room, and I think you fit that bill," he laughs.

"Thank you," I reply, and steady my eyes ahead on the speaker. I can sense his sideward glances. I feel my heart pounding, sitting so close to a strange man. I say strange, but he is actually quite handsome.

A second or two later I feel him shift in his chair and cross his legs. I turn my eyes slightly to observe him. He is holding a notebook and he has completely disengaged with me. I now realize he was only teasing me. What possibly could have made me think a handsome man like him would actually be flirting with a woman my age?

I hear an unexpected applause and I realize I was not paying attention to the speaker. I clap along with them and turn full attention to the front. Reverend Sherrill is sitting down and Harry Crowell steps up on the platform to speak.

"Ladies and gentleman," he begins and clears his throat. "I, too, agree with Rev. Sherrill. We certainly do not want to open up our fair city to the addition of more barrooms or gambling hells. However, the YMCA is hardly an establishment that will corrupt our city. Nor is the YMCA a church, or does it pretend to be. What the YMCA does provide is a facility for young men to spend their leisure time enjoying affordable reading and innocent games in a wholesome and polite social setting. I ask you mothers and wives, do you not prefer this over 'the houses of ill repute' in Gold Hill?"

Some of the audience look shocked at his remark. Others shake their heads and applaud. The man turned to me and remarked, "Good point." I did not want to begin a pointless conversation, so I simply shook my head.

Before Mr. Crowell could sit down, a middle-aged woman stood up in the audience. I had seen this pinched-faced woman before around town. She is dressed richly and a fur capelet is draped over her shoulders. She is obviously of the upper crust and I am sure she would be quick to remind you of the fact. "Mr. Crowell," she calls. "Might I remind you, we already have a men's social club here in town. I can hardly see why the city would even entertain the thoughts of funding another one."

"My dear woman," Mr. Crowell responds. "The New South Club is hardly a facility for the common man. The dues alone are more than some of us make in a year."

At his remark, there is an outburst of laughter. The woman gathers up her purse, sticks her nose up in the air and marches out of the room. Her mealy mouth little husband stands up, tips his hat and follows her.

Mr. Crowell steps down and the mayor comes to the platform. "Folks, I think we have seen the end of what the government has called reconstruction. As you all know, Charlotte has closed their barrooms and saloons, but for what good? Last month two wagons were confiscated coming from Statesville hauling barrels of illegal whiskey. Just last week here in Concord (and I will call no names) the revenue collector broke up one of the largest moonshine stills on record. I can only ask, is this the reputation you want for our city? People, the laws are changing. As good citizens, it is our individual responsibility to abide by them. Now if I may, allow me to introduce to you Mr. Colin Collins, our next speaker."

My seat-neighbor rises out of his chair. "Excuse me," he whispers and squeezes past me. I feel his knees against mine and observe his fit figure. I hold my head down to prevent any additional eye contact.

When he steps up on the platform, he turns to address the audience. "Good evening, everyone!" he says, in an optimistic tone. "I am with the Concord Electrical Company and we supply your city with the means for which to light your streets. Your mayor has asked me to address your concerns regarding the recent complaints of burned-out bulbs. I have a bill I would like to respectfully submit for approval for the replacement of such bulbs. There are presently 56 electric streetlights in Concord and of those, 19 are burned out. The total cost for the labor and replacing the 19 bulbs is $32.50. I think...."

"What about that $800 a year the city is already paying your company for the use of them lights?" a man shouts from the back.

Mr. Collins does not flinch in his response. "Sir, with a town of 4,200 people, $800 is certainly not too much to pay for safe streets and walkways. However, as wonderful as electric lighting may be, the bulbs do not last forever."

Henry makes an attempt to stand, but Lilly holds onto his hand. He frees himself and stands to speak. "The moonlight is free and there ain't no bulbs to change."

Everyone laughs, including Mr. Collins, who now replies, "Well that is fine, but what happens on cloudy nights?"

Henry thinks for a moment, "I reckon we could catch a tumbler of lightning bugs and hang them on the trees to light the walkways. Maybe we could just all stay at home like decent folks."

Mr. Collins does not respond to that statement. Why should he? Henry's ridiculous comment has just sealed the deal for the electrical company. Mr. Collins hands the bill to the mayor and the meeting is adjourned.

The crowd is pushing to the door. I feel like a lost little lamb following behind Henry and Lilly. "Mrs. Simpson," I hear someone call out. It is Mr. Collins and I am surprised he knows my name. "I have been meaning to come by and see you," he says, pulling me to the side to speak to me.

"To see me?" I question.

"Yes, I knew your husband, Joel. I was working on the electrical installations in the mill before he got sick. He loaned me a fishing rod and I would like to return it to you."

"Oh, I see," I reply, feeling a twinge of sorrow rise up in my heart. "Anytime will be fine. If I am not home, you may leave it on the porch. I live on Peachtree.

"I know where you live. I gave Joel a ride home a couple of times. If you would grace me the pleasure of your company, I would like to bring it by when you are expecting me.

A lump develops in my throat. I cannot answer and fear my eyes will tear up in embarrassment. Lilly calls for me. When I turn to answer her, I discover Mr. Lee is standing behind me. I am trapped between Mr. Collins and Mr. Lee.

"How about tomorrow night around 6:30?" Mr. Collins asks.

"That should be fine," I respond.

"Excellent, tomorrow it is," he says, and turns to leave. When he passes by Mr. Lee, he speaks and pats him on the back.

I have no time to recover my wit before Mr. Lee approaches me. "Have you got a moment?" he asks.

"Actually no. Henry and Lilly are waiting for me," I apologize. "If it is important I will tell them to wait."

"No, no, you go on. I just wanted to tell you I have some reports to drop off for you." His voice drops as though his feelings are hurt.

"That is good news," I say, trying to sound reassuring. When he smiles, I hurry off to catch up with Lilly and Henry.

On the way home, Henry is quiet. I am worried about him too. Maybe his job has gotten to be too much for him. Perhaps he should put in for a retirement.

When I walk in the front door, I am reminded of my empty stomach. I am pleasantly surprised to see Dovie has food warming in the oven for me.

Dovie is nowhere to be found, but I am thankful she prepared supper. Still this does not forgive the last couple of weeks. It is late and I will deal with Jasper and her tomorrow.

That night before I sleep, I pray,

Dear Lord, I often wonder why the path in front of us is shaded from our eyes. I do not question your ways, only question my own. I am sinfully fearful and all too aware of my many weaknesses. Give me eyes to see your way. Amen.

Chapter 11

The Fishing Rod

Odd how it is this morning. It is as if Jasper and Dovie knew I was going to give them a grand scolding. As soon as my feet hit the floor, I can smell breakfast cooking. Jasper had already collected the mail and my paper lay next to my plate.

"Goodmor'in Miss Lizzie!" Dovie says, in a high tone as if it is the fourth of July.

"Good morning to you, Dovie," I reply, knowing she is trying to butter me up.

"I's fixin' hot cakes fer yous. Jasper he's gone to da barn," she says smiling.

"That's nice," I reply. I feel my grudge starting to soften after a sip of coffee. Oh well, I think to myself. Looks like they are shaping up. No use in ruining a good day with stern words.

I sort through the mail and see a post card from Victoria. I make it my first piece of business to read.

January 12, 1893

My dearest Mother,

I have the most exciting news. I am going to the World's Fair in Chicago! Our chapter of Woman's Suffrage here is arranging the trip. We will all take part in Susan B. Anthony's march. I am even thinking of entering the women's swimming competition. How bold will that be! The World's Fair is being organized to celebrate the 400th anniversary of

Christopher Columbus in the new world. What better time to raise awareness for the emerging "New Woman." Oh, Mother, please consider coming with us. There is to be a 264-foot ferris wheel, musicals, wild west shows and all sorts of splendid modern wonders.

Please write soon,
I hope to hear that you and the family are well.
Arrivederci and love to all,
Victoria

I admire her boldness and I see some of my younger self in her. Joel loved Victoria as much as he loved his own two children, but she is different. As much as I hate to admit it, she is high-spirited like her father. I see in her the same passion, but I pray she will make better choices.

I can only imagine what it would be like to go to Chicago. Joel would have not approved and besides, I cannot afford to spend money on a trip. I will ask her to take her Kodak and send me some pictures. I say a prayer in my heart for her safety and then open my newspaper. I chuckle softly as I read over the front page.

Dovie cuts her eyes my way, *"What's be so funny?"*

"Nothing terribly funny, just a poem. Today is February 2, Groundhog's Day," I reply. She nods and I read the poem aloud.

Swine or squirrel I do not know,
When he peeps out to say hello,
Pray not his shadow show,
For back in the hole he will go.
Six more weeks of winter, oh no!

She smiles slightly and returns to her cooking and I to my paper. My eyes scan over the headlines. "You would think with all the trouble in this world, this paper would have more important things to talk about than just the goings and comings of ordinary folks," I say to Dovie.

"*Yes'um, you sho thinks so,*" she says and darts out the door toward the pantry.

I do not know why I initiated such a conversation with Dovie. She has never shown an interest in things outside her own little world. I suppose that is good; you have less to worry about. I return to my paper and read to myself:

Capt. Jonas Cook, from Mt. Pleasant, was seen in town on Monday having lunch with Capt. Odell and Gaston B. Means.

Cannon Mfg. Co. is thriving even with the fear of another depression. There is talk of building more mills in the area.

If there is a War with Chile, will the Cabarrus Black Boys be called up?

Government proposes a new tax to pay for telegraph business. Why should the ordinary man or farmer have to pay for such luxuries of rich folks?

Black measles in Charleston, public schools shut down.

Personals: I, Geo. Tilley, forbid anyone from offering entertainment or lodging to my wife. She is neglecting her household, running around town and passing the care of the children to strangers.

I am appalled by the last ad. What kind of husband would air such dirty laundry in the newspaper? If I were that wife, I would be running as far away from that husband as I could.

Dovie sets a plate down in front of me. "*Cans I gets you anything else?*" she asks, looking rather sheepish. "*I's gonna make a egg custard fer supper. Jasper says de hens he gots out back are laying fools."*

From experience, I know she wants something. I lay down the paper and look her directly in the eyes. "Alright Dovie, what is it?"

"Jaspers and I's gonna have a baby!" she blurts out, clapping her hands together.

"Good Lord in heaven! Dovie, did you not tell Jasper about the rubber sheaths I told you about?"

"Jasper told me dem things don't work for colored folks."

"If you would have asked me, I could have told you different. Now how do you think I can support you, Jasper and a baby?

"Momma says if you was mad, we could live with dem tills we could get our own place. I's can gets a job somewheres."

"Well, you just might have to do that!" I said angrily.

Dovie drops what she is doing and runs upstairs crying. A few seconds later, I hear Jasper come in the back door. He walks in the kitchen. When he does not see Dovie, he sets the eggs down quietly and goes to look for her.

I can hear her crying upstairs and I begin to feel guilty. I know it is a sin to slander an unborn child. After I finish my breakfast, I will talk to her. We will manage somehow. One child will not be so bad. She will have to promise they will make every effort not to let it happen again until they are able to support themselves.

When I go upstairs, Dovie is crying. Jasper is sitting on the bed watching her pack up their things in an old suitcase. I walk over and take the suitcase out of her hand. When I go back downstairs, we have an understanding. One child means Jasper will have to work more hours at the blacksmith's. Two children means they have to find somewhere else to live.

In a short while things are back to normal. Dovie is in the kitchen making egg custards, Jasper is on his way to Mr. Tom's to ask for more work and I am in the office working on my book.

1877-1878

When the mill was on short time, Joel would take odd jobs and farm himself out. Supper might have not been on the table some nights, if it had not been for my piano business.

After silver was discovered in Tombstone, Arizona, Joel would tease about striking out for the Wild West. He said he could get a job as a lawman and ride with Wyatt Earp. If he had been a single man, it might not have been a joke. If he had gone, I would have followed him.

In 1877, there was a great dispute over who won the presidential election between Samuel J. Tilden and Rutherford B. Hayes. In those days, I did not follow politics very closely, but almost overnight reconstruction ended and the military occupation was gone. Shortly after that, the remaining Southern states were readmitted to the Union and Hayes became the president.

Joel said the end of reconstruction was not much of a compromise. Plain and simple, the North was done with the South anyway. The money was all gone and there was nothing to gain. What the war had not robbed, the depression of 1873 had claimed. The speculators had turned their interest to more profitable ventures, such as silver, gold and the railroads.

President Hayes may have skated through the election, but his handling of the railroad strikes did not go so smoothly. When the railroads began to cut salaries, the workers refused to work. President Hayes used federal troops to control the riots and hundreds of workers were injured or killed.

In spite of all we had endured, I believe Southerners to be among the most optimistic people on earth. I give to reason that it be our firm foundation of faith and the solid soil upon which we were born.

When the Federal troops vanished, towns and cities were left to govern over themselves again. Slowly, law and order returned and women and children felt free to travel about town.

The mill had been a slow sinking ship for years. In 1877, on the courthouse steps, Captain John Odell purchased the mill. With the prospect of steady work, there was finally a feeling of ease in the community.

Mr. Odell became known as the "Master Mill Man." The mill grew and the community grew up around it. Word spread and people came from all over to live in the booming town of Concord. New employee houses were built with running water and electric lights.

There were company picnics, Easter egg rolls, baseball games and prizes such as silver dollars. It was the first time in our children's lives that we could offer a few luxuries.

The girls were grateful to update their wardrobes and I bought them books for pleasure reading, such as Oliver Twist and Tom Sawyer. Joel and Robert liked to read dime novels about cowboys and Indians and the Wild West. I was not so approving. I was afraid all the adventures might turn Robert wild too.

I think this would be a good time to tell you about the young souls I call my children.

I will begin with Victoria at age 14. She was a tall, willowy girl, with a figure suited for a ballerina. Her mass of curly blonde hair was a becoming frame for her soft hazel eyes.

One could easily be fooled by her soft and dainty appearance, in thinking her to be the same. She was outspoken and borderline abrasive at times. She chose her words carefully and took pride in her grammar.

Factoring in her above-average intelligence and her quick temper, she did not readily make friends. Fortunately, either she did not notice or it simply was not a concern of hers. In short, Victoria was a scholar. She questioned all things and would spend days researching fact or fiction.

Robert at age 12 was more likely to cut-a-fool than follow the rules. He was a dark-headed, handsome boy, smallish in size, but wiry and fit. With his smart wit and comedian tendencies, he had no trouble making friends. He was often a ringleader of mischief.

Like any mother, I will tell you my son was a good boy. But I learned to keep an eye on him. Robert could do no wrong according to Joel. He was the apple of his daddy's eye. I suspect Joel was just as rotten when he was a little boy too.

Which brings me to last, but not least, my little Tessie. At age 10, she was already set in her ways. She was soft spoken, shy and otherwise a wallflower. I will never figure it. She had all the traits to be the very belle of the ball, a charming little package of coal-black hair and eyes with rosy cheeks and pearly white teeth.

Still, Miss Tessie was often too afraid to speak and was most happy at home in her safe, domestic setting. She would rather be in the kitchen than in the parlor. Joel used to tease. The fellow that finds Tessie will have himself a good wife. The fellow that finds Victoria best hold on to his hat; it is going to be a wild ride."

Now that I have set the stage, I feel I can go forward. It was the summer of 1877 when Mr. Brown, or "Uncle Billy," moved into the neighborhood.

Joel was working full time again and I had a full book of piano students. With the children being older and the present state of things, I felt it safe to let them be free to themselves.

A typical day began like this: Joel left for the mill before six, my first lesson began at 10, Victoria took to her books, Tessie played with her dolls and Robert roamed over the neighborhood with his friends while I prayed he would not get into trouble.

Two weeks after the house two doors down was vacated, the new folks were moving in. Robert and his friends sat on the hill across the street and watched the wagons unloading.

He and a couple of boys would show up around lunchtime, looking for a handout. In turn, they felt it was their duty to give me an account of the new neighbor's belongings. I supposed it was innocent spying and at least it kept them out of trouble for a few days.

According to Robert, the only occupants of the house were an old man at least 100 years old, a dog without a tail and a daughter who looked about Tessie's age. I assumed by his description the child must be a grandchild who was left in his keeping.

I gave them a week to settle in their home. Then I baked an apple cake with plans to take the girls down to welcome the child. I would introduce myself as the piano teacher. It never hurts to scout for potential students.

Robert had taken off early that morning and I

determined I would see him around noontime. I was surprised to find him waiting on the front porch, with intent to accompany us to the new neighbor's house.

I thought it endearing and sent him inside to comb his hair and wash his hands. The girls expressed their resentment. Nevertheless, we all knocked on the door of our new neighbors that spring morning.

I recall we waited for some time before I knocked again a little louder. "Just a minute, I hear you!" came a small high-pitched voice from behind the door.

The handle rattled and creaked and it appeared that whoever was on the other side of the door was having difficulty. Robert stepped up and gave the door a push.

The door flew back and we heard a squeal, which sounded more like a cat than a human. The house was dimly lit and there was no one in sight. Tessie was frightened and ran back down the steps.

In a few seconds I heard, "Oh me! Oh my! Excuse me. The door has knocked me off my feet." Then from behind the door she stepped. The children's mouths dropped and I tried my best not to show my own astonishment. Standing before us, as only seen in books, was a miniature lady. I was certain she was not a child, even though she was smaller than Tessie.

"Hello," she said, smiling. She reached out her tiny hand to shake mine and then waved out to the children.

"We are the Simpsons," I said, regaining my voice. We live in the gray house two doors down. We have come to bring you an apple cake."

I nudged Robert and he cautiously extended the cake.

"Please come in," she said, and gestured for us to enter. I nodded my head and the children filed in behind me. We followed her into the sitting room and she offered us a seat. Once we were seated, she excused herself to go have "Jing" prepare tea.

As soon as she left the room the children began whispering. I cautioned them to be quiet. For an extended time the four of us sat in silence looking over the strange room. From the best I could guess, the room was eclectic decor of things from foreign lands.

We were so involved in our viewing that we did not see them enter the room. When the little woman called out, "here we are," we turned to see another marvel. Carrying the tray was the very first Oriental lady our eyes had ever seen. She was so stunningly beautiful that before Tessie could control herself she gasped and clapped her hands.

The child's reaction seemed to please her. She smiled softly and bowed her head. Then skillfully she went about setting up the tea table. I, too, had to control my gasp when I saw the exquisite hand-painted teapot.

The little woman took a seat in a rocker, which was intended for a child. "My name is Dora."

I introduced the children and myself. Then she stood up as if she was on stage and posed. "Good evening, ladies and gents. I am the Duchess Dora of Amsterdam. I stand 36 inches tall and weight 32 pounds. My father was a giant of a man standing over six feet tall, my mother nearly his equal. When I was born, I was so small that Mother bathed me in a teacup. I speak six languages, including the language of the fairies. I am over 300 years old and I can never die. I am known throughout the world for my rare miniature paintings and I write poetry so sweet that it will melt the hardest of hearts."

She took a bow. I clapped, understanding it was a performance, and the children followed suit. She began to giggle and a button popped off her blouse, slightly exposing the cleavage of her tiny breasts. "Well, not really, that is all circus talk," she said. "I am just little old Dora Brown from Guntersville, Alabama."

"You were in the circus?" Tessie asks.

"Well, of course darling, it is the best career for midgets. This lovely lady that pours your tea is Jing. We met when I was performing in China. When I left to come back to America, she came with me. My husband, who you will meet shortly, was a lion trainer. Quick, before he comes in, say nothing of the way he whistles when he talks. He is very self-conscious of it. You think I would be the one to be self-conscious," she said, giggling again.

Joel used to say, "curiosity can be as dangerous as a butterfly hovering over a flame." As always, it was Robert who could not restrain his curiosity. "Why does he whistle when he talks?" he asks.

"Shall I tell, Mrs. Simpson? Are your children brave enough to hear about the attack?"

Thinking only of Tessie I was preparing to say no. But, Tessie spoke up, "Yes, do tell!"

Dora looked around a moment and then lowered her voice to a soft whisper. "Every day for over 30 years he went in and out of the pens, feeding and caring for the animals. But on this day, when he walked by the fence the beast jumped over the fence. He pounced upon his chest and with his massive teeth, ripped into my husband's throat. He would have surely been killed had not another worker ripped up a fence post and beat the animal off him."

"Did they shoot the lion?" I asked.

"Oh, it was not a lion, it was a donkey! You see, he was so embarrassed that we left the circus. Who wants to hear that Alexander William Brown, the great lion trainer, was taken down by a little donkey?"

She had barely finished her story when Mr. Brown came through the door. He was a man of normal size and not a likely mate for little Dora.

We talked and enjoyed the tea and apple cake. I could hardly wait for Joel to come home that night. I had something exciting to tell him.

Some of the neighborhood children were afraid of Uncle Billy and his tiny little wife, but not our children. Uncle Billy would tell them stories and make them funny hats out of newspaper. Tessie loved to dress up in Dora's fancy circus dresses. In fact, I think one of those little dresses is still in the attic.

I think it was Joel who liked Uncle Billy the most. He claimed that old man had more tolerance in him than any man he had ever known. He saw people for what they were and just accepted it. Proof being, not every man would marry a midget and take on the care of a Chinese girl.

I have since found some of Uncle Billy's quotes that Joel jotted down in his journal:

"I believe that all folks are entitled to their own personal liberty. If a man wants to chew tobacco that is alright by me, as long as he don't spit in my standing room. If a man sits in the barroom on Saturday night, then on Sunday morning he is sitting in the front pew in church, that is between him and the Lord. He can eat snakes and onions and go around knocking things down with this breath. I don't care. Just as long as he leaves my dog and me alone.

Uncle Billy, little Dora and Jing lived down the street from us for only one summer. We will always remember them fondly and consider ourselves blessed that our paths had crossed.

Thinking of Uncle Billy and Dora brought back some fond memories. I pull the last page out of the typewriter, number it and place it in the notebook. I had an excellent day of writing, a whole chapter to my credit.

I think about Dovie and Jasper. Who knows, a little baby in the house might be enjoyable from time to time. Then a fear comes over me. What if I get attached to the child and they move away? Stopping for a moment, I go to the window and look out. The days are growing longer. Dovie and Jasper will not be here forever and I will be alone.

I pull down the shade, walk over and start to pour myself a small brandy. I glance up at the clock, 5:45. "Colin Collins!" I scream aloud, running down the hall to change clothes.

Dovie crosses my path in the hall, *"What in tarnation is wrong with you?"*

"Nothing, is supper ready? Did you make the custard? Please bring it and coffee in the front room at 6:30. I am expecting a guest."

I put on my navy dress and redo my hair. I stop and look in the mirror closely; I can see a few strands of gray in my hair. Sitting at the desk all day has left me looking hallow. Perhaps a little rouge might brighten me up a bit. I am not trying to impress Mr. Collins. I would certainly hate for him to go away with a bad impression, especially since he and Joel were friends.

Dovie and Jasper are eating in the kitchen when I come in. Jasper's eyes widen to see me dressed for company. I prepare a plate and eat standing over the stove.

"Miss Lizzie, is Lilly and Henry coming to visit?" Dovie asks, but she really is just fishing.

"No. A gentleman is returning a fishing rod he borrowed from Joel," I respond, and set my plate down on the counter.

I reach up over the sink for the tooth powder and head out to the back porch for the bathroom. Dovie calls out, "Do you want me to answer the door for you?"

"No, I will be out in time."

When I come back in the house, Dovie is waiting for me. *"Miss Lizzie, I lets him in and he is waiting."*

It is only a little past 6 o'clock and he is early. I smooth out my skirt and walk slowly toward the front room. I open the door and see the back of a man's head, but it is not Mr. Collins. It is Mr. Lee. "Lizzie," he says, rising to his feet. "I just dropped in to go over a few things on this report with you."

"Oh, well, I...," I stumble around trying to decide what to say.

"Oh, I am sorry. It looks like you are dressed to go out. I can just come back later," he says, and starts to leave.

Before I can give a response, there is a knock at the door. I know who it is, but Mr. Lee smiles as if he does too. Dovie goes to the door and I hear her say, *"I's let her knows you are here."*

I call out to her, "Dovie, show Mr. Collins in."

"Mr. Lee, are you acquainted with Mr. Collins? He was a friend of my husband's. He has come to return a fishing rod he borrowed from Joel."

"Oh yes, Colin is a traveling man, like me," Mr. Lee laughs.

It would have surprised them to know that I understood what he meant by a traveling man. Joel had been a Mason too.

"What kind of fishing rod is it?" Mr. Lee asks.

"You know this is really embarrassing," Mr. Collins says, smiling back at me. "I was in such a hurry to leave the house I forgot the fishing rod."

"Is that so?" Mr. Lee says, looking at him suspiciously.

Dovie comes in with a tray of custard and coffee. She sets it down on the coffee table. On her way out the door, she rolls her eyes at me. Before Jasper, I could be certain she would be sneaking down the hall to hear what was going on. Maybe Jasper will keep her occupied; well not too occupied. The last thing I need is to hear the bed banging upstairs tonight.

For over an hour, the three of us sit together in the front room, trying to make small talk. The two men talk about the possibility of another depression. They talk about the need for a city bank, telephones and the wonders of the electric lights.

Mr. Lee somehow seems to be taking on the role of host. He gets up, puts a log on the fire and straightens up the rug with his foot. He leans back and crosses his legs in the chair. If I did not know better, I would swear that Mr. Lee was trying to outlast Mr. Collins' visit.

One on one, I would enjoy chatting with either of them. I feel like asking them to take their conversation down to the club. Of course, I do not. Mr. Collins attempts to pour himself another cup of coffee, but the pot is empty. I offer to make a fresh pot, but he says he must be on his way. He promises he will remember the fishing rod next time.

Mr. Lee stands up and shakes his hand and I see Mr. Collins to the door. When I return, Mr. Lee has his coat on and his hat in his hand. "Good night, Lizzie. This has been a most enjoyable visit. Thank you for your hospitality. Please give my regards to Dovie and Jasper."

He makes his way to the door as I follow. "What about the reports?" I ask.

"Oh," he says, reaching in his pocket. "Now isn't this embarrassing," he smiles, and moves closer toward me. "I was in such a hurry to leave the house that I forgot the reports."

Standing by the door in the dim light, he was now close enough to kiss me, and for a moment I thought he might try. I am distracted by a noise overhead and realize it is Dovie and Jasper again. "Good night, Mr. Lee. Feel free to drop the reports off at your earliest convenience."

I open the door, he tips his hat and I lock the door behind him. I call for Rebel. For sometime that night, I lay awake trying to sort out the events of the night.

Chapter 12

A Reluctant Spy

The next morning when I let Rebel out, I noticed the fishing rod on the porch with a note attached:

Dear Mrs. Simpson,

It was truly my intent to return the fishing rod to you last night. I admit that subconsciously I may have forgotten it on purpose, hoping it would afford me yet another opportunity to see you again. My innocent ploy was to acquire your friendship, but I did not expect to encounter a rival. With that in mind, I will be straightforward. If you would give me the honor, I would like you to dine with me at the hotel on Saturday night. You may send a response to my office- 21 Depot Street.

Yours truly,
Colin Collins

For a portion of the morning, I went around pretending to myself that I was blindsided. Actually, I was not, but it seemed like the proper thing to do. Handsome men like Colin Collins are often philanderers. How well I should know.

I spent the morning arranging my office and sorting through old letters and cards. It is strange how someone's voice is imprinted in your memory. I could almost hear mother say, *"A young woman knows a man's intentions, but an older woman better beware. He is likely after her money."*

Mr. Lee's showing up was a surprise, but my guess is it was just a coincidence. As soon as I respond to Mr. Collins' note, I will erase the whole thing from my mind.

I walk slowly toward the office, contemplating my answer. On my desk is a box of stationery. The first sheet I remove is imprinted with a wide black band across the top. The second piece I remove is printed with a spray of pink roses. The mourning stationery is too serious, but the other is too romantic for a refusal, but who says I should refuse? A sheet of linen white seems most appropriate.

I am distracted by a knock at the front door. I remain seated hoping Dovie will answer. The knock comes again. I slip the note in my desk drawer and go to the door. The thought crosses my mind it may be Mr. Lee with his reports.

I pull the curtains back and see that it is not. It is Mr. Lee's mother. I open the door quickly and bid her to come in out of the cold. She is shivering and I encourage her to have a seat by the fireplace.

"Would you like a cup of hot coffee or tea?" I ask.

"Coffee would be nice if you have it, but don't make a pot especially on my account," she says, slipping off her coat. I leave her and go for the coffee.

When I return, she is studying my painting hanging over the mantle. "Would you like cream or sugar?" I ask.

"No, no, black is fine," she says, reaching out her gloved hand for the cup. "Lovely portrait, Mrs. Simpson. Quality work such as this is quite expensive. I am sure it will someday be a family heirloom."

I smile and we both sit down. I knew what she meant. She is bewildered how a mill worker's wife could have afforded the luxury of having a portrait done. It would have taken a month of Sundays to explain. Some things are just best left to mystery. "Mrs. Lee, it is a delight to see you. On a cold day like this, I fear this is not just a social call," I open up, filling in the silence.

"Well, as a matter of fact, I am here on behalf of William. He is not well and he asked me to pay a call on you."

"Not well?" I ask, hearing the pitch of excitement in my own voice.

"Well, I should not have sounded so serious in my tone. He has a bit of a head cold, nothing more. But, you know how men are; they are all big babies. He took his dog to the country yesterday morning to take instruction from Captain Smith, the bird dog trainer from Lexington. I told William it was too damp and cold for the dog, much less for him. I cannot imagine why, but it was after 9 o'clock when he got home last night. This morning he woke up sneezing his head off."

It is hard not to laugh, since Mr. Lee was at my house last night. I hold my head down so that she will not see my smile. He must have come straight from the field to my house.

When I regain my thoughts, I look at her calmly. "I am pleased to know that is all that pales him. But even a head cold can turn wicked this time of year."

"Indeed," Mrs. Lee agrees. "Well, the reason I am here, William needs your help. Because of the delicacy of this matter, he sent me to explain the details.

She reaches in her pocket and hands me a newspaper clipping. "Read this first."

I, Geo. Tilley, forbid anyone from offering entertainment or lodging to my wife. She is neglecting her household, running around town and passing the care of the children to strangers.

"Yes, I recall reading this in the paper yesterday. I thought then, how odd that a man would put such nonsense in the newspaper."

"Well, I feel the same way!" she adds. "I have had a total of three husbands to date. If any man of mine would ever put an ad in the paper about me, I promise you, he would not live to talk about it."

My laughter escapes me and Mrs. Lee laughs too. "I suppose you are shocked that a woman my age would consider another husband. My dear, I might be old, but I am not dead. I am surprised a pretty woman like you does not already have a ring on your finger. I was just telling William the other day that he better...," she stops and clears her throat.

"Now let's get down to the business at hand," she says, reaching in her bag and handing me a small black box. "William says it is easy to use."

I look at it briefly and hand it back to her. "My daughter, Victoria, had her Kodak camera here at Christmas."

Mrs. Lee attempts to hand the camera back to me. "William asked me to give you this one."

"I appreciate the offer, but what do I have to take photos of now? Rebel?"

Rebel is asleep lying by the fireplace. When I say his name, his head pops up.

"Mrs. Simpson, have you heard of Pinkerton Detective Agency?"

"Yes, of course," I answer.

"William would like to ask you to do a little detective work for him today.

It seems this Mr. Tilley has hired William to investigate his wife. If William can prove that the wife is unfit or unfaithful, Mr. Tilley plans to divorce her and take the children," explains Mrs. Lee.

"So, he wants me to track down this woman and photograph her committing some marital offense?"

"Yes, but it should be fairly easy. She is said to be seen lunching at the hotel several times a week with unknown men. All you need do is position yourself in a seat that you might overhear their conversation and take a photo. Then turn your work in to William. He will take care of the rest."

"Oh, I don't know. That sounds like dirty business. I would not want to be dragged into such an affair. I will need some time to think this over Mrs. Lee."

"Mrs. Simpson, the man fears his wife is planning to leave him and take the children with her. If he does not act quickly, then he may never see his children again."

"I see. If she is a bad sort, that would not be in the best interest of the children. But, I hardly think I am qualified for such a task."

"Mrs. Simpson, why don't you and I go to the hotel for lunch together? Maybe we will get the story. If not, we will leave it for William when he gets out of the sick bed." Mrs. Lee is smiling and I see a spark of excitement in her eyes.

I agree. In a short time, I am riding to town with Mrs. Lee or "Agnes" as she wishes to be called. I discover my new friend to be a fast and reckless driver. I nearly lose my breath when she cuts in front of another buggy, causing a near collision.

At last, we arrive safely at the hotel. My knees are so shaky I am fearful I will tumble over as I step out of the buggy. I look over at Agnes who is not the least rattled. I steady myself against the carriage and ask, "How will we recognize Mrs. Tilley?"

"I come here often and I know all the wait staff," she boasts.

As soon as we walk in the door, the host runs up to take our wraps. Agnes goes across the room and whispers something to a young woman who is folding napkins in the corner. The girl drops her work and leads us into the restaurant. She seats us next to the window. "Coffee?" she asks.

"Please," Agnes replies, and I nod.

The girl does not go to the wait station, but circles over the restaurant. Shortly she returns and announces in a full voice, "Yes, Mrs. Lee, we do have a table by the fireplace. Please follow me this way."

A few people look up as we are relocating, but such a request for an elderly woman does not seem unusual. The table she directs us to is close quarters. We must squeeze in next to the wall to be seated. "Now, while you look over the menu, I will go get your coffees," she says. Before she walks away, she taps on our table and ever so slightly motions to the table directly across from us.

There is a man and woman seated there. Apparently, it is Mrs. Tilley and possibly the man in question. I lift up my menu to shield my face. She is decent looking, not the type one would suspect as a rounder. The man is much older and beside his chair rests a cane.

Agnes carefully takes the camera out of her bag and covers it up with her napkin in her lap. She is prepared to take the photo. The girl returns with our coffee and Mrs. Tilley looks over and smiles at us.

Something is just not right about this scene. No woman with any self-respect would arrange a rendezvous with her lover in broad daylight in a public place. The couple is engrossed in a serious-looking conversation. I glance over at Agnes and see she has the camera in position to snap the photo. "Wait," I whisper.

I tap my ear indicating that we should listen. Leaning forward and holding my breath, I strain to hear what the man is saying. "Mrs. Tilley, when we met here last week I would have hired you on the spot, if it were not for your children. I have since talked with my wife and we agree that having children in the house again will be nice. I came here today with full intent to offer you the position as my wife's nurse and housekeeper. I misjudged my travel time and I arrived in town nearly an hour early for our meeting. While I was waiting, I occupied myself reading over the local newspaper. I must say I discovered something very disturbing." He reaches in his vest pocket and hands Mrs. Tilley a folded newspaper.

Mrs. Tilley's hands begin to tremble as she reads. She quickly lays the newspaper down and turns to look out the window. I myself have been in such delicate positions and I recognized her posture. She is fighting to hold back her tears. Whatever her answer is, I know in my heart she is an innocent victim.

After a few seconds, her shoulders raise, she takes a deep breath and turns to face the man. "Mr. Hatley, I understand your concern. I had not wished to give reasons why I had such a strong desire to leave town. Now, I feel for the sake of my children I should not factor in my pride. First, let me say, yes, I am married. My husband of over 12 years is a good provider. We have a nice home, there is money in the bank and he is a respected man in this community. But, I wonder what people would think if they knew what happens behind closed doors. He has no patience with the children or me. He screams at the children for speaking over a whisper. I know the Bible says spare the rod, spoil the child. But, a four-year-old little girl does not deserve to be beaten until she is black and blue. My dear little boy has scars on his back from being beat with the strap. I shall not plea for myself, but...," she stops speaking and pulls her bottom lip down to expose her missing teeth. Then she turns quickly to face the window.

Agnes slowly puts the camera back in her bag and we wait for the man's response. "Mrs. Tilley, I had not bargained on all of this. My wife is a sick woman and she cannot handle undue stress. However, I have no tolerance for a man who would abuse his wife or strike a child. As a Christian, I certainly cannot just ignore what God has revealed to me. I feel I am obligated to take you on as planned."

At first, I see Mrs. Tilley's face lighten, then seconds later it darkens again. "Mr. Hatley, I appreciate your kindness, but let me relieve your burden. I will decline your offer. Something else will come along," she says, gathering up her coat and purse.

"Good day," she says to Mr. Hatley. As she passes by our table, I drop my eyes to avoid hers.

Her head is level and her shoulders are back as she walks toward the door. What a fix for such a lovely young woman, I think to myself. I turn my head toward the man sitting at the table. He has returned to his coffee as if nothing has happened.

My heart begins to pound as I see her walk past the window. Somehow I must help her. Mrs. Lee's eyes warn me that to interfere would not be wise. I pay her no heed and stand up to follow Mrs. Tilley. In my haste, I upset my chair. It bangs on the floor sounding like a gun shot. Along with half the men in the restaurant, Mr. Hatley's head rotates quickly toward my direction. Even though it has been 28 years since the war, old soldiers never return to the ease of being civilians.

When Mr. Hatley identifies the sound, he jumps up to upright my chair. I thank him and hurry quickly out the door. I see Mrs. Tilley reaching in her purse for a coin to give the boy who has just brought around her buggy.

I call out "wait!" She turns her head and I see the puzzled look on her face. I walk slowly, praying for some divine guidance.

"Yes," she says as I approach her.

"Are you Mrs. Tilley?" I ask.

She nods cautiously, "Is something wrong?"

I reach in my pocket and hold up my own handkerchief. "Did you drop this?" "No, it is not mine," she answers, and pauses briefly to see if I have anything else to say.

"Nice day isn't it?" I say politely, even though it is cold and damp.

"I suppose it is, compared to the last couple. Winter is not my cup of tea," she says, smiling sadly. I notice that she is a pretty woman in spite of the suppressed look on her face.

Very awkwardly, I make another attempt to engage her in conversation. "Spring is just around the corner."

"I hope so; we could use a little sunshine." With that statement, she cuts off the dialog and opens her buggy door. "Good day to you ma'am."

I am now forced to step out on a limb. "My name is Lizzie Sanders. Someone told me you were looking for a housekeeping job."

She has one foot on the runner and turns halfback my way, "Who on earth told you that?" she asked, looking edged.

I cannot recall his name," I say nervously. She does not answer, but looks over my head. Her distracted eyes cause me to turn around and I see Mr. Hatley coming our way in a fast trot.

"Mrs. Tilley, can I speak to you?" he asks. When she steps down off the runner, I turn quickly to leave them alone. As I walk away, I hear him say, "Can you be prepared to leave with me on the 8 o'clock train tomorrow?"

Agnes is smiling when I sit back down at the table across from her. "See, I told you so." Her tone was not that of arrogance, but more motherly. I have a feeling we are going to be very good friends.

We made an agreement to forget what we have seen today. If we report this to William, he will be legally obligated to tell the husband. Yet we felt obligated to see that Mrs. Tilley and her children have a chance for a better life. Tomorrow's news will only state that Mrs. Tilley and the children have vanished. By the grace of God, I hope she is never found.

On the ride home, Agnes invites me to accompany her to the opera house on Saturday night. She says she has been yearning to hear the well-known Negro pianist who will be appearing. I quickly accept dinner and the Saturday night show. It has been a long time since I have enjoyed such a pleasure.

When I walk in the front door, I hang my hat and glance over at the clock on the mantel. It is nearly 3 o'clock. The biggest part of my day is gone. I had planned to spend the day writing. At this rate, I will not be finished with my book by spring as I had planned.

There are still several hours of daylight and I have never been shy about burning the midnight oil. When I retreat to the office, I suddenly remember Mr. Collins' invitation is awaiting my answer.

With time, unanswered questions often seem to answer themselves. Mrs. Lee's invitation is perhaps an omen I should refuse Mr. Collins. I will compose a note and Jasper can deliver it this afternoon to Mr. Collin's office.

Dear Mr. Collins,

Your haste in returning the fishing rod was admirable, but it was not necessary. I knew you would return it in due time. I am flattered by your invitation to dine with you on Saturday night. Unfortunately, I will be chaperoning an elderly friend to the opera house on that same night. Perhaps another time.

Best wishes,
Theodosia E. Simpson

I give special thought to the last words. Should I say, perhaps another time? It may sound bold, as if I am asking for another invitation. Yet to just refuse closed-ended would be rude. I decide the note is fine, slip it in an envelope and address it to Mr. Colin Collins.

My search for Jasper ends at the barn. He heard me drive up and is in the process of stabling the horse for the night. Rebel is following along behind Jasper; a dog likes man's work. I hand Jasper the letter, he nods his head and I head back inside.

The wind is getting up, feeling like a knife cutting through my clothes. The only good place to be on a night like this is by the fire. It will be a good night to write. Yes indeed!

1879-1880

The winter of 1879 was a mild one. Spring brought on the promise of a prosperous crop of wheat, cotton and corn. It was almost as if the dark cloud that had hovered over the South for so long was slowly being lifted.

The old hotel began the year under new proprietorship in 1880. Mr. Ritch, the new owner, expanded the dining room, refurbished the room and opened the halls for dances. Having a first-class hotel in Concord attracted travelers with cash in their pockets. The town was growing with new houses and businesses.

It was that year I first realized I was part of the fading past. There was a new generation emerging, whose youth afforded them little memory of the war years. They were tired of the old depressed ways and had high hopes. My Victoria was one of them. She, too, was braced to take on a new modern world. There are always those that reject new ideas, but by the end of the year, nearly every home enjoyed milk in glass bottles, Ivory soap and Scott's toilet tissue and paper towels. Some even replaced sugar with a new noncaloric compound called "saccharine."

Victoria was a bright-eyed, intelligent young lady at 16 and the first of my children to graduate from school. Her angelic appearance attracted a host of suitors. However, her independent nature scared away all but the bravest and the most desperate.

Sister Tessie was developing well for her age and was quickly becoming a rival to Victoria in beauty. However, because of her pleasant and too-agreeable disposition, she was far more approachable than Victoria.

Such was the case of Victoria's graduation class dance. John Whitley first asked Victoria to the dance. When she refused him, he then asked Tessie. For Victoria, it was a lesson well learned. *There are only three ways to answer a request—*

to grant, refuse or promise. To do any in haste may bring later regrets.

The first week of June 1880 will always be one for my memory. It all began a few days before Victoria's graduation. Joel did some odd jobs for Mrs. Davis to pay for Victoria's dress. When Mrs. Davis paid him with four silver dollars, Joel went straight downtown to pick up the dress Victoria had placed on hold. Victoria had resolved to being escorted by her younger brother, Robert. Perhaps Joel felt sorry for her, so he surprised her with a matching hat and gloves.

On the afternoon of June 6, the whole family rode into town to attend the commencement exercise. We were all proud of Victoria and it was a grand affair. The Concord Band furnished the music under the leadership of Professor Frankenfield.

When John Whitley came to collect Tessie to go to the dance, Joel insisted that Victoria and Robert ride along with them. It was an honest mistake. Joel had no idea of the trouble that had brewed between the two girls. As the four of them rode off in the buggy, Joel said, "Now that is a pretty picture."

I replied, "Darling, you are only looking at the frame." I was just about to explain my remark when the sheriff walked up.

"Mr. Simpson, I need to speak to you," he announces and pulls Joel aside.

When Joel walks over to me he is smiling, but I knew that smile. Something was wrong. He tells me the silver dollars Mrs. Davis paid him with were apparently counterfeit. He would have to go with the sheriff to clear up the misunderstanding.

I wanted to ask more questions. However, when the sheriff started to walk toward us, Joel helped me in the buggy and assured me he would be home shortly.

I had been home less than an hour when the front door burst open and I heard Robert calling for me. I quickly jump from my seat and see him ushering in a crying Tessie. Her face was flushed and her eyes and lips were swollen. Seconds later, I discovered her distress.

Poor Tessie was too shy to speak up that she was being attacked. All the way to the dance, her sweet perfume had caused her to be the victim of tiny stinging bees. She thought she could endure the evening, until she began to suffer a poison reaction to the stings. Robert borrowed John's buggy to bring Tessie home and left Victoria with him to enjoy the dance.

I spent the next two hours taking care of Tessie. First, I made a compress of tobacco and placed it on the stings, and then I gave her catnip tea to counteract the reaction. I continued with cold compresses to her eyes and lips until finally I closed the door, leaving when she fell asleep.

In the meantime, Robert returned the borrowed carriage and John brought Victoria and Robert home. When they came in the door they were singing, "Oh Dem Golden Slippers." I had to quiet them to prevent them from waking Tessie.

They were in the middle of telling me about their exciting evening when they suddenly realized their father was missing. I told them what I knew. Then I spent the next half hour arguing with Robert why he should not strike out at that time of night to look for his father. Robert and my own fears were just about to wear me down when there was a knock at the door.

I sent Robert to the door, but when I heard him talking to the sheriff, I followed. It was then we learned Joel had been arrested for passing counterfeit money. The sheriff said he believed Joel, but his story could not be verified because Mrs. Davis was away visiting her sister. Since Waddell's store had pressed charges, he was obligated to hold Joel until the issue could be resolved. Therefore, Joel spent the night in jail.

The next morning I went to visit him and take him some food. I walked right into the jailhouse. To my surprise, there were Joel and the sheriff sitting in the jail cell playing cards.

Joel saw me first and said jokingly to the sheriff, "Roy, lock the door quick! There are criminals out there!"

The sheriff jumped up quickly, turned the barrel over with his big belly and the cards flew across the room. "Just a matter of legal ins and outs and we will have this cleared up, Mrs. Simpson. Sorry for any embarrassment this might have caused you and your family, but I am just doing my job."

"Oh, I understand," I said, as I eyed over the cell. I saw a small jug and a couple of tin cups on the floor. I turned to Joel, "Oh darling, spending the night here must have been awful, with nothing but the 'moonshine' to light your cell."

Joel knows what I meant by moonshine, I had seen the jug. I was angry. I had lain awake all night, recalling the stories he told about the prison camps during the war. I imagined Joel lying on the filthy cold floor with rats running across his back. Little did I know he was having a holiday.

I did not wait for them to say a word, but plopped the food down on the table and marched out. As I was leaving, a reporter from the Concord Standard approached me. "Ma'am, can I get your name please?" he asks.

I was still miffed and I replied quickly, "No!" He followed along behind me as I walked briskly back to my buggy. "Do you know anything about this ring of counterfeiters?" he asks.

There was not a lot of news to report in town and the reporters were often accused of peeking in people's windows to get a story. "No!" I said, turning around quickly to face him. He jumped back as if he was afraid I would strike him, but continued to follow along behind me.

He offered to help me up in my buggy, but I refused. "Ma'am, I hear tell that the sheriff has locked up a whole gang of outlaws. Can you verify that story for me?"

I looked down from my seat at the man in the ill-fitting plaid suit. He was a young man with a head of red hair and a freckly face. He may have been just eager to do his job, but it was time someone taught him a lesson about people's privacy. I leaned out of the buggy and whispered,

'Jesse James.' I then motioned my horse toward home and the man took off running in the direction of the newspaper office.

Joel was still in jail on Sunday morning and we did not go to church. I would rather people wonder where we were, than ask questions where Joel was. Around 4 o'clock the sheriff came riding up with Joel.

Mrs. Davis returned and confirmed that she did in fact pay Joel with the silver dollars. Waddell's store agreed to drop the charges, but insisted Joel put something up for collateral. Joel was without a pocket watch for six months, until he paid off the debt. Now you see why I am not fond of shopping at Waddell's.

The sheriff could hardly arrest Mrs. Davis, but there was still the job of tracking down how the silver dollars got in circulation. Mrs. Davis said she had gotten them in change at Mr. Wilson's produce stand. The search came to a dead end, when Mr. Wilson said he got the coins from a stranger passing through here on his way to Raleigh.

....

I look back over my work for a moment and then pull the page out of the typewriter. I number the page and carefully place it my folder. It is 11 o'clock. All is quiet upstairs, and Rebel is asleep on the couch.

Thinking back over the events of June 6, 1880, I can laugh now, but it was not a joke that day. I look over the room in which I sit. All around me are bits and pieces of my family stored here. It is like a museum of artifacts, fingerprints, handwritten notes and worn out furniture. The rest have escaped this place. I am now the keeper of the past, alone, listening to the walls and the wind.

Chapter 13

A Rose Newly Bloomed

Wednesday morning when I let Rebel out to explore, I discover that Mr. Lee has dropped off an envelope for me. I am delighted on two accounts: one, I could use the distraction and second, I am hoping to have the money to visit Victoria this spring. The thought had even crossed my mind to start up piano lessons again, if Mr. Lee did not have work for me soon.

After breakfast, I inform Dovie I will be working in my office all day. I look up at her and for the first time I see she is showing. "Best go and see Dr. Baker soon," I tell her.

She is reluctant until I tell her I will pay for the visit. She then says she will have Jasper make an appointment. As I walk out of the kitchen, she says she will bring lunch in for me around noon.

"Thank you," I respond. Thinking in my head, "This baby is going to cost me my trip to Charleston and who knows what else."

It is a warm sunny day, not at all like mid-February, but more in keeping with the last of March. I start up a fire to rid the room of the damp smell and open the blinds so the sun can shine into the room. Even though it is just 9 o'clock in the morning, I could crawl up in the old chair and take a nap. It might be a nice way to soak up a sun-filled morning, but old ladies take naps. I am not ready to be old or take up that habit.

Brushing off the idea, I sit down at the desk and open the envelope. I see there are two handwritten letters. The first is Mr. Lee's.

Good morning Lizzie,

I would like to thank you for assisting my mother with the Tilley case. It is unfortunate we were not able to help Mr. Tilley. The poor man was heartbroken when he came home finding his wife and children were gone.

Please make three copies of my enclosed final report and Mrs. Boyd's letter. This is a sad case, but interesting. When Mr. Boyd retained me, I would have bet a nickel he was guilty. I guess the old saying applies here: "Evil doings and spiteful words are like boomerangs— they will always come back to hit you in the head.

Thank you,
William

I stop for a moment with the letter still in my hand. Mr. Lee and his mother both insist on being on a first-name basis with me. Still, I do not think I fall in the same class as they, at least not these days. Nevertheless, it would be rude not to ease my own formalities. William is a smart man.

I prepare my desk, insert the carbon paper between the pages and slip the paper under the roller. It has been several months since I made duplications and it takes several tries. At last, I have it perfectly aligned to begin typing:

*I, William T. Lee, Attorney at Law of the State of
North Carolina, present to the grand jury of Cabarrus
County my plea that my client, Mr. Moses K. Boyd, be
pardoned of all previous charges against him.
Furthermore, I hereby am demanding that the above
stated be released from incarceration immediately;
based on my findings.*

Respectfully,
Mr. William T. Lee

I remove the sheets, reload the typewriter and take out
the next letter. The handwriting is so poor that I must read
over it several times before I can transcribe it.

February 8, 1893

*Since 1890, I, Silda Boyd, have been employed as post-
mistress by the county of Stanly. I am no longer fit for
work, as I have been recently diagnosed with a leaky
heart, which shall prove fatal within days of this letter.*

*That being said, I am making full confession of my
wrongful and sinful deeds. Having involved myself in
a shameful affair, I planned to abandon my husband,
with a man I know now was nothing more than an
instrument of the devil.*

*With this man's encouragement, I stole a sum of
money from the post office, giving part to him and
placing the balance in my unsuspecting husband's
shirt pocket.*

*I then sent for the sheriff and reported the money
stolen. When asked who had been in the post office on
that day, I told them only my husband. The money I
planted was discovered and my husband was arrested.*

*If all had gone as planned, my lover and I would have
vanished. However, days after the crime, I became ill*

and the diagnosis is as I have said. My evil lover left as
soon as I told him the news and has since not been seen.

I am pleading from my deathbed that my faithful and
true husband be released from any wrongdoings. I am
the one and only guilty party and for that I must now
answer to the Lord.

Yours Truly,
Silda Boyd

When I finish the letter, I walk over to the window and look out across the street. Poor Silda, was she so wrong or was she just so weak? She had a hole in her heart and the devil found his way in. So many souls are misled in the fever of passion.

I am reminded of the time when Dovie comes in with my lunch. She tells me Jasper has arranged to take her to see Dr. Baker this afternoon and afterwards they will visit with her mother. I tell her to have the doctor send me the bill and she backs out of the room quietly.

I study over the plate of fried potatoes, a piece of chicken and a biscuit. I will be happy to see spring. I am in need of some fresh vegetables and fruit.

I eat half of the potatoes, part of the chicken and give the rest to Rebel. After wiping my hands, I stand up and stretch. A quiet house is a good place to write another chapter in my book.

1881- 1882

First, I must apologize for the length of this chapter. In the years of my children coming of age, there is much for a mother to remember.

I will begin with the great state of political affairs in 1881. In spite of Ulysses Grant's costly trip around the world to improve his popularity, he did not make a comeback.

The Republican Party nominated James A. Garfield. They were victorious in campaigning Garfield as a man of humble beginnings and Major General in the Union Army. On March 4, 1881, he became the 20th president of the United States.

However, at 9:30 on the morning of July 2, 1881, President Garfield was shot at the Sixth Street Train Station in Washington. By his side ironically was the Secretary of War, Richard Todd Lincoln. Not only was Richard the son of the first president of the United States to be assassinated, he had now witness the second. Garfield, unlike Abraham Lincoln, survived for 80 torturous days before he died of complications two weeks before his 50th birthday on September 19, 1891. Vice President Chester A. Arthur stepped up as President.

Some folks claim there is only a fine line between politicians and criminals. Therefore, I could not write this chapter without giving mention of two others that were assassinated: Billy the Kid on July 14, 1881, and Jesse James on April 3, 1882.

I suppose it was fitting with the state of affairs that the weather should follow suit. 1881 was the worst year to my memory for threats of high storms and tornadoes.

In Stanly County, the wind blew over a house,

forcing the family to crawl out the chimney to save their lives.

The mill in Concord was expanding under the new ownership of Captain John Odell. For the first time workers could buy stock in the company and Joel took advantage of the opportunity.

Alexander Graham Bell and Thomas A. Edison were names in the news. It was the new age of technology: electric lights, indoor plumbing and telephones.

Joel said what a man did in his own back yard was no business of the government. In addition, if a man was peculiar, that was his business too. Just like old Colonel Earnhardt. Even in the dead of the winter he never wore a coat. He said he had been robbed of his coat once and he was not going to give the next fellow the chance.

The Colonel was known for making the best whiskey around. He told Joel in order to grow good whiskey-making corn, you have to fertilize the fields with dead snakes. The whiskey will have a good bite to it, but go down smooth.

One day the revenue agents came and busted up the Colonel's still. In less than a week, they found him stone dead lying across his bed. Joel said the old man just gave up on living.

That fall of 1881, there were many strange things happening around town. People were afraid to bury their dead for fear of body snatchers. Some 40-odd graves had been dug up and the bodies were missing.

It had started a panic all over town. Some thought it was the beginning of the end, while others said the dead had risen to revenge any wrongdoings against them. Even though most people believed it to be nonsense, it certainly had reduced the traffic on the streets at night.

It was a serious crime, but since the robberies were occurring around Halloween, people found it reason to poke fun. Robert had teased Tessie so that she was afraid of shadows the moonbeams cast at night. She insisted that the windows always be closed and the curtains pulled.

For over a month, bodies were subject to be missing all over town. It was not until late November the case was solved. The sheriff set up groups of men to stake out at all the cemeteries. At last, they caught two men digging up a fresh grave in the colored cemetery. The men were Germans. They could barely speak English, but when the sheriff held up a noose, they quickly spilled the beans. Mr. Hughes, the cabinet and coffin maker, had hired the men to exhume the bodies, rob them of the valuables and lastly sold the bodies to a medical institution. It was a gruesome ordeal and we were all glad when it ended.

The summer with all three children out of school had been busy. I suppose I cannot describe Victoria as a child any longer. She had first said she wanted to go to a Union School of Stenography and Typewriting. It was expensive and Joel was not the least bit fond of her going to New York. She had applied for funding, but nothing had come through. That fall, Robert and Tessie went back to school leaving Victoria alone at home.

I tried to offer her some options, but nothing seemed to appeal. Joel said my energy would be better spent encouraging her to find a good husband.

It was with great excitement the day I opened the letter from Dr. Fannie announcing she was coming to visit. She would be staying for the whole month of December and through the holidays.

I felt like a child as I decorated the house and prepared for my long-awaited visit with my dearest friend. Joel even bought a string of the new electric Christmas lights for the doorway. I wanted everything to be perfect by the time she arrived.

The children were excited too. They had heard so much about Fannie and now they could put a face with the stories. The day she was to arrive the children did not understand why they could not go with me to the train station.

Joel explained to them that the moment belonged only to Dr. Fannie and their mother. I appreciated his consideration, but Joel also knew I needed to speak to Fannie alone. I had a problem. It was Victoria. She had no idea that Joel was not her real father. When she hears the truth, I want it to come from me.

I recall worrying over what to wear and fretting over my hair until I was nearly late leaving for the station. Joel kept reassuring me that I looked fine, but it had been 17 years since we had last seen each other. It was hard to explain, but I wanted her to see me as I once was. Seeing a wrinkle in my brow or showing up in downgraded attire would hurt Fannie. She had always admired me.

Joel kissed me goodbye and I left for the station. I arrived just in time to see her step off the train. The moment I saw her I burst out in joyous laughter. She was wearing that same funny little hat!

With tears in my eyes, I begin to shout out over the crowd, "Fannie, over here! Over here!"

"Theodosia!" she screamed, coming full force my way nearly knocking people over in her path.

For some unknown time, we stood embracing each other in the middle of the train station. If God had called me home right that very moment, I would not have felt cheated.

Fannie paid the attendant to collect her luggage and load it in the buggy. People were staring at us as we walked arm in arm across the street to the cafe. I could care less, for my world had stopped. I was with my best friend once again.

We took a seat by the window. It was as if all the years suddenly were washed away. I watched across the table as the sunlight danced across her ebony skin. She was still the same: her voice, her mannerism and that laugh. The effects of time had not left her unscathed. I detected a few gray hairs and wrinkles, but they only added wisdom and dignity. When she lifted her teacup to her lips, I was reminded of the first time I saw her in New York City. She still amazes me.

We talked for hours, pondering over the lost years. We laughed and we cried. At last Fannie mentioned Edmond Cook. When she spoke his name, his memory suddenly appeared like a dark cloud hanging over the horizon.

It was then that I opened up the issue that Victoria did not know Edmond was her real father. Fannie sat back in her chair and stared out the window for some time. The waiter brought our food and she pushed the peas around on her plate.

"Lizzie, did you raise this girl to understand the grace of God?" she asked.

"Of course," I answered.

"She is still young and sheltered by your wing. Wait until she has experienced the trials of life for herself. With a little wisdom and grace, she will be understanding of the circumstances of her birth. Your secret is safe with me, my friend," she said, as she reached out across the table and squeezed my hand.

Nothing more needed to be said. I had my peace, Edmond's memory would remain buried in the sandy soil of Charleston, until I decided to resurrect it.

When we finally arrived home, Joel and the children were waiting. Cindy Lou and her family had come to be part of the reunion, too. There was food and rejoicing.

Fannie gave each of my girls a rose-colored conch pearl necklace and Robert was awarded a telescope. They were quite possibly the grandest gifts my children had ever received. Fannie may have been a stranger, but they accepted her as family the moment they met.

Fannie loved all my children, but she was fondest of Victoria. When she saw Victoria for the first time, she reached down and cradled her fair face in her dark hands. "You are the breath of your mother," she said, as the tears streamed down her face. "Such beauty is born again in you."

Victoria was embarrassed at Fannie's flattery and blushed. Fannie looked at her and recited a line from a poem: *"Accepting a compliment with grace is a sign of refinement. Accepting criticism with consideration is a sign of wisdom."*

Robert and Tessie did not understand Fannie's affection for Victoria, but Joel and I knew. She was recalling the innocent little baby she had rocked in her arms before the war swept her away.

Joel was kind enough to keep himself and Robert occupied while Fannie, the girls and I toured the town. We visited Sallie and her family in Stanly County. I can still laugh remembering the occasion Fannie met the mayor.

The mayor, campaigning for re-election, was roving over the cafe making grand introductions. When he came to our table, I presented to him Dr. Frances Holloway from Charleston, educated in London and well-known activist for the women's suffrage movement.

"Is that right?" he said, pulling up a chair backwards and straddling it to face us. "Do tell me more about your work, Dr. Holloway."

I was afraid he was mocking her, but I remained silent, feeling sure Fannie could hold her own.

"Mayor, instead of me telling you about the issues of women's rights, perhaps you could arrange a lecture for me to speak to the fair women of your city. I am sure they would find my speech enlightening."

"Oh really," he says, raising his eyebrows and rocking his chair back. "I don't think the females in these parts are a bit interested in that sort of thing."

"Females!" Fannie said, standing up so she can tower over the mayor. "I beg your pardon not to describe women with the same term as one uses to describe an animal!"

By this time the whole cafe is silently looking over at Fannie and the mayor.

He looked around the room and laughed. Because of his fat belly and short legs, he nearly tumbled over when he tried to get out of the chair. Fannie reached down and steadied the chair so he could free himself.

"Are you married, Miss-Dr. Holloway?" he asked.

"No, I am not," she answered.

"I did not think so," he said, as he straightened up his waistcoat.

"And what do you mean by that?" asked Fannie.

"A wife knows she is the weaker sex and her husband is the stronger. She gets what she needs and there is not a one in 100 that has to do a lick of work to earn it. There ain't a woman in this town that's got the nerve to upset that apple cart," he said, and backed up and crossed his arms across his belly.

"N-E-R-V-E!" Fannie said, with bullets coming out of her eyes. "Let me tell you something, sir. As a doctor I can tell you that a woman is by far the stronger and braver of the sexes; might I just mention childbirth to you, sir."

Fannie is prepared to continue, but the mayor shouts out, "Look behind you! That is the biggest rat I have ever seen!"

Fannie screams and jumps in her chair. Within seconds the mayor is doubled over laughing; there is no rat. A few people laugh, but I notice some stern faces among the onlookers.

Fannie sits back down and attempts to resume eating, but her hands are shaking. We had just finished our meal when a well-dressed woman approached us. "Dr. Holloway," she said, and extended her hand. "I am Eve Coltrane, president of The Woman's Club of Concord. On behalf of myself and the ladies of my club, I would like to apologize for our mayor." She pointed toward a large table of women. They were all smiling our way. She lowered her voice to a whisper, "Sometimes he can be a real horse's ass."

Fannie rolled her head back and laughed. "Indeed!" she said.

Before we left, Fannie and Mrs. Coltrane scheduled an engagement for Fannie to address the club on the marvels of modern medicine and women suffrage.

From the beginning, Fannie and Victoria got along splendidly. Victoria was scholarly and a no nonsense-type girl. She enjoyed greatly debating with Fannie, but on most subjects they agreed.

When the day arrived for Fannie to speak at the women's club, I did not allow Tessie to come along. I did, however, feel Victoria was mature enough to hear whatever Fannie chose to present.

Fannie began her lecture on women's health. The topics were most informative and I must say provided a sound argument for why women must demand equal rights.

She began by discussing the number of women who suffered from narcotic addictions. She faulted the heavy-handed doctors who so quickly wrote prescriptions to their unknowing victims. She stated that doctors dismissed women's real ailments, brushing them off as mere nervousness or hysteria. Thus treating them with mood-altering drugs, such as opium, laudanum and morphine. Even though their symptoms may have been relieved, blazing eyes, pale and pallor complexion are not signs of health.

Her talk included natural remedies for common colds, sore backs and wormy children. She spoke up against the so-called 'poison' medicines containing arsenic, mercury, snake venom, turpentine and coal oils. They offered no cure and ingesting them was the same as putting one foot in the grave.

Victoria held on to every word, but some of the women began to twist in their seats when Fannie spoke on birth control and sexual-transmitted diseases. "Ladies, there is only one way to contact gonorrhea or syphilis," she said frankly.

"From your husband or lovers during sexual intercourse. I warn you, many doctors conspire with husbands to keep the nature of your complaints a secret. They may give you false information or tell you it is a simple case of the whites, honeymoon cystitis or even lack of female hygiene. If you have symptoms, it is wise to schedule a private consultation with a doctor unknown to your husband."

She closed to a group of women cheering and clapping on why women should have the right to vote and run for office. I have a feeling Fannie's visit ruffled a few feathers in the community.

On Christmas Eve, we had a grand celebration planned with family, friends and neighbors. Les Lester was our honored guest. He had successfully completed his schooling and soon would begin an internship with Dr. Jones in Davidson.

The fire was glowing and there was food on the table. The front door was ajar and people were coming and going all night. We had all gathered around the piano to sing Christmas carols when a beautiful apparition appeared in the middle of the room. Some of the guests gasped and others began to cry. The only reasonable explanation was the figure standing before us was an angel.

Her long blond hair hung loosely to her waist, her feet were bare and her only protection from the night air was a long white dressing gown.

Her blue eyes seemed to be in a fixed position. We all held our breath waiting for her to deliver us a message. At last, I made an attempt to communicate with our heavenly guest. "You are welcome in our home. Please tell us why you have come tonight." To this she did not answer and continued to stare straight ahead.

Fannie moved closer to the angel. She waved her hand across the girl's eyes and took hold of her limp wrist. Fannie then looked at us and smiled. "Here I am a doctor and I have been as foolish as the best of you. This poor child is from another world all right. It is dreamland. She is sleep walking. Les, will you help me get her to a bed?"

Les carried her into my room and we covered her with warm blankets. Who she was or where she came from, we had no idea. Long after the others had left, Les sat by her side stroking her hand and gazing into her sweet face.

When she awoke, it was Les she saw first. At first, she was alarmed, but in a soft tender voice he calmed her fears. The girl regained her senses and asked that we send for her grandfather.

Joel knew the address and in a short time he returned with the grandfather. He went at once to her bedside, cradled her up in his arms and with tears in his eyes said, "Oh my sweet Jeanette, I love you so."

Les looked down at the girl and repeated the words, "Oh my sweet Jeanette, I love you so."

By the look on Les' face, we knew he had spoken the truth. Les and Jeanette are proof of love at first sight. They were married two weeks later in the front room of our home. Today, Les has a successful medical practice in Davidson. He has three beautiful little girls and an angel for a wife, who sometimes is known to wander in her sleep.

We rang in the new year of 1882. The clock was ticking and soon it would be time for Fannie to leave. Before she returned to Charleston she was first heading to Washington for meetings and lectures. Joel, Robert and Tessie might have been ready for our household to return to normal, but not Victoria and me.

Fannie had become a part of my heart again. The week before she was to leave, I could hardly control my crying. I was afraid Victoria would miss her even more than me. Fannie had opened the door to the world to her. Victoria wanted more than to be a wife and raise a family. She wanted to see things, go places and discover the world. So, when Fannie approached me I was open to her offer.

She wanted to take Victoria with her to Washington. The trip would only be for a few months. She promised to have Victoria back in time for school. Joel did not readily consent. After he spoke of all the reasons she should not go, he looked up and winked at Fannie. "That girl of ours is just as pigheaded as the rest of you liberal-minded women. Take her with you. I am tired of seeing her sit around here twiddling her thumbs."

There were cheers, tears and packing to do. Two days later, I watched my oldest and my best friend board the train to Washington.

The first week or two were the hardest, but I knew the trip would be good for Victoria and she would be home soon.

It was August 2 when they were due home. It was hot as blue blazes and this time the entire family went to the station. First Fannie stepped off the train and we waved wildly. My heart stopped, for I did not see my Victoria.

Fannie picked up her bag and spoke to the passenger behind her. "Look, that woman is Victoria!" Robert shouted. He was right. There she was in all the glory of a rose newly bloomed. She was dressed in the highest fashion of the day. Her braids were gone and her hair was coiffured high upon her head.

They approach with Fannie grinning and Victoria gliding as if she is on skates. "Well?" Fannie asked, pointing at Victoria.

Before I can say a word, Victoria comes running up and gives me a big hug.

"She may look like a princess, but she is still my girl, Victoria," I said, as I push her away to take a good look at her.

Tessie stomped her foot and ran back to the buggy crying. At that moment, I feared it was going to be a hellish homecoming. As always Fannie was wise; she had the foresight to acquire a wardrobe for Tessie, too. Again, another thing added to the list of things I owed to her kindness.

It was to be a short and final visit for Fannie. I would be left with a grown-up Victoria, who may or may not adjust back to our domestic life. My hope was once she was enrolled in school she would settle back down.

The week Fannie was to go home, Victoria received a letter from the school. She eagerly opened it, thinking it to be an orientation letter. When I saw her eyes tear up, I knew she had been rejected. I tried to tell her there were plenty of other schools, but nothing seemed to calm her.

At supper, Fannie was in a serious mood and Victoria barely spoke. The evening brought a soft summer shower and we sat out on the porch to enjoy the breeze.

Fannie waited until the children had gone to bed before she made her announcement. "The girl is too intelligent to rot here in this house. I want to take her back to Charleston with me."

"To Charleston!" I said, alarmed, looking over at Joel for his reaction.

"Now Lizzie," Fannie said. "Don't be thinking just of yourself. You know the schools in Charleston are some of the finest in the country. I have worked hard and I have no children of my own. I can certainly afford to see Victoria gets a proper education."

I stood up, walked to the edge of the porch and turned my back on Fannie.

"She is 18," Joel said. "Think of where you were at 18."

I turned back and smiled at him, wondering if he remembered the night we first met at my debut party. "Yes, she is 18," I said softly.

"She has had a taste of freedom," Fannie said. "And like they say, once the baby bird is ready to leave the nest, it must learn to fly."

"Fannie, my answer is yes," I said and Joel nodded.

She assured us we would not be sorry and extended the offer to Tessie when her time came. As for Tessie, it would not be right for her, but I was confident it was for Victoria.

Two days later, we said farewell to Fannie and Victoria. At first, I felt like there was a hole in my heart. Like all mothers, I loved my children equally, but Victoria was once my only reason for living. She brought me comfort in a world where comfort could not be found, she was my earth and my sky. God in his perfect timing sent her to me, and now I must be brave to let her find her own way in the world.

Time has a way of filling in the spaces. Soon, I had her letters and cards to look forward to and a trip to Charleston come spring.

Chapter 14

A House That Just Keeps on Giving

Saturday, February 18, 1893

It had been a busy week, but I had not forgotten about my date with Agnes Lee. In fact it had been on my mind all week. For the first part of the week, I fretted over what to wear.

Then I decided to be resourceful. I eyed some of my latest magazines and went to work at remodeling one of my older frocks. My brown velvet suit showed little wear. Now with its slimmer skirt, lace collar and cuffs, it looked as modern as the ones in the fashion plates.

It was easy to rework my accessories, but my old boots would have to do. Once we were seated, no one would take notice of my feet anyway.

At 6 o'clock, I am dressed and waiting for Agnes's carriage. Right on time, I hear it drive up. I grab my cape and open the door expecting to see a servant, but I am most surprised to see it is William Lee. He has come to escort us to dinner and the opera house. I judge it awkward at first. However, once we are at the restaurant, I relax and find that I am enjoying the company of Agnes and her handsome son William.

Not since Victoria's last visit had I engaged in such intriguing conversation. We discuss the fear of another national depression. I had read the predictions in the newspaper, but it is informative to hear William's take on the subject. He says a crash is near certain, unless President Grover Cleveland makes it his first priority the moment he steps back in the White House. The causes and effects, in his opinion, are due to a too eager society trying to rebuild after the war. Banks were far too enthusiastic to hand out mortgages. There were too many new businesses at once, resulting in an overproduction of commodities flooding the market. This, combined with the gold and silver issue, is a sure disaster.

Before we move on to talk about lighter subjects, William speaks of the inappropriate use of US Marines to overthrow the peaceful kingdom of Hawaii.

"Nothing but greed," Agnes says. She slams her fist down on the table and looks at us both. "If you ask me, this country will collapse because of greed." It was a good point, but not a great revelation.

We arrive early at the opera house and the usher directs us to our seats. I find myself seated between William and his mother. I determine he is quite popular judging by the number of people who stop to speak to him.

Even though Agnes and I are engaged in conversation, I glance up occasionally and smile at the people passing by. However, when I hear a woman's shrill voice, my ears are redirected. "William, I am so delighted to see you out and about. I heard from my father that you were ill. Now I see you here before me, fit as a fiddle," she says giggling.

I cannot help but turn my head to put a face with the voice. She is a tall, blondish woman, perhaps some younger than myself. Her pink satin dress is hanging off her shoulders. I deem it inappropriate, but she and the dress look expensive. Our eyes meet briefly and she smiles, but not necessarily at me. I am certain I would not like her and turn my head.

The pink-dressed woman bends down so her lips are nearly touching William's ear. "Glad you were able to find someone to help out with your mother. Good help is hard to find these days," she says, knowing I can hear her.

"Yes, it sure is," William replies.

I did not turn my head again, but I could feel her looking at me. After a second, I hear her satin dress ruffling off. I am appalled she thinks I am the nurse and that William did not set her straight. Then the sickening thought occurs to me: maybe the reason I was invited in the first place was to help take care of mother.

William excuses himself saying he will return shortly. Agnes continues talking to me, but it is hard to concentrate on our once-enjoyable chat. I am lost in a fog of emotions and embarrassment. I see William standing next to the woman in the pink dress and her group of socialites.

"Did you hear me dear?" she asks, shaking my arm gently

"Oh, sorry Agnes, I seem to have developed a sudden headache," I reply.

Just before the curtain goes up William returns, but this time he sits on the side of his mother. I was glad when the evening came to a close. When we arrive at my house, I graciously allow William to walk me to the door. Agnes insists that she call for me for lunch next week. I lie and tell her I am expecting guests.

"Sometime soon?" she calls out.

I do not answer, but make haste to the door. William takes the key out of my hand and unlocks the door. "It was a pleasure having you join us tonight, Lizzie," he says, as the door pops open.

"Thank you," I reply. "Good night, Mr. Lee."

I am halfway down the hall when I hear a soft knock at the door. It is William and I open the door. "You must think I am awful," he says.

I am prepared to receive an apology until he continues, "I forgot to leave your check in the drop box. I will bring it by first thing Monday morning, along with a few reports."

"That will be fine, just drop them in the box Mr. Lee," I say respectfully. He is no longer William to me. This is business and he is Mr. Lee.

I do not bother with a light, undress in the dark and slip in the bed. What a fool I was to think I had been invited for my entertainment. I am just a hired woman, Mr. Lee's secretary and now nursemaid to his mother.

I close my eyes and pray:

Dear Lord,

I, who once had everything, know all too well of the sin of pride. I am thankful for my humble surroundings and the lessons that I have learned. If it is your will for me to be Mrs. Lee's companion, nurse or friend, I will abide. Please help me to have compassion for those that nurse such fine taste. Amen.

I find myself tossing and turning most of the night. Sleep does not always come easy for a lonely woman with no one to hold.

Sometime in the wee hours of the morning, I must have fallen into a deep sleep.

I was dreaming I was on a steamship sailing across the ocean. I was stretched out on a sun couch basking in the sun and the view was glorious.

I awoke suddenly hearing a noise, which I soon detected as Dovie's voice.

"Miss Lizzie, is yous goin' to church? It is a nearing 10 o'clock ands I's ain't heard a peep outs of yous. Hello," she said, knocking a little louder.

The sun is streaming through the window across my face, but there is no ocean view and the room is cold. I debate if I want to leave the comfort of my warm bed to go to church. Then I recall something the preacher once said. The devil plants all sorts of ideas in your head to romance you away from the church. I sling my feet over the side of the bed and call out, "Just give me a bit and I'll be ready."

"I's heat ups da grits warm fer yous," she says. I sit there on the side of the bed and listen to her walk away. Her footsteps used to sound like a little squirrel on the roof, but she is walking heavier and slower these days. A belly full of baby flattens out the feet.

Rebel is lying at the foot of the bed and he raises his lazy head. I stroke his ears and say, "You are a good boy, Rebel. You don't have to go to church; heaven will be waiting for you."

On the hook behind the door hangs only my robe. I finally packed Joel's away. I slip it on and one of my slippers, but the other is missing. I look under the bed, under the chair and then around the room. When I look back at Rebel, I see he is lying on it. He must have taken it to bed with him last night. I roll him over to retrieve it and he growls at me. "I take that back Rebel, you might need some churching up," I say, giving him a shove off the bed.

He is at my heels when I walk through the kitchen and out on the back porch. I have to wait a moment for Dovie to come out of the bathroom. *"It is cold in dar,"* she says, when she comes out.

Jasper drives to church and Dovie sits up front with him. I have been going to the colored church with them since before Christmas. I like it. At my old church, the members could be pretentious. Speaking of pretentious, I think back over the events of last night. I think I feel sorry for Mr. Lee. He must be a very insecure man to have to put up such pretenses.

This Sunday is the same as most. After church, Dovie scratches up a bit for lunch and then she goes to her mothers. They always ask me to go along. I typically say no. Today I will go. It will be nice to see Cindy Lou. Dovie is finishing up in the kitchen and I hear the buggy pull up around front. I assume it is Jasper, but when I look out, I see it is Tessie and her family who have come to visit.

Odd I think, since I have not seen them since Christmas. As soon as I open the front door, her two children jump out of the buggy. Walter helps Tessie out of the carriage and at once, I see she is expecting again.

It was a pleasant visit, but a bit too long. Tessie's husband Walter is 20 years her senior. He was a widower with grown children when they married. Walter is painful religious and I find him just as boring. I suppose Tessie does not; two children and a baby on the way is proof in the pudding.

I thought after supper I would work on my writing, but I was drained. I wondered if it was the visit, the late night before or just old age. I went to bed early.

Early Monday morning I see Mr. Lee's carriage drive up. He knocks at the door and Dovie starts to answer. "No," I caution her and place my finger over my lips. I hold on to her arm and we stand frozen in the hall listening to him knock several more times. When no one answers, I hear him open the drop box.

When he is out of sight, I collect the contents. Mr. Lee's instructions inform me to make three copies of an uninteresting will. My check is attached to the note. There is no personal message, nor does he even bother to sign the note.

"This is all just fine by me," I say aloud. His money spends well and I was not looking for anything else from him in the first place. Well, nothing more than the use of his typewriter. If he should decide to dismiss me, I will bring down my old typewriter from the attic and finish my book. I let my thoughts run to Victoria. That girl would not take any such business off any man, and I will not either!

I have nearly achieved expert status at this typing. In little over an hour, I had completed the reports, sealed the enveloped and dropped them in the box on the porch.

With the task well done it gave me a new sense of self-worth. I took Rebel for a brisk walk. When I came back, I was refreshed and ready to work on my book. It is important work, even if it is only important to me.

1883-1884
Even though we did not have Victoria home for Christmas in 1883, it was a grand one. Joel surprised Tessie and me with train tickets to Charleston. As soon as the school year was over in June, Tessie and I would spend the summer with Victoria.

It was a delight to think of being in Charleston again. Not once had I stepped back on the soil of my birth since I came to North Carolina in 1867. I could not help wondering how much it may have changed. My only worry was leaving Robert and Joel.

In January, I received an unexpected letter,

January 1, 1884
Vila dos Americanos, Brazil

Dear Aunt Lizzie,

I am writing to you with sad news. My father, Thomas Wilson Huneycutt, departed this world on 28 November 1883. Please take comfort in knowing that after the doctor's diagnosis his death was not long in suffering.

The last week of my father's life, I spent sitting by his bedside, day and night. In those final golden hours, he told me about his life in North Carolina.

Imagine my surprise to find that in his youth, Papa had fathered another child with your sister, Annabelle. He had tears in his eyes when he told me she died during the delivery of the baby. I now know I have a sister in North Carolina.

I was then to learn my father did not come to Brazil alone. He came with his young bride Betty Jo. He laughed as he described her as a fiery redheaded, straight-shooting girl from the hills. He said his heart was broken when she died of yellow fever not long after they came to this country. He wanted me to tell you Betty Jo loved you and left this world as your best friend.

After a couple of years, he married my mother. She is Brazilian and I have her dark complexion but Papa's blue eyes. After *The War Between the States*, many of the Confederate soldiers came to Brazil. So, Papa being an American or a 'Confederado' was not unique.

I hope you will accept my apologies for the delay of my correspondence. Since my mother had died two years prior, I was left with the burden of mourning my father's death. Finding that I was the sole executor of the estate has been a trial for my 16 years of age.

At the risk of sounding boastful, I must tell you my father worked hard and died a wealthy man. I have been well provided for and I am educated well beyond my years. I speak Portuguese, Spanish and fluent English. Fortunately, I am by no means left destitute.

Papa longed to go back to North Carolina to see his family. He was remorseful for leaving and not staying in touch. Since I have no living family here, it was Papa's desire for me to come to America to be with my family in North Carolina.

I shall be leaving tomorrow. I ask that you pray for my safe travel and my heavy heart. If all goes well, you should expect me to arrive in Concord, North Carolina, on the noon train, January 30, 1884.

Your niece,
Angelina Marie Huneycutt

It was all sad news. I had often wondered what had happened to my friend Betty Jo. I suppose her death explains why I never heard from her once she reached Brazil. I cried thinking if only Thomas would have stayed in contact with us.

Still, Joel and I were confused why Angelina wrote to me. I am not her actual aunt. My sister Sallie is married to Ransom who was her father's brother. Sallie is her aunt by marriage.

Regardless of the reason for the mix-up, the girl was on her way and I was left to break the news to Ransom that his brother had died.

Then it was the matter of what to do with the girl when she arrived. Even though Sallie was two years older than I was, she still had two young children at home. Sallie said if the girl was willing to help with the children, they would take her in. They had an extra room since Ransom's mother had passed away.

Somehow based on Angelina's letter, I did not expect that to be a fit. It was decided she would stay with us in the city at first. When we got to know her, we could determine what to do with her.

Tessie and Robert read over the letter many times. They were excited about meeting their foreign cousin. I had to keep reminding them the girl was not really their true cousin.

Early Monday morning on January 30, Joel went to the station. The attendant informed him there had been a delay. She would not be arriving until Wednesday.

That night during supper, we heard a commotion outside. Joel jumped up and ran to the window, at which time he saw a carriage parked out in front of our house. Before he could get to the door, the two men had begun unloading trunks, bags and packages on our front porch.

I stood in the doorway as Joel questioned the men. They pointed to the carriage and just at that moment, a young woman stepped out. She was dressed in luxurious fabrics and under her arm was a small white dog with a ribbon around its neck.

Her long dark hair was blowing freely in the wind. She looked around to observe her environment, then reached in her velvet purse and paid the driver. When I heard her say, "Muchas gracias," I knew it was Angelina.

"Aunt Lizzie?" she asked, approaching as if she was a queen. When she reached out to take my hand, I saw she has her father's blue eyes.

"This is a welcomed surprise," I responded. "The station said that there had been a delay."

"I am a resourceful girl," she said, with a heavy Spanish accent. "Did I not say in my letter that I would be arriving on January 30?"

"Yes, but," I saw it was pointless and motioned for Robert and Joel to collect her bags.

"Aunt Lizzie, most things are possible if one is willing to pay."

I ushered her in the house out of the cold. She dropped her cloak on the chair and revealed her dress with a plunging neckline. Her striking features and figure did not go unnoticed by Robert.

I told Tessie to show her to Victoria's room and Robert gathered up her bags.

Joel whispered in my ear, "Now this is going to be interesting."

Interesting it was. Prior to her coming here, I tried to explain to Robert the girl was not his cousin. Now, I kept reminding Robert she was family and to stop following her around like a little puppy dog. Speaking of puppy dog, she held the dog constantly, even during the meals. I think the only time she sat him down on the floor was to pee on the carpet.

She and Tessie were like oil and water from the moment she arrived. Angelina was a small girl, but she was larger than life. Tessie said she treated her like a servant, and, in fact, I felt much the same. Just to make a trip to the post office was an ordeal. We had to wait for her to frizz her hair and dress as if she was going to the opera.

When we took her to the country to meet her relatives, she could not believe they lived in such poverty. Sallie and Ransom were not rich, but they lived as well as most. They had a comfortable home and Ransom earned a fair living. Sallie was insulted when Angelina offered to give Ransom money to help feed their children.

So disposing of the girl at Sallie's was not going to be possible. Another week passed with us catering to her and trying to entertain her. The worst of it was seeing Robert make such a fool of himself over this little Brazilian beauty. If she had turned her hand to help or even offered, it might have been tolerable for a week or two more. I suppose she felt her time was better spent primping and weeping over the heroines in her romance novels.

At last I had to ask her, "Angelina, what do you want to do with the rest of your life?"

She looked at me odd and said she did not know. I then explained that I thought this was not the kind of town for a sophisticated girl like her. A bigger city would be more to her liking. To this, she readily agreed. When I told her of Charleston, the French shops, the theater and the beautiful sandy shores, she was intrigued. However, when I spoke of the handsome and wealthy young men, she was eager to take the next train.

The next morning I sent a telegram to Victoria asking if she could make arrangements for Angelina to be enrolled in a nice boarding school.

I did not feel the least bit guilty. It was the best thing for her and certainly for my family. Two days later I received a reply from Victoria. She had it all arranged and would meet her at the train station.

The next day, Robert took Angelina and all of her luggage to the depot. "Adios," I say cheerfully, as I watched them pulling out of the drive. Robert was heartbroken. She promised to write, but as the old saying goes, "out of sight, out of mind." In a few weeks, Robert had forgotten her and he was looking forward to his school graduation.

Robert was not much of a student, but he was

good with his hands. He liked to build things and he was not shy of hard work. He was planning on working in the mill for the summer and save his money to open up his own cabinet shop.

I will enclose the next two letters as they tell the story perhaps better than I can myself.

May 1, 1884

Mother dearest,

I hope all is well in North Carolina. I wanted to let you know that I will be traveling with Dr. Fannie to Atlanta for a few weeks. Do not fret, for I will be back in plenty of time for your arrival on 9 June.

I must tell you that young Angelina is fitting in finely in Charleston. I have personally given her opportunities to mingle and make new friends. She has become quite popular. She is happy here, although school does not agree too well with her.

I have some exciting news to share with you. I have met a very promising young man. His name is Peter. He is most eager to meet you when you come to visit. Do not tell the rest, but if all goes well, you may be hearing wedding bells in Charleston soon!

Arrivederci for now,
Victoria

I shall never forget the day this next letter came. I was upstairs with Tessie, helping her sort through her things for our trip to Charleston. It was still two weeks off, but I wanted to make sure her summer frocks were still suitable.

Joel called up the stairs to let me know a letter had arrived from Victoria. I told him to lay it on the foot of the steps. I would be down shortly. An hour or so later, I went downstairs, picked up the letter and slipped it in my apron pocket. After supper, I went out on the front porch to read the letter.

May 20, 1884

My dear only mother,

There is no easy way to tell you the saddest news. I can hardly write for my heart is so heavy. Fannie and I went to Atlanta as planned. However, she took ill while we were away and we were forced to cut our trip short. When we got home, I begged her to let me send for the doctor, but she refused.

She had a cough for sometime, but I assumed it was from that silly pipe she smoked. The cough became constant, with spitting of blood. She was in great pain and by the end of the week, she was bedridden. I sent for the doctor in Summerville.

When he arrived, he told me that Fannie had come to see him about a month ago. She had already diagnosed herself. She knew she had cancer of the lung. He did not expect her to go down so quickly. He said there was nothing he could do, but give her something to make her comfortable.

Yesterday morning at 8:15, one of the finest souls that ever walked this earth departed this world peacefully. In her dying hours, she spoke of you, Mother. She told me to tell you she would see you on the other side.

If it was not enough for my heart to be broken by the death of our beloved Fannie, there is more. I know it is low in comparison, but on my return, not once had Peter come to call.

When Fannie died, I sent for him, but there was no word. Desperate to speak to my friend, I went on my own to his home. His sister invited me in and at first denied knowing of his whereabouts. However, when she learned why I had come, she showed me the card she had just received from Peter. It was dated May 15, from New Orleans. Peter and Angelina had run off together and were married the day before.

You can only imagine my shock and shame. Angelina has damned me to live a life without the only man I shall ever love.

Oh dear mother, please promise me you will come quickly. I cannot bear the days to come without you.

Your oldest and truest,
Victoria

I made arrangements to leave for Charleston the next day. Under the circumstances, I felt it best that I go alone. Tessie did not seem terribly disappointed. In fact, she may have been relieved. She was always uneasy about being away from home. Sadly, I would miss Robert's graduation day.

The trip was much easier than I had imagined. The transportation system had certainly improved since my last train trip. I was due into

Charleston the day of the funeral.

It was around 1 o'clock when I arrived. I had planned to go to the house first, but with the funeral at two, there was not time. I hired a taxi to take me directly to the church and to deliver my bags to East Bay Street.

If it had not been for the somberness of the day, I would have enjoyed the carriage ride. I had almost forgotten the enchantment of spring in Charleston. The trees were blooming and birds were singing.

When we turned on King Street, I began to recall how the Battery looked the day I left in '67. I tried to erase the memory of the burned-out buildings, streets filled with hungry people and the sounds of the distant bombs.

In 1884, the city was much as it was before the war. Most of the buildings had been restored, homes were not blackened by soot and people were walking along the streets merrily.

I closed my eyes to inhale the salty air. It may have been just imprinted in my senses, but I thought I detected a lingering stink of war.

When I arrived at the church, I reached in my bag and placed my black lace mantilla over my head and shoulders. The door was opened and I walked in alongside both whites and Negroes. Only the first few rows were full, but I did not see my Victoria. She saw me first. The perils of the last week had stolen the brightness of her youthful complexion and I nearly did not recognize her.

I squeezed in the pew next to her. As soon as I

was settled in my seat, Victoria took my hand and laid her head on my shoulder. When I turned my head, I saw a Negro man and woman sitting on my left. In a very clear and distinct voice the man simple said, "Lizzie, it so good to see you again." The woman nods.

I knew at once that it was Simon and Millie. Sitting there beside them, the years melted away. They were once my servants, or better placed in my mind as my dear friends. There was still a bond between us that not even the years of time could destroy.

It was not a fancy service or burial. Fitting I suppose, for my dear friend.

Fannie liked simplicity, but she was far from being simple herself. The depth of Fannie's love and understanding could never be measured, even six-feet under, she still towered over most.

It was an odd feeling stepping back inside the house for the first time. Much was still the same. The paintings of the original owners Fredrick and Anna Bullwinkle were still hanging in the hall. In the parlor I saw the old furnishings. The creaking boards on the steps and the sun shining in from the bay window made me feel like I was home again.

Victoria took me upstairs to the room she called the "blue willow" room. Yes, I knew the room well; it was once Mrs. Bullwinkle's room. Little did Victoria know that she was conceived and born in that very bed. A thousand memories flashed through my mind as she closed the door behind her. Her father, Edmond Cook, was dead, but he was still alive in my memory.

Quickly I freshened up. Victoria said she was expecting people to drop by. Oh, how well I knew the Charleston style; there would be visitors stopping by all day dropping off cards and food.

I walked over to the window and looked out over the city. I came to this house as a young girl, only to be it's caretaker while Dr. Clarence Bullwinkle was away at war. I knew the doctor was fond of me, but the depth of his affection would not be revealed until after he was killed. In his will, he had left all his earthly belongings to me. The house and his money were a reasonable fortune, but between the war and Edmond Cook, I left here penniless.

Yes, that old house had seen its share of marriages, births and deaths. It had survived raging storms, the war and the nights of endless weeping. Now, respectfully submitted to the memory of those walls was another faithful servant, Dr. Frances Holloway.

The afternoon brought on a steady stream of old familiar faces, but mostly patients of the good doctor whose healing hands had changed their lives forever. As the evening dragged on, I could see it was taking its toll on Victoria.

I had nearly convinced her to go upstairs and rest when the doorbell rang. Simon had assumed his old role as butler of the house and answered the door. I was alarmed when I heard him shout out, "Dear Lord, I cannot believe my eyes!"

Victoria was standing by the fireplace when he escorted a petite dark-headed woman into the room. She stood there with a suitcase in her hands and smiled. Her eyes looked familiar, but I could not place her.

"Lizzie?" she asked. I detected what I thought was a slight Irish brogue. Could it be? I wondered.

Without waiting for me to speak, she calls out, "Lizzie, it is me, Molly."

My heart stops. Before me stood a vision. There in the grown-up flesh was little Molly, the Irish girl Fannie and I took in so long ago. Fannie trained her to be her nurse, but she thought the girl capable and arranged for her to attend medical school in London.

To my knowledge, she was not heard from again.

We were to learn Molly has no knowledge of Fannie's death. She had come in response to Fannie's letter. Victoria wept as Molly took out the letter and read aloud.

To Dr. Molly O'Neal,

I am sorry to hear about the recent death of your husband. Given the timing, I thought you might be interested in coming back to Charleston. I shall be retiring by the end of May from my medical practice. I know of none other that I would rather turn it over to. If you agree to accept my offer, I think you will find it has grown into a successful practice. The house is presently in the hands of Lizzie's daughter, Victoria. I am sure she will be agreeable to lease the clinic to you, as well as offer you room and board in the Bullwinkle house. Please do not delay your response.

Your true friend,
Dr. Frances Holloway

Pieces of the puzzle were fitting together for Victoria, yet I feared the biggest piece could slip out with Molly's next words. Molly was not only there when Victoria was born, she was the hands that delivered her into this world.

I insist that Victoria go upstairs to rest. When we are alone, I explain to Molly the urgency of my actions. Simon shook his head. "Fannie told us to be mindful of what we said around Victoria. She has been asking questions. Sooner or later, she is going to find out the truth. I only pray she does not turn against you."

Not only were we to learn Fannie had taken care of what was to happen to the clinic; she had also taken care of us. The house, as she had promised, was deeded back to me. She had left a sizable bank account for Victoria, allowing for household expenses and taxes. She had also left $500 to each of my children and to Simon and Millie.

Simon said there was something magical about that old house. It just kept on handing out unexpected blessings. I thought about what he said to me when I first moved into the Bullwinkle house. "Once this house casts its spell on you, you can never leave."

How right he was.

In a few short weeks, Molly had transitioned into the resident doctor. Victoria and Molly were getting along splendidly. Fannie was wise to pair them. Victoria was to start teaching in the fall and continue working with the Women's suffrage. I felt sure with her busy life, soon she would be happy again.

I remained in Charleston for the summer. We visited the remains at Sandy Ridge and I told Victoria about my life before she was born. I told her about the first time I met Joel. I spared few details about the night Mammy's daughter Violet was raped or how my cousin Gerald was murdered. But, I never found the courage to tell her about Edmond Cook.

Chapter 15

1885-1886

You Ain't Worth Killing!

Friday, February 24, 1893

I had not seen Mr. Lee since last Saturday night. Our agreement was he would drop off the reports in the box, but this entire week he was persistent in disturbing my privacy. He would knock several times, and then finally drop the reports in the box.

Last night he knocked, then sat on the porch and waited for nearly an hour. Dovie did not question why we all had to stay shut up in the house every afternoon from 5 to 6 o'clock. By Wednesday, Jasper's curiosity had gotten the best of him. *"Miss Lizzie,"* he said, *"Yous can't hides behind these walls fer ever. Whats is you afraid of?"*

Jasper was right. I could not allow anyone to keep me prisoner in my own home.

With that in mind, today I will answer the door and invite him in.

Dovie is dusting the furniture in the hall when he knocks at the door. I glance at the clock; it is a quarter past five. Dovie stops what she is doing and sits down on the edge of the chair afraid to move. "Dovie, you can go check on supper. I'll answer the door."

She picks up her rag and watches me put down my knitting, smooth out my skirt and start for the door. She does not move until I motion for her to scat.

Once she is out of sight, I open the door. The look on my face was of surprise. It was not Mr. Lee. It was Mr. Collins. "May I speak to you for a moment?" he asks.

"Yes, please come in," I say, and gesture toward the front room.

"Mrs. Simpson, I stopped by to invite you to a program tomorrow night at the Presbyterian church. A colored girl by the name of Mary Jane McLeod is to be the speaker. She will be graduating from the Scotia Seminary and has been awarded a scholarship to Moody Bible Institute in Chicago, Illinois. "

"Sounds interesting," I say, and offer him a seat.

"Some of the teachers are hosting the event in her honor. They say she is an extraordinary commentator. There will be music and refreshments following. I thought if you would like to go, I would be happy to drive you."

"This Saturday night?" I ask.

"Yes, tomorrow. I am sorry for the short notice. In fact, I just found out about it myself."

Before I could answer, I hear the door open and Dovie clears her throat. I look up and standing behind her is Mr. Lee.

"Well, Lizzie. No wonder I could not get you to the door. You are entertaining the likes of my old friend Colin Collins," he says, laughing. He walks over and extends his hand. Mr. Collins rises and shakes his hand, but he does not look happy.

"My dear Lizzie, you must be a busy lady." Mr. Lee says, taking a seat uninvited.

"I have stopped by every day this week to see you. Today I came to the kitchen door. I thought I might be at least able to speak to your darkie."

"Dovie?" I ask, raising my eyebrows at him.

"Yes, Dovie, that is her name," he says. "My mother, God bless her, is all excited about hearing some dark..., or colored girl, speak tomorrow night. She wants to know if you will escort her."

"I assume you are speaking of Mary Jane McLeod?"

"Sounds right," Mr. Lee says. "Dinner first?" he asks. "You know Mother enjoys her food."

I look over quickly at Mr. Collins. He is sitting quietly looking out the window. I make a bold decision. "Oh, I am so sorry. I have already made plans to go with Mr. Collins. Tell your mother maybe next time."

Mr. Collins' head turns quickly in my direction. I smile and he looks at me nervously. I can see Mr. Lee is embarrassed. Seeing him sitting there with his hat in his hand gives me a slight feeling of superiority. After a few wordless seconds I speak up.

"Well, Mr. Lee, do you have any work for me today?"

He reaches in his coat pocket and extends an envelope in my direction. "Thank you very much," I say, standing up to take it in my hand. "I will have it ready for you by Monday."

Mr. Lee is not a stupid man. He knows that in one sentence I have made it clear I work for him, and I have politely asked him to leave.

"He stands to his feet, places his hat on his head and says, "I will let mother know. She will be disappointed. Good day, Mrs. Simpson, Mr. Collins. I'll see myself out."

I stand and watch him go down the hall and out the front door. If he came in the back door, I would have preferred he leave out the same door. It may be just silly superstition, but Mammy always said it was bad luck.

When I hear the door close, I turn back to Mr. Collins.

"Now, where were we?"

He laughs at my come back. "I was saying, I would be by to pick you up tomorrow evening around five. And you were saying you would be happy to have dinner with me before we went to the meeting."

"Oh, I did, did I?" I say in good humor.

"Well," he says, jumping to his feet. "I have found our little chat most agreeable, but I will not intrude any longer." He slips his hat back on his head. "So we are on for tomorrow?" he asks, leaving it open ended.

"Yes," I confirm.

He walks toward the hall and I follow him as he makes his way to the door. "Oh, by the way, I always leave out the same door I entered. Superstitious, I guess."

I have a funny feeling in the pit of my stomach as if he had read my mind.

Saturday, February 25, 1893

It is unusual to see Lilly and Mrs. Davis at my front door before the 9 o'clock hour. I invite them in. Lilly burst into tears before I could even offer them coffee.

"Henry has been shot!" she cried out.

"Shot?" I ask, taking hold of her hand and guiding her down in a chair.

"Where?" I ask.

"In the buttocks!" she screams out.

"That was not exactly what I meant, Lilly. Please tell me he is going to be alright."

Mrs. Davis spoke up, "Yes, the doctor thinks so. A man from the railway just came with the news. He says Henry is still at the doctor's office. We were hoping you would take us to pick him up."

"Where is he?" I ask, remembering my engagement that

night.

"He is about 10 miles out of town on this side of Charlotte. I have the directions," Lilly says, pulling a piece of paper out of her pocket. "Lizzie, say you will take us. Our buggy is so small. Yours is large enough for him to lie down in the back seat. Mother could ride up front with you and I will sit in the back, so Henry can lay his head in my lap."

"I see," I reply, thinking the situation over. If we left now and there were no complications, I could be back by 3 o'clock.

"Very well, as long as there are no delays. I have plans for this afternoon."

"We are ready!" Lilly responds, jumping to her feet.

"I will get changed and have Jasper bring the carriage around." I say quickly, leaving them sitting in the front room. As I am changing my clothes, the thought runs through my mind: Why not just let Jasper drive them?

I find Jasper in the barn and he agrees to take them. Jasper brings the carriage around front and I have full intentions to tell them there has been a change of plans. However, the moment Lilly sees me, she throws her arms around my neck and weeps. "Lizzie, I could not get through this without you. You are my dearest friend."

I look up at Jasper and he gives me a half-cocked smile. I tell him to take care of things while I am gone and to expect us back early afternoon.

Thankfully, it is a sunny day and not at all cold for February. I even see a few daffodils in bloom along the road. I think about what I read in the paper the day before. Scientists are predicting winters will be getting shorter and summers will be longer. It is all right by me, but I wonder how it will effect the growing season.

We have little trouble finding the doctor's office, but the

trouble begins when we arrive to pick up Henry. When the good doctor learns Lilly is Henry's wife, he presents her with the bill for $7.50. Lilly looks at me stunned. "I will have my husband take care of this bill as soon as he is able."

"Soon as he is able?" he says, excitedly.

Lilly tries to remain calm and replies, "$7.50 is a lot of money. I cannot pay the entire amount today." She begins to dig in her purse and Mrs. Davis in hers. I follow suit and combined we have a total of 43 cents. Lilly hands it over to the doctor.

"This is robbery!" he shouts. "Highway robbery. I am an old man, in retirement for over 15 years. Still, I was able in the wee hours of the morning to pluck the bullet out of your husband's behind!"

From the rear, we see Henry approaching. He manages to make it to the doorway and props himself against the frame, "Dr. Ledbetter, if I recall correctly I heard you accept Mr. Hinson's terms when he brought me in. He told you the railroad would pay your fee of $5.50. Now it appears you have since jacked up your fees and are trying to double dip from my wife and the railroad." Henry starts to stumble and Lilly runs to catch him.

The doctor makes a feeble attempt to help her lay him down on the floor. "Well, I will need some type of collateral. Might I add I am retired and have little income of my own."

Henry reaches in his pocket for his watch, but Lilly stops him. "No," she says, taking her wedding band off her finger. The doctor is quick to take possession of the prize.

We collect Henry and very gingerly load him in the back seat. Henry is angry over the loss of Lilly's wedding band. Her words were all Henry needed to hear. "*A golden wedding band holds little value, but what it represents is*

210

priceless."

The ordeal at the doctor's office has cost us over an hour. I now realize I must travel slowly to prevent from jarring our patient. It is approaching 2 o'clock by the time we are on the main road.

On the way home, we find out the events leading up to the shooting. Henry as always was walking his 12-mile stretch to inspect the track. When he approached the crossing, he noticed at least a dozen spikes were missing. If he could not replace them quickly, number 67 could derail.

With time running out, he went to work immediately replacing the spikes. He had just nailed down the last one when a shot came out of nowhere and landed in his backside. The impact pitched him off the track and into the ditch. Seconds later he heard the train go by.

He may have bled to death had not a passenger seen him lying in the ditch and told the conductor to stop the train.

Before he could be rescued, the robbers came charging out of the woods firing their guns in the air. Their surprise attack failed when they met up with a few passengers named Smith & Wesson. In view of all the recent holdups, the railroad had planted a couple of marshals aboard.

When we return home, it is already after four. I help Lilly get Henry in bed and run across the yard. I have barely enough time to wash the dust off and get dressed before Mr. Collins arrives. I run through the front door calling "Dovie!" In a flash, she comes out of the kitchen as if she is expecting to see me on fire.

"Dovie, please press my navy skirt and my gray-striped blouse. I am in a world of hurry."

"*Is yous going somewheres?*" she asks.

"Yes, yes, with Mr. Collins to dinner!" I reply, on my way to the bathroom. I know she is still looking at me. So I call back "Hurry!"

After washing up and arranging my hair, I slip into the bedroom. I am hoping to see my clothes laid out on the bed, but they are not. I sit down on the side of the bed and wait for Dovie to deliver them. It is 4:45. The thought runs through my head: please don't be early. It was not a thought. It was a prediction. The doorbell rings.

"Dovie!" I call out. She does not answer. I call out again, "Dovie." Again, there is no answer. I peek around the bedroom door. The front door is a straight shot up the hall. I can see Mr. Collins through the oval glass. If I come out to look for Dovie he will see me prance by in my chemise.

When he knocks again I will have to go to the door myself. I have just slipped my old dress over my head when I hear Dovie running down the stairs. She answers the door with my skirt and blouse draped over her arm. *"Uh, Miss Lizzie, she ain't quites ready. Comes on ins and have a seat."* I close the bedroom door slowly and wait for her to deliver my attire.

When I enter the room, Mr. Collins smiles, but it is awkward. I redirect the moment by telling him the story of Henry, of which he seems most interested.

Dinner goes smoothly. I find Mr. Collins an engaging conversationalist, but not quite as charismatic as Mr. Lee, which is a relief. When we arrive at the church, the street is full and we have to park a distance away. Even though he does not take my arm, he is mindful of my every step.

The church is filling up and we find a seat on the third row. I have barely gotten arranged in my seat when someone sits down beside me. I look to my right and it is Mr. Lee. He is alone. "Well, lookie here. What a surprise seeing you two here," he says, giving us both a big grin.

"I am sure," Mr. Collins says, in a not too polite tone.

I am wedged in between the two of them. Mr. Lee is a big man. When he crosses his legs he takes up a good part of my space. He raises his arm in the air allowing it to flop down on the back of the pew behind my head. I would like to speak my mind, but instead I say, "Was your mother not up to coming?"

"Oh, she is fine. She just did not want to come without you," he replies.

"Tell her I am sorry." Secretly, I think he is only trying to make me feel guilty. My guess is he did not want to be bothered with her.

I redirect my attention to the front as a woman from the school is introducing a dark Negro girl. "I would like to present to you tonight a remarkable young woman from Mayseville, South Carolina. Her parents, Samuel and Patsy, were former slaves and Mary Jane is one of 17 children. She will be graduating with honors from the Scotia Seminary here in Concord in June."

For the next hour, you could have heard a pin drop as the girl of wisdom far beyond her years told her story. It was a story of faith, determination and hard work. At only 11 years old, she walked five miles to and from school and then spent the evenings teaching the rest of her family. Her hard work did not go unnoticed. She was given the opportunity to come to the Scotia Seminary in Concord. She has since received a scholarship to the Moody Bible Institute in Chicago. She bravely accepts, even though she knows she will be the only Negro student. Her plans after completing her education will be to go to Africa and teach. She concluded her program by speaking of her mission. She plans to spread the word to all people that education is the key to a better life.

As the program ends, my eyes are filled with tears.

There is so much about this girl that reminds me of my dear friend Fannie. I will always miss Dr. Fannie. May God rest her sweet soul.

When Mr. Collins walks me to the door it is not very late, and I invite him in for coffee. He is considerate and declines. I suspect he has seen me yawning and knows I have had a long day. We say our goodnights and I agree to have a second dinner with him soon.

Sunday, February 26, 1893

When I wake up the next morning, I fear I am coming down with a cold. I send Dovie and Jasper on to church without me. Since I am not tagging along, they will go straight to her mother's from church.

In contrast to yesterday, it is raining and cold. After having a bite to eat, I bundle up in a wool blanket and go down the hall to my office. I start up a fire and lay down on the couch with Rebel. Sometime around noon I am feeling better, and decide to type Mr. Lee's reports. When I have finished, I lay them on the hall table; it is too damp to put them in the box.

With the blanket around me I venture out to the bathroom. As I come back in the house I notice the door to the attic is open. Strange, it was not open before. At first I think only to close the door, but then my curiosity says take a look.

I start upstairs in my gown and bare feet, and then the thought crosses my mind: what if someone has slipped in the house and is hiding in the attic? I turn around and go for my pistol. It is in my nightstand by the bed. The room is dim, but as soon as I slip my hand in the drawer I feel the handle.

As I start back up the stairs, I hear a noise and my heart begins to pound. Suddenly an old memory comes to haunt me. I turn quickly and press my back against the wall. I freeze, recalling the day I crept up the stairs of Joel's house, pistol in my hand, and seconds later the intruder shot me in the back. It is all real again, even though it has been 30 years ago.

I stand still and listen. There is definitely a noise. Once I have regained my nerve, with my back to the wall, I scale up the stairs. When I reach the top, I see no one. I step up carefully and slip behind the rafters to get a better look. Still there is no one.

Oddly enough, a trunk is standing open and a letter is lying in the middle of the floor. Assuming my fears were only the wind, I step out in the open to pick up the letter. When I lean down something swoops over my head, which causes me to scream and fall to my knees.

When I discover it to be only a bird, I am relieved. Looking over the space, I see the window is open. The little bird lands on the back of an old chair and turns its head to look at me. I pick up a broom and after several tries, I am successful in sweeping the bird out the window. I start back down the steps, thinking someone has been up here. I remember the letter and turn around to go back for it.

Once back downstairs and the excitement is over, I am reminded I am not feeling well. I go into the kitchen, make a cup of hot tea and return to the office.

I throw another log on the fire and slip on my glasses. When I take out the letter and focus my eyes on the envelope, a chill runs down my spine. I see the return address clearly—The Theological Seminary in Columbia, South Carolina. I am stunned by what I see. I would have thought Joel would have destroyed the letter. For some reason he must have tucked it away in this trunk. One day soon I will have to go through that trunk to see what else might be hiding there.

Finding the letter is odd timing. I have been suffering a writer's block not knowing if I should include those dark days in the next chapter of my book. The bird, the open window, is it a sign? Perhaps it is time to set the bird free.

I walk over to the desk and slip a sheet of paper into the typewriter. Just before I begin, I stop to pray.

Dear Lord,

Some things in the pages of our history are not pleasing. As we are reminded of our transgressions, please give us the understanding to learn from our mistakes and the courage to share that wisdom with others. Amen.

1885 and 1886

I will only share a few lines of this next chapter on national news. You shall see our personal happenings over the next two years could be a book all on its own.

On March 4, 1885, Grover Cleveland became president. At last, the South felt like they had a friend in the White House. The day of the inauguration, the newspaper said the streets of Washington were filled with soldiers in Confederate uniforms. General Fitzhugh Lee led them in a rebel yell when Cleveland rode by. On July 23 of the same year, former President Ulysses Grant died of throat cancer.

Mark Twain published two books that year. "The Adventures of Huck Finn" and the "Personal

Memoirs of Ulysses Grant." I thought a first edition of both would be a good investment, so I purchased them for Joel's birthday. I will never forget what he said when he unwrapped them. "I heard enough from Grant when he was alive and I for damn sure don't want to hear anything from him now. As for your Mark Twain to call himself a Southerner is mockery. He enlisted as Samuel Clemens in the Confederate Army, stayed two weeks and then high-tailed it out west." With those words, he wrapped the books back up and told me to put them on my own shelf. I was hurt that he did not consider my feelings, but never again did I underestimate the depth of old war wounds.

The so-called "Gilded Age" was not without its share of trouble. Progress always comes with a price tag. It seems to me if a country does not have a war to fight, then they will fight among themselves. Indians, women, Negroes and the Chinese immigrants were all fighting for their piece of the pie. Papa used to say: *Any fool can start a fight, but a wise man knows when to walk away.*

Now I shall begin where I left off in my last chapter of 1884. My time in Charleston with Victoria was well spent, but I was glad to be on my way home that fall.

The house on Peachtree Street looked the same.

However, Robert appeared to have overnight transformed from a boy to a man. As planned, he had worked all summer in the mill. He had become a popular man around town, with a busy social calendar and a host of new friends.

When Mr. Oliver asked if Tessie would be interested in taking a job in his grocery, Joel gave his consent. I was amazed at how Tessie had blossomed. Her shyness seemed to be repressed. She too was enjoying new friends and social outings.

Lastly, I must turn my thoughts back to the joy of being home again with Joel. A part of me had been restored. Those first couple of weeks were like a second honeymoon. With the children off and about, the two of us enjoyed our afternoons alone.

Tessie and Robert were delighted with the provisions Fannie had left them in her will. To them having $500 was the same as a million dollars. Robert worried about how he would spend it and Tessie worried about saving it.

Robert first talked about going out west with his money, which I discouraged. Then he made inquires about acquiring a franchise to install burglar alarms. Joel discouraged this. He said it might be a booming business up north, but he doubted there would be much need for it in the South.

Tessie decided to save her money until she was married, which I felt was wise. With a little battle, we encouraged Robert to do the same or at least until he had a sure investment.

In September when school sessions began, Tessie refused to enroll. She said she would lose her job at the grocery if she went back to school. Tessie was a smart girl. It seemed a shame with only one year to graduation. She put up a convincing argument and Joel gave in to her.

I knew Joel's thoughts. She would be married soon and she certainly had enough education to be a wife. He was from the old school and I understood his ways. Still something inside of me was uneasy. I knew Tessie had loved school and I feared she felt she had to work. I reassured her she was no burden to us. Still, she insisted she preferred her job over going back to school. I let it go. Now looking back, I should have trusted my instincts.

For reasons unknown to us, Tessie dismissed herself of her job around the first of October. I questioned her why she did not want to stay on and help Mr. Oliver at least through the holidays. I was concerned why her answer did not satisfy my inquiry.

She had always been a quiet girl. My fear was she was withdrawing more into herself. I tried to encourage her to get involved in church activities or take a class of china painting with Lilly and myself. Nothing seemed to interest her. Joel was worried too. Yet, I have learned men handle things differently than women. When he tried to talk to her, he wound up angry. He insisted that after the Christmas holidays she would enroll in the late semester of school.

Tessie had always been an obedient child. This was the first time she protested against her father. In the end, Joel had the final word. If Tessie was to live under his roof, she would be back in school come January.

I was hoping Christmas would perk up her

spirits. She appeared to be going only through the motions. Other than church, she rarely went out of the house. She took very little pride in her appearance and sometimes would stay in her robe all day. All she cared about was eating and sleeping.

By the time January rolled around, I told Joel I had made Tessie an appointment to see the doctor. It just was not natural for a young healthy girl to be in such a state of gloom from sunup to sundown.

The morning we were to see Dr. Baker, Tessie came downstairs and I could tell she had been crying. I assumed she was afraid of the doctor's visit and I tried to reassure her. Her hair was neatly arranged and she was wearing her navy dress. I recall clearly seeing the buttons bulging across the back and thinking that before she wears it again, I will let it out a bit.

When we arrived, Dr. Baker's nurse came out to collect Tessie. I stood up and the woman gently touched me on the shoulder and said, "I will be with her in the examination room."

I sat back down. Tessie looked over at me and followed the nurse into the examination room. Even though I still saw Tessie as a child, she was 18 and considered by most an adult.

I had expected the doctor to be with her for at least an hour. In less than 30 minutes, I saw the nurse come out of the room. She did not look up at me and I was afraid something was terribly wrong. She went into another room and closed the door behind her. Another 30 minutes passed and I began to get angry, thinking the woman had left Tessie to suffer through the exam alone.

I looked at the clock and decided I would knock on the door and make my presence known. I stood up, walked across the hall and was just before knocking when the door opened. The doctor stepped out and closed the door behind him. He looked at me and said, "Mrs. Simpson, may I see you in my office?"

Not knowing what to expect I followed. He asked me to take a seat and walked over to the cabinet. He took out a bottle of whisky, poured a small glass and handed it to me. He then sat himself down behind his desk. "Please," he said, pointing at the glass. "You might find it helpful." Upon the doctor's advice, I tipped the glass back.

"Mrs. Simpson, I have always seen you as a rational and understanding woman. Sometimes things in life just happen. We cannot blame ourselves or God for things which are out of our control."

My heart stopped. "Doctor, is it serious, and will Tessie be alright?"

"Oh, your daughter will be alright; most women are, after about nine months," he replied. He leaned forward and crossed his arms on his desk.

"You cannot mean what I think you are implying?" I ask, feeling I have misunderstood.

"Yes, Mrs. Simpson. I think you understood me correctly. If you remember, I delivered Tessie. I watched her grow up and I am upset over this, too. We cannot abandon her. We must remember she is a victim. It is her innocence that was robbed. The young man is unscarred and she is left suffering the consequences. Mrs. Simpson, this is an age-old problem and from my experience, it is best to embrace her with love and compassion. If you would like, I will be happy to speak to your husband, too."

"You are wise, Dr. Baker," I said, and reached out and shook his hand.

Before I left the room he spoke his final spill. "Mrs. Simpson, may I suggest that you and Tessie go on a nice long holiday, visit friends or relatives until after the baby is born? When you return you will be the proud new mother. In society, it is a polite way to handle this sort of thing. Your secret will be safe with me."

When I opened the door to the examination room, there sat Tessie on a little metal stool. She did not lift her head to speak to me. I went over, dropped to my knees in front of her and cradled her up in my arms. I lifted her up on her feet and we walked out of the doctor's office arm in arm. Yes, I understood how Tessie felt. I had made my share of mistakes, but abandoning Tessie would not be one of them.

On the way home, I thought of the day we found out my baby sister Annabelle was pregnant. So many times Mother wished she had never sent Annabelle away. Nothing could have saved Annabelle. Still mother always blamed herself.

I told Tessie I would handle her father. Joel was not an easy case, but he agreed he would not humiliate Tessie. When I shared the news with Robert, he understood. We were a family and we would all stand by Tessie. I was proud of his compassion.

Joel insisted on one thing. He wanted me to find out from Tessie what happened. I think it was a relief for Tessie to have it all out in the open. It began when Mr. Oliver's son, George, came to work in the grocery. He was working temporarily until he went on to theological seminary. As Tessie told what happen, I could see it all too clear. George was a handsome boy, older and more experienced. He must have planned his game as soon as he laid eyes on Tessie. He flirted, teased her and eventually coached her into the stock room for a kiss or two. Tessie trusted him and thought his intentions were true. She never dreamed it was only lust. One night as they were closing, he pulled her aside and of her own free will she followed him. However, this time things were different when he kissed her. His hands began to run wildly over her body. When she tried to push him away, he got angry and thrust her down on the floor. When the deed was done, he left her to lock up the store alone. She blamed herself for what happen, even though I tried to convince her what he did was a crime. It was called rape.

With what Tessie told me, I knew Joel would have to know. I waited until Tessie had gone to bed, took Joel in the front room and closed the door. As soon as he heard the whole story, he marched upstairs and woke Robert.

While Robert was getting dressed, Joel went out and saddled up the horses. By the time Robert came downstairs, Joel was in the kitchen loading his pistol.

Joel would not listen to reason, even though I begged and pleaded with him. He was like a wild man unleashed. He left me standing in the kitchen and seconds later I heard the back door slam.

It was after midnight when they returned home. Joel came straight in the house and poured himself a drink. When he sat down at the kitchen table he begun to cry. The only thing Joel said was, "If I was any man at all, I would have pulled the trigger."

When Joel left for work the next morning, he said nothing about the night before. I knew he would have to come to terms with himself. When he got home that night, he was ready to talk.

Joel and Robert had gone to Mr. Oliver's house. They first spoke to Mr. Oliver and were told George was not home. Joel sat down prepared to wait.

Their voices woke up Mrs. Oliver and just as she was coming down the steps, George walked in the front door. The boy was quick to claim he had been at church when he found out Joel was Tessie's father. Joel could tell the boy had been drinking and asked, "Do they serve whisky at your church?"

The boy got defensive and Mr. Oliver said he was going to send for the sheriff. Joel then asked George, "Are you sure you want the sheriff involved in this?"

Even though George looked a little nervous he kept a cool head. "Well, Mr. Simpson, please tell us what is on your mind."

Joel told them Tessie had confessed to her mother what had happened. Now as a result of George's unscrupulous conduct, Tessie was expecting his baby. When he used the word rape, Mrs. Oliver started crying.

George played the part of the righteous son. While patting his mother on the shoulder he said, "Mother dear, I am sorry you had to hear such a hurtful thing. I was afraid something like this might happen to that poor girl. She was such an impressionable little thing and with all those miners in town, she was easy prey. I warned her about hanging around those bars," he said, as he shook his head.

Joel said he felt a rage come over him. He pulled out his pistol. His every intention was to send George Oliver straight to hell. Just before he pulled the trigger, he looked over at George's mother and hesitated. Robert stood up, slugged the boy and knocked him to the floor. Joel said he walked over, held the pistol to the boy's head and watched him whimper like a baby. "You ain't worth killing," he said, and gave him a sharp kick, which was certain to have broken a few ribs.

Before he left, he warned George if he said one damn word about Tessie, he would hunt him down and skin him like a rabbit.

The hardest thing for Joel was knowing George had gotten away with the crime, but Tessie would have to serve the time. Tessie was already starting to show by the time we left to spend the summer at Sallie's house in the country.

Several days after we had left, Joel learned the power of a mother's scorn. He received this letter.

Dear Mr. Simpson,

Your wife wrote me some time back with some distressing information about a man named George Oliver. A young man's reputation is of utmost importance to us here at the seminary. In view of the seriousness of the accusations, we certainly could not let it go without investigation.

In organizations such as ours, things do not always happen quickly. Your wife's letter was presented to our board for review. This, coupled with the need to prove the legitimacy of the claim, prolonged our action.

The following chain of events I think may be of keen interest to you. Two weeks after I received your letter, I was awaked in the middle of the night by the sound of a gunshot.

The next morning the origin of the gunshot was revealed. While the caretaker was out making his nightly rounds, a man broke in his home, entered his daughter's sleeping room and attempted to assault her. The caretaker was steps away and heard her scream. He shot and killed the man. Later the body was identified as your George Oliver.

We are sorry we were unable to help you with your concerns. Please know that your daughter and your family will be in our prayers.

Your obedient servant,
Rev. J.B. Mason

Joel never told Tessie about the letter and as far as she knew, George moved away and never came back.

Before I close this chapter, there is more to Tessie's story. The day we arrived at Sallie's house, Ransom and a man named Walter Barringer were in the process of fencing in a new pasture. Sallie told us she invited Walter to stay for supper. He was a widower and she knew he would be grateful.

Looking back, I knew Ransom had told Walter of Tessie's circumstances. For the next several weeks, Walter came almost daily to help Ransom with various projects. It became a routine that he would stay for supper.

I began to notice he favored Tessie's conversation and his concern for her welfare. Walter spoke to me first about his intention. He wanted my approval to ask Tessie to marry him and he would raise the child as his own. I told him it was not my approval he needed, it was Tessie's.

July 15, 1886-Walter Moses Barringer and Tessie May Simpson were married.

July 30, 1886-Travis Lee Barringer was born.

Walter had put all his eggs in one basket. Before he asked Tessie to marry him, he hired a woman to come in and prepare his house in anticipation of his new wife and baby. I suppose if Tessie had not agreed to marry him, he would have had an empty nursery and a lonely bed.

I stayed to help Tessie with the baby until August 20. I was ready to come back home, but I was afraid of what I might find. Joel and Robert were hardly housekeepers and the moment I opened the front door, I knew I had my work cut out for me.

Dovie was still living with her mother, but she was happy to be hired out. She came to stay with me for a couple of weeks to help restore law and order to the Simpson household.

On Tuesday, August 31, Dovie and I finished most of the work. It was a job well done and the next day I would take her home. It was around 10 o'clock when I went to bed that night.

I recall tossing and turning for quite sometime. It was a hot and humid night and the sheets were sticking to my skin. I finally drifted off to sleep, but awoke suddenly, feeling the floor shaking and hearing the sound of broken glass. I thought at first I was dreaming, until Joel sat up in bed as if he had been shot.

Seconds later Dovie and Robert were knocking on our door. Joel said it must have been an earth tremor. I recalled a few tremors when I was a girl in Charleston and assured Dovie and Robert it was nothing to worry about. A photograph of Victoria had been knocked off the mantel and the frame and glass broken. I swept up the pieces and went back to bed.

The next day people were talking about the tremor all over town. It was not until the evening paper came out that we learned the frightening news. Charleston had a massive earthquake. There were over 100 known dead and an undetermined number injured. Although the quake lasted only about a minute and a half, there were buildings and homes destroyed, fires raging through the streets and people were left homeless. Reports of the shock had been felt as far as Maine and Bermuda. Furthermore, they feared aftershocks would follow. Southern Telegraph Company had worked all night to get a line out to let the world know of the disaster.

When Joel finished reading, my heart sank. My Victoria was all I could think about. I would have paid any price just to know if she was alright. I sat up all night praying for not only Victoria, but all the people of Charleston. I could not help but ask why God could let one city suffer so much.

Early the next morning we received a telegram from Charleston. My hands were trembling as I read:

We are all fine—house spared—except for chimney. Volunteering at hospital with Molly—much to do—will write soon. Love Victoria.

The aftershocks lasted for several months, although none were as damaging as the first. On September 9, we had a shaker here in North Carolina. Some people were hysterical, fearing they would die of what they called the "shaker sickness." Still others were sure they would soon hear Gabriel's horn.

I was glad it was not the end of the world, but I was glad when the year 1866 finally came to its great end.

Chapter 16

Let Your Heart Be Your Guide

March 1, 1893

The last couple of days have been uninteresting as far as my activities are concerned. I have not heard once from Mr. Collins. Even though it is fine by me, I wonder if I have offended him in some way.

Mr. Lee dropped off one report, which occupied my time for the whole of one day. It was regarding the accidental shooting of a young woman by her husband. Mr. Lee was representing the grieving man, who claims to have been cleaning his gun at the time of the accident.

Dovie is not doing well with the carrying of her child. She is having difficulty breathing, which I felt was due to her enormous size. Yesterday, Jasper carried her in to see Dr. Baker.

When they came home, Dovie was crying and ran straight upstairs. I knew she must have received alarming news, but I was not prepared to hear what Jasper was to say. According to Dr. Baker, Dovie would deliver twins.

I knew that having a baby in the house would be an adjustment. But, I was gambling that Dovie would learn to juggle things in a few weeks. All bets are off now, since there will be two babies. I expect I will be working for Dovie, plus paying to keep her and the babies up!

Such is the way of life. We think we have smooth sailing, only to find a storm is brewing in the west.

Speaking of storms there is one brewing next door. Henry is still flat on his belly, suffering with the slow healing of the bullet wound in his backside. Not only is Lilly waiting on him all day long, she is also nursing her mother.

I am afraid her mother's illness is partly my fault. As an attempt to be a good neighbor, I sent over a few magazines for Henry to read while he was laid up. One of the magazines he passed on to Mrs. Davis, "A Modern Woman's Guide to Good Health." After she read the magazine, she confined herself to her bed.

She is now convinced she is suffering from rickets, because her bones are stiff, her back is curved and she requires an afternoon nap. Not knowing what to do, Lilly asked Dr. Baker to see her mother. After a brief examination, he very kindly told Mrs. Davis her complaints were normal findings for a woman of 80 years.

His diagnosis only served to make her angry. She called him a quack and demanded to see another doctor. The next day another doctor came and another one two days later.

I questioned why they did not send for Les. Lilly said her mother did not feel comfortable with a boy doctor. She needed someone with more experience. Les was hardly a boy, he was 38 years old. He had been practicing medicine for over 10 years. I suppose Mrs. Davis still sees him as that little orphan boy.

The last doctor showed up and saw his opportunity to milk the cow dry. He agreed it was indeed rickets, which seemed to make Mrs. Davis happy. He said if her condition was not treated carefully, she would surely die.

My first clue something might be questionable was the doctor's expensive medicine. He left only a small bottle of "calomel" and at three doses a day, it will not last long. In addition, he would be coming twice a week with his machine to administer "electopuncture" treatments to Mrs. Davis. Lilly said the machine is supposed to stimulate her muscles.

The first treatment was on Monday. It was so painful that her mother screamed each time he zapped her with the current. Today I am to go over and help hold her down for the second treatment.

I have finished my noon meal when I see the doctor's buggy pull up next door. Since Jasper is working at the print shop, I run upstairs quickly to check on Dovie. She is lying in bed with her head propped up on a pillow. She is not asleep, but her eyes are closed. "Dovie, would you like some lunch?" I ask.

"Nos, I'll be downs in just a bit," she says, even though I was not certain it would happen.

I promise not to be gone long, grab my wrap and run over to the Davis house. When I knock, Henry calls out, "Come on in, the door is open."

When I step into the parlor, I see Henry, stretched out on the sofa on his stomach. Around him is an array of comforts, a tray of half-eaten food, a few books and his pipe. "They are upstairs," he says. "I don't hear any screaming yet, so they are most likely waiting on you."

Mrs. Davis' bedroom door is open. I stop briefly and knock on the doorframe. She is lying on the bed on top of the covers. Lilly is sitting on one side of the bed and on the other is a tall gray-haired man, who I assume is the doctor. Lilly looks up at me, "Oh Lizzie, thank you for coming. Can you hold mother's feet?"

I nod, but I am not feeling good about being part of this operation. Slowly I walk over, sit down on the edge of the bed and take hold of Mrs. Davis' ice-cold feet.

"Are we ready?" the doctor asks, looking down at Mrs. Davis.

"Yes," she says in a feeble voice. I am amazed how quickly she has gone down. Just last week she was sweeping off her porch and walking to town. The next thing I hear is a loud scream and her body jolts. It takes all my strength to hold her feet down on the bed. Lilly is franticly patting her mother on the head and seconds later the next jolt occurs and Mrs. Davis shouts out, "Dear Jesus!"

It is more than I can stand and before I can control myself, I shout out, "Stop this! This is insane!"

The doctor turns to face me. "Ma'am, medical science is not always easy to witness, but I assure you it is for the greater good of the patient."

"Doctor, you have no idea the things I have witnessed in my lifetime, but I will not sit here and witness you torturing this old lady," I retort.

"Mrs. Davis, Lilly," he says ignoring me. "Do I have your permission to continue?"

I know my face is beet red when she looks over at me. "Well, I don't know," she replies. "Maybe that is enough for today. Don't you think so Mother?" she says, patting her mother again.

There are tears streaming down Mrs. Davis' face. In a clear voice she says, "I think I would rather just go on and die of the rickets than be electrified."

The doctor begins packing up his things. "Very well, it is your choice to live or die. Let me remind you, Mrs. Davis, my fee includes four jolts. You have only received two, but my time is important. I will have to charge you for all four jolts."

At this point Lilly is mad. "I have an idea for you doctor. Why don't you offer the other two to my husband? If you are successful in jolting him off the sofa and back to work, then maybe we can pay your bill!"

Before he can answer, Mrs. Davis sits up in bed and throws her feet over the side of the bed. Slowly she stands and leans to the left, then to the right. "You know," she says, "them treatments have done me some good. And I know for sure it would do some good to see Henry take a jolt or two." She begins to laugh so hard that she rocks herself back down on the bed.

"Me too!" Lilly says. "Doctor, bring your machine downstairs!"

I pull on Lilly's sleeve to stop her, but she gives me a wicked little laugh and follows the doctor. Mrs. Davis creeps down the steps behind her.

The doctor enters the room and quickly begins hooking up the machine to Henry, the unknowing sleeping victim of medical science. Seconds later I hear, "What the hell?" coming out of Henry's mouth. Then with the next jolt, Henry jumps up on his feet and begins running all over the room.

"It is a miracle!" Mrs. Davis says, doubling over laughing.

Lilly holds her face serious as Henry rants and raves. "What kind of trick is this?" he asks her.

"It is not a trick, but a marvel. A few seconds ago, you could scarcely turn over and now you are strutting around the room like a peacock in June."

When Henry notices me standing behind Mrs. Davis, I give him a quick little wave. "Good to see you are all doing so well. I will see you later," I say, and dart out the front door.

As I make my way across the yard, I am thankful to be out in the fresh air. If I stayed around there much longer they might decide I need a jolt or two.

When I open the front door, my heart stops. There lying at the foot of the steps is Dovie. "Dovie!" I scream, but there is no answer. I quickly run over to examine her. She is breathing, but she is unconscious. "Dovie," I say, giving her a little shake. I am relieved to see her eyes open. She tries to speak, but her words are scrambled.

"Don't move, I will go for help." I jump to my feet and run out on the porch. I am just in time to catch the doctor loading up his buggy. "Help!" I shout. "Please doctor, we need you!"

When he sees I am serious, he grabs his bag and runs across the yard. The moment he enters, he sees Dovie lying on the floor. He pulls out his stethoscope and listens to her heart. She begins to stir. "Did you fall?" the doctor asks.

"I ain't sure; alls I 'members is havin' dis big pain and den the next thang I knows is Lizzie standing over me."

With our help, she is able to stand to her feet. There is blood on the floor and I am afraid she has hit her head. When she is up, I see the back of her dress is covered in blood. "Do you have a bed downstairs?" the doctor asks.

"Yes," I say, and point to the little bedroom where Tessie used to sleep.

Carefully we begin to lead her down the hall, leaving a trail of blood as we go.

She doubles over halfway down the hall in pain and buckles down to her knees. It then takes all my strength to hold on to her as we drag her to the bed.

After the doctor examines her, he reaches in his bag and places some medicine under her tongue. After a few minutes, she is calm. He motions for me to join him in the hall and closes the door. "Twins, it looks like to me. My guess is one of the babies is dead, or maybe even both." I had not liked him before, but now standing before me his face is sorrowful and concerned.

"Can you do anything for her?" I ask.

"She is in labor now. By the looks of things it should go fairly quickly. Do you want me to stay and deliver the babies?"

"Yes, please," I reply, nearly begging.

He says nothing more, but goes back in the room with Dovie and closes the door. There is a long period of silence and then the screaming begins. I know all too well the force of those screams, having bore three children of my own.

The doctor comes to the door once and asks for some hot water. His hands are bloody. I am pacing the floor when I hear the back door open. Jasper! In the excitement, I had nearly forgotten about him. I quickly explain to him that Dovie is in labor and the doctor is with her. I decide it is best not to give bad news as long as there is hope.

I sit down in the hall and rest my back against the wall. Jasper does the same. Dovie's screams vibrate the wall behind me. Shortly, there is silence. We wait.

My fears are growing that both babies are dead. Then there is the tiniest of whimpers. It is the voice of a newborn baby."

Jasper jumps to his feet, but my previous knowledge causes me to caution him.

"Wait until the doctor comes out," I say softly. Jasper slides back down to the floor.

When the doctor comes out of the room he is carrying a moving bundle in his arms. He looks down at Jasper, "You are the father?" he asks.

"Yes!" Jasper says, proudly.

The doctor hands him a lone child. "Here is your son, sir."

Jasper takes the baby in his arms and holds him gently.

"My wife, is she alrights?"

"Yes, she will be fine," he replies.

"Buts da other doctor says theys wuz two babies," Jasper says, looking at the doctor fearful.

"My good man, the Lord is wise, but sometimes he makes a mistake and sends to this earth one of his own angels. Such is the case I have witnessed today. A beautiful little girl was returned to heaven."

The doctor walks over and opens the door. "Sir, I expect your wife would like to see you now. You may hold the little girl; it makes it easier."

Jasper hands the little boy to me. He wipes his eyes and quietly disappears into the room with Dovie.

In my arms is a healthy looking baby boy, with dark eyes and coffee-colored skin. "A good-looking boy," I say to the doctor.

The doctor makes no response. He gathers up his things and starts for the door.

"I will send the coroner over. They like to write these things up nowadays, even on the Negroes. Wrap the baby up tight in a couple of sheets. It might be a day or two before he can get by here."

The thought of a dead baby in the house for an undetermined number of days is unnerving. I walked the doctor to the door holding the living one, "Thank you," I said. "Please send me the bill."

"Oh, you can be certain of that, Mrs. Simpson," he says, as he walks out the door.

It was after midnight before I went to bed. Dovie and Jasper were upstairs with their new baby boy, which they have named Levi. Across the hall is a baby girl, who will be remembered only as Angel. Before Dovie and Jasper wrapped the baby in a blanket, they first cut off a tuft of her hair. Then they placed the baby in a basket, as if she is sleeping.

Early the next morning I am awakened by voices. After the day before I am braced for almost anything. I slip on my robe and follow the voices to the kitchen. I am amazed to see Dovie standing over the stove stirring a pan of fried eggs.

"Mornin' Miss Lizzie," she says. Jasper is sitting at the table with the baby in his arms.

"Dovie, what are you doing up?" I ask. "You should give yourself a few days to recuperate." When I had my children the doctor insisted on a week."

"Is be alrights. I am a whole heaps stouter dan you," she replies in a cheery voice, but her face is tired and worn.

I walk over and take over the job. "Sit down. I won't be responsible for you falling out on us." Dovie obeys and slowly walks over to the table. She is weak and her knees are trembling. At last, she makes it to the seat. She does not really sit, but braces herself on one hip.

I hear Jasper and Dovie whispering, but I do not look up. Just as I take the pan off the stove, Dovie calls out to me. *"Miss Lizzie, cans Jasper takes da buggy fer a couple of hours?"*

I am curious where he is going and why he cannot just walk or ride his horse. In view of all that has happened, I just nod. He hands the baby over to Dovie and leaves the room quietly.

In a few minutes, I see him coming down the hall with the deceased baby in the basket. Before I can stop him, he slips out the back door. Dovie is nursing her baby boy and does not look up until I speak. "Dovie, did you not understand what I told you about the coroner?"

"Yes'um, buts we donts need no body to tell us da baby

is dead; we knows it."

At first, I think I will try to explain that it is a matter of public record. Then I decide it will be just a waste of time. "What is Jasper going to do with the baby?" I ask.

"He is a going to see da preacher's house and den burry da baby in da church cemetery." It seemed reasonable and I asked nothing more. I had learned a long time ago it is best not to question the colored folk's ways.

I set a plate of food down in front of Dovie. She shakes her head, but I push it closer to her. "Eat, you need your strength."

When I see she is eating, I sit down at the table with my plate. I open up the paper and take a sip of coffee. The headlines capture my attention.

Charlie Sherwood of Forest Hill has been appointed as the new manager of the County Poorhouse.

Rev. W. S. Grisson was welcomed with a pleasant pounding on Wednesday. The church ladies filled his larder with can goods and earthly comforts.

Thanks to the brilliant mind of Thomas A. Edison, the great electrician, it is now possible to receive and send telegrams on a train.

Another mill accident at R. A. Brown. It was a narrow escape for death for Henry Hunter when his left arm was caught in the machinery.

People are questioning if the hens have stopped laying. The price of eggs has gone up from 10 cents a dozen to 15 cents.

The colored preachers are doing much good, preaching against drinking and gambling.

Rumor has it that a fellow was quoted to say the prettiest thing in town was a certain young lady in a prim and proper new calico dress. So, let this serve as an example to the young ladies who feel baring of the bust or wearing short sleeves catches the eye.

I am pondering over whom the young lady might be when the baby begins to cry. The baby is still cradled in Dovie's arms, but she has fallen asleep sitting up. I lay the paper down and walk over to roust her up.

I am in process of helping her upstairs when the back door opens up. Jasper has returned, but he is not alone. Cindy Lou greets me, telling me she has come to help until Dovie is back on her feet.

In less than an hour, baby and mother are sleeping. Jasper has gone to work, the kitchen is cleaned up and Cindy Lou is clearing out the birthing room. I am thankful Cindy Lou has come to stay for a while.

The house is quiet at last. I tiptoe down the hall to my office. I close the door and sit down at my desk. I am hoping my mind will clear to write a chapter in my book. I flip back over my previous work to see where I left off. "Let's see. Yes, here we go, the years 1887 and 1888," I say aloud.

With one sheet of fresh paper in the typewriter and my scrapbooks out for inspiration, I am deep in thought. I jump when I hear a thump on the door. Rebel is standing outside the glass door wagging his tail. I get up, let him in and close the door again.

I have just gotten back into my work when I see movement out of the corner of my eye. Cindy Lou knocks softly and I open the door. She asks if she can set up her photo painting in the front room. When I agree, she thanks me and closes the door behind her. In a few minutes, I see her spreading out a drop cloth over the table by the window.

She pulls her paints out of her bag and sits down to work. Seconds later the baby begins to cry; she rushes upstairs.

After returning to my work, I am disturbed again by a knock at the front door. Rebel is barking and I say to myself, "Good Lord, what next?" I jump from my chair and go to the door. Carefully I pull back the curtains and see a man I do not recognize. I crack the door just enough for him to speak his business.

"Mrs. Simpson?" he asks. "I am the county coroner."

When I invite him in, he asks in a stern voice to see the deceased colored infant.

"I am sorry, but I cannot do that," I answer. I can tell by the way that he raises his eyebrows he is not going to be sympathetic to the circumstances.

"Mrs. Simpson, I can assure you the examination will only take a few minutes. Then all I will need is your signature as the witness and I will be on my way."

We are standing at the foot of the stairs and he is looking over my shoulder into the other rooms. It is clear he will not be easily brushed off and I will have to provide more details.

"Sir, I am sure you know that the Negroes have mysterious ways. Last night my house girl did have a baby, but..." I stop in the middle of my sentence when I see Cindy Lou walking down the stairs with the baby boy in her arms wrapped up in a "cannon cloth."

The man bypasses me to view the infant in Cindy Lou's arms. I see at once that he thinks he has found his evidence.

"Cindy Lou, this man is from the county and he has come to take a look at Dovie's baby." Cindy Lou is puzzled, but she pulls the towel back to expose a kicking and whimpering very-alive baby boy.

The man jumps back as if he has been stung by a bee. I walk over and open the front door. "Like I said, the Negroes' ways are mysterious. Good day to you sir."

The man does not waste any time in getting himself out the door and down the steps. Cindy Lou and I laugh as we watch him run across the yard, jump up in his buggy and take off in a flash.

"We don't have to worry about him again," I say, and close the curtain.

The humor in the event seemed to lighten up the gloom of the house. After lunch I am in good form to begin writing.

1887-1888

The years 1887 and 1888 were the best years since the war. The economy was on an upswing. There were new houses and businesses being built. In an odd way, it gave me a sense of pride seeing the fine houses on the main street. It served as a memory of grander times in Charleston and it was good to see our Southland flowering again.

Mr. Coltrane came into town and opened up a new bank. I must make mention of P. B. Fetzer, who had put in the water works. Now we could all enjoy fresh water in our homes.

Odell Manufacturing was expanding and there was a new mill, Cannon Manufacturing Company. With more opportunities for employment, the population was growing. As the wages went up, so did the people's spirit.

Concord socialites were emerging, forming charity organizations, becoming spokeswomen in the churches and holding rallies for the temperance movement. It is always the wealthy that enjoy that sort of thing. It may serve as an opportunity for them to give back to society, but in my personal opinion, it better serves as an opportunity for them to be seen in their fancy clothes. Nevertheless when there is good being done, one should never question the motivation.

When Captain Odell bought a shipment of fine-blooded horses, he was in need of a trainer. Through the grapevine, he heard of Joel's skills and offered him the position. Joel accepted and for the summer of '87, he did not work in the mill. Joel said Captain Odell had a splendid sense of humor. He named one of his horses "Congress," and when Joel asked why, he told him it was because the horse, just like "Congress," would not pass anything. I was sorry when the summer was over and Joel went back to work in the mill.

North Carolina as a whole was seeing a light at the end of the tunnel. Widows and disabled soldiers were slowly receiving small pensions. It was still a struggle for the Confederate soldiers, even though the Union soldiers got their pension as easy as pie.

That summer we had lemonade socials and we attended baseball games. Robert was a team member and it helped to fill his leisure hours. Still, being the last at home, Robert was restless. Joel offered to help him buy a piece of land, but Robert said farming was not his calling.

Summer passed and it looked like Robert would finish up the year working at the mill. That fall we learned that Ransom had an outbreak of cholera in his hogs. With slaughter season right around the corner, unhealthy animals meant no meat for the winter. Tessie's husband delivered an infusion of tobacco and buttermilk which he guaranteed as a cure.

Ransom was in the pen with the hogs when a large male attacked him, knocked him off his feet and bit a gash out of his leg. He managed to crawl out of the pen and lock the gate before the beast lashed at him again.

A day or two later, Ransom sent word asking if Robert would like to buy his dry good store. Joel and Robert looked over the numbers and by the end of the week, Robert had made his decision. Ransom agreed to teach Robert the ropes and we felt he could make a go of it.

Ransom explained that before he and Sallie were married, he had lived upstairs in the store. Robert liked the idea and with a little remodeling, he moved in shortly before he took over the management.

About two weeks later Joel and I drove down to see how Ransom was getting along. We found him sitting on the front porch and complaining only slightly of the wound. The visit was pleasant until Ransom told us he heard of Robert rambling around town and even going down to Gold Hill. When Joel saw I was upset, he reminded me that Robert was a grown man. He was just sowing a few wild oats and he would be fine once he found a good girl. I was hoping Joel was right, but Sallie said she had smelled whisky and tobacco on Robert's breath a time or two.

I was even unhappy when Lilly reported seeing Robert in the alley with a girl that worked at the hotel. Lilly said she met the girl at Patterson's store. The girl was buying a handful of groceries and came up a few pennies short. Lilly said she gave her the extra money and the girl said her name was Mary and that she had moved here from Gold Hill.

I tried to hide how upset I was with her news. Lilly changed the subject and I did not ask any more questions. I knew the reputation of Gold Hill and anybody coming out of that town had to be trouble or running away from it.

The next day I took 10 silver dollars out of my savings and rode into town to have lunch at the hotel. When I arrived, I told the waiter I would be waiting on a friend and he sat me at a table for two. It was a lie when it left my lips, but before the day was over, it became a truth.

I took out a book to read and delayed ordering. After sitting there for over an hour, the only employees I had seen were a couple of Negro girls, the cook and the waiter. No one could I tag as Mary.

If I did not order soon I was afraid they would charge me rent on the table. When I was called upon again, I would have to order. Suddenly I was inspired when I saw a young woman approaching me.

"Are you ready to order Ma'am? The kitchen will be closing soon," she says, looking down at me with soft green eyes. Her dark blonde hair was tied at the back of her neck, but pieces were hanging astray over her face. She looked tired and unkempt, but not unclean.

I had not once looked at the menu, so I asked for the Wednesday special, even though I had no idea what it might be. She looked at me odd and then left for the kitchen.

I watched her work over the restaurant as she waited for my order to come up. She was wearing a new apron, but the balance of her attire had seen many washings and numerous repairs. She was not wearing stockings and her slippers were scarred and run over.

I was not to wait long before I see her heading my way with an enormous plate of food. "Here you go, Ma'am," she said, setting the plate down.

I looked down at the plate and asked, "Is this what I ordered?"

"Yes Ma'am, you asked for the special. Wednesday's special is double meat, potatoes, green beans and an extra-sized piece of apple pie. I'll be back with your biscuits in a second." She looked as if she was going to laugh, but turned quickly for the kitchen.

It was a plate of food nearly enough for a whole family. In fact, during the war, it would have been two meals. When she came back with the bread, I had not yet touched the food.

"Mary?" I asked, catching her off guard.

"Yes, I am Mary." she replied.

"I am Robert's mother," I said, expecting her to deny knowing him. Instead, I see her lips start to tremble and she makes attempt to curtsy as if I am a queen.

"What time is your shift over?" I asked.

"When the lunch customers are cleared," she replied.

I looked around and the restaurant was empty. I told her I needed an extra plate and she left without asking questions. When she brought the plate, I divided my meal and insisted that she sit down across from me.

She sat down, but only on the edge of the chair. I motioned for her to eat and she obeyed. Once she began to eat, it was clear she was nearly starved.

I saw the waiter first and I knew he was angry. "Mary, this is certainly not acceptable!" Mary jumped out of the chair and began to apologize.

I stood up and faced the waiter. "Sir, did I not say I was waiting for a friend? I have sat here all afternoon waiting for my friend Mary to get off work, so that we might share a plate of food. Is that not acceptable?"

The waiter's face turned beet red. "Oh, yes Ma'am, so sorry." He pulled the chair out for Mary to sit back down and left us alone.

I watched across the table as Mary finished the last of her food. Her features were pleasant, but she was not a beautiful girl. Even though she spoke with a country dialect, she handled herself mannerly and politely.

When she laid her napkin down it was my cue to speak. "Mary, I hear you are from Gold Hill," I say.

She did not answer, but asked a question of me, "I suppose you don't think I am good enough for Robert?"

"Mary, let me be honest with you. I know about Gold Hill. It is like all mining towns. There are far more barrooms than churches and far more dishonest women than honest. I don't know why you came here, but I suspect it is to escape your past. I cannot blame anyone for wanting to better themselves, as long as they don't drag anyone else down in the efforts."

She held her head down and said nothing. My plot to rid her from my son's life now seemed cheap and dishonest. I hesitated, but thinking of Robert's best interest, I reach in my purse.

My original plan was to offer the girl five silver dollars and negotiate with her up to the 10. With her sitting before me, I felt sorry for her and decided to offer her the entire 10. "Mary, do you care for Robert?" I asked.

She then looked up to face me, "Yes, very much so," she says, clearly.

"Then Mary, let your heart be your guide," I stop and study her face.

The coins are in my hand, but something in her eyes has control of my heart. I cannot lift my hand to the table.

"Mrs. Simpson, your words remind me of my mother. She was Cornish and a woman of much faith. Shortly after she came here from England with her parents, she met my father.

Unfortunately, he was killed in a mining accident before I was born. My dear mother mourned that loss the rest of her life. Before she died, she said an angel told her to send me to Concord. She said she could not die in peace unless I made her that promise. She gave me all she had left in the world, which was 10 silver dollars and her last words were, "Mary let your heart be your guide."

I slipped the coins back in my purse. "Mary," I asked, "What does your heart tell you to do about Robert?"

"My heart is Robert's. I love him. He needs a strong woman to keep his feet on the narrow path and Mrs. Simpson, in my heart I know I am that woman."

In my heart, at that very moment, I knew she would be the hand that rocked the cradle of my grandchildren.

December 24, 1887: Robert Edward Simpson and Mary Anne Moyle were married.

November 11, 1888: Aarron Edward Simpson was born.

Dovie came to live with Joel and me in December of 1888.

....

Chapter 17

Midnight Rider

Friday, March 3, 1893

When I open the door to let Rebel out to make his morning rounds, it is 7 o'clock. It is slightly overcast and I can smell the remains of the early morning shower. To tell the truth, I like these soft, cloudy days; it is easier on my eyes. Sunny days make me think I should be going somewhere, but a rainy day gives me permission to stay at home.

Rebel begins barking at something in the ditch. I call him back, but his back bows up and he jumps back. Quickly he darts in and out of the ditch. If he has trapped some sort of varmint, it could be rabid.

I am still in my gown, but I run in the house and grab the fire poker. As I approach the ditch, I hear Rebel yelp and I see the trouble. There is a copperhead coiled up against the bank.

Thinking of my bare feet, I feel a fear rise up inside of me. I grasp hold of the fire poker and close in on the snake. Rebel is in the way and I am afraid I might hit him. "Back Rebel!" I command.

When my view is clear, I raise the fire poker high in the air and come down with a mighty blow. When I recover, I realize I have missed my mark. The snake has coiled up tighter and is hissing at me in retaliation. This excites Rebel more and he is barking nonstop.

Again, I raise the poker and strike. This time I hit the ground so hard that a clump of grass flies up in the air and hits me in the face. I scream, fearing the flying object might be the snake.

Adding to the moment, I hear someone call out, "Did you kill him?" When I spin around, I lose my balance. I am at once struggling to keep from falling in on top of the snake. A large hand reaches out and takes hold of my arm to save me. It is Mr. Lee.

"My dear woman, what a surprise to see you!" he says, smiling.

Suddenly I am aware of my appearance. I brush the dirt off my face and smooth over my hair. My white cotton gown is blotched with red mud and my feet are padded with wet grass.

"Step back," he says. "Let's see if you killed the devil." Without warning, he pulls out his pistol and shoots the snake. "You missed again," he laughs.

My human brain cannot resist looking upon the gruesome sight and the bloody snake makes me nauseous. I drop the poker and run toward the house, hearing Mr. Lee laughing in the background.

When I reach the door, Cindy Lou and Dovie, with the baby in her arms, are standing in the hall. Seeing the look on my face, they step back, giving me a clear path to the bathroom.

After splashing cold water on my face, the feeling passes. It was not the snake, but the sickening memory it brought back. The last time I raised a fire poker was to kill a snake also, but it was Edmond Cook, my first husband.

I comb my hair and brush my teeth. In the midst of the ordeal, I had forgotten about Mr. Lee. Hopefully, he has dropped off my work and has gone on his way. When I step back in the house, I hear him talking to Cindy Lou. He invited himself in.

I slip past the door and into the bedroom to change. When I walk into the front room, he is standing over Cindy Lou admiring her painting. He has one hand on his hip and in the other hand is a cup of coffee. He has made himself at home.

"So there she is," he says, in a teasing tone.

Cindy Lou looks up and smiles, *"I'll leaves yous two alone."* Before I could say anything, she is up and out the door.

Something has caught Mr. Lee's eye out the window and he walks over to get a better look. "Your man is out there collecting the snake. Surely he is not going to eat it," he says.

I glance out the window and see Jasper hauling off the snake. "Mr. Lee, I see you don't know much about Negroes."

"And why would that be?" he asks.

"He is going to extract the poison from the snake. When I was a little girl there were snakes all over the plantation in Charleston. One of the slaves saved Papa's life by making medicine from the very snake that bit him.

"Slaves? Plantation in Charleston?" Mr. Lee asked, squinting his eyes and tilting his head to one side.

"Let me get you some more coffee." I take the coffee cup out of his hand and head quickly to the kitchen. When I return with the coffee, he does not ask any more questions. I am glad. It was a slip of the tongue and I hope he will forget it.

"Lizzie, my mother sent me over to persuade you to have Saturday lunch with us. She has had some fits of melancholy lately. She needs some company and she favors yours. Please say yes for an old woman's sake," he says, stopping to wait for my answer.

"Yes, I will come, Mr. Lee."

"Then for the sake of a foolish and selfish middle-aged man, will you agree to go horseback riding with me after lunch?"

It was the first time Mr. Lee had directly asked for my company. I could see he is serious. "Aah, horseback riding?" I ask, trying to buy myself time before answering.

"Well, if you are not able, we can take the carriage for a ride," he says, trying to encourage my answer.

"Yes, of course I am able to ride a horse," I say, without realizing I have just accepted full heartily his proposal.

"Grand!" he says. "I will be by for you around 11 o'clock tomorrow."

When I close the door behind him, I stand back from the window and watch him mount his horse. He is a fit and handsome man, but I am afraid he is arrogant and prideful. One thing I am sure of, he is a clever lawyer. Today he put me on the defense and I was quick to testify I was young enough to ride a horse. He is clever indeed.

As he rides away, I feel an excitement rise up in my throat. I can no longer deny the attraction between Mr. Lee and myself. It has always been there, but I chose not to acknowledge it. The question in my mind now is, should I ever allow it to come to the surface?

When I turn around, Cindy Lou is standing behind me. She is taller than myself and over the years she has widened too. I feel almost like a little girl standing face to face with her. *"Yous sho got a frisky look on yous face,"* she says.

I push her out of my way gently. "Don't you have better things to do than spy on me?" I tease.

"I reckons I mights, if I had me a good lookin' man likes dat to gets hold of," she says, fanning her face.

"Cindy Lou, we are both too old to have such silly talk. Get yourself upstairs and hush up," I reply.

"Maybe yous is olds, but I ain'ts," she responds, marching up the steps.

Saturday, March 4, 1893

A split skirt and a calico blouse are not the perfect attire for a lunch date, but surely Mrs. Lee will be forgiving. Just to make sure, I will make mention of the afternoon plans shortly after we arrive.

When Cindy Lou sees I am dressed to go out, she is distressed. Her bag is packed and Jasper has brought around the carriage. She says she needs to go home, but she would be back Sunday after church. She assumed it would be my job to take care of Dovie and the baby. It did not set well with them when I said that Jasper should assume the job. After a few huffy remarks, they decide that they will all go to stay at Cindy Lou's for a couple of days.

As they are leaving, I tell Jasper to bring my buggy back this afternoon.

Cindy Lou throws up her hand and they take off. She is annoyed, but she will get over it. We are like sisters and we can afford to be mad at each other. We know each other's history and nothing will ever come between us.

I think back to the old days growing up on the plantation. Mammy was her true mother, but in so many ways, she was mine too. Mammy used to say: *When da Lord made colored children he sprinkled dem with cinnamon, but Miss Lizzie is so sweet, de Lord rolled her in sugar."*

Mr. Lee arrives just on time to pick me up. He smiles when he sees me. "You are ready to ride, I see. Are you a modern woman or just a good old country girl that never took up the notion of riding sidesaddle?"

I laugh at his comment. "Oh, I suppose you will see." I would like to say my Papa once owned some of the finest horses in the country. Furthermore, by the time I was 14, I could ride sidesaddle as well as the queen and astride as well as most men.

Instead, I say nothing of the kind and we walk out together. "Take a look!" he says, pointing at his vehicle. "Just bought this two-wheeler this week. You will be my first passenger. Let me help you in, if you dare. I must warn you she is fast."

I take his hand and climb up in the rig. He runs around and squeezes into the seat beside me. "Is this a French Chaise?" I ask.

He looks at me oddly. "No, but you are close. It is a one-horse shay. Folks call it a "Whisky" because a fellow can whisk all over town in one of these with ease."

The rig is off balance by the weight of Mr. Lee. When we first take off, I grasp the door, thinking we may turn over. Mr. Lee chuckles. I am sure he feels he is impressing me.

As we pass by Mrs. Davis' house, I see the doctor's carriage is parked out front. I turn briefly to look back at the door. "Anything wrong?" Mr. Lee asks.

"No, I guess not," I reply. "I would not have figured on it, but I suppose Henry is getting another electrical jolt." My line opens up the conversation of the electopuncture treatments. Mr. Lee says it sounds like a thing that could stop a person's heart.

It is a windy day, as can be expected for March. I begin to worry if Dovie has the baby's head covered. I have always heard cool air is not good for newborns. Then I consider how warm the day has turned out to be. The baby should be fine.

I learn Mr. Lee lives in the Poplar Tent area of town. When we turn off the main road, he explains that the land has belonged to his family since before the Revolutionary War.

When we cross over a small bridge, I see the house sitting on the hill. It is impressive by its size, but not by its architectural design. It is square with no front porches or pillared columns. On both sides of the door are two pairs of windows.

As we approach the door, Mr. Lee tells me his grandfather designed and built this house as a surprise wedding gift for his grandmother. When they returned from their honeymoon, it was furnished and ready for them to move into.

Men think practical and in straight lines. If the wife had a say so, there would have been at least some nice shutters and a front porch to sit on.

When we walk inside, I smell years of living. There are two Chippendale chairs sitting next to the wall and an oval mirror hangs over them. The wallpaper is old and there are no rugs on the worn plank floors. The vast hall feels cold and damp.

"Come, let's look for mother," Mr. Lee says.

I can hear my steps echo as I follow him to the end of the hall. The door to the small closet under the steps is standing ajar. He closes the door and latches it.

"Mother," he calls out, but there is no answer.

The next room we walk in is far more to my liking. It is a stately room with built-in bookshelves and rich wood paneling. The furnishings are comfortably arranged and well suited for the room.

"Mother!" he calls out again as we walk by the adjacent room. It is a parlor room with upholstered furniture and a pianoforte sitting by the window. I like this room, too.

Mr. Lee shrugs his shoulders. "Maybe she is in the garden."

I follow him around back to a sunny veranda. We stop for a moment and I admire the raised garden beds perfectly aligned in rows. We take the brick pathway through the garden. This time in the loudest voice he calls out, "Mother!"

At the edge of the hedgerow, I see a head pop up. "Aye?" A small dark-skinned man calls back.

"Sam, have you seen my mother?" Mr. Lee shouts back.

The man lays down his rake and starts toward us. "Not since she asked me to cut her some flowers."

"Thanks, Sam. Tell her we are looking for her if you see her."

We walk back in the house and are greeted by Amy, who I learn is Sam's wife. She, too, is looking for Mrs. Lee. "Billy, your mother told me to set the table and then she disappeared." Amy must have worked for the Lee's a long time. I doubt if many people call William Lee "Billy" these days.

Amy goes to check for Mrs. Lee upstairs and Mr. Lee directs me toward the sunroom. By the window is a small table set for three. In the center of the table is an arrangement of buttercups and sweet bubbies. "Lizzie, make yourself at home. Mother has got to be here somewhere. I'll be right back."

He rushes out the door and I sit down to relax. The room is restful, but I am becoming increasingly uneasy. I hear scratching and bumping sounds coming from the hall. The noises get louder and louder. At last, I cannot contain myself. I step out in the hall, but there is no one there. Slowly I start down the hall expecting some sort of beast to attack me. The sound seems to be concentrated underneath the stairwell. Yes, I am certain the noise is coming from the closet. I have my hand on the latch, when I think of Papa's old saying: *"Curiosity can be as dangerous as a butterfly hovering over a flame."* My hand freezes for a second. Then, as if I cannot help myself, I jerk open the door. With one thump, Mrs. Lee flops out on the floor in front of me.

Amy runs out of the kitchen and we help Mrs. Lee to her feet. Her hair is stringing down in her face and perspiration is dripping from her brow. I pull one of the Chippendale chairs out in the middle of the hall and she sits down.

We are waiting for her to catch her breath before we collect the story. She has just begun to speak when Mr. Lee and Sam come in the front door. Seeing his mother in such a state, Mr. Lee rushes to her side.

"I was just looking for my sheet music when someone locked me in the closet!" she cries out.

"Who in the world would do such a thing?" Mr. Lee asks.

"Not me," says Sam.

"And you know I surely did not!" Amy says defensively.

"Then if you two did not, who did?" Mr. Lee asks.

"Maybe it was a ghost!" Sam says, excitedly.

I have solved the mystery in my mind. "It was no ghost," I say. "It was you, Mr. Lee! Do you recall latching the door when we came in?"

All eyes fall on Mr. Lee. He grins sheepishly and folds his arms across his chest.

Mrs. Lee jumps to her feet. "Well, Billy! I was afraid that someday you might lock me up in the insane asylum, but never did I dream you would lock me up in a closet!"

At first we all gasp. Then Mrs. Lee graciously extends her hand to me. "Nice to see you again, Lizzie. Shall we adjourn for lunch? I am starving."

The meal is wonderfully prepared and is presented without incident.

The conversation is engaging. Mrs. Lee tells of the misfortune of a pretty young lady. She married a likely fellow who took her to Augusta, Georgia, but after the honeymoon he deserted her. Her father had to go and deliver her home. They have since discovered the so-called husband has two other wives. If he is caught, they will charge him with bigamy.

"Yes, it is shameful how some men take advantage of our young girls. As parents, we cannot shelter them from everything, but time takes care of a lot of things," I say, ending the conversation. I am thinking of my own dear Tessie.

After lunch, Mrs. Lee gives us a concert on her pianoforte. When she asks if I play, I reluctantly say "yes." She insists I play for them. I know I am by far a better pianist. If I play, I will overshadow her.

Seeing that she would not take "no" for an answer, I walk over to the piano with full intent to miss my notes. However, after I sit down, I glance back over at Mr. Lee. He leans back against the sofa and crosses his legs. His blue eyes are sparkling as he smiles encouragingly. Now I am faced with the battle of my pride.

I am weak-willed to my own vanity. I begin playing by memory "Beautiful Dreamer." When I have finished, I have missed not a single note. When I look up, Mr. Lee is not smiling but his expression is bright. Mrs. Lee claps and says, "Your mother must have been a wise woman to raise such a charming daughter."

Mr. Lee says that we should be heading out if we are to go riding. Mrs. Lee agrees. I ask to freshen up and she sends me in the direction of the bathroom. As I am walking out of the room, I hear her whisper to Mr. Lee, "It is just not typical."

"Shh," Mr. Lee cautions.

I did not turn around and pretended not to hear. I knew what she meant. My upbringing exceeded my status. I was not trying to hide my background, but it would seem boastful to explain.

When I return, they are engaged in a quiet conversation. My calculations tell me they are talking about me. Mr. Lee jumps up. "Shall we take the high road?" he asks, trying to redirect the awkward moment.

The sun is warm as we crunch across the gravel path toward the barn. Mr. Lee asks if I would like to see his new puppies. He says there are six in the litter. When we enter the dog kennel, three fat puppies come waddling out to greet us. Mr. Lee looks around nervously and calls out, "Belle!" Shortly the mother comes out of the shed.

"Where are the rest of your children?" he asks her, patting the dog on the head.

"I can tell you, but you ain't gonna like it." We turn to see Sam standing behind us with a sack in his hand.

"I reckon they squeezed through the fence and something got hold of them," he says, and shakes his head.

"Damn!" Mr. Lee says.

"Yep, and last night something killed a half-dozen chickens."

"Do you figure it was a coyote or a wolf?" Mr. Lee asks.

"Can't be sure, but I am sure this will be the last meal that critter gets." Sam holds the sack up in the air. "I have filled these carcasses with broken glass and wolf poison. I'll hang the meat down by the chicken house tonight. When they grab their free meal, the glass will open up their gut for the poison to do its work."

"What is wolf poison?" Mr. Lee asks.

"It's an old Indian trick, nothing but dried sweet bubbie flowers."

"Who would have thought that a sweet-smelling flower could kill a wolf," Mr. Lee says.

"Lots of things white folks don't know," Sam says as he walks away.

As Mr. Lee and I walk toward the barn, he tells me that Sam and Amy are Cherokee Indians. His father brought them here over 50 years ago. They are still here and he supposes they will die here. "They are like family," he says.

"I know what you mean," I reply.

"Lizzie, the other day you mentioned your father's plantation in Charleston. Are you from Charleston originally?"

"Yes, we came here after the war."

"Do you still have family here?"

"I have only one sister living; she is in Stanly County."

"Is she as pretty as you?" he asks, being coy.

"Prettier," I say, and pick up my step.

The afternoon is enjoyable, but it is sorrowful, too. It is the first time I have been out riding since Joel died. After an hour or so, we arrive at a creek with fresh running water. In the clearing is a cabin.

"Let's take a break," he says, turning in.

We tie off our horses and step up on the porch. The cabin is nicely furnished and it looks as if someone lives there.

"I built this cabin myself," Mr. Lee says.

"I am sure you are proud of your handiwork," I say, as I walk around looking over the place.

"Yes, we were," he replies in a serious tone. "I built it as a getaway for my wife, Ellen."

Not knowing what to say I reply, "I see."

"You look like you could enjoy a place like this, too, Lizzie."

"Yes, it is peaceful here." I know the look in his eyes as he approaches me. If I stand still I am certain he will attempt to kiss me. He reaches out, touches my arm, and for few seconds gazes down at me. Slowly he backs off after giving my hand a slight squeeze. "Lizzie, you are a dear."

"Thank you Mr. Lee."

At my words he responds, "Must you call me Mr. Lee! My name is William."

"How about Billy?" I tease.

I am afraid he is angry when he turns around so quickly. He takes me in his arms and I see passion in his eyes. He lowers his lips to mine and kisses me. It is not a childish peck, but the kind of kiss exchanged between a woman and a man that know the intimacy of marriage.

I did not resist and he pulls me closer, nearly lifting me off my feet. I close my eyes, allow him to stroke my back and kiss my neck. Until that moment, I did not know how much my body craved a man's touch.

The moment is disturbed by a clash of thunder. I push away gently, leaving him panting in the middle of the room. "Looks like a storm is heading this way," I say, and clear my throat.

"No need to worry," he says. "The roof is sound and I even have a bit of whisky in my saddlebag. "Let's just wait it out," he says, smiling and moving again toward me.

"No!" I say forcefully. An image flashes in my mind of my first night with Joel many years ago. I am feeling guilty and I want to go home. My hands are trembling.

"What are you afraid of Lizzie?" he asks, reaching out to stroke my hair.

"Nothing, but it is getting late." I slip on my jacket and head out for the horses.

He stands in the doorway for a moment and watches me mount my horse. Then he follows my lead. There are a few drops of rain, but it appears the storm will pass over us.

His horse is in front of me and I follow. Something inside of me starts to rage. Was this all a plan to take advantage of a poor lonely widow? Did he think I would be weak enough to let him bed me?

When the house is in sight, I slap the horse to speed him. He takes off in a flash, but then begins to buck. I try to hold on, but I feel my body being thrust in the air. My breath leaves me when the earth comes up to greet me.

It is dark when my eyes open again. I have never seen this room before and the bed in which I am lying is unfamiliar. The door is open and I can hear voices in the hall. In a few minutes my mind clears and I determine the voices belong to Billy and his mother.

It is slowly coming back to me. The horse threw me and I was rendered unconscious. I must be in the Lee's home. When I sit up I am at first dizzy, but then the feeling passes and I try to stand. However, there is a sharp pain in my ankle, which causes me to moan.

At once Mrs. Lee appears at the door accompanied by Dr. Ledbetter. I remember him as the doctor that cared for Henry after he was shot. I hope he does not remember me.

He runs to the bed and insists that I lay back down. "What is your name?" he asks, speaking to me as if I am a child.

"Lizzie Simpson," I reply.

"And can you tell me how old you are?" he asks.

I look around the room and I see Mr. Lee standing in the doorway. Mrs. Lee is hovering over me and the doctor has his long nose in my face. "Yes, of course I can, but I see no reason to!" I am increasingly becoming agitated.

"Mrs. Simpson," the doctor says loudly. "You have had a fall and you hit your head. Amnesia is sometimes a result of such accidents."

"My name is Lizzie Simpson. I live on Peachtree Street. I have three children and a dog named Rebel," I say bluntly.

I hear Billy laughing. "May I come in?" he asks.

I look down and pull the sheet up over my chest. I see someone has undressed me down to my chemise. "Yes, please," I say, trying to sit up.

"Lizzie, I feel terrible. That horse has never done that before. Please accept my apology."

"Of course, it was my fault. Now I am feeling so very foolish. If someone can help me get dressed, I will beg you to take me home."

"Home?" the doctor speaks up. "I am afraid that would be a bad idea. I strongly suggest that you stay put for at least two or three days. With your medical history it could jar things in the wrong direction."

"How do you know of my medical history?" I ask, feeling that my privacy has been invaded.

"Mrs. Simpson, the scar on your back is indicative of an old gunshot wound. There could be fragments of metal remaining. I must insist that you give things time to settle, before you submit to being bumped around in a carriage," the doctor says, looking at Mrs. Lee for her approval.

"A gunshot wound?" Mr. Lee asks, looking at me flabbergasted.

"A home invasion following the war," I say softly, hoping that there will be no more questions.

Mrs. Lee speaks up, "Lizzie, you need to rest. Amy and I will tend to you."

"Well, I suppose I have no choice but to impose," I say, accepting my fate.

The doctor begins to gather up his things. "I don't think the ankle is broken, but when the swelling goes down, we can better tell." He turns to Mrs. Lee on his way out. "An ice pack will help. Send for me at once if she becomes lethargic."

They leave me alone to rest. No one in this world but Joel could understand how I feel. But he is not here. If he were, none of this would have happened. I feel helpless and it is as if a bad nightmare is happening to me all over again.

For an undetermined amount of time, I lay there weeping silently. I fear they have forgotten me. I want to go home and I am hungry. If I lay here much longer I might starve, but first my bladder will burst.

Slowly I sit up. My back is sore and my head is throbbing. I raise up my leg and evaluate my ankle. It is bruised and swollen, but since I can move it, I am fairly sure it is not broken. With the help of the nightstand, I am able to lower myself to see under the bed. I am praying there is a chamber pot under the bed.

I am in luck. Just as I drop down on the floor to reach under the bed, the bedroom door opens. It is Amy carrying a tray of food. "Good heavens!" she calls out. She sets the tray down and drops down beside me. "Did you fall?"

"No, I am trying to reach the chamber pot!"

She begins laughing and reaches under for it. "Here you go," she says. "I will be back in a second."

When she returns, she helps me back in bed and sets the tray of food in my lap. While I am eating, she sits down in the chair by the bed. Then she begins to talk. Long after I am finished eating she is still talking. I am to hear her whole life story. She tells of when she was only 16 years old her people were driven off their land. She and Sam hid out in the caves until the soldiers left. Shortly after that Mr. Lee's father was one of the missionaries that found them. She said she had three babies, but they were all born dead. For her,

Billy is like her own son. What else she may have said, I am not sure. I drifted off to sleep thinking my life has became a human comedy.

Sunday, March 5, 1893

There is a faint knock at the door before Amy steps in the room. "Good morning!" she says, in a cheery voice.

She goes to the window and opens the curtains. The fresh sunlight hurts my eyes. "Mrs. Lee and Billy have gone to church. I will fix you a toilet, if you wish."

"Yes, that would be nice. I would like to dress. Where are my clothes?" I ask.

"I have washed them. They were covered with mud. Seems the horse slipped and caused the whole thing."

She left the room and returned with a washbasin and my clothes. "Holler if you need me," she says, closing the door behind her.

My body is sore, but I have little trouble taking care of my needs and dressing. It is impossible for me to put a boot on the injured foot; it is too swollen.

In my stocking feet, I hobble over to the mirror. My hair is a tangled mess and there is a bruise on the left side of my face. I feel like a spy, but I open the dresser drawers hoping to find a comb, brush or a few hairpins. The drawers are all empty. I am sure that no one stays in this room.

I sit down in the chair and wait. What I am waiting for I am not sure.

From the window, I have a bird's-eye view over the property. I see fields laid out and a number of outbuildings. There is no sign of life except the horses in the pasture.

It is not long before Amy is back. As if she has read my mind, she hands me a brush and some hairpins. "Oh, I almost forgot," she says, and steps back outside the door. "I found these in the attic. See if you can use them."

She hands me a pair of handmade crutches. "Thank you," I say. I stand up and try them out. "I think I can manage."

"I will help you downstairs if you like."

"Yes, maybe I can go home," I reply.

"We will see," she says, making up the bed.

First, I try to balance myself with the crutches on the steps. Amy steps in front to make sure I do not fall. The steps are slick and I anticipate a disaster if this be my only choice. She reaches for the crutches and leans them against the railing. "Sit down on the step and lower yourself step by step," she says.

It is a most ungraceful process and my arms tire after the first few steps. I plop down on one and then wiggle forward to drop down on the next step.

I am halfway down when the front door opens. I hear Mrs. Lee before I see her. She is talking loudly to someone behind her. I feel my face turning red, expecting to see Billy behind her. Then flipping in through the door, waving her arms, is a slim-figured woman in a big hat. The moment I hear her voice I know who it is. It is the pink-dressed woman.

She had referred to me as the nursemaid that night at the opera, but now she will take me for the scrubwoman. What else will she think when she looks up and sees me mopping up the floor with my bottom. Amy and I both freeze. She knows I would rather not be seen in such an impolite position.

When Billy comes in, the woman is too busy flirting to look up the stairs. I watch him help her with her coat and Mrs. Lee starts down the hall. Then quickly Billy turns around. "You ladies go on in the parlor and I will join you shortly."

The moment he starts up the stairs he sees me. "Lizzie! What in the world has happened?" The tone of his voice sparks curiosity in both women and they come rushing to look up the stairs.

There I sit, flat on my bottom and the three of them peering up the stairs at me.

Amy speaks up, "I was helping Mrs. Simpson down the stairs. She can't bear no weight on her foot."

"Here, let me help. I think we can do better than this," Billy says, laughing. Then with one quick scoop, he picks me up and carries me down the stairs.

He walks past his mother and the woman. I can hear them whispering as they follow along behind us. Once in the parlor, he sits me down in a chair by the window. "I'll be back down shortly," he says, and heads back upstairs.

"Mrs. Simpson, it is?" she asks. I only nod. "Agnes tells me you have had some sort of riding accident. It must have been quite serious, judging by the sight of you," she says, squinting her eyes.

"Not terribly; the horse slipped and tossed me off," I said, covering up the bruise on the side of my face with my hand. Women of her kind are often talented in dishing out insults that look like compliments. I am braced, waiting for her poison comeback.

Oh, but this time I may have underestimated her skills. She does not answer at all, but turns directly to Mrs. Lee. "Darling, I had something like this happen once. A man slipped on my front stoop. He said he was not hurt and I thought nothing more of it, until he came back a month later dragging his lawyer with him. He said as a result of the fall he was rendered unfit, he lost his job, his wife left him and he was in debt with medical bills. It could have gone worse for me. Still the judge made me pay all his medical bills. If only I had called a doctor as a witness the day of the accident, I would not have had to pay a penny."

I could tell where she was going with this and my blood was boiling. If I could get out of this chair, I would walk home.

She leans forward and pretends to whisper to Mrs. Lee. "William being a lawyer himself, I am sure he knew to send right away for the doctor."

"Yes, but nothing like that occurred to us. We were only concerned for Lizzie," Mrs. Lee says, looking over at me tenderly.

"Oh, and rightfully so," the woman says. "A bruise like that is nothing to be taken lightly. I hope it does not leave a permanent mark." She walks over and looks down at me. "I am sorry with the drama of your entrance, we were not formally introduced. I am Bertha Harris Collins. I know you may have heard of me, as a shameful sort," she laughs. "Yes, thanks to William I am now divorced and fancy free. I say life is too short for any woman to spend it unhappy. Do you not agree, Mrs...?" she says, leaving an opening for me to finally speak.

"I am Theodosia Simpson," I reply, without feeling any need to supply her with any of my own personal information.

"Are you a divorced woman too?" she says, thinking she is being clever.

"No no, my husband Joel died."

"Oh well, I was afraid my husband, Colin, would have lived forever just for spite. That is why I had to divorce him," she says. I know she is teasing, but I find her comments in the worst of taste. She laughs at her own joke and ends with an embarrassing series of snorts. Mrs. Lee as the hostess feels obligated to snicker, but I turn my head. I see no need to reward bad manners.

Mrs. Lee makes an attempt to engage in a more genteel conversation. Bertha is bragging about the dress she will be wearing for her daughter's wedding. The dressmaker claims there have been only two other women who have ever owned a dress made of American silk. One is Mrs. Garfield and the other is Mrs. Tom Thumb. I think it is likely humbug. Her lips are flapping, but I have stopped listening to her words. I am thinking about what she said earlier. She is Colin Collins' former wife!

I am trying to work it all out in my mind. It is slowly making sense to me. It was never about me. It was all about Bertha. I have the feeling Billy and Colin were once friends, but the divorce must have iced up their friendship.

My temper begins to rise, just thinking about how they both have used me. Neither one of them are interested in me. They just wanted to make each other jealous. In Charleston, we called men like them "hound dogs." One thing for sure: those dogs will not be running this rabbit again.

As soon as I get a chance to talk to "Billy," I am going to speak my mind.

From now on, it is strictly business between us, "Mrs. Simpson" and "Mr. Lee." I hope I never see Colin Collins again.

My thoughts end when "Mr. Lee" enters the room. "Ladies, I hope you have not missed me too much," he jokes. The truth is, he likely thinks we are pining over him. In his mother's eyes he can do no wrong. My guess is he is having an affair with Bertha Collins and yesterday he plotted to seduce me. Maybe he had to run upstairs after church and add a few more names to his list.

As soon as he sits down I ask, "Mr. Lee, can I trouble you to make arrangements for Sam to take me home?"

"Oh no, Lizzie, the doctor said you should not be jarred for several days."

"I really need to go home and besides, I am intruding on your day." I look over at Bertha and my words bring a satisfied grin upon her face.

Mr. Lee walks over and kneels down beside my chair. "Lizzie, I will not hear of it. You are welcome to stay as long as you like. I must insist you stay at least one more night." I am confused by the sincerity in his voice, but like they say, watch out for a wolf in sheep's clothing.

I am trapped in the Lee's house at least for one more night. There is nothing to do but make the best of it. Lunch is served and I make my way to the table with the use of the crutches.

As soon as the meal is over, Mr. Lee announces he has some pressing business and he will need to be gone for a couple of hours. Mrs. Lee looks disappointed, but Bertha just smiles. "Hurry back, love, or else I will be gone when you return."

Mrs. Lee suggests we play a card game. I accept, but Bertha declines. She prefers to relax and chat in the sunroom.

In the beginning, Bertha is the only one talking. She talks in circles of random things. We hear about her daughter's wedding plans and the trip they will take to see the World's Fair. She agrees that women should have more rights, but disagrees with the temperance movement. She thinks if a person wants to have a drink it is their right.

She says, "Most of the women that are in favor of the temperance movement are ugly old bats. It is not strong drink that keeps their men away from home." I try not to laugh even though her statement may hold a great deal of truth.

By the time she gets around to talking about bustles and hats, I am yawning. Mrs. Lee is working on her needlework and I wager she has not listened to a word of it.

For some reason, I start to feel sorry for Bertha. I cannot quite decide why she is here. She goes over to the table and picks up the newspaper. She shakes out the paper loudly and spreads it out to read.

On the stand next to me is a stack of books. I sort through the titles hoping to find something of interest. For a few minutes, the room is filled only with the sound of turning pages and Mrs. Lee's knitting needles clicking together.

Then Bertha begins to share the news with us. "The county coroner has resigned," she reads out. "Says here, he retired due to a sudden onset of nerves. They are accepting applications for the position."

I start laughing and they both look up at me surprised. "Do you know something about this?" Mrs. Lee asks.

"No, no, but I can certainly see how that could be a nerve-racking job," I lie.

But secretly, I suspect it has something to do with Dovie's baby. I guess we scared the daylights out of the old fellow.

There is a knock at the door and Bertha jumps up and looks at her watch. "Well, here is Willie right on time to pick me up." She walks over to Mrs. Lee, gives her a peck on the cheek and then nods to me. "Nice to see you, Theodosia."

Mrs. Lee does not get up to walk her out. After the door is closed, she walks out in the hall and calls for Amy. When she returns she folds up her knitting and lets out a loud sigh. "That girl never stops talking. After she leaves I feel like I have been run through the mill!"

I am trying to think of a proper response when Amy comes in with a tray. I see a bottle of wine, cheese and bits of bread. "Let's drink to some peace and quiet."

We spend the afternoon alone; Mrs. Lee dozes in her chair and I read. When supper is served, Mr. Lee is still not home. It is after dark when he returns. He offers no explanation to where he has been, but he is polite and of good spirit.

Around 9 o'clock, he retires to his room. Mrs. Lee offers to have Amy help me upstairs, but I ask to sleep on the sofa. I explain that first thing in the morning I must go home. I have left my house unattended too long. She is agreeable to my request and in a few minutes, Amy brings me a blanket, a pillow and a glass of water.

In less than 30 minutes, the house is quiet. I make myself a cozy bed and pick up the book I started earlier. It is a clever book, "Peck's Bad Boy and His Pa." The boy's mischievous escapades remind me of Robert when he was a boy.

I have just read a few pages when I hear a noise. I gasp when I see a huge, ghostly figure moving around in the hall. I pull the blanket up around my neck and listen. I hear a rustling sound moving up the stairs and in a few minutes it is back down again.

As the footsteps get closer, I am afraid I might scream. When the figure steps out in the dim light, I see it is not a ghost. It is Mr. Lee. He is dressed in a long, white robe and in his hand is a white cap. I draw up as he passes down the hall; he does not see me. Shortly I hear a horse leaving.

There is much I do not know about Mr. Lee, but tonight I know one of his secrets. He is a midnight rider with the Ku Klux Klan.

Chapter 18

Marriage Bond

Monday, March 6, 1893

I am awakened the next morning by the aroma of coffee and the savory sweet smell of bacon. I sit up quickly and search around for my purse. Once it is located, I take out my mirror and a handkerchief. I have no basin to wash my face, but I am a woman who has learned to be resourceful. I dip my handkerchief in my glass of water and wipe over my face. I take my hair down, run my fingers through the tangles and pin it back up.

When Amy walks in, I am standing up trying to smooth out the wrinkles in my clothes. She asks if I would like her to press them. "No, that will be alright," I reply. "I don't think I look too unsightly. I will be going home this morning."

"Oh," she says, looking surprised.

"Amy, would it trouble Sam too greatly to drive me home."

"I am sure he will be happy to take you home, but I insist you stay for breakfast."

"Then I insist on staying; I am starving," I joke back at her.

I follow Amy into the kitchen; there is no one at the table but Mr. Lee.

"Good morning," he says. He looks at me intensely for a moment. I wonder if he is trying to read my mind or eyeing my morning appearance.

"Good morning. Will your mother be joining us?" I ask.

"I expect not; she likes to sleep late. Amy usually takes something up to her room."

I hear the back door slam and Sam comes in quietly and sets a basket of eggs on the counter. He nods and walks back out. From the window, I see Amy walking up to greet him. Sam kisses her on the cheek and they walk off toward the barn hand in hand.

Mr. Lee notices I have witnessed the scene. "They were put on this earth for each other." I make no reply and stare out the window, thinking of Joel.

"Lizzie, look at me," he says. "I need to explain to you about Bertha."

"There is nothing you need to explain," I say, turning to look him in the eye.

"Yes there is. Bertha is my cousin," he says and reaches across the table for my hand.

"Cousin?" I look up surprised.

"Yes, bless her heart. Her father was nothing but a drunkard. When her mother died, she came to live with us. She was 12 or 13 years old at the time. She was rough as a cob and Mother took it upon herself to mold Bertha into a social butterfly. I am not sure if Mother went too far or Bertha tries too hard. The point being, I would like to offer my apologies if she said anything offensive to you."

"Poor dear, I had no idea," I say. "Do you think her past haunts her?"

"Of course. Does the past not haunt us all?" he comes back with.

"Indeed it does," I say, softly. I pull my hand back and return to my food.

"Lizzie, this town is full of pretenders like Bertha. All hoping to better themselves by their ways, means and the company they keep. I myself have been guilty of the same sins. However, I am in a position now that it makes little difference to me what anyone thinks. Do you know what I mean?"

"I have given up long ago on such fruitless worries, Mr. Lee."

"I know, Lizzie, that is one of the things I admire about you. You are like an open book and make no pretense about it."

"Is that how you see me, an open book?" I ask.

"Well, not exactly. What I am trying to say is I admire you for not trying to "up" yourself by pretending to be something you are not."

"Mr. Lee, let me tell you one thing. I feel no need to "up" myself. What would you say if I told you my father was once one of the richest men in Charleston? Or if you knew, I once lived the grand social life of a Charleston Belle?"

"Lizzie, I was not attacking you. There is no need to make up fantasies."

"Fantasies! First you imply I am sociably beneath you, now you are questioning my sanity." Before he can offer up a rebuttal, there is a knock at the kitchen door.

Amy sticks her head in the door. "Lizzie, there is a colored man at the front door asking about you." I jump from the table, hobble to the door and see Jasper standing on the porch.

"Misses Lizzie, we's wuz worried!" he calls out, when he sees me.

"I know, I should have sent word. I had a riding accident, but I am all right now.

"I's gots bad news. Misses Davis is deads," he blurts out.

"What happen?" I ask.

"Theys fount her dead in da bed, on Satday mornin," he says, shaking his head.

I think back quickly and remember seeing the doctor's carriage out front when Mr. Lee came to get me. I have only been gone two days, but suddenly I feel like it has been years. "Rebel!" I call out.

"Yous dog is fines, but Misses Lilly sho needs yous. Da funeral it bes todays."

"Wait here, I'll get my purse," I say, turning around to see Mr. Lee and Amy standing in the hall behind me.

"Amy hands me my purse, "Thank you for everything," I say, reaching out to give her a quick hug.

"You come back to see us," she says.

"Lizzie, I am on my way into town now. Let me drive you," Mr. Lee offers.

"No thank you, I'll ride with Jasper." I open the door and Jasper helps me to the carriage. "Good-bye all," I call back.

I briefly give some thought to the doctor's warning of being jarred, but I feel no pain on the way home.

As we turn down the lane, I see a line of buggies on the street. There is a funeral wreath on Mrs. Davis' door and the curtains are drawn.

Dovie greets me at the door. *"Miss Lizzie, Momma says yous mights be at da lawyer's house. We had an awful times finding yous. I's afraid yous gots mads and left us all."*

"I pat her on the back. "No, not hardly."

Cindy Lou comes out of the kitchen and I explain briefly about the accident before I go to prepare myself for the funeral.

When I walk in Mrs. Davis' house, there is a soft buzz of voices. In the parlor I am hoping to see Mrs. Davis sitting by the fireplace laughing, but this time she did not cheat death. I see her casket.

I do not see Henry or Lilly, but Les is standing in the corner. Before I can limp my way through the crowd, he sees me. He waves and starts my way. I want to find out what happened and Les will know. Before he can reach me, I see Lilly coming down the stairs.

"Lizzie!" she cries out. "Where have you been?"

I am not able to answer before she grabs hold of me and begins to weep. My ankle is having enough trouble holding me up, but now I have the weight of Lilly too. Our entwined bodies stumble, but she does not notice. I grab hold of the stair railing to keep us from falling.

Les comes to my rescue and takes hold of Lilly. "Lilly, let's go sit down. It will be time to go to the church soon."

As he guides her into the kitchen, he looks over at me. His eyes are saying, "I have something to tell you."

Lilly plops down in a chair. Les walks over and pours us both a cup of coffee.

"Where is Henry?" I ask.

"He should be back anytime now. He had a meeting with his new boss. I know it is poor timing, but it was urgent."

"New boss?" I ask.

"Yes, he has taken the job as the county coroner. It seems the old one resigned unexpectedly. Mrs. Davis' doctor knew Henry was looking for work and they offered him the position. He was to start today, but under the circumstances he will begin next week."

"Oh I see," I reply to him. Then I turn to Lilly, "I am so sorry. You are holding up so well, dear." I see she is not, but perhaps my comment will give her some encouragement.

We sit quietly sipping our coffee until Henry comes in the back door. When Henry and Lilly begin to talk, Les motions for me to meet him in the hall. He slips out first and I join him.

"Lizzie, I am so angry I don't know what to do," he says, wringing his hands.

"What has happened?" I ask.

"That damn doctor should have known better than to administer such controversial treatments to an old woman. You can be certain those electopuncture treatments damaged her heart. "Her heart just stopped." He would have liked to say more, but Lilly and Henry interrupted us.

Lilly insists I ride with the family to the church. The funeral was more elaborate than I would have expected for Henry and Lilly's budget. I assumed Les had taken care of the expenses until he made a similar comment. We agreed that it was odd. He said he was going to ask them if they need his financial assistance.

When we return it is after 5 o'clock. I am tired and ready to go home, but Lilly begs me to stay for supper. She begins to pull out food the neighbors have brought and sets the table. None of us have much of an appetite, but I suppose she needs to keep busy.

While we are eating, Les brings up the funeral. "I don't know when I have seen such a nice service, Lilly. I hope it did not stress your budget too badly."

"Oh no," she says. "I paid for it with my spare money."

"Spare money?" Les asks.

"My widow's pension. I saw no reason to turn it down after all these years, just because Henry and I got married. When the checks started coming I just kept them."

I see trouble and so does Les. It is more his place to deal with the issue than myself. It seems to be of no concern to Henry, who is busy stuffing his face with a piece of pie.

"It is getting late and my ankle is giving me pain. I suppose I should hobble back home." I stand up and make my way to the door.

"Would you like me to take a look at it Lizzie?" Les asks.

"No, it is only a sprain. It will just take a couple of days to heal. Good night all."

When I return home, I find Rebel lying on the doormat waiting for me. The last couple of days have been like a whirlwind. I left Saturday to go out for the afternoon and here it is Monday night. I have been laid up in a stranger's home and Mrs. Davis is dead.

Dovie's baby starts to cry upstairs and then I hear the rushing sound of footsteps running across the hall. What would Joel say about the state of things? I have lost control of everything, the children rarely visit and I have given up my home to Dovie and Jasper.

On the hall table, I see three letters addressed to me. I pick them up and walk across to the front room. The light in the hall is like a halo illuminating my painting hanging over the mantle. With the letters in my hand, I flop down in a worn chair.

There she is smiling down at me. My thoughts go back to the days when I sat for Antonio to paint my portrait. Our paths crossed for only a few short weeks, but his presence is still here living in the brush strokes of my face. I recall what he said the day he left, "A Gypsy's never in one place long enough to own its grief." He was mysteriously handsome and in my mind, he is forever young. I wonder if he ever thinks of me.

In the dark I pray softly, *"Dear Lord, please give me the wisdom, the courage and the strength to do your will."* (The words of my favorite hymn run through my mind— I once was lost, but now I am found.) *"Find me Lord; I am lost, Amen."*

After a few minutes, I turn on the light. The letters are from Mr. Collins, Victoria and an insurance company. I have no idea, why the American Insurance Company would be sending me a letter. Joel had a life insurance policy, but it has already paid out. I nervously open the letter.

Dear Mrs. Simpson,

It has been called to our attention that the life insurance policy owned by Joel E. Simpson has not been claimed. Our records indicate he died on August 5, 1892.

We apologize in our delay in contacting you. However, the circumstances of the policy required legal considerations before the death benefits could be properly assigned.

This policy was issued 1859 and at that time, Joel E. Simpson was married to Amanda Cooper Simpson. Our investigation finds that she is also deceased and there were no children from that marriage.

It is our belief that you were Mr. Simpson's lawful wife at the time of his death. Therefore, you are entitled to all and any benefits payable from this policy. We kindly ask that you provide us documentation of your marriage. Once we receive this information, we will promptly make payment directly to you as the beneficiary.

Most sincerely,
Jack M. Taylor

I think back to the day Joel and I were married on Sallie's front porch. To the best of my knowledge, the marriage bond is in the family Bible. I lay down the other two letters and go across to the office.

On the top shelf is the old leather Bible. I can smell the old paper as I gently turn the gold-gilded pages. I see my grandmother's handwriting in fancy old English lettering. On the pages are tears of my ancestors as they recorded deaths and marriages of their loved ones.

There it is. I take it out of the envelope and read over it. *On this day May 2, 1865, I, Reverend Herman Furr, joined in holy matrimony, Theodosia Elizabeth Sanders Cook and Joel Edward Simpson.* Underneath I see the names Ransom and Sallie Huneycutt as witnesses.

This should do. I attempt to slip the marriage bond back in the envelope, but it catches on a folded piece of paper. I gently unfold the yellowed paper, but it tears in the creases as I open it up. I lay it down on the desk and piece it together to read.

Joel, I wish you and Lizzie the best. May God bless you with many happy years together. Please take the marriage bond to the Stanly County Courthouse to be recorded.

Your friend,
Herman Furr

I feel my face flush as I realize this document was never filed. In the excitement, it was placed in the Bible and never opened again. Could it be after all these years we were never legally married? If so, all our children are illegitimate, too.

After pacing back and forth across the floor, I decide the only thing to do is go to Mr. Lee. It might be embarrassing, but surely he will be able to advise me.

I walk slowly down the hall toward the bedroom. I am thinking in my head: death takes the body, but those we love live forever in our hearts. "Joel," I say aloud. "You will always be in my heart."

I undress and slip under the covers when I remember the other two letters. I close my eyes with thoughts of waiting until the morning to read them. After a few minutes, my eyes pop open. I run down the hall to read the letters.

I open Mr. Collins' first, thinking it will be brief and of little importance.

Dear Lizzie,

I have thought of you often since the last time I saw you, even though I tried not to. I know it has been less than a year since your husband died. Most women feel it proper to wait a year before thinking of the future.

Forgive me if my words sound unfair, but at our age most of life is behind us. A year is a long time. Perhaps I am being selfish, but if you feel your heart and mind are ready, I would like you to consider me as a serious suitor.

I seldom find company as delightful as yours. If romance is not in our future, I am certain a friendship will be.

Say you will do me the honor in having dinner with me again this Saturday night.

I await your response.
Most humbly yours,
Colin Collins

His letter is odd timing. Maybe we have more in common than I thought. If the truth is known, people could shun us both. He is a divorced man and I was never legally married to the man I lived with. I think I will accept his invitation. He sounds lonely, but I suspect he does not miss his former wife Bertha.

I find myself laughing over the whole thing as I tear into Victoria's letter.

Dear Mother,

Sit yourself down, for the words I am about to tell you will surely come as one of the greatest shocks in your life. It was a most unexpected happening for me too. I have wanted to write you before now, but until I was certain, I restrained.

Mother, I am in love! The grandest news of all is that my love loves me too.

He has asked me to marry him and I have said YES! Oh, Mother, I hope the news fills you with as much happiness as it does me.

Mere words cannot explain how wonderful he is. He is most kind and a talented physician. I met him while volunteering at the hospital following the earthquake. Of course, we spent long hours together working and aiding the needs of others.

He is from England and has the most charming way of speaking. He calls me "Vicky." Isn't that dear?

We are planning on a June 6 wedding and a honeymoon trip to England to meet all his family. Please say you will come to Charleston for the wedding or else I will come to North Carolina and drag you back with me. If you need me to send money for the train ticket, just let me know.

With love,
Vicky

PS: Please tell Robert and Tessie I am not going to be an old maid after all.

"Vicky" is right. This is a shock. I never dreamed she would allow herself to fall in love again. She seemed so settled in her ways. Nothing will keep me from going to her wedding. I am beyond happy with her news. I hope she has made a wise choice and nothing happens this time.

By the time I am back in bed, even though my body is tired my mind is racing. So much for one day: a funeral and Victoria's wedding plans. If that is not enough there is the issue of my marriage bond. Lastly, I know soon, I will have to seriously consider my feelings for Mr. Collins and Mr. Lee. One thing for sure, life is constantly changing. No wonder we are taught to take it one day at a time.

I drift off to sleep wondering if the insurance money could be enough to pay for a train ticket to Charleston.

Tuesday, March 7, 1893

It is just before 7 o'clock in the morning when I open the door for Rebel. He runs out barking and nipping at the wheels of a bicycle passing by on the street. At first, I did not recognize the rider, until I hear Henry's voice. "Damnit Rebel, you are going to cause me to run into the tree!"

"Rebel! Come back here." I shout.

Henry drops his foot and brings the cycle to an awkward stop. "Lizzie, sorry I did not see you standing there. How do you like my new wheels?"

"Rather impressive. Is this how the new County Coroner makes his rounds?"

"Yes. Cheaper to keep than a horse, and with the new brakes, this thing will stop on a dime," Henry laughs.

"I hope you don't have to haul any bodies in that little luggage rack," I call back.

Henry waves goodbye and Rebel runs past me on his way to the kitchen.

Seconds later, I hear Dovie in the kitchen, *"Getz downs or I's gonna bat yous with dis spoon."*

I run to the kitchen. I see the baby sleeping in a basket and Rebel on his hind legs trying to reach the bacon on the counter. "Rebel!" I call out. "You are being a bad boy this morning."

"He sho is. He's done and ate two pieces fer I coulds getz hold of him," Dovie says, in a frenzy.

"Let it be my two pieces," I reply, and pick up the newspaper.

"Where is your Mother?" I ask, as I spread the paper out across the table.

"Jasper took her home fer good."

"So soon?" I ask, looking up at her.

"Da baby is done a week old, Miss Lizzie. We is managin' fine."

"I will miss her," I reply, and turn back to my newspaper. My eyes scan over the main headlines:

The cigarette business is doomed: People wise up to the health hazards and the smoking craze is rapidly declining.

Yellow Fever and Temperance: those that drink liquor are less likely to recover.

The Baptist Church rejects man with wooden leg: It appears the Baptist preacher refused to baptize a veteran of the late war in the holy water. He claimed his wooden leg was not flesh and blood. The man has since joined the Methodist Church where they welcomed him, flesh, blood and wood.

The Hinson's milk cow was struck by lightning in Friday's storm.

Social Equality: will it ever be reached?

Divorce rate in U.S. is highest in the world: Laws are expected to tighten up all over the country. North Carolina now prohibits divorce altogether.

The last headline reminds me of Colin Collins and Bertha. If the union was unfit, it is best they got their divorce when they did.

I close up the paper when Dovie sets a plate of pancakes down in front of me. My first bite tells me something is different. "Dovie, why do these pancakes taste strange?"

"Yous ain'ts used to da new butter," she says.

"Do you mean margarine?" I ask.

"I reckons. It taste all rights once you gets used to it ands its a sight cheaper dan real butter."

"Dovie, this bogus butter is nothing but hog fat mixed with yellow dye. Don't buy this stuff again. President Cleveland tried to pass a law against it. Not only is it bad for you, it is putting the dairy farmers out of business."

She shakes her head and watches me scrape it off my pancakes. I take a second bite and again I ask, "The pancakes still taste odd. Is this a new recipe?"

"It bes Aunt Jemima ready mix. Alls you do is add water," she says, proudly.

"Don't buy that either. If you do not want to make the pancakes from scratch, I will make them myself. I don't want these things again," I say bluntly, and push the plate away.

"I's sorry," she says, with tears in her eyes.

At once, I realize how harshly I have spoken. "No, it is I that should be sorry. I know you were just trying to help. Let's just stay with the old ways as long as we are able."

I pull the plate back in front of me and begin to eat. I lost my bacon to Rebel and these modern pancakes are all there is. Best not to waste.

After breakfast I dress and go straight to the office to write a reply to Mr. Collins. I also compose a letter to Tessie and Robert to tell them of Victoria's wedding plans. They will be as shocked as I was. Once Jasper is on his way to the post office, I turn my mind toward the rest of the day.

I part the curtains so I can see if Mr. Lee comes by to drop off a report. I have considered the marriage bond issue over night. First, I will ask Mr. Lee to inquire about the amount of the benefits. It is likely it is not even enough to rectify the trouble it will cause. In my eyes, the marriage was legal. That is enough for me.

I have been away from my writing too long. Since I will be going to Charleston in June, I now have a new incentive to finish my book. Perhaps I could give a copy to Victoria for a wedding gift. Unfortunately, the hardest year to write about is yet to come. For the year 1892, I will not need a scrapbook to refresh my memory.

When I reach up on the shelf for my scrapbooks marked 1889 and 1890, I see a thin line of mouse droppings. I put down the books and go to the pantry to look for rat poison. There is none there. I leave a note for Jasper along with 15 cents.

Jasper-please go to Wadell's for a box of "Rough on Rats."

I return to my office. I take out a sheet paper and open up the first scrapbook. The headlines are neatly pasted on the pages:

With today's modern conveniences, Americans are enjoying more leisure time.

Everyone is playing ball! Baseball, football, golf, tennis and now the ladies enjoy lawn tennis and croquet.

Thomas Edison has given the world another wonder! Moving picture show.

March 4, 1889 Benjamin Harrison becomes the 23rd president of the U.S.

North Dakota and South Dakota dispute over the order they will be admitted into the Union. President Harrison chose the order alphabetically. North Dakota as #39 and South Dakota as #40.

More states admitted to the Union: Montana #41 and Washington #42.

St. Helena, Montana, has more millionaires per capita than any other city in the world.

The great race to the west continues! More former Indian lands are opened up to white homesteaders. It is getting wild in the west lands!

1890-Indian braves say the solar eclipse has made them invincible to the white man's bullets. The darkening of the sun is a sign from the Great Spirit.

September 2, 1889: Charlie D. Graham goes over Niagara Falls in a wooden barrel.

I have just picked up my pen to begin my outline for the next chapter when there is a knock at the door. I glance out the window hoping to see Mr. Lee, but it is a young man in a courier's uniform. He has a small package in his hand.

I am not expecting anything; perhaps it is for Jasper or Dovie. When I open the door the young man ask, "Are you Mrs. Simpson?" I nod and he hands me a small package. "Good day," he says and hurries back to his wagon.

I take the box into the office and open it. Wrapped in a white handkerchief I am amazed to see a gold locket that belonged to my mother. I discovered it missing shortly after a man came from Lancaster's to install the linoleum floor in the kitchen. Joel said that he may have stolen it, but I assumed I had lost it.

There is a note accompanying the locket:

Dear Mrs. Simpson,

Two years ago you trusted me in your home to install flooring. When I saw this locket on the windowsill, I stole it. Most recently, I have received the Gospel and my heart has changed. I wanted to return it to you.

The locket is shined and polished. I clasp it around my neck. "Yes, good will always rise to the surface," I say aloud. I return to my writing:

1889-1890

It was a hot afternoon in late September of '89. I was walking to the post office when an old gray-haired Negro man driving a wagon passed by. His woman was sitting high on top of their few precious bales of cotton they hoped to turn into cash. It was not an unusual sight to see Negro tenant farmers crossing the intersection of Spring and Barbrick on the way to the cotton warehouse, but something about this sight seem to evoke a feeling of sadness.

The man was missing a leg and in its place was a home-made wooden peg. His face was weathered and his expression was one of only survival. The woman was small and fragile with a distant look on her face. She looked familiar to me.

As they went on down the road, I disregarded the emotion as only the woman reminded me of Mammy. Then it hit me. It was Violet! I took off running after the wagon, forgetting I was a grown woman and people would be staring.

I know you have forgotten Violet and her husband Harper, so I will refresh your memory. They were former slaves of Papa's. When Ransom and Sallie got married, Papa sent them to North Carolina. After the war, they took up sharecropping and we lost contact with them.

I had given up running and was out of breath by the time I was in sight of the cotton warehouse. The woman was standing by the wagon and the one-legged man was negotiating terms with the supervisor.

The one-legged man turned away from the supervisor and started hobbling back to the wagon. I was afraid they would drive off. I called out at the top of my voice, "Violet!"

Slowly the woman turns her head and looks my way. I pick up my step and start running again. She points to me and the man starts to smile. Just as I near them, I hear Harper say, "Lizzie!"

They were not just slaves to me. It was a reunion of family. The three of us huddled together and for a moment, I was transformed to the days of my youth in their arms.

The supervisor calls out, "Mr. Harper, do we have a deal or not?"

Harper calls back, *"I spects so."*

Violet and I visited while the men did business. She told me Harper had lost his leg in a mining accident while working at the old Rocky River Mine. She smiled when she told me they finally had a son, 20 years ago.

After the cotton transaction, we walked up to the drug store. Violet and Harper waited outside and I went inside and got us all a fountain Coca-Cola. We sat down under a tree and enjoyed the drink. Violet said it was too strong for her, so Harper drank hers, too. When they had to leave, Harper gave me an Indian head penny. I carry it in my purse always. I told them where we lived and they promised to visit, but I have not seen them since.

'89 and '90 were golden years for Joel and me. The children were all out on their own and we were alone except for Dovie. It was a gentle time for us. I had carefree days to work in my garden, to read and visit friends.

Joel was made a supervisor at Capt. Odell's Mill. The mill now had 5,000 spindles and 356 looms in operation.

Some of the workers left Odell Mill to work for the Cannon Mill. It was an impressive new two-story building, with 130 looms and 4,160 spindles. The factory was built on 40 acres and there was land for workers to build homes and tenant houses to lease. The grounds were kept neat and clean and the company store was a draw, too.

With the mills using 30 to 40 bales of cotton a week, the cotton market was a busy place. The whole town was mushrooming around the steady growth of the cotton factories. Its money trickled down to every business, every home and every pocket.

Robert was becoming quite the merchant. His business was growing and he was working long hours. I think things were not easy for Mary with Aarron just over a year old and an another baby on the way.

When the new St. Cloud Hotel went up, Robert was certain it would bring in more people and more business. He began making frequent business trips to scout out new and better merchandise for his customers. He borrowed money from the Concord National Bank to expand his business and to build a nice new home on North Union Street.

We were proud of his success, but Joel was never one to borrow money and he was worried. At last, he tried to talk to Robert and encourage him to slow down, enjoy his family and be a little more cautious of his finances. Robert got angry with his father for interfering.

For several weeks, we did not hear a word from Robert or Mary. Then one afternoon they drove up and took us to the newly opened St. Cloud Hotel for dinner. After the meal we had a tour of the grand hotel. There were 27 guest rooms with wrought-iron balconies, electric lights and fine furnishings and carpets. The hotel had at least one bathroom on every floor with hot and cold water and for a quarter, a Saturday night bath could be had. There was even a barbershop on the first floor for guest convenience.

To my knowledge, Robert and Joel never discussed Robert's business again. I let it serve as a lesson to me, to never tell Mary how to raise her children.

Speaking of children, those years gave me two more grandchildren to add to the family Bible.

Born November 1, 1888–Louisa May Barringer to Walter and Tessie.

Born December 31, 1889–Anna Grace Simpson to Robert and Mary.

With the children gone, Joel and I had become attached to Rebel number three, almost as if he were our own flesh and blood. I am not certain if Joel was more devoted to the dog or the dog was more devoted to him.

Rebel was getting on in age and he preferred to spend most of his days sleeping. In the summertime his favorite spot was under the front porch. I suppose the ground was cool and he could watch people coming and going.

One day in July, I was coming home from the neighbor's when I saw a boy poking a stick under the porch. I called out to him, but before I could reach the scene, I heard Rebel growl and the boy scream.

When they saw me, both Rebel and the boy ran off down the street. I spent the rest of the afternoon looking for Rebel and the boy. When Joel came home we continued the search. It was long after dark before we gave up the hunt. It was not to the next morning that we found out what happened.

The boy ran home and told his Papa he was being chased by a mad dog. The father, seeing a dog running down the road, shot and killed our dear old Rebel.

When the man made inquires about the dog, one of the neighbors identified him as our animal. The man came to our house red in the face, declaring he would press charges against us for letting a vicious dog run loose in the neighborhood.

When Joel heard the man had shot his dog, he sat down on the steps and wept like a child. I then explained to the man that I believed his son was to blame.

The man said nothing and simply turned around and left. Later that afternoon he came back with a bundle under his arm. "I can't replace your dog, but I knew Mr. Lentz had a litter of beagle pups and under the circumstances he let me talk him out of one."

Nothing could replace Rebel number three, but time heals many things. Therefore, Rebel number four found a place in our home and our hearts.

In closing, I shall speak only briefly on a few national affairs. The Indian Wars raged on and there was talk of war with Spain. In the news was a progressive-thinking young man, Theodore Roosevelt. Joel said he would wager that Roosevelt would be president one day.

On December 6, 1889, the South mourned the death of our Confederate President, Jefferson Davis.

Chapter 19

The Angel's Wings

Wednesday, March 8, 1893

Lilly came to visit. She had retired from her job when she and Henry got married. Now since her mother died, she was lonely with time on her hands. At first, I did not even mind her rattling on, but by midmorning, my nerves were thinning.

I suggest we ride into town for lunch. She hesitates, until I say it will be my treat. Lilly says she needs to close up her house and I throw on my wrap to go hook up the carriage. We have just stepped out on the front porch when a buggy pulls up. Lilly and I stop on the steps. "Seconds later, Colin Collins steps out. "Going somewhere ladies?" he asks smiling.

"Yes sir, we are heading downtown to the hotel for lunch," Lilly speaks up.

"What a coincidence, so am I," he says. He walks up and stands at the bottom of the steps to look up at us.

It is awkward not knowing the reason for his visit, but I feel I must at least introduce him to Lilly. He returns with a flirtatious remark, "nice to meet you young lady." To which Lilly blushes and giggles. Then he reaches behind his back and hands me a bouquet of buttercups. "I saw these early bloomers and I stopped to pick them for the Queen of Peachtree Street."

Lilly looks at me with baited breath. She is like her mother; she loves to plunder into other people's business. I purposely avoid looking at her, "Thank you, Colin. I will put them in water. Lilly, run on now and lock up; we don't want to miss the lunch special."

I have lived next door to Lilly for over 20 years. She will not let this pass. I can expect her to bring up Colin's name a hundred times today. She should know by now that her tactics will not work on me.

When Colin follows me into the house, I feel trapped. I ask him to have a seat in the front room, while I go for a vase. I return with the flowers, set them down on the table and see Colin has made himself comfortable in my chair.

I sit down, but only on the edge of the sofa. I am hoping my posture will serve as a clue that I am not eager to relax into conversation. He, however, appears to have all the time in the world. If his claim to be in the neighborhood checking on the electric streetlights is true, then he should need to get back to his job.

We are still sitting when Lilly comes back. Colin does not take a hint. Finally, I say, "excuse me, Colin, but I need to go and hook up the carriage. I have promised to treat my friend Lilly to lunch."

At once, he stands to his feet, "How rude of me. Ladies, if you would do me the honor, I would love to have you both as my guests for lunch."

I respond quickly, "No, no. We could not possibly take advantage of your kind nature."

"Take advantage of me! Why any man in town would jump at the chance to be seen around town with you two lovely ladies."

I am searching for my words of refusal, when Lilly pipes in, "Then we certainly cannot disappoint."

"Shall we?" he says, looking my way.

Lilly places her hat on her head, clinches it down with her hatpin and walks out the door. I follow her and Colin tags along behind me.

When we arrive at the hotel, we take a table by the window. I did not know Colin to be such a talker. I assume it was either because he felt he had to entertain Lilly or he was nervous. Then I see the reason. Sitting across the room are Bertha and Mrs. Lee.

My hope for going undetected is destroyed when Bertha leans over the table and whispers to Mrs. Lee. She tries to be discreet and drops her napkin. When she leans over to pick it up, she glares directly at us. I could have acted as if I had not seen her, but I was not guilty of anything. I acknowledge her by offering up a tiny little finger wave.

She looks insulted, but she manages to smile. Mrs. Lee then turns around and waves as if she was unaware we were behind her.

"Bertha is my..." Colin whispers.

"I know," I stop him. I do not want to give Lilly more fuel for gossip.

"Who?" Lilly asks, turning around looking in their direction.

"Nothing Lilly, nothing. Have you had the soup?" I ask, trying to redirect her attention.

When Bertha and Mrs. Lee finish their meal, I hold my breath as Bertha approaches. "Hello there Mrs. Simpson, fancy seeing you here. I must say, you sure do get around for a widow woman."

"Now, Birdie," Colin says, scolding her by a pet name as if she is his child.

Bertha looks down at Colin, "You are looking fit, my dear. New suit?" I see by Colin's expression that it is hard for him to resist her flattery.

"Colin, I hate to bring up a personal manner, but I am sure your lady friends will forgive me. It is your goat. He got out of the fence yesterday. He wandered down the road and got a swift kick by Mr. Gibson's old mule. Mr. Gibson has your goat locked up in his barn. I don't suppose you can go fetch him?" she says, looking at him sweetly.

"I'll take care of it later," he says, turning back around to face us at the table.

"Good. Don't be too long; Mr. Gibson might charge me stable rent." She laughs, and then looks my way. "Sorry to interrupt your meal."

Mrs. Lee, who has stood quietly, speaks up, "Lizzie, may I call on you tomorrow?" she asks.

"It would be my delight," I respond. Mrs. Lee spins around and follows Bertha out of the door.

Our food arrives and Lilly and I carry the conversation for the balance of the meal. Colin is distant and barely touches his food. My suspicions tell me Bertha still has a hold on Colin.

When we arrive back at my house, Lilly looks at the time and says she has work to do. "Would you like to come in Colin?" I ask, feeling sure he will refuse.

"I suppose not. I need to be getting on my way," he says, in a weak voice.

"I understand," I reply and start toward the house.

"Lizzie," he calls back to me. "About Saturday night."

I stop him before he has to say more. "Oh yes, Colin, I almost forgot. I am sorry to say, but something has come up. Maybe some other time."

"For certain," he says, taking a deep breath.

I walk to the front door alone. He stands frozen in the yard as if he is in a trance. Before I disappear behind the door, I stop and turn around to look at him. He squints his eyes to see me clearly in the sun.

I wave goodbye. Our eyes lock. At that moment, we both know that what could have been will never be. The past still haunts us both.

"Goodbye, Mrs. Simpson," he says. He gets in his carriage and rides away. I sit down in the rocking chair on the porch. I lay my head back and close my eyes. Colin's past still holds him. If he chooses, he can still return. For me the past is buried and the future is all I have.

I am a bit surprised to see Mr. Lee on the porch at 5 o'clock. He has a report in his hand, but he does not drop it in the box. He knocks on the door. My first thought is not to answer, but when he knocks again, I go to the door.

He asks to come in and I show him to the front room. "Would you like a brandy?" I ask.

"After the day I have had, that's exactly what I need," he replies.

When I return he is leaning over the table smelling the buttercups that Colin delivered earlier. "My mother said she saw you today. Did you have a nice lunch?" he asks, never looking up at me.

"It was pleasant enough."

"What did you have?" he asks.

"Soup," I answer, knowing that it really makes no difference to him. I have begun to figure him out. His courtroom manners spill over to his personal life. He is making small talk, but hopes to find out something else.

"I have a report for you. I wanted to deliver it myself, because it is rather urgent. It is lengthy and I am afraid it might tie up your weekend. You can say no, if you have plans." He sits back and watches my expression carefully.

"I will start on it this afternoon," I assure him.

"Good, I have to be away on businesses, but I will stop by on Sunday."

"That will be fine, Mr. Lee."

I get up to walk him to the door. He steps in front of me blocking the door. "Lizzie, I would like to stay for supper on Sunday, if you will have me," he says uneasily.

"Then I will be expecting you, Mr. Lee." I smile and close the door. There is a rush of excitement in the pit of my stomach. Collins may be out of the picture, but Mr. Lee may be a different story.

Friday, March 10, 1893

A visit from one of my children is always welcomed. In all the years since Robert left home, he has never showed up at the door at 7:30 in the morning. It is a known fact; he is not a morning person. His wife, Mary, says it takes all her effort to make sure he is on time to open up the store. I am concerned.

He rushes in and I can see he looks weary. His hair needs trimming and he is unshaven. He stays for breakfast, but he eats little. Before he leaves he has confessed to me that he is in deep financial trouble.

His store had been most successful. The bank eagerly loaned him money. He had expanded twice and built a new home. The booming economy in Concord is also attracting new merchants. Since Christmas, the city had licensed four new stores.

Now his once-loyal customers were going from store to store. He had overextended himself, trying to stock his store with the best merchandise and then was forced to sell it at the lowest cost.

Mary had no knowledge of the state of things. He just kept his nose to the grindstone, hoping things would turn around. If something did not change quickly, he will lose his house, his family will be out in the street and he will have to close the store.

I find myself wondering if he can hear his father's warning as loud as I can. Robert's lips were trembling when he spoke. He most hated to disappoint his wife and children.

Even though Robert was a grown man, a mother's love does not end just because her boy becomes a man. He left that morning with the reassurance if his empire crashed, he and his family could find refuge here.

I had grown used to my peace and privacy when it was just Dovie and me. Now with two children, Robert, Mary, Dovie, Jasper and their baby, there is going to be little room left for me.

When Mrs. Lee arrives, I am not much in the mood for entertaining. She is good company, but it is hard to keep my mind on the conversation. I agreed to go with her to the opening of the traveling art exhibit in two weeks. After we had our cocoa, she leaves.

The balance of the evening found me working on the lengthy report that Mr. Lee had delivered. It seemed familiar and halfway through I realized I had typed it before.

I held it up to the light and I could see where Mr. Lee had erased the date. For the life of me, I could not be sure why he would do such a thing. Was it because he thought I needed the money or he wanted to keep me busy while he was away. It was after midnight when I complete the document.

I slip in bed, lay my head on the pillow and close my eyes. The house is quiet, but it is hard to stop the noise in my head. There are many things I like about Mr. Lee, but his mysterious side worries me. I think back to the night I stayed in his home and watched him ride off to join the Klan.

What else does he hide behind those cool blue eyes? Can he be trusted? He is clever and manipulative. The night does not bring me a peaceful sleep; my back is aching from the hours of typing.

Saturday, March 11, 1893

My project weighs heavy on my heart. If my words come easy, today I will complete my book. On Monday, I will take the manuscript to Mr. Roberts at Brentwood Publishing and negotiate terms. It is my hope to have a copy to present to Victoria when I go to Charleston.

1891- 1892

The year 1891 was a typical year for us. Often on Saturday evenings after Joel got off work, we would ride to Sallie and Ransom's and spend the night. The four of us would drink fruit wine, play cards, sit on the porch and watch the sunset. Then on Sunday, before we came back to town, we would go for an afternoon ride.

New houses were being built on our street and new families moving in to work in the mills. There were summer picnics, fall festivals and church socials. Most of the families were happy, but some claimed they felt like the "Mill Man" owned their souls. They worked all week and then turned around and spent their last dime at the company store.

Thanksgiving Day, Mr. and Mrs. Bost hosted a turkey dinner at the Grist Mill to raise money for the mission. There was a barn dance afterwards and Joel and I danced until we could hardly stand.

When the table was set for Christmas Dinner 1891, Joel announced it was the grandest meal he had ever seen. We had enough food to feed an army. In fact, our house was host to a small army of family and friends. There was Mrs. Davis, Lilly, Henry and Sallie, Les, Tessie and Robert's families. Finally, yet importantly seated at the table, was Victoria. She had just arrived the night before and surprised us all.

Joel was happy. After many years of struggling we had enough to eat, our bills were paid and we had the joy of our family around us. When Joel gave the blessing, he could hardly choke back the tears. Looking back, I know that the meal was God's special gift to Joel.

After the meal, the children wanted to go outside and play. Louisa had just turned four and she begged her mother to let her play with the big children. Tessie looked at me for my approval. "Bundle her up. A little fresh air will do her good," I said.

So many times, I have wondered if things would be different if I had encouraged Tessie to keep her inside.

From the front room, we could hear the children outside, playing fox and the hounds. Maybe an hour passed before Tessie's little boy, Travis, comes in to say they cannot find Louisa. Tessie's husband jumps up, grabs his coat and follows Travis outside. Time passes and he does not return. Tessie puts on her wrap to go out to look for her, too. Joel tells her to stay inside; he will go help look for her. An hour or so later the front door bursts open and Joel has Louisa in his arms. She and Joel are both soaking wet.

Quickly we strip her wet clothes off and wrap her in a warm blanket. When she is dry, Joel goes to change his clothes. When Joel comes back, he tells us what happened. When it was Louisa's turn to be the fox, she ran around back to hide. She got too close to the creek and fell in.

The evening ended and Joel went to bed early. He said he felt a chill coming on. Since Victoria was to leave the next morning, we stayed up talking until after midnight. By the time I crawled into bed next to Joel, he felt warm. I was afraid he had caught cold.

The next morning he was up early and ready to take Victoria to the train station. He said he felt fine, but as soon as he got back, he went back to bed. He was running a fever, sneezing and coughing.

With the mill being closed for the Christmas holiday, he would have plenty of time to recuperate. Tessie sent word that Louisa had a cold, too, but in a few days she was feeling better. On January 2, Joel went to work even though he was still sick.

When he came home that night, he went straight to bed without supper. Later that night I saw his coat was still hanging over a chair. It felt damp. When I hung it up to dry, a folded document fell out of his pocket. Across the front was the name Mountcastle Insurance Company. I thought that perhaps it was a fire insurance policy. I sat down at the kitchen table to read over it. I quickly realized it was not. It appeared to be a personal insurance policy Joel had taken out on himself. It was not a life insurance, but some sort of sick man's policy that paid doctor or hospital bills.

I thought it strange on two accounts, one being it was taken out in November and second I did not know a thing like this existed. When I folded it back up, I laid it on the table. I planned to talk to him about it. It might be the kind of thing that Robert and Tessie need to know about, too.

Joel coughed all night long and neither one of us got much sleep. Sometime in the early morning hours, Joel finally drifted off to sleep. He was still asleep when it was time for him to go to work, but I did not wake him. I sent Dovie to report him sick and to fetch Dr. Baker.

It was 9 o'clock when Dr. Baker arrived. Joel was still asleep and I had to wake him. At first, Joel said he did not need to see the doctor, but when he tried to stand up, he could offer little resistance.

Dr. Baker's diagnoses was as I had suspected. Joel had pneumonia. He gave Joel some laudanum and prepared a plaster for his chest. He asks if I had ever cared for a sufferer of pneumonia. I said yes and we talked briefly of the protocol. He left saying he would be back the next morning.

That night I greased his chest and kept a steam pot going all night by his bed. By the next morning when the doctor made his rounds, Joel was sitting up in bed and the fever was down. Dr. Baker cautioned Joel to follow all his instructions and told me to keep up the good work.

For a week, I continued the treatments. Joel would be a little better by morning, but by evening, his fever spiked again and he suffered with violent fits of coughing.

I sent for Dr. Baker again and this time he recommended warm salt gargling and whiskey and honey for the cough. He told me things like this just take time.

The third week, when Dr. Baker came I could tell he was worried. Joel had lost at least 10 pounds and he was sleeping most of the time. He gave him a blood tonic and an ether inhalant to break up the congestion.

In desperation, I sent Robert to find Minerva, the Indian woman who lived down by Rocky River. She was not a young woman when she delivered Tessie, so I was afraid she had passed.

When Robert returned, he said he had found the woman, but she was too feeble to make the trip. She remembered us both. She sent a sack of potions for Joel: an asafetida pouch to wear around his neck, cough syrup made from sweet gum and mullein, a salve smelling strong of eucalyptus and lastly, instructions to make an onion poultice to be placed on his feet and chest at night.

After a day or two of the Indian woman's medicine, Joel improved. His appetite had returned and the coughing was improving. I was hopeful that this was all behind us. It was against my will, but the following week he went back to work.

He no longer ran a fever, but the coughing and wheezing was constant. He barely made it through the door in the evenings and he was in bed before dark. I began to fear this was something more than the lingering effects of pneumonia.

Again, there was a glimmer of hope with Spring. The fresh air seemed to be just what Joel needed. His humor was improving but he was not out of the woods yet.

While Joel was laid up sick, there was a steady stream of visitors. Some were fellow Masons, others friends, but mostly people from the mill.

There was a Negro man named John who said for two years he could not find work. Joel hired him to work in the basement opening up the cotton bales. Then the young couple who had just got married and Joel were kind enough to let them work side-by-side in the weave room. I opened the door one Sunday evening to a young boy with a handful of wild flowers in his hand. He was the spokesman for the kids at the mill. They wanted to tell him he was the best boss man. He never cursed or jerked them around like the other supervisors.

When June brought on the endless days of summer and the humid nights, Joel's breathing worsened. The summer before, he could have easily ran to town and back; now it was difficult for him to walk to the barn. Joel just kept pressing on, even though I begged him to see another doctor.

At 2 o'clock on a hot July day, our world came crashing in around us. The front door flew open with two men carrying Joel in the house. They said he had just collapsed on the mill floor.

He was conscious, but too weak to stand. Not long after we got him to the bedroom, there was a tall elderly man standing in the hall. Seeing I am alarmed, he quickly identifies himself. "Mrs. Simpson, excuse me for letting myself in. I am Dr. Lilly. Captain Odell said I should come right away."

Dr. Lilly's examination was not favorable. He felt certain we were dealing with consumption, or as he called it, tuberculosis. He immediately suggested Joel be sent to a sanitorium as soon as possible.

I told the doctor I had read about such facilities. The private ones were often referred to as health resorts. They were located in picturesque mountain locations with luxurious hotel accommodations. The state sanitoriums were prison-type environments, housing patients suffering with infectious disease, lunatics and criminals.

He looked at me with the tenderness of a father. "Dear lady, I will see what I can do. In the meantime, keep the shades down, try to keep him comfortable and see that he rests."

I walked him to the door. Just before he left, he turned around quickly, "Mrs. Simpson, is it true you worked in the hospitals during the war?"

"Yes, I am afraid that is true," I replied.

"Thank you," he said, and hurried off to his buggy.

It was a dreadful 24 hours. Joel coughed most of the night; finally, I resolved to give him a dose of laudanum. It offered him some relief and I fell asleep in the chair next to the bed.

Early the next morning, Dr. Lilly returned. He examined Joel and then called me out in the hall. "Mrs. Simpson, arrangements have been made for you and your husband to go to the Mountain Sanitorium for Pulmonary Diseases, in Asheville, North Carolina.

"Doctor, Joel would surely die if I were to subject him to such conditions. Is there any way I can keep him at home?"

"My dear lady, this hospital is far from being a public ward. It is a lovely Queen Anne mansion overlooking the French Broad River. I think your husband will be quite pleased with his accommodations."

"Thank you very much Dr. Lilly, but I am certain such a place will be out of the question for our budget."

"Did I not say I had made the arrangements?" he said, looking at me and raising his eyebrows.

"Yes, but...," I started.

"According to Captain Odell, your husband was one of the few men in the mill that had the good sense to take out the health insurance policy. The hospital is run primarily by the Sisters of Mercy and the physician in charge, Dr. Schmidt, is a personal friend of mine. I was able, reach him yesterday by telephone. He agreed to accept Joel as his patient, but health insurance being a new concept, he was a little reluctant. However, when I mentioned your experience as a nurse during the late war, his interest was sparked."

"My experience?" I asked.

"To put it more plainly, I have bargained you to volunteer to work in the hospital to offset your husband's medical fees. That is if you are willing?"

I was stunned. Working in a hospital was the last thing on earth I ever wanted to do again. I had put those years behind me, but for Joel it was not a sacrifice. "Yes, of course I will do it." I said bravely. "But even with the insurance and indenturing myself, I am sure it will not cover all the charges."

"Mrs. Simpson, it will all depend on the length of stay. Some patients recover quickly in the high altitudes. The fresh air and good nutrition can do wonders. However, for others the healing is slower and can take over a year. Let's just pray Joel is one of the lucky ones and the stay is short."

"My husband's health is the most important thing. If need be I can sell the house," I resolved.

"Then where would you live when you returned?" he said, in a teasing sort of way. Before I could answer, he took up my hand in his. "Mrs. Simpson, a private source has agreed to be responsible for any outstanding balance that is not satisfied."

"A private source?" I question.

"Yes, but I am afraid the source wishes to remain anonymous." His words took me back. I suspect it is the same private source that paid for Les' education, after his accident. I will not confront him, but he is a good man.

"I will be accompanying you and your husband to Asheville on the morning train."

"The train tickets?" I asked, thinking of the cost.

The doctor reached in his pocket and held up three tickets. "I will be here to deliver you to the station at 6 o'clock sharp in the morning. Now, do you have enough laudanum to keep Joel comfortable for the night? The trip is going to be hard on him and he needs his rest."

"Yes," I replied.

"Good, then I will leave you. I am sure you have much to do before the morning comes. Good day."

He was right. I put Dovie to work at packing my bags. I instructed her to pack only a few blouses, skirts and dresses. I was certain I would be issued a uniform, but my personal items and underthings could not be left out. Fortunately the day before had been washday.

I then had the job of breaking the news to Joel. I was prepared for him to be rebellious, but he was not. I am not sure if it was because he knew it was his only hope or he was too weak to put up a fight. He lay in the bed and instructed me in packing his bag. His final request was that I include the photo of our family, which was taken at Christmas.

He was asleep before I finished packing. I then had the task of writing a letter to Tessie, Robert and Victoria to tell them the news of their father's illness. I explained where I would be and that I would write to them as soon as I arrived. To Robert, I left the responsibility of the household finances. Dovie would maintain the house, but she would need money to manage. In my letter, I left Robert instructions where he would find a sum of money. I prayed it would be enough to sustain things until we returned.

The next morning with Dovie's help, we dressed Joel. His trousers were so loose that we had to pierce another hole in his belt to keep them from falling to the floor.

Dr. Lilly was right. The trip was especially hard on Joel. Looking back, it was equally as hard on me, watching him struggle to restrain his coughing. I will never forget the piercing stares of others at his constant coughing.

I heard one woman say, "We paid good money to ride this train and we should not have to sit here and listen to that death rattle." Others complained that he could be contagious. Upon the first stop in Salisbury, several passengers collected their luggage and demanded to be put on another train. It was humiliating and I was thankful that Dr. Lilly had traveled with us. We could have never made the journey without him.

As we neared Asheville, Joel had a window seat. I could see the beauty of the rolling hills reflecting in his eyes. I recall how gently he held my hand, softly patting it from time to time.

Perhaps it was my hopeful imagination, but it seemed that from the moment we stepped off the train his breathing improved. Dr. Lilly ordered our luggage and we sat on a bench looking over the river. The soft summer breeze blew through Joel's dark hair, which was now peppered with silver. In his face, I could see the strength of a soldier and the compassion of a man who had been blessed to see the faces of his grandchildren. Even in his frail condition, he was still a handsome man.

We took the new electric street railway to the square, and then hired a coach to take us to the sanitorium. When we arrived, Dr. Lilly left us in the coach while he went in to announce we had arrived. Minutes later a young colored girl came out pushing an invalid chair. She said her name was Beth and helped Joel into the chair. I looked up to see three nuns approaching. The smallest of the three reached out and shook my hand. "I am the Reverend Mother here. We are pleased to have you. We can always use an able body around here," she said, and smiled at the other two. "Beth, if you would be so kind as to take our patient to room 8, then I will show Mrs. Simpson to her quarters. Sisters, please gather their luggage."

I hesitated to let go of Joel's hand until he winked at me. "Go on, I'll be fine."

Obediently I followed the Reverend Mother down a gravel path toward the back of the three-story house. I forgot myself once, stopping to look over the beautifully manicured gardens. There were beds of herbs, compact vegetable gardens and an assortment of flowers. Reverend Mother noticed I had stopped. "Tending of the earthly soil is one of God's most pleasurable chores. Our Sisters are glorified with a green thumb."

"Indeed they are," I replied.

312

Under the back porch steps was a small door. She gave it a push but the door was jammed. Again she pushed and the door flew open, nearly spilling her to the ground. Her wimple fell down over her face. She reached up, restored it back to the proper position on her head and laughed. "Here we go," she said, extending her arm out in the room.

I see before me a humble room with two small beds. There are no paintings on the wall, only a small crucifix hangs between the two beds. There is a chest of drawers, two wash basins and a small fireplace. The floor is brick, but the room is clean and tidy.

"I think you will find this suitable," Reverend Mother states. "You have met Beth. She will be your roommate. Through the kitchen doors, just down the hall, you will find two bathrooms with four shower stalls. You may use the one on the right. The other is reserved for our male patients. Beth will be your mentor and instruct you of your duties. In consideration of your reasons for being here, you will be responsible for the delivery of all your husband's meals, at which time you may take yours as well. Breakfast is at 6, lunch at 12, and supper is served at 5. After supper, you will have two free hours before the night rounds begin. Lights out at 9 o'clock. Do you have any questions Mrs. Simpson?"

"No, I think I have it," I answered. Reverend Mother's face was kind, but I knew she meant business. I was to earn every dime of my keep.

"Good," she said. Without warning, she reached out and clasped her hands around my waist to measure me. "I will send down a uniform for you shortly. After lunch, Beth will put you to work." She nodded slightly and then turned and left.

I had yet to unpack my bags when there was a knock at the door. I opened to see a broad-faced nun standing at the door. She came straight in and spread out two gray dresses and two stiffly starched bib aprons. "Reverend Mother said to tell you there is a laundry bag under your bed. Hang your soiled clothing on the door. The maid will take care of your laundry. You will need to stitch your initials on your personal things."

I thanked her and she nodded in the same fashion as the Reverend Mother and slipped out the door. The first dress I tried was too large, but the second fit perfectly. I put the apron on, pulled my hair back tightly, sat down and waited.

It was 12:30 when Beth finally came to collect me. She apologized for the delay. "Sorry I am late. There was much to do to settle in your husband. The doctors are with him now." I took note that if I had not been looking at her directly, I would have not known she was colored. Her pronunciation was perfect.

"Doctors?" I asked.

"Yes, Dr. Schmidt, Dr. Fletcher and your doctor."

"Will I be able to speak with them?" I asked.

"She pulls out her watch from her pocket to check the time. "Are you willing to skip lunch?"

"That is acceptable with me."

"Then follow me," she said.

I followed her up the back steps and in through the back door. I could smell something cooking and my stomach began to growl.

"Smell that?" Beth asked. I nodded and she said, "Wait here." In a few minutes, she returned with a couple of fresh baked rolls with a piece of meat inside. "Here you go; there is no need in starving." She keeps walking, eating on the way. I followed suit, feeling like an orphan that just received a handout.

We walk up three flights of steps and then down the hall to room 8. I can hear men talking inside and then I hear

Joel's voice. I immediately started to open the door, but she placed her hand over mine. "We never enter a patient's room without knocking. It is one of Reverend Mother's strictest rules."

I stepped back and she knocked on the door. "Enter," comes a man's voice from behind the wall.

She opened the door. "Dr. Schmidt, the patient's wife wishes to see you."

There was a pause, and then I recognize Dr. Lilly's voice. "Please send her in."

When I walked in the room, all eyes were upon me. I saw Joel dressed in a hospital gown and propped up in the bed. He patted the side of the bed for me to come sit down next to him.

"Mrs. Simpson," Dr. Lilly began. "After the doctor's examination, they do not feel that your husband is suffering from tuberculosis."

"Then this is good news?" I asked. I looked at each of the doctors, hoping to see smiles of encouragement, but their faces are stern.

After a moment of silence one of the doctors walked over to the bed. "Mrs. Simpson, I am Dr. Schmidt. We are seeing more and more of these cases mistakenly diagnosed as tuberculosis." His dialect was most likely German in origin. "What we are dealing with here is a disease called byssinosis or brown lung. The breathing difficulties, chest tightness and coughing all mock other diseases."

Over the next few days, I was to learn more. They called it an occupational disease of cotton mill workers. The lungs are affected by years of exposure to cotton fibers and dust. Joel most likely had the disease for sometime, even though it was silent. His pipe smoking and the recent onset of pneumonia had ultimately caused it to flare up.

There were some controversial treatments, but Dr. Schmidt was not in favor of any of them. They would proceed with the same protocol as for tuberculosis: rest, fresh air and sound nutrition.

For the balance of June and July, I scrubbed everything from floors to patients. I rushed upstairs every morning to bring Joel his breakfast. Most days, I missed my own lunch, having only time to bring Joel his, give him a kiss and rush back to my duties. Supper was most often the same.

However, without fail I spent the hours 5 to 7 in the evenings with him. When the weather was good, I would take him outside in a roller chair so that we could enjoy the gardens together. Those were precious hours. If I could muster the strength, I would go back to his room once my night shift was over. He would most often be asleep, but I wanted to be there with him. I would pray for him and use this valuable time to write to my children.

His progress was up and down. Just when I thought he had taken a turn for the better, he would start back the coughing. By the end of July, the wheezing was constant. I suppose I knew, but I refused to let my mind believe it for one moment. However, when the doctors asked if we would like to go home, I knew they were giving up hope and were sending him home to die.

I begged them to please try something else. Dr. Schmidt said he would consult with his colleagues. I think Joel would not have agreed to the surgery if it had not been for me.

On August 8, Plombage surgery was scheduled. The doctor would make an incision into the diseased lobe of one lung and physically cause it to collapse by filling the cavity with olive oil. It was hopeful that this would allow the lung time to heal. If the surgery was successful, then they would do the second lung once he regained his strength. We knew of the risks, but it was our only hope.

They sat about to build Joel up and to prepare him for the surgery. He was given a diet high in nutrition, supplements and tonics. The nuns visited him twice a day to pray for him. I was encouraged.

Six o'clock on the morning of August 5, I was on my way up to Joel's room with his breakfast. As I came down the hall, I could hear excited voices coming from his room. The door was ajar. I knew at once that something was wrong. I dropped the tray in the hall and ran to the room.

When I walked in Joel was lying face up with his eyes closed and the doctor leaning over him listening to his breathing. The nurse did not look up at me when she walked out of the room carrying a pail filled with blood.

"Mrs. Simpson," Dr. Schimit said, as he looked up at me. "He is resting comfortable now. I will speak to you in the hall."

I could not hear much of what he said. I was near deaf from my heart pounding in my head. "Mrs. Simpson, it is out of our hands now. The lungs are hemorrhaging and he has lost the battle. Before this day is over your husband will be with the Lord. Go to him now. I will let Reverend Mother know you will not be returning to your duties. Please try to keep him quiet. It will be easier that way." He took my hand and kissed it tenderly. "These things are never easy." I tried to collect myself before I entered the room. I watched the good doctor make his way down the hall. His silver head bobbing up and down over his bowed back. I wondered how many times he had witnessed this scene.

I sat by Joel's bed all day. When the nuns came in to pray, Joel's glassy eyes would open and he tried to smile. The sun grew dim and the room was silent when suddenly he wheezed out, "Lizzie, do you see that bright light?"

I jumped up and sat down gingerly next to him on the bed. "No darling, I do not."

"Listen," he said. "I can hear singing. I feel the cool breeze of the angel's wings."

His trembling hand reached out for mine, but his voice was uncannily strong. "Don't cry, my rose. Hold my hand until I breathe my last breath, then walk away and promise not to look back on my frail body. I will see you again in heaven."

I recall nodding and biting back the tears. His eyes fixed upon my face. At 7: 05 p.m. on August 5, 1892, he departed. I stood up and walked out of the room, as I had promised.

I never once looked upon Joel's body, not even during the wake or the funeral. I will always remember him as he was. He was my lover, my best friend and my rock. He taught me how to love, but most importantly, he taught me how to love myself. He often said that on this earth his greatest job was to make me happy. It is my responsibility and my gift to him to continue his work.

The End

I pull the last page out of the typewriter. Yes, this is where I will end my book. Shall there be another book, it will be called "Lizzie." It will be my journey, built on the foundation and strength of the years and lessons I have learned from the past.

Chapter 20

Get Out of This Mess!

Sunday, March 12, 1893

Today is the first day Dovie and Jasper will take their baby to church. The baby is almost two weeks old, but until now has only been known as "Baby." In their church the preacher is responsible for naming all the babies.

Dovie and Jasper bring the baby up to the altar. The preacher takes the child in his arms. "Children are our future! Our God is alive! He has a plan for this child and as God's people, it is our responsibility to see this child is brought up to know the ways of the Lord. If he is sick, we will care for him; if he is good, we are to praise him and if he strays, we will forgive him. I now give this child the son of Dovie and Jasper Jackson the name which I have chosen to bless and bring him honor. He shall be called Phoebus."

It is a beautiful ceremony and afterwards there is fellowship and food. When we return home, Jasper cares for the baby while Dovie and I start on the supper preparations.

They are aware that Mr. Lee is coming to supper. It seems of little concern to Dovie, but Jasper seems worried. When Dovie takes the baby upstairs, he comes in the kitchen where I am working.

"Misses Lizzie," he says softly. *"Dos you knows dat Mr. Lee owns one of dem whore houses in Gold Hill?"*

319

"Jasper! Mr. Lee is a lawyer. That is certainly not true."

"*Da town mens say it be so.*"

"Have you been out there?"

"*Nos ma'ams.*"

"Then you don't know it is true." Jasper shakes his head and leaves me alone. I am angry with him for even believing some silly rumor like that.

Jasper is nowhere in sight when Mr. Lee arrives. Dovie stays downstairs and helps me with the meal. When the table is cleared, she disappears.

The evening has its share of uneasiness, but for the most part it goes well. Mr. Lee talks a great deal about the economy. He says we are facing another depression. The banks have been too eager to loan money to every fool that could sign his name on the line. Not only that, but half the businesses in operation now will be closed by the end of the year.

"Lizzie, how is your son Robert's business holding out?" he asks bluntly.

"Stressed" is my only answer. I wonder if he thinks my son is a fool, too.

"This is why I always say a man cannot put all his eggs in one basket. There are some businesses that will thrive even in the worst of times."

"And what would those be, Mr. Lee?" I ask.

"Bars and Brothels," he laughs.

I change the subject quickly. "Mr. Lee, I have a small matter that I would like your advice." I reach in the drawer and hand him the letter from the insurance company regarding Joel's life insurance.

He reads over the letter. "Maybe your ship has just come in," he says.

"Really?" I ask.

"No, I was teasing you. My guess is it could not be

much. Policies that pay big benefits are expensive. I doubt seriously if Joel could have afforded such a policy. I am, however, surprised that this company is still in business after all these years."

He is most likely being truthful, but his assumptions are in poor taste. I have observed from the first day I met Mr. Lee that he is not shy in dishing out his opinions.

"I see, well would you mind making an inquiry on my behalf?" I ask. I watch him read over the letter again and look at the envelope. He folds it up and slips it in his pocket.

"In what county is the marriage bond filed?" he asks, taking a sip of his coffee.

"Let's not trouble with all that now. I would like to find out if the benefits are worth the effort," I reply, hoping he will just take my word at face value.

"Lizzie, if it is a dime and you are entitled to it, then it is worth the effort. Just tell me where the bond is filed and I will take care of this for you."

I turn to study his face. "I am not sure," I lie.

"Well, what county were you married in?" he pries.

"Stanly," I say, knowing I am getting in deeper.

"Well, that is where it will be. I will ride out tomorrow to the courthouse."

"No, it will not be there. Excuse me for a moment." He watches me walk across the hall. When I return, I hand him the marriage bond. The note from the preacher is still in the envelope.

"Oh, this is all we need," he says, as he looks over the document. Then his eyes fall to the blank line, where it should have been recorded. "Lizzie, is this the original copy?"

"Yes, I have reason to believe it is," I reply, sitting down slowly. I wait for his response as he reads the note from the preacher. At first, the look on his face is serious and then he bursts into laughter.

"Well, just when I thought you were pure as snow, I find out you have never been legally married," he says joking.

"Mr. Lee! This is hardly the kind of thing a woman wishes to turn into a joke. It was a mistake. You can plainly see that." I walk over to the window and turn my back on him.

He sees he has made me angry. "Lizzie, I am sorry. I was only trying to make light of this little blunder. It will be a simple matter of taking the document in and having it recorded. The trouble is going to come in with trying to collect the insurance money. It may look fishy when the records show you have just married a dead man."

The words dead man ring in my ears, but I understand what he means. "See what you can do." I reply softly.

The evening closes and I walk him to the door. "Lizzie, he says. "It is time we stop pretending. We both know where this is heading. Then without permission he takes me in his arms and kisses me. "I will see you tomorrow," he says, opening the door to let himself out.

I am burning with emotion. It is a mix of excitement and anger. I doubt that Mr. Lee asks permission for many things. I respect a man with ambition, but I hope he knows where to draw the line.

That night as I lie in bed, I think of the many nights I spent laying next to Joel. Mr. Lee has made his intentions clear, but mine are not clear, not even to myself. I speculate if Mr. Lee's comment about the bars and brothels was just in jest or was Jasper right.

It is just after 10 a.m. when I walk out the door of Brentwood Publishing Company. Jasper had been working for Mr. Roberts for over a year. He told me Mr. Roberts would make me a fair offer to print my books. He was right.

I stroll down the streets in a cheery mood, knowing I will have my books by June. I am in the frame of mind for shopping.

The styles have changed. If I am going to Charleston in June, I will need to update my wardrobe. Joel had his theory on store-bought clothes. He thought people should be self-sufficient. When the children were young I made all our clothes. However, in the later years he was a little broader in his thinking.

My first stop is Miss Fannie Fisher's millinery shop. She is with a customer and I take a seat to wait. I have just picked up a recent copy of Cosmopolitan magazine, when something catches my eye.

Miss Fannie sees it too. "Take a look at the fancy rig!"

It is drawn by a pair of fine horses and loaded with packages and crates. A man emerges from the driver's seat. We can only see the back of his dark head, but he is a trim figure and richly dressed. He ties off the horses and walks across the street to the hotel.

"My, oh my! That must be the artist that has came in to set up his exhibit," Miss Fannie says.

"I for one will be going to see that exhibit," the customer boasts. I make no comment, but I remember my invitation from Mrs. Lee to see the exhibit.

Two hours later, I am walking down the street with my new hat in the box. The hat was more expensive than I had planned. I am to learn quickly the price of everything has gone up. Mrs. Cross' shop has a nice selection of silks, gloves, fans, bustles and handkerchiefs, but the merchandise is all dear. I leave with only a few accessories and two Butterick patterns. I then walk toward Robert's store hoping to find some yardage of nice calico. Joel was right, one should always be self-sufficient. With a little work, by June I can make myself a sizeable wardrobe.

When I get to Robert's store, the door is locked. He may be still at lunch. I have an apple in my purse, take it out and sit down on the porch to wait. After a few minutes, I see the fancy rig we saw earlier go down the street. This time I see the profile of the man and he appears to be a handsome sort.

By 2 o'clock, I tire of waiting and head back. Maybe I have some fabric in the attic. Just across from where my carriage is parked, I see a crowd forming. As I near, I hear offensive language and insults shouted out.

Old James Lineberger is intoxicated and attempting to ride his mule on the porches of the stores. He is destroying property and breaking plate-glass windows. People are running in all directions. I am fearful someone is going to get hurt.

When he pulls out his pistol, a group of white men interfere. They jerk him off his mule and give him a thrashing. When they finally drag him off to the jailhouse, he is kicking and screaming. The people are excited over the happenings, fearing it will stir up trouble with the Negroes again.

When I return home, Dovie tells me I have had two visitors, Robert and Tessie's husband. *"Yous is a grandmammy again. Tessie had a boy last night,"* she informs.

"Did he say anything else?" I ask.

"Yes'um, he says alls is good and da baby is fats."

I look over at the clock. It is too late to go out tonight. If she needs anything, Sallie is nearby. I will ride out in the morning.

I change into my housedress and go up in the attic in hopes of finding some fabric. The attic is cool and damp, but there is still enough light to see over the space. I stop for a moment, remembering the night I saw Robert talking to Moses McGraw. In a joking tone, I call out, "Mr. McGraw, are you still with us?" There is no answer and I laugh aloud to myself.

I dig through a trunk and discover a nice piece of plaid, some white sheeting and a few smaller yards suitable for a blouse. I will go to Robert's next week for more material. I reach for the lid of the trunk and it falls down with a thump, nearly hitting the top of my head. I jump back, lose my balance and fall to the floor. Before I regain myself, I hear a noise at the top of the stairs. I am alarmed until I see Lilly.

"Dovie said I could find you up here," she says. "What are you up to?"

I show her the fabric and tell her about my plans for a new wardrobe for my trip to Charleston. Lilly is an excellent seamstress and she offers to assist me. "Between the two of us, we will have you looking like you stepped out of a magazine by June."

I am delighted with her offer and give her a big hug. We are coming down the stairs laughing when we see Mr. Lee standing in the hall talking to Dovie. I had forgotten he said he was coming by. My hair is hanging down and I am in my housedress.

"Hello, looks like you forgot I was coming for supper," he says. I have an idea he is joking, but perhaps he is not.

"You will have to take pot luck, I am afraid," I return in the same tone.

"Lizzie, I came to invite you over for supper. It would be a pleasure to have you too, Mr. Lee," she says, politely.

"Don't look to me to turn down a meal," he says, giving

Lilly a pat on the back.

"Good, then come on over when you are ready," she says, and darts out the door.

My plans for sewing are dismissed. I tell Mr. Lee to have a seat and go to change my clothes.

Lilly has a nice supper, but Henry is in a dark mood. When the meal is over, he talks nonstop about death. It appears this new job has taken a toll on him. He talks about all the gruesome things he has read recently in his novels and newspapers. He says he now believes in ghosts and magic. He even shows us an article about the great Harry Houdini. When he runs out of human oddities to talk about, he ponders over what happened to the giant body of Jumbo the elephant."

Mr. Lee listens to it all, but in a condescending sort of way. I am glad that Lilly and Henry do not notice. Mr. Lee is the one to end the visit. He says he has to call on a sick friend on his way home. It seems odd, but there are no questions asked.

Lilly hands me her Sears catalog to look at the styles of dresses. She agrees to go to Tessie's with me in the morning and Mr. Lee and I walk in silence back across the yard.
He sees me to the door, but tonight he does not attempt to kiss me. "Good night, see you later sweetie," he calls out as he runs to his carriage.

The next day Mr. Lee did not stop by. When I read the evening paper, this headline caught my eyes:

Ku Klux Klan fills the streets of Concord last night. It is suspected that their presence was to serve as a reminder that violence from the colored community will not be tolerated.

I would be willing to bet Mr. Lee was one of the white caps on the street last night. Perhaps he was too tired to visit after his late night work.

For the balance of the week, he stopped by, sometimes twice a day or even three times.

He seemed to be larger than life. He asked personal questions. What I did not tell him somehow he found out on his own. It was as if he was taking control over my life. If I was not home, he came back later wanting to know where I had been. Where it was going I was not sure, but I was sure I wanted it to end.

Friday, March 14, 1893

Early morning, Robert came back to visit. He carried the sad news that the bank had sold his house. It came as a complete surprise to him. Just last week he talked to the bank manager and he had agreed to give him a few more months. Now it seems someone found out about the mortgage being in arrears and assumed the loan. The bank manager said that with the state of current affairs, they had to accept the offer. Robert left saying that he and his family would start moving in tomorrow.

It was not only a blow to Robert, but to me, too. I had three bedrooms. Dovie, Jasper and baby were in one. Robert and Mary would take the other. Then there was Robert's two children. The only thing to do was to give up my bedroom to the children. I would sleep on the sofa in the office.

In between taking care of the baby, Dovie helped me convert the office into my sleeping quarters. We are in the process of hanging a privacy curtain over the glass pane doors when Mr. Lee invades me again.

The house was in an upset and he had to step over boxes to get through the hall.

"You are working too hard," he says, looking around with an inquisitive look on his face.

"Yes, to that I agree, but some things are out of our control," I reply.

"Is that so?" he says, in a tone of mockery.

"Well, for some of us it is," I counter, only to satisfy his ego.

"Mind telling me what is going on?" he asks.

"Robert is moving in here. Someone bought his home out from under him."

Mr. Lee smiles. "It was the best thing that could have happened to him. It got him out from under that debt."

"What?" I stop and look up at him.

"Lizzie, why put yourself through this?"

"Do you suppose I throw them out in the street?"

"No Lizzie. I am asking you to come live at my house. Get out of this mess. Have you not had enough living among coloreds and crazy neighbors? I have done my homework on you. This old house is a far cry from the way you were raised. I can put you back in your rightful place in society. They will accept you, if for no other reason than because I say so."

"Mr. Lee, I am going to try to hold my tongue," I say, fighting back the tears. "But I would like it very much if you would leave."

"Lizzie, I understand you are upset, but you are a sensible woman. I will give you a day or two to think it over. I am confident you will come around to my way of thinking."

He reaches in his pocket and hands me an envelope. "The life insurance money, $500."

"Thank you very much, Mr. Lee," I say, and reach for it.

"Lizzie, please call me William, I don't want my future wife calling me Mr. Lee."

That night it occurs to me, Mr. Lee may have been the one that bought Robert's house. If he thinks this little trick will force me into marrying him, he is badly mistaken. I am my Papa's steel magnolia. *I am strong as steel and my roots are planted deep in this southern soil. Time may have weathered me, but I will always bend with the wind.*

Chapter 21

The Art Exhibit

Saturday, March 18, 1893

Mrs. Lee's promise was to come for me at 5 p.m. An additional family of three moving into a small house has turned everything upside down. The moving has been steady all day. With Jasper's help, Robert has stacked the furniture in the barn. The children are chasing Rebel over the house and Robert's wife has cried all day. The floor is covered with boxes and crates. Now Dovie's baby is crying.

I am trying to get ready to go out for the evening, the bathroom is always occupied and I cannot find my shoes. For the first time, I am seriously considering Mr. Lee's proposal. "Mr. Lee's house or the lunatic asylum?" I ask myself aloud. If I did not have the visit to Charleston coming up, I might consider eloping with Mr. Lee tonight. I laugh to myself.

I open the front curtains and I am sitting waiting for Mrs. Lee by 4:30, with my wrap in my lap. I will make sure that I meet her on the porch as soon as the carriage drives up. I have not the strength to explain the reason my house is in such disarray.

Straight up 5 o'clock her carriage pulls up. When the driver gets out, I am relieved to see it is Sam and not Mr. Lee. I gather my things and go out the door at once.

We dine at the hotel and then walk to the lobby to view the art exhibit. The paintings are as lovely as any I have ever seen. There are paintings of mountains, seashores and portraits of handsome men, women and children.

I am wandering up and down the aisles at my leisure. Mrs. Lee is ahead of me, I see her stand back to admire one of the paintings. Soon another woman joins her. I think nothing of it and continue my viewing. Before I join Mrs. Lee, she has a small group gathered around her.

As I am approaching, they are looking directly at me. One man calls out, "It is uncanny."

I slowly walk to the back of the group, but all heads turn my way. "Lizzie, I think you need to see this painting," Mrs. Lee says.

The people part and I step forward. The painting is in plain view. It is of a young woman seductively posed on the front porch steps of a farmhouse. I have a strange feeling that the house is Sallie and Ransom's. When I step closer, I gasp. The woman in the painting is me.

From the back of the room comes a familiar voice, "It is strange when one sees the hands of time rewind." The voice is smooth as velvet and I detect a slight accent.

The chatter of the crowd ceases and the only sound in the room is the sound of his heels clicking across the wooden floor. I do not dare turn around, until I hear him call my name, "Lizzie."

I turn around slowly and before me he stands. "Antonio," I say softly.

He lifts my hand to his lips and gently kisses it. Suddenly I am transformed back to the days of my youth, to the time when a young woman posed for a romantic gypsy to paint her portrait.

If the people were staring I did not see them, if they were talking I did not hear them. He takes my hand and guides me through the crowd. We walk quickly until we are alone in the garden. "Lizzie, I have dreamed of the moment we would meet again," he says smiling.

"And I have thought of you often, too," I reply.

"A lifetime has passed, but it seems like yesterday," he whispers. His face is aged by time, but serves only to make him more handsome than I remembered.

"Lizzie, forgive me, but I have made my inquiries. I know you are widowed. For many years, I prayed that if God would ever let our paths cross again, this time I would not walk away."

"This is all so sudden," I whisper.

"Is it?" he says. "Or is it a dream that we both have shared for many years."

"I loved my husband," I say, knowing I am being honest.

"I know it was he you loved when we met, but if he had not owned your heart, would you have given it to me?" he asks.

I look up into his dark eyes flickering in the moonlight, "Yes, Antonio, yes."

He gathers me up in his arms and kisses me. I first resist, but the passion overcomes my reservations. We are interrupted by voices and I gently push him away. I feel no guilt, no shame or remorse when I hear Mrs. Lee call my name. "Lizzie, I am ready to go now."

I quickly begin to tell Antonio how to find me. He smiles. "Did I not tell you I had made my inquiries? Dine with me tomorrow, breakfast, lunch or dinner?"

"Lunch will be fine," I reply tenderly.

"No, too many meals have passed. So, I may come for you early and bring you back only if you beg."

"Eight o'clock?" I say, smiling.

"Eight o'clock it is," he says, kissing my hand as I walk away.

Mrs. Lee and I walk silently back to the carriage. Sam is waiting. I feel like a child waiting to be scolded by her mother. Mrs. Lee and I sit in the back and Sam takes hold of the reigns. The night is cool, but I feel a hint of spring in the air.

After a few minutes Mrs. Lee speaks. "My son is a horse's ass," she says bluntly. "When I first met you, I was only thinking of my son. I thought if he could marry someone like you he could at last settle down. He toyed with the idea, but just like his father, he was reluctant to give up his drinking and nights at the brothels."

"Mrs. Lee, you don't have to tell me all this," I said, feeling sorry for her.

"No, I do," she reply quickly. "You see, I had a change of heart when we became friends. I like you Lizzie," she says, and pats me tenderly on the hand.

"And I like you too, Mrs. Lee."

"Frankly, I wronged you. I knew my son would never make you happy, but by then he had set his cap for you. William is used to getting his way and I was afraid you would fall to his manipulative ways."

"Mrs. Lee, it is alright; you meant well."

"I have righted the wrong tonight, my dear," she says, laughing.

"What do you mean?" I ask.

"Lizzie, the first time I came to visit with you, I asked you about the fine portrait of you hanging over your mantle. I was amazed by the detail and the passion in the artist's brush strokes. When you left the room, I wrote the name of the artist down. I put William to work at tracking him down. He reported to me that the artist in question was from humble beginnings, but his work had earned him worldwide fame. In short, he is a very wealthy man.

Several weeks ago, I saw that he was to have a showing in Columbia. I took the train and went to see the exhibit. It was then I first saw the painting we viewed tonight. When he saw it had captured my attention, I mentioned your name. Lizzie, I arranged for him to come to Concord and for the two of you to meet tonight."

"Why?" I ask.

"Because we are friends and I want you to be happy. Lizzie, Antonio has loved you for many years. Life is short and time grows more precious as the years go by. Follow your heart."

She takes hold of my hand and we ride in silence for the balance of the ride. When the carriage pulls up in front of my house, she gives me a motherly little kiss. "Goodbye sweetheart," she says.

They wait until I have unlocked the door before they drive away. Something told me I would never see her again.

December 15, 1893
Paris, France

To: Agnes Lee
    Poplar Tent, Concord, NC

My Dear Friend,

I hope this letter finds you well and in good form. I wanted to tell you what has happened to me since our eyes last met. After all, my extraordinary story begins with you.

Antonio was only in Concord for two short weeks, but time does not govern the depth of the heart. When it came time for Antonio to leave, he pleaded with me to go with him.

When he spoke of the romantic places we would travel, I could hear the rolling rivers, feel the wind in my hair and taste the salty air as we sailed across the sea.

Once I could have easily allowed myself to take to the road like a gypsy, but change does not come easy for a woman my age. I wanted nothing more than to follow my heart and spend the rest of my life in search of rainbows. I had a responsibility to my children and my grandchildren. I could not forsake them.

At the time of Antonio's departure, it was decided that once his summer tour was complete, he would come back and plant himself next to me.

I kissed him goodbye and was happy knowing he would be returning in the fall. However, as the weeks went by, a gloom came over me. Antonio was a man who lived in the region of the moonbeams. He was a dreamer. For the first time in his life, the earth would own him, not the wind.

When I received his letter in May, I had full intention to respond with a sorrowful goodbye. However, it was that letter that changed everything.

My Darling Lizzie,

My tour has delivered me to a spot on earth that I am sure is most near to heaven. I will be in the fair city of Charleston until August. Please say you will come and share this time with me. We can marry here and then you can finish my tour with me as my bride. Then where the road leads us from there, I place in your hands.

> *I await your response.*
> *Antonio*

I knew at that moment God had given his blessing for me to go to Antonio. The path was laid out before me and my view was clear. My bags were already packed and the train tickets bought, to leave for Charleston the next week for Victoria's wedding.

First, I gathered my children around me. I read them Antonio's letter and I waited for their response. There were no harsh words, no sad faces, only words of encouragement and well wishes. I made no promises to when I would return, only that I would.

My leaving came at a good time. Robert and his family now had the house to themselves and Dovie and Jasper proudly moved into their own home.

The day before I left, I went to say goodbye to Cindy Lou. She was part of my past and she would always have a place in my heart.

On the morning I was to leave, I gave each of my children a copy of my book. Sallie and Ransom drove me to the train station. Sallie and I sat quietly side by side on the bench. When the whistle blew, there were no words left to be said.

We were more than sisters, we were best friends. We had shared the best of times and suffered through the worst. If it were God's will that our paths never crossed again, I would forever be blessed to have a sister named Sallie.

When I stepped up on the train, I knew a whole new world was unfolding before me. I turned once more to look at my dear sister.

She gives me her best smile. "We shall all look forward to our '*Letters from Lizzie.*'"

So, I will close my letter to you, Mrs. Lee. I

again thank you for what you did for me. After we left Charleston, we set sail for a European tour. We will be in Paris for the Christmas Holidays. I want to wish you and Mr. Lee a Merry Christmas.

Yours most sincerely,
Theodosia

Oh P.S.: Robert says to tell Mr. Lee he may come for his typewriter.

Enclosed you will find a copy of my book.

The future of Concord is to be made and assure by the action of home people. No external or miraculous influence will ever build her greater. As the making of a man is within himself, so must the future life and solidity of Concord come, primarily, from her people.

John B. Sherrill
- editor of the *Concord Times* January 4, 1889